Into the Wildewood

To all who keep our forests alive, the conservators and the foresters, especially the USDA Forest Service and the National Park Service. May you grow many rings.

And to Tolkien, the most stubborn Siberian Husky on the planet. I miss you and your barking, beloved boy.

Acknowledgements

It takes a lot of help to get a book from idea to store shelf, and I would not have been able to write this book without the amazing editorial eyes of Andrew Karre and Sandy Sullivan of Llewellyn, the encouragement and support of agent extraordinaire Richard Curtis, and the love of my number one fan, my amazing husband. Much assistance also came from my long-time critique group, Maureen, Nancy, and Carla, who read draft after draft as if it were new each time and never griped. Well, seldom griped.

Thanks, too, to all the Renaissance Faire workers who transport their visitors to another era, one day at a time—the pirates and jousters (yum, the pirates and jousters!), the wenches and pub lurkers and strolling minstrels, the kings, queens, courtiers and turkey drumstick vendors, the rascally jokesters and the poor sod stuck in the stinky foam-rubber suit on the hottest day of summer. I love you all.

GILLIAN SUMMERS

Into the Wildewood

THE FAIRE FOLK TRILOGY

flux™
Woodbury, Minnesota

First Edition
First Printing, 2008

Book design by Steffani Sawyer
Cover design by Kevin R. Brown
Cover illustration by Derek Lea

Flux, an imprint of Llewellyn Publications

The Cataloging-in-Publication Data for *Into the Wildewood* is on file at the Library of Congress.
ISBN-13: 978-0-7387-1332-8

This is a work of fiction. Names, characters, places, and incidents are either the product of the author's imagination or are used fictitiously, and any resemblance to actual persons, living or dead, business establishments, events, or locales is entirely coincidental. Cover model used for illustrative purposes only and may not endorse or represent the book's subject.

Flux
Llewellyn Publications
A Division of Llewellyn Worldwide, Ltd.
2143 Wooddale Drive, Dept. 978-0-7387-1332-8
Woodbury, MN 55125-2989, U.S.A.
www.fluxnow.com

Printed in the United States of America

one

CANOOGA SPRINGS, NEW YORK
WILDEWOOD RENAISSANCE FAIRE CAMPGROUND

Five days on the road with Dad, and Keelie Heartwood still didn't have a belly button ring. Her sort-of boyfriend Sean hadn't called her even once, and now she was stuck at another Ren Faire. Worse, her best friend from California would soon arrive to see her in all her misery.

A horn blatted in the rain outside, followed by raucous laughter from the Merry Men's cram-packed little party tent next door. She added a line to her journal about not being allowed to party with the other Rennies, and being confined to the camper.

Life sucks, Keelie wrote. She closed the book where she'd been documenting her pitiful existence, then leaned back in her cramped bunk and stared into space. It wasn't a long stare, because it was limited to the trailer's cozy eight-feet-by-six-feet. She'd been working hard at thinking "cozy" instead of "claustrophobic." It wasn't fair. She was stuck camping, but she'd heard that all the other elves, including the nasty elf girl Elia, were staying at some luxurious lodge in town down the road from the Faire. They had room service. She barely had room.

Keelie was supposed to wait inside for her dad to return from his errand. It had been hours. She'd spent the time listening to the loud fun next door at the Wildewood Renaissance Festival's party headquarters.

If her friend Raven were here, they could join in the fun. But Raven had gone to Manhattan after the last Ren Faire, to work an internship at Doom Kitty, the famous Goth record company. It was a better gig than digging up herbs with her mother, Dad's old friend Janice the herb lady. Janice would be joining them soon, but Keelie really missed Raven. She was beautiful and confident, and treated Keelie like an equal rather than a fifteen-year-old tagalong.

The Wildewood's theme was Robin and his Merry Men, and Robin's partners in crime were singing (or what they optimistically considered singing) a rousing song that had something to do with married women and beer. Every chorus ended with a shout of "hey nonny!" They'd been at it for the past two hours, getting louder and more off-key by the minute.

Keelie sensed the trees stirring around her, and apparently they weren't happy with the concert either. She'd been able to sense them all her life, but it was only since she'd moved in with Dad that they'd actually talked to her and allowed her to see their spirit faces. The ancient oaks, larger than the trees in Colorado, pressed their energy around her now, wanting her to come out and open herself to them.

There were whispering birches and silent elms, too, and small cherries and drooping willows that liked to keep their roots wet by the banks of the river that flowed, deep and silent, at the edge of the Faire's campground. Sir Davey's Earth magic lessons had helped her block the trees most of the time, so that she wouldn't go crazy, but tonight she was tired, bored, and lonely, and she couldn't concentrate on the simple words her father's good friend had taught her. She had three more lessons to get through, from the notebook he had left her, but she couldn't focus on them.

Keelie reached up and groped around on the little wooden shelf (cedar, from the north woods) built into her bunk. Her fingers closed over the smooth sides of the pink rose quartz she'd impulsively bought at the High Mountain Renaissance Faire. She held it in front of her, closed her eyes, and concentrated, trying to center herself. She inhaled and released her breath, then imagined that her feet were like tree roots seeking the dirt, grounding her. Her hands tingled, and there was a small ringing in her ears like tiny bells, which eased away most of the green tree-energy that surrounded her. The exercise would have been totally effective, but she was interrupted several times by shouts of "huzzah" from next door.

"Huzzah" was apparently the medieval equivalent of "You go," and the Merry Men made full use of the word. Keelie opened her eyes. The room was bathed in a pinkish glow.

Yes! She'd done it. She'd been working with Sir Davey

for weeks to summon the crystal's protection. She couldn't wait to show him how far she'd come. She slumped back against the wall with a sigh. If only she could use the stone to send herself to the beach, or, for that matter, to bring her dad home from his errand.

Her father's ridiculous little homemade camper was fine for overnight stays, like the ones they'd had on their trip from the Faire in Colorado to here, the Wildewood Renaissance Festival in upstate New York. This Faire was the last stop in her dad's annual summer Tour de Ren Faires. He traveled to three a year, selling the beautiful and unique wood furniture that he made during the winter. When they finished here, they'd head for his winter home in Oregon.

She'd gotten over the embarrassment of people seeing her stepping out of the elaborately decorated little fairy-tale camper perched on the bed of the old pickup truck. But it was dollhouse-sized—too tiny for the three days they'd spent cooped up here while Dad set up his shop. She missed the spacious apartment of the High Mountain Renaissance Faire. She wistfully recalled their claw-foot bathtub and the tapestries depicting unicorns and flowers.

Outside, rain thrummed on the metal roof and the wooden sides of the camper, and against the tiny windows. Even the little cat door, unlatched now to let Knot in and out, creaked slightly. Raindrops pelted it as if tiny water soldiers were laying siege to the camper.

Keelie shuddered, remembering the water sprite she'd rescued in Colorado. *That* reminded her of the Red Cap, the destructive evil fairy she'd defeated. Not bad for a girl who until two months ago hadn't known she had magical abilities.

She checked her watch, a contraband object according

to the rules of the Faire. Everything the visitors saw had to be in keeping with the theme: "*... nonperiod items must be left in the staff living area so as not to distract from the period ambience...*" That's what the Players' Manual said.

What a joke. If that were true, then everyone over fifteen could forget about having teeth. She'd taken history; she knew what it had been like back then. The world of the Renaissance Faire was a fabulous fake. Fun, but not to be taken seriously, so she figured some rules were better ignored.

According to her forbidden timepiece, it was just after midnight. Zeke, her dad, had left at ten to see Sir Davey and show him the way to the rock and gem shop's new location. Sir Davey had just arrived in his mammoth Winnebago, and was parked in the motor home section of the campground. It would be great if they could stay in his RV. She'd have to sleep on the pull-out sofa, of course, but she'd heard that Davey's RV had a real bathroom in it. A hot shower sounded fabulous, not to mention going to the bathroom without crossing the entire campground. Maybe if she stayed in Sir Davey's "cavern on wheels" she'd sleep peacefully—without sensing trees and having magic tingle through her body.

Dad had promised Keelie her own room in their supposedly beautiful tent. She hadn't seen it yet, since it had been too wet to set it up. The tent was stashed in his shop, along with the furniture he'd shipped here to sell.

He was late. May he'd gotten so busy that he'd forgotten her, or some tree had distracted him. Or worse, some woman. Dad was a babe magnet, and Keelie didn't want to share him with anyone now that she'd rediscovered him.

She needed to replace her destroyed cell phone. She

didn't want to use Dad's, a small wooden rectangular box that he used to call other elves. The one time she'd tried to use it to call Sean at the Florida Ren Faire, she'd ended up telepathically linked to a spruce tree in Alberta, Canada.

After that, she tried talking Dad into buying her an iPhone. Mom had used a BlackBerry, which Dad might have been interested in because it sounded so natural and earthy, but none of her friends would be caught dead with one.

Mom. Keelie sniffled, wishing for lightning, thunder, some kind of weather drama. The plain old rain was making her maudlin, reminding her that her mother had only died three months ago. Not that she was over feeling sad; on the contrary, lately she'd been weeping over every little thing. She thought she'd gotten used to being without Mom, and to life without malls, friends from private school, tennis lessons, and the beach. Maybe she just needed to stay busy, to postpone the worst of her grief.

She missed Ariel, too. Keelie had bonded with the blind hawk that she had cared for in Colorado. Cameron, the birds-of-prey expert from the High Mountain Faire, had taken Ariel to a specialized rehab facility in Pennsylvania. No vet could help the bird. Ariel suffered from an elven curse, and so far no one had been able to break it.

Another loud "Hey nonny!" interrupted her thoughts. Keelie covered her ears to muffle the men's singing, but it was no use. They were bellowing so loud that the townies could probably hear it.

"I put her forthwith over my knee
And the naughty wench began to plea,
A little harder, master, pleeeaaaase..."

Keelie put her pillow over her head. It didn't sound likely that the Merry Men would get depressed and go to bed.

Something smacked the side of the trailer. She imagined her dad's hand holding on to the wall, injured, trying to find help and unable to reach the door. She held up her glowing quartz crystal. It shone brighter, and little rays of prismatic pink flashed around the room.

Ridiculous. But the image of her hurt dad lingered. Keelie pushed away the light blanket that covered her and sat up, leaving the bunk to open the door. Fat raindrops pattered on the ground beyond the wood-gingerbread encrusted overhang. The rain gleamed in the darkness, illuminated by lights from the Merry Men's tent. Out here, she could also hear feminine laughter coming from it, along with the deeper rumble of male voices. She wasn't going to look.

A Budweiser can gleamed in the light from the tent opening. No doubt this was the source of the thump on the wall. The morons in the tent had heaved an empty can out their tent door. It wasn't even period ale, as if she cared. She sighed. No Dad. Just a bunch of late revelers. She was tempted to disobey Dad and join them, but he'd have a fit if she did.

She'd gone with Raven to one of the infamous tent parties at the other Faire. For Keelie, that party had been an eye-opener. Bottles of mead, a strong, honey-flavored wine, had been passed from person to person, followed by a shared cigarette that she knew wasn't tobacco. And the guys who played the pirates at the Faire had been there. They were every bit as handsome as the jousting knights, but they took their rascally personas too seriously. Raven had danced for them, and one of the pirates had taken advantage of Raven's distraction to sit close to Keelie. It had been fun, and scary, and exciting. But when Raven saw that the man had started feeling her up, she stopped dancing and got her out of there, at least without making a scene. Keelie appreciated that, and now knew that she wasn't about to attend a tent party alone. Not that she'd want to go to this one.

Earlier, Keelie had overheard some of the Merry Men say that the Rivendell party area was quiet now, but that's where the action would be once the Faire opened. The jousters kept the horses corralled in the meadow next to their tents, the section jokingly named Rivendell by some insider who knew that most jousters were elves. Jousters. She had a soft spot in her heart for one in particular—Sean. Her heart fluttered when she recalled their kiss. But her chest tightened when she remembered that Sean hadn't called since their departure. He'd promised he would.

Keelie needed to talk to Raven. But Raven wasn't here, and she was stuck at this Faire with no phone. She couldn't even escape and find one, because she didn't have a driver's license. This was another sore point. Dad hadn't given her any driving lessons, and was always making excuses whenever she approached him about it.

Something moved in the forest behind the tents. Holding up the rose quartz crystal like a lantern, Keelie squinted, but saw nothing. She was about to step back and close the door when the shadow stepped out of the forest. It was a horse, although not big and brawny like the jousters' mounts. Maybe it was an Arabian. His white coat gleamed brightly, even in the darkness and deep shadows of the woods. It was probably one of the trick horses, the swift ponies that performed clever tricks in between jousts. Maybe he had broken free from the meadow.

Someone was going to be in big trouble for letting it get loose from the Rivendell corral. Keelie wasn't about to get soaked trying to catch it, either. The roads around the Faire were far from busy, so what trouble could the horse get into? It would be safe enough until morning.

The trees began to sway, although there wasn't any wind. Then Keelie felt green whispers trying to form in her mind. The rose quartz grew warm against her palm, and magic washed over her. Her hand tingled as the protective stone grew brighter and brighter. Suddenly, the light disappeared, and the night was black once more. As Keelie's senses dissolved into spiraling green energy, even the sounds from the Merry Men's tent disappeared. She was alone with the trees.

A heartbeat later, a single beam of pink light, like a laser, shot from the rose quartz. It reached across, turning into a bright silver glow that surrounded a slender spiral horn on the horse's head. Then the horse turned sharply and ran into the woods, the glowing horn still visible.

Heart pounding, Keelie realized what she had seen. Oh. My. God. Adrenaline rushed through her body. The muscles in her legs tightened. Poised. Ready. She took a step toward the woods.

But, overcome with an overwhelming anxiety that screamed *danger*, she found that she couldn't move. Something magical was forcing her to stay in place, rooted to the ground. The scent of cinnamon surrounded her.

A minute later, that's where Dad found her, holding the rose quartz aloft and still staring blankly into the indigo shadows.

two

"A unicorn," her father repeated, his eyes wide as he leaned back against the soft cushions on Sir Davey's sofa, a bottle of mead in his hand. "The guardian of the forest. I've never seen it here in Wildewood. I'd heard rumors from the human girls who claimed to have seen it. Are you sure?"

"I saw it." Keelie shivered, although it was warm in Sir Davey's RV, and the stone walls blocked the trees just as she'd hoped. She'd seen a unicorn. She was awed. The thought echoed in her head.

Sir Davey poured more tea into her cup. "I believe you, lass. It begs the question, though, why you? Unicorns are powerful beings, and mysterious. You must not wander through the forest alone."

"Alone? She must not enter the forest at all." Zeke frowned at his bottle of mead, and then looked down at Keelie sitting on the floor. "As Sir Davey said, we don't know its purpose in showing itself to you. You've just come into your magic. Whatever the creature has in mind, you won't be able to handle it, not yet."

"I can't stay out of the woods. What if the trees call me? I'm a Tree Shepherd, right?" Keelie looked from her father to Sir Davey, who was nodding wisely. "And why is the unicorn dangerous? If it's the guardian of the forest, don't we have, like, a shared cause?"

She studied both men. Her father was tall and slim. His long, wheat-colored hair was pulled into a ponytail, covering his pointed ear tips. Sir Davey was dark and handsome, and four feet tall if he stood on tiptoe. When the Faire was open, Davey wore a musketeer costume. The white feather of the musketeer hat always stayed pristine, even around the Muck and Mire show.

Sir Davey cleared his throat. "Traditionally, unicorns show themselves only to—" He blushed. He went back to examining her rose quartz.

"*Virgins.* I get it." Keelie rolled her eyes. "I've read a book or two."

"What we need to understand is why it showed itself to you." Sir Davey stroked his short beard.

"Hey, I'm a virgin, just to let you know." How insulting.

Dad didn't look at her, but she could see that his shoulders were more relaxed than they were a while ago. The old hypocrite. Until she moved in with him he'd been a real party boy.

"Are we going after it? I want to go after it. I want to see it again." Keelie's feet itched to run into the forest.

"No." Her father slammed his fist on the sofa arm.

Keelie was startled by the violent gesture, but recovered quickly. "Why not?" The desire to see the unicorn was almost a physical ache—a yearning she had to fulfill.

Dad sipped his mead, then looked at her. "'Because I said so' isn't going to cut it, is it?"

"No."

He sighed. "You're as stubborn as your mother."

Keelie sat up straighter. "Thank you."

His lips lifted a little at the corners as if he was trying to suppress a smile, but then he became all serious. "Keelie, unicorns can be good, and they can be self-serving, especially male unicorns once they set their sights on a young female they want."

"Sounds like some of the Merry Men. Did you hear them whistling at the belly dancers when they walked through the campground yesterday?"

Sir Davey grinned. "I saw them this morning." He swiveled his hips in imitation.

Dad rolled his eyes. Keelie wondered if the belly dancers had shimmied over to the campground just for Dad's benefit.

"This is different," he said. "The unicorn could place an enchantment on you to make you forget your dreams, your family, yourself. It makes you want only to be with it."

"That's so narcissistic."

"Exactly! Stay away from it."

Easier said than done. Keelie really, really, really wanted to see it again. It had been so beautiful. The way its spiral horn seemed to glow with some source of internal magic. And she wanted . . .

Dad waved his hand in front of her face. "Your energy

field is up. Tell me exactly what happened when you saw the unicorn."

Keelie leaned back against Sir Davey's sofa, still somewhat lost in her unicorn musings. "I wanted to run after it." Her voice seemed far away, even to her own ears. "I would've, too, but then I smelled cinnamon. I couldn't move."

She blinked and looked up at Dad.

He sighed, almost in relief. "My guess is the unicorn has some form of Dread magic, which he uses to keep humans out of his forest."

Sir Davey tugged his beard. "Aye, but why would the unicorn run if he was trying to get Keelie to come to him?"

She closed her eyes and the image of the unicorn formed in her mind, his white coat gleaming as if he'd been bathed in moonlight. She couldn't imagine that anything so lovely could have any connection to the Dread, the potent spell elves used to keep humans away. It was called the Dread because people felt panic building the closer they got to Dread-protected areas. Her brush with it in Colorado had made her want to run away screaming.

She had to find the unicorn. Opening her eyes, Keelie stared directly at Dad, who watched her warily. His forehead was etched with worry lines.

He took another sip of mead. "The unicorn's already worked his enchantment spell on you."

"I'd know it if he'd put a spell on me." Or at least she hoped she would. She really couldn't see herself forgetting everything and running away into the woods like a lovesick girl chasing after some guy—or in her case, a unicorn.

"She'll be okay, Zeke. The rose quartz protected her."

Keelie sighed with relief, although the atmosphere in the

room was as heavy as a smoggy Los Angeles afternoon in August. "Hey, look at it like this. Most dads have to worry about their girls dating horny teen boys. You just have to worry about a unicorn."

Her attempt at humor failed. Dad took another sip of mead. The worry lines deepened on his forehead.

Sir Davey stood up. "If she sleeps here, it should neutralize the unicorn magic for tonight." He motioned to the stone-clad walls. "And once the sun is up, she'll be safe enough around humans." He handed the rose quartz back to Keelie. "Keep this on you at all times. It protected you tonight, and it'll continue to protect you."

Dad frowned again, and his voice seemed determined. "As will Knot. He'll be with you wherever you go."

"No way, Dad!"

His baleful fatherly glare said there would be no further discussion.

Keelie was glad to see a full-size bed in Sir Davey's room. Just as she was beginning to nod off, a loud purr came from around her feet, where Knot was curled up. Moonlight streamed through the parted curtains over the window above Sir Davey's bed, illuminating the cat, his fur stuck up in wet devil points. Strange. A normal cat would have groomed himself, but Keelie wasn't surprised. Knot was not a normal cat.

She hadn't figured out exactly what he was, but she'd been told that he was her guardian, as he'd been her mother's. The cat was some kind of magical being, a fairy, maybe, and some day she'd figure out his secret. One thing was clear: he was obnoxious. She strained to hear the combined sound of Dad and Sir Davey's voices as they spoke in the living area of the RV, but she couldn't make out any of their conversation. She couldn't sleep. She sat up and pulled aside the curtains to look out into the night. From a hilltop far away she saw a sparkling silver light, like a small earthbound star glimmering. Was it the unicorn?

Something sharp clawed her ankle. Keelie gasped. Two green eyes glowed at her.

"What's wrong with you?" Keelie picked up Knot and dropped him off the bed. She closed the curtains and lay back down. Loud purring filled the room as Knot hopped back onto the bed and walked up alongside her body, purring louder and louder with each step. Then he settled down on her pillow.

"Gross! No way am I going to sleep with a wet cat on top of my head." She moved her head to the other pillow and closed her eyes. It was probably futile, with the unicorn in the forest waiting for her. She reached down for the rose quartz that she'd brought into the bed with her. With it clasped in her hand, she finally slept.

■ ■ ■

The following morning, Keelie stood next to Sir Davey's RV and stared at the trees. Hemlocks, birch, and spruce grew together to form this patch of forest near the campground, with a few oaks sprinkled in. Trees carpeted the rolling hills, and the blue and purple Catskill Mountains loomed in the background.

She walked closer to the tree line behind the camper, glancing behind her to make sure Dad wasn't watching. Under the low branches of the spruce trees, it was dark and the scent of loamy earth tickled her nose. A tingle of magic jolted her. She stepped back, wary. Wind rustled the leaves on the birches, and the branches on the hemlocks trembled in the cool air. Above her, the spruces danced in the breeze. She heard green whispers; the trees were aware of her presence. There was an undercurrent of sadness, deep grief, and pain in the green energy of the trees. Something tragic had happened to the forest, and it hadn't healed from the trauma.

Keelie was leery of these unknown trees. The aspens in Colorado had helped her, and she'd helped them, although it had been weird to have them inside her head. But there was a very creepy tree vibe coming from this forest. Keelie didn't want to go in, but she sensed the unicorn was there, waiting for her. The heart-shaped amulet that hung around her neck, the heart of the aspen Queen Reina, grew warm against her chest.

Magic prickled over her skin once again. Keelie wondered if the unicorn was nearby.

Her fear faded as she remembered how he'd glowed in the moonlight. She longed to see his horn glimmer in the sun, and wondered what color his eyes were. She heard the crunch of dry leaves as someone or something walked nearby. If she hiked into the woods, she might be able to find the unicorn. A longing to do so welled up within her. Then the dry leaves crackled even louder, as whomever or whatever came closer. Keelie's heart raced. She reached into her jeans pocket and pulled out the rose quartz. Warmth flooded her. Unicorn or Red Cap, she was protected.

Staring at the base of the spruce trees, Keelie noticed a moss-covered rock. It was standing upright, as if it had sprouted roots deep into the soil. At the rock's base, several tiny red mushrooms grew in a circle. A fairy ring. She looked around, but saw none of the stick-like fairies she'd met in Colorado—the *bhata*.

Suddenly, Knot landed nearby like a furry ninja. Keelie jumped back, and her bare arm brushed the bark of a spruce. Green filled her mind, but not the peace of the green woods she'd known before. This was an agitated presence.

Knot dug up one of the mushrooms, his tail twitching. It was time to go, before the fairies discovered that their ring was broken.

"You never learn, do you? Remember what the *bhata* did last time they caught you?" She'd look for the unicorn another day. Right now, she needed to find Dad. He'd told her to meet him at the new shop. She backed out of the forest, careful not to touch any branches or bark, and headed for the Faire.

Using the map her dad had given her, Keelie quickly found his shop. It was located in the congested Enchanted Forest Loop, across from a small grove of oaks. Zeke's shop was one of many lined up together, sort of like houses in California subdivisions where homes were so close together you could reach over and tap your neighbor's second floor window. All around her, Keelie saw artisans and craftsmen busily preparing for the opening of the Faire.

Her dad's shop was crowded with crates, some already opened, and the vine-and-crystal-embellished chairs she loved stacked haphazardly around. Keelie was amazed at how different this plank-floored structure was from their half-timbered, two-story place at the High Mountain Faire. This little shop had a wide, open front, a small counter in the middle, and shelves on the back walls for the dollhouses and wooden castles Zeke had brought to sell. A door in the rear wall probably led to a storage area or a workshop.

The place seemed empty, so Keelie ducked back out. Down in the cul-de-sac area of the Enchanted Forest Loop she found a familiar spot, Janice's herb shop. At this Faire it was called the Apothecary Shoppe, and—yuck—it was right next door to the privies. She bet Raven and Janice would be burning incense and scented candles by the barrel-load before the end of the summer.

One good thing about the loop was that it was going to be filled with busy foot traffic as the mundanes (the uncostumed Faire goers, according to the Rennies) made their way to the privies. Even now, activity hummed in the air, accompanied by the sound of hammers, electric saws, and conversation as everyone rushed to finish before the crowds appeared.

Majestic old oaks lined the path, shading it with their canopies of leaves. Hundreds of acorns blanketed the muddy roadway, a hazard worse than throwing bags of marbles around. Two men in yellow shirts, with "Security" written in black letters on the back, were raking and sweeping the acorns up.

The taller of the two kicked at an acorn with his heavy black work boot. "You'd think these stupid trees would run out of these dad-blame acorns."

The other one kept raking. "It ain't natural for trees to make this many acorns over and over, day after day."

Keelie closed her eyes and sensed the sentient presence of the trees, but something was wrong. These trees were older, much older than the ones near the campground. According to what Dad had taught her about trees, old trees were more cognitively developed, could wield more magic, and could telepathically communicate with each other and with tree shepherds. But these oaks, old as they were, seemed almost primitive.

And they were angry.

three

Keelie pressed the rose quartz against her chest as rage like hot sap flowed through her veins and poured into her mind. Then the anger stopped as a cool green energy flowed through her. Something furry was rubbing against her leg. She looked down expecting to see Knot, but to her surprise it was a skinny white cat.

"Where did you come from?" Keelie reached down to pet the white kitty. "You probably saved me from having some kind of green lava eruption." The cat arched its back against her outstretched hand, and then raced into the woods across the lane.

One of the security guards stopped and looked up at the

trees. He wiped his forearm across his reddened forehead. "I don't see why Finch doesn't chop these trees down. She's always blowing a gasket over these oaks because the shop owners complain about the acorns."

Keelie sensed dark green anger sweeping through the trees. The oaks brandished their branches as if a high wind were blowing through their leaves, and suddenly a barrage of acorns rained down on the two security men. One acorn landed, with a hard thump, on her scalp. Arms covering her head, Keelie ran back across the lane to Dad's shop.

From the safety of the enclosure, Keelie watched the two security guys run down Enchanted Lane like their pants were on fire. Merchants and workers stopped what they were doing to watch them. Keelie noticed several gazing at the trees and shaking their heads. A woman in jeans and a tank top crossed herself and hurried into her shop.

"Huzzah, huzzah, the King is in his chamber and the Queen is in the privy, and what see we here, but a lovely little pretty," sang three Merry Men dressed in green tunics and matching tights. They'd stopped and circled a woman wearing a bodice that made her bosom pop out of the top like two apples in a tiny fruit basket. She giggled as they crooned more disgusting lyrics and carefully tiptoed through the acorns, followed by the Merry Men. They, too, watched their footing among the nuts.

This Faire had more nuts than those strewn on the ground. Thank goodness she didn't have to work with that bunch. Keelie planned to take it easy at this Faire.

She looked up at the Heartwood shop's wooden sign, which had an oak tree with little heart-shaped acorns dangling from the branches. Maybe Dad chose this location so he could be a tree shepherd for the errant oaks. They looked like ordinary trees, but Keelie noticed the roots were gnarled like arthritic hands. Even without magic, a person could see wizened facial features in the knots and lumps on the trees' trunks.

Next door to Dad's shop, to Keelie's delight, was a leather goods booth named Lady Annie's Leather Creations. Curious, she went to explore. It wasn't like she needed boots. She had her mother's old pair, and a pair of everyday boots Janice had given her at the High Mountain Faire.

Lady Annie's shop was ready for action, and the smell of freshly worked leather cut through the green of the crushed acorns outside. Keelie inhaled deeply. It reminded her of the smell of a new car, which in turn reminded her that she hadn't had a single driving lesson. Then all thoughts of cars vanished as she caught sight of Lady Annie's wares. Her mouth dropped open.

Awesome, designer Renaissance footwear filled the shelves—mainly incredible boots, hand tooled, with carved bone buttons all down the sides, in dozens of designs. A framed poster from the Lady Annie's Boots catalog showed how they fit the wearer's leg like a second skin. Keelie closed her mouth for fear she'd start drooling, and picked up the handwritten price tag on a gorgeous dark red pair trimmed in black. Her stomach bottomed out when she saw the price: nine hundred dollars.

Wait a minute. Her inner-California girl gave her a mental smack across the face. She'd been hanging around elf daddy, trees, and an obnoxious cat for way too long. This was custom footwear. Think designer prices. This she could go for, and they would work perfectly with the garb Janice and Raven had given her. Maybe this place was new and Raven didn't know about it. She was all about leather. Keelie smiled as she recalled Raven's spending spree at a leather shop in Colorado.

"Can I help you?" asked a young woman with tanned skin and long, straight black hair. Dressed in a T-shirt and jeans, she wore an absolutely stunning squash-blossom turquoise choker and a pair of Lady Annie boots with worked leather eagles on the sides. A little pin on her shirt read, "Lady Annie."

"Do you make these boots?" Keelie asked.

"Yes, I'm Lady Annie, and every pair is leather-crafted by me or one of my family members."

"Wow. I love your necklace, too. Are you Native American?" She'd met a Zuni woman who looked just like Lady Annie when she and Mom had taken a trip to Arizona

"I sure am. Navajo." Lady Annie stared at Keelie. "You're Zeke's daughter aren't you?"

Keelie nodded. "How did you know?"

"You look like him." Her eyes glinted. Another of Dad's conquests. "I met your father and your cat, yesterday."

Okay, not an old Zeke girlfriend. Yet. "My cat must have made an impression."

"He sure did. He knocked over a display of boots." She smiled. Obviously a forgiving cat lover. "I just saw him across the street."

Keelie turned around and saw Knot batting at some acorns on the ground. Stupid cat! She saw a *feithid daoine*, a bug fairy, buzzing nearby. It was shiny bronze and looked like a beetle if you didn't look too closely. Knot didn't have a good relationship with the bug fairies—his fault, since he loved to torment them. Not her problem. Knot could have the fairies, Dad could have the unruly trees, and Keelie could have new boots. The thought thrilled her. She breathed in and focused on the displays, trying to decide between the soaring hawk and the rearing unicorn emblems.

"If I were to design a pair of boots for you, I would have to suggest tree leaves, with hand-carved buttons shaped like acorns—sort of like these." Lady Annie pulled out a really beautiful pair of boots, green, with tooled brown leaves climbing up the sides. The buttons were silver oak leaves.

"Those are gorgeous." Keelie hoped she wasn't actually drooling. In a nonchalant movement—a contemplating-a-purchase kind of gesture—Keelie checked for drool. Whew, none.

"If you want a pair, you need to place your order early. I can only make so many each Faire season."

"Custom-made boots. This is so Italian."

"Yeah, I've even made boots for rock musicians when they're on tour."

"Impressive." Maybe Keelie had discovered a designer side to the Faire: California Cool meets the Middle Ages.

"How long would it take for you to make me a pair?"

"Three weeks if I start today. You have to make a three-hundred-dollar deposit before I measure you, or you can pay in full using your Lady Visa or Master Card."

Dad had confiscated all of Keelie's credit cards when she had gone online and ordered new clothes from La Jolie Rouge. She'd been feeling really sad and upset about Mom. Dad had gone all parental unit when he saw the total—$400.00. But Keelie had bought everything on sale. He hadn't understood how much money she'd saved. Dad had absolutely no shopping logic whatsoever. It had to be because he was all elf.

She didn't need credit cards. She had a bank account bursting with cash. Talbot and Talbot, her mom's California lawyers, had sent a letter saying that Mom's estate had been put in trust until she turned eighteen and was attending college. Her eyes had bugged out when she saw how much money was there. Maybe Dad could front the cash, and she could go ahead and put her order in so that she could have them for this Faire. He'd want her to have themed footwear to coordinate with the business.

"I'll have to get the money from Dad. He's going to love the leaves and acorn theme. I'll come back later to get measured." He shouldn't have a problem with her ordering a pair of boots she was paying for with her own money.

Lady Annie motioned casually with her hand. "Since you're Zeke's daughter, we can go ahead and measure you now, and I can start cutting the leather today, because once the Faire starts tomorrow, it's going to be crazy."

"Let's get started." Keelie sat on a small wooden stool (birch from West Virginia) and Annie got to work.

As Keelie left Annie's booth an hour later, she almost ran into a man carrying a stack of boxes. This was one busy footpath. Up the lane, three hunky actors read from scripts, practicing their lines. They were part of Prince John's guards. This Faire's story line was that Prince John's betrothed, Princess Eleanor, was coming and there was to be a wedding. Robin Hood and his Merry Men were going to disrupt the ceremony to rescue Maid Marian, who was being held prisoner and was serving as Princess Eleanor's handmaiden.

Underneath the veneer of modern-day medieval madness, Keelie sensed the trees' magic edging on her mind. Her hands were tingly from it. She reached inside her pocket and touched the rose quartz. Instant calm enveloped her. Remembering the lovely boots, Keelie smiled in anticipation. Just wait till Elia got a load of Keelie's new boots. Perfect Elf Girl's forehead was going to crinkle up with envy. Maybe she'd get some permanent wrinkles. Keelie would be more than happy to make Elia look her full sixty years, instead of seventeen.

Keelie peeked into her father's shop. Dad wasn't in, and she needed to get her cash. Here again, if she had a cell phone she could've called him to ask about the boots. If he had a problem with her ordering them, well, it was his fault because he should've replaced her cell phone by now so that he could've told her not to buy them.

On the other side of Dad's shop was a bright Pepto-pink building, with a trellis of dark green ivy growing up one side and a sign that read, "The Gingerbread House." Her mouth watered until she saw that there were no gingerbread cakes or cookies here. Instead, the shelves were filled to overflowing with something else she loved: puppets. There were fluffy white unicorn hand puppets and marionettes in the form of knights and princesses and dragons. They all looked so fun.

Keelie found herself on the shop's porch, although she couldn't remember climbing the three wide steps. From up here she could see Sir Davey walking down the path.

The shop drew her attention once more and she drifted inside. The walls were lined with shelves, which were draped with bright colors and crowded with hand puppets and stringed marionettes, as well as with the little puppets that could sit on your shoulder. The shop was so cute, and smelled like cookies, too, which added to the enchantment. Keelie could imagine the little puppets all coming to life.

A woman with blonde hair piled up in a disheveled bun came out and smiled at Keelie. "Hi, I'm Lulu, the puppet lady." Her eyebrow was pierced with a little silver hoop, which had a tiny red heart dangling from it. She gave off a really cool vibe. Keelie's anxiety melted away, and she was filled instead with a languid warmth as fuzzy and sweet as cotton candy on a hot summer's day.

Their hands touched with a zap of static and Lulu jumped back from the shock. She waggled her hand in the air. "Hey kid, you have some zing there." Her face had gone splotchy as if she'd eaten shrimp and was having an allergic reaction.

"Are you okay?" For some reason, Keelie really liked Lulu; she genuinely seemed like a nice person, someone Keelie could hang out with when the Faire got boring.

"I'm fine. You work here? What's your name?"

"I'm Keelie Heartwood. My dad's shop is next door."

Sir Davey saw her and waved, although he frowned when he saw Lulu. "You okay, Keelie?"

"Fine. Just visiting the neighbors." Keelie wondered why Davey looked so wary. Knot hissed and arched his back.

"Is it safe to have that cat loose? He should be on a leash or in a crate." Lulu looked queasy.

"You can't walk a cat on a leash." But the idea of Knot in a crate was actually pretty good. "Besides, he's part of my dad's business."

Keelie sensed the oak trees across the lane. Green energy was building up, and the oaks were definitely angry. She looked around, but didn't see anything that would anger them. Not a lumberjack or beaver in sight. Acorns began pinging on the tin roof of the puppet shop.

Lulu groaned. "Not again. I've complained to the Faire director, and she said it's being handled, but whatever she's doing is not working."

Keelie looked out. The trees were now like multi-limbed wooden creatures aiming their acorns like little projectiles at the gingerbread shop. Another tingle shot through her, making her shiver. A major dose of tree energy was coming their way. Keelie grabbed her rose quartz and stepped out onto the path. She addressed the trees.

Stop it. Leave the puppet lady alone. Her unspoken command rang through the clearing.

No response. Worse, it was as if she'd hit a wall. She was being ignored.

Shocked, Keelie turned around. This was the first time the trees had rejected telepathic communication with her, and she didn't like it one bit. It was like calling someone and having them rudely hang up on you.

Lulu's gaze traveled past Keelie and up to the branches of the oaks. A breeze swept down the winding lane and acorns showered down around them like green hail. Keelie threw her arms over her head, but no acorns hit her. She looked up.

An invisible umbrella surrounded her. She could see the acorns hit the air a foot above her, and then careen off as if they'd bounced from something solid. Lulu was gone, fled back into her shop, and Keelie was trapped in a bubble in the middle of an acorn storm. This wasn't her magic, so who was protecting her?

four

Through the haze of green and brown nuts, Keelie saw Dad come out from the back room of the shop. He frowned, then held out his hand. Waves of calm rippled past her, then up into the trees. The anger melted, vanishing into calm silence, then subsided into sleep.

Relieved, Keelie ran toward him. She was going to have to learn how to do that hand thing. She kicked acorns out of the way as she went. They even covered the shop floor.

"Did you do that?" Dad's eyes were bloodshot now, and the whites had a green tinge. A side effect of the green magic? Keelie stared, afraid to say anything. It was hard to tell what passed for normal in her crazy new life.

"No, it was the trees," she answered. "They blasted us." Keelie touched one of the wooden support beams: hemlock, local to the forest. *An overgrown logging road, and the stumps of ancient trees around her, and sorrow, rooted deep*. Whoa. She shook the wood's memory from her head. She needed more plastic in her life. A credit card would be a good start.

Dad leaned against the smooth polished pine counter. "I know what the trees did, but did you put up the protection shield?"

"The what? You mean that invisible umbrella? I thought you did that."

Knot sauntered out from behind the counter, his furry tail held high. Hadn't he just been across the street?

They both stared at him.

"Do you think he did it?" Keelie looked down at the stupid cat. "I thought he was the one who made the trees mad, using one for a scratching post or something."

Knot batted at a huge green acorn that had rolled in with Keelie. It skittered across the pine floor like a rolling marble. Knot ran after it, pawing it until the acorn twirled round and round like a lopsided top.

"No, it wasn't him." Dad was talking to her, but looking over her shoulder. Keelie turned to follow his gaze.

He was staring at the puppet woman and the hundreds of acorns carpeting the ground in front of her shop. He obviously thought something was up. Dad closed his eyes. When he opened them, he frowned. His eyes looked spooky. "The oaks will be quiet for a while."

Lulu's splotches had disappeared, and she was hanging marionettes on a spinner rack. The woman stared back, but turned away with a fearful look in her eyes.

"Come with me, Keelie," he said loudly. "I'm opening these crates in the back, and I want you to see where I keep my packing supplies." He lowered his voice and put his head near hers. "What did she say to you?"

"Nothing, really. She told me her name is Lulu. She has the greatest shop with all these cool puppets. What's up with the oaks, though? They're totally cranky."

"More than cranky. And they're not responding to us. They've been like this for years, but usually a little care comforts them, calms them down." He shook his head. "I'm not sure what's going on, but I fear it may be serious. If only I could speak to the unicorn."

"Want me to find him?" She cringed inwardly. Her voice had come out high-pitched, like an eight-year-old begging for a treat.

"Stay out of the forest, and don't ask again. These trees are old, Keelie, the survivors of a logging camp which existed here about thirty years before they built the dam and power plant upstream. The Faire is built over the old logging campground, and some of these buildings stood then. It'll be a long time before the forest recovers."

That would explain the hemlock post's image. "The trees aren't this obnoxious every year, are they?" If so, this would have been called the Haunted Forest instead of the Wildewood Faire.

"It was a beautiful forest." Dad's eyes grew misty as he remembered. "There were no elves to perform the tree Lorem, so the energy and spirits of the fallen trees haunt these lands, and something has awakened them. That's one reason why I don't want you going near the unicorn. He's powerful and protective of the forest, and he may not hesitate to use your magic for his purpose."

Fear skipped up Keelie's spine. "There's not another Red Cap, is there?"

"No, no evil fairies, just the Faire director that I have to get ready for. She's a beast of a woman."

Keelie had filled with yearning when Dad said "unicorn." She knew he was in the forest, and even though Dad had warned her about his glamour, she didn't want to resist the compulsion to go into the woods. What could the unicorn do to hurt her? Dad watched her with a suspicious expression that said *I know you're up to something*. If she did go into the forest, she'd need to divert his attention.

"Why were the oaks throwing acorns at Lulu? She's really nice." The puppet lady had a right to be freaked about the acorns.

"I don't know. She's new. The children's costume shop used to be there, but the owner got sick this spring. Admin scrambled for someone to fill the slot, and Lulu was looking for a new home for her puppet business."

"Is she an elf?" Lulu didn't look like an elf, and she was too nice to be one, but there was something magical about her.

"No, she's human, but she makes me uncomfortable. She's odd. Steer clear of her until I know what it is, okay?"

"But she's so nice. I like her. "

"Keelie!"

"Okay, but can I at least buy one of her puppets? I want a shoulder unicorn." Mom would have bought one for her. She'd loved stuffed animals. Moments later, hot tears rolled down Keelie's cheeks, as if on autopilot. She hated how she cried without warning.

Dad pulled a wad of tissues from his pocket and gave

them to her. These days he always carried tissues in his pocket for his waterspout daughter.

"Sorry." She blew her nose.

"It's normal, Keelie. You're grieving. Three months isn't that long. You've been through a lot since losing her, too."

"No kidding. Like finding out I'm not human?" That had been a shocker.

"Half human," he corrected. "It might do you a world of good to do something other than hang out at the shop. I'm stuck here, getting ready for opening day and waiting for Scott to arrive, but you're free. Why don't you get a job?"

"I just wanted to hang."

"If you had a job working in the Faire, you could earn some pocket money. I saw the shopping gleam in your eyes."

"What a coincidence. I was just at Lady Annie's looking at boots."

"You already have your Mom's and the ones Janice gave you. Why don't you buy a bow and learn archery?"

"Archery?" Leave it to an elf to think archery was fun. And he would bring up the fact she already had two pairs of boots. Dad just didn't get shoes and females. Two pairs weren't enough.

"I thought I'd use some of the money Mom left me. And besides, they're not so expensive."

"I've seen the price of those boots." Zeke quirked an eyebrow, as if he thought it was funny that she wanted a pair. "But if you really want them, you can get a job."

"I just ordered a pair." Keelie blew her nose as she said it, trying to disguise the words.

It didn't work.

"I hope you're joking." His voice rose to "you're grounded" volume.

She couldn't believe Dad was picking a fight. She was the one who'd lived in close quarters with him and his cat, without a refrigerator and without a bathroom for the past three weeks. She'd pointed out every piercing and tattoo parlor in eight states and Dad had driven past every single shop, eyes looking straight ahead, never once glancing at where she was pointing. She'd *earned* those boots. "I *have* ordered them, and Lady Annie has already cut the leather." Well, she didn't know if Lady Annie had actually started, but she might have. Too late now.

"Really." Dad's face had paled, but Keelie noticed his neck was beginning to turn green. This was not normal.

"Are you okay, Dad?"

"Don't change the subject."

"Fine. It's my favorite subject right now. I have money in the bank, so what's the big deal? They're going to be really great, with leaves and acorns. They'll go with the shop." Although she might need to rethink the acorns after this last incident.

"Keelie, that's your college money. If you want the boots, you have to work for them."

"Excuse me?"

"You heard me. You're going to work for those boots."

Keelie's mouth dropped open in outrage. "It's my money. I can do as I please. I'll call Ms. Talbot, and she'll tell you that I can spend my money as I see fit."

Dad shrugged. "Call her. She'll tell you that you can't touch the money until you're eighteen."

Knot abandoned his wild game of acorn hockey and sat down in front of Keelie to wash his butt.

"Fine. I will call. Mom would've let me have them." The tears were back.

Dad grabbed the crowbar and pried the lid off a nearby crate with more force than was necessary. The lid went flying and bounced off a post, splintering on the floor. "You're living with me now. Ms. Finch, the Faire coordinator, has an office in the administrative building. She's in charge of hiring."

Fresh tears made Keelie dab at her eyes, and she blew her nose with the tear-dampened tissue. "You're kidding, right? You want me to get a job?"

"Ms. Finch. Go. Now." Dad's face had gone stern.

"Yeah, right, Zeke. It'll take me a hundred years to pay it off working just on weekends." Keelie scowled at him. She'd just downgraded him to a first name basis. Forget calling him Dad until he acted like one.

"You need to learn the value of working for something. I think you've had too many things just given to you."

"How dare you? Mom loved me. She took care of me." Keelie spun on her heel and started to march away.

Her right foot slipped on Knot's acorn, and she hit the ground hard on her backside, her teeth clacking together painfully. Winded and jarred, Keelie concentrated on inhaling and exhaling as her tailbone spasmed with pain.

Dad dropped the crowbar and ran to her. "Are you okay?"

"I'll live." She groaned, too rattled to pull away as he helped her up. From beneath her, the acorn rolled across the floor. The sadistic orange feline sauntered out of the shop, not bothering to look back at the havoc he'd caused. At least he was acting normally.

Keelie limped to the end of the street, studied a map of the Wildewood Faire, and found the Admin building. She knew that calling the attorneys was hopeless. They'd never let her have the money. Dad had called her bluff, and now her leisurely summer plans were a bust.

Soon she stood in front of a white cottage that must have once been part of the logging camp. A sign on the door read "Hiring." Knot ran past her in a blur and stopped on the porch. Keelie marched up the steps, barely looking at the pots of herbs that lined them.

She glared at the cat. He had some nerve, following her as if he was all concerned. She'd probably be bruised for a week from his stupid acorn.

"You're never, ever going to sleep with me again." She realized she'd been shouting when two really hot hunky guys in jeans and polo shirts stopped to stare at her, as did a teenage girl with long brown hair. The girl glared at Keelie with a look Keelie was familiar giving, not receiving—the "you're such a dork" look. The trio exchanged glances that plainly said, "What a loser!"

Keelie quickly retaliated with a hand on her hip and the bored "who gave you permission to stare at me?" glare. If Laurie were here, she'd startle them with something smart.

The trio got the hint and moved on. Keelie overheard the girl say, "Can you believe I got a job at Francesca?"

Francesca, the coolest shop at the Ren Faire.

Now *that* was a place she could work. She loved their clothes—beautiful interpretations of period clothing. Ubercool for Rennie garb, the La Jolie Rouge of the Ren Faire. The kind of costume that would go with her boots.

Keelie winced as she climbed the porch steps. She needed

a guardian to protect her from her supposed guardian. Knot sat at the door as if he were daring her to go inside.

"Get!" She shooed him away with her foot. He purred.

The wooden door suddenly opened, and cool air rushed out. Admin had air conditioning. No fair. The cool air became downright cold as Keelie looked up at a large woman with flaming red hair and flashing green eyes.

"What in the hell are you doing? Were you planning to knock, or just stand there?" The woman looked as if she was having a bad day and was about to take it out on Keelie.

"I'm here to apply for a job," Keelie managed to squeak.

The woman's red eyebrows narrowed as her gaze went down Keelie, and then back up again. "How old are you?"

"Fifteen."

"Hmm. Do I know you?"

"I'm Keelie Heartwood. My dad's—"

"Zeke Heartwood." Her frosty voice warmed up a couple of notches. "You're one of them. Come on in, the others are inside. I hope Heartwood can do something about those belligerent oaks."

Keelie followed the woman, who was wearing jeans, too, but paired with a white blouse under a blue tapestry-patterned bodice. Keelie noticed that she had a pair of Lady Annie's boots. A rising red sun, over a black mountain range, was tooled into the brown leather that clung to the formidable woman's thick calves. More determined than ever, Keelie knew she'd work for boots. She'd show Zeke she could do it.

The woman walked behind an ordinary metal office desk and plunked down into a swivel chair. There was nothing Renaissancy about it. She motioned toward a ladder-back chair with stuffing poking from its torn seat cushion.

"So you're Zeke Heartwood's kid."

"Yes."

"I'm Ms. Finch. Why do you want a job at the Faire?"

"I need to earn some money."

"Why aren't you working for your dad?"

"Dad has an apprentice. He thought it might be good for me to do something different. He wants me to meet new people, experience new situations."

She beamed. "I have the perfect job for you. You understand you've come a little late. Most jobs have been filled."

Keelie leaned forward. "I've got a great job in mind, too. Do you have any openings at Francesca? I would love to work there."

"Sorry kid, but those positions have been filled. You just missed the last spot. I gave it to a girl who was here just a few minutes ago. You must have seen her. Mall brat. Abercrombie & Fitch type."

Keelie wondered if Knot would go and pee on the girl on her first day on the job. Maybe if she bribed him with catnip. Then Keelie could show up and really show the Francesca people what she could do. Maybe she'd even have her boots by then, and she'd really fit in with the Ren Faire designer crowd. An image of her riding bareback on the unicorn flashed through her mind. Again, the urge to go into the woods washed over her. She forced her attention back to Mrs. Finch's arched red eyebrow.

"Then what do you have in mind for me?"

"You've heard of a Jack-of-all-trades?"

"Yeah."

"Well, you're going to be my Jill-of-the-Faire. You're going to fill in wherever and whenever I need you."

"What does that mean?" That sounded either fun or awful.

"Here's the job description: One day you're filling in at the joust, holding horses because one of the squires has called in sick. Or you'll be serving up turkey legs because one of the local high school kids has a hangover, or I may need you to fill in at the juggling show because the juggler has dropped a bowling ball on his head. Or you'll be helping Sir Brine with his pickle cart. I put you where I need you."

"Pickle cart? No way. Are you sure you don't have anything else? A permanent job, maybe?"

"I do have an opening for an assistant to the privy cleaner." Finch leaned forward, eyes locked on Keelie's.

She shuddered. "Jill-of-the-Faire works."

Finch sat back. "Good. Your first job is tomorrow, opening day, by the front gates. You'll need to be there at eight-thirty to greet customers. Pick up your costume at the garb shop this afternoon, and I'll walk you through your duties."

"Costume?" She envisioned a beautiful gown. This could be sweet. Whatever it was would be worth it for the boots.

"Plumpkin the Baby Dragon." Finch waved a hand in the direction of the other side of the house. "It'll be the purple fuzzy one in the other room. They should've gotten the vomit out last year. If not, spray some more Febreze in it, and you'll be good to go. Better take a bottle with you in case the smell comes back."

The embarrassment of wearing a fuzzy purple dragon suit was one thing, but entertaining little kids sounded awful. And the Febreze had not killed the smell. Keelie thought maybe now would be a good time for the unicorn to rush over, pierce her heart with its horn, and end her life.

five

That afternoon, Keelie returned to the Admin building. The potted lavender by the porch wafted its soothing scent over her. Janice said lavender was good for stress, but the flower's purpley spikes reminded her of what was coming: Plumpkin the Baby Dragon.

She crept past the office, not anxious to see Ms. Finch again. At the end of the hallway, a sign read "Costume Shop." Opening the door, Keelie was greeted with a beehive-swirl of activity. The room was crowded with women. A thin woman with graying brown hair buzzed about with a yellow measuring tape around her neck, a pincushion on her wrist, and a notepad and pencil in her hands. She wove through the others, all of whom were trying on costumes.

Keelie kept to the edge of the room, scooting around a plastic table laden with luxurious bolts of velvet, lace, and silk. Racks overflowed with cloaks, women's voluminous gowns, and men's doublets. Another woman was cutting fabric at a long waist-high table, using stiff plastic pattern pieces. No one looked at Keelie, and that was perfect. She wanted to grab the Plumpkin costume and get out of there.

Fabric heralds decorated the walls. These tall vertical banners with tasseled, pointy ends were paraded around on horseback before the jousts. One of them had stylized silver branches against a black background and bore the words "Silver Bough Jousting." Next to it was a green one with a silver hawk. Sean o' the Wood's crest. Keelie sighed and thought of Sean at his Ren Faire. Right now he was probably practicing jousting with the other knights, his chest emblazoned with his silver hawk. She hoped he missed her as much she missed him.

Keelie scanned the room, trying to zero in on the Plumpkin costume. It wasn't here. She was startled to see a unicorn head in a corner, and then realized it was just a realistic costume piece. The image of the real unicorn formed in her mind; she closed her eyes as a longing to find it inundated her, obliterating the noise and people in the costume room. Maybe Dad was right and the unicorn had enchanted her.

No! She had to focus on her Jill-of-the-Faire job. She'd ordered the boots, and she was going to show Zeke she could earn the money to pay for them. Maybe after she proved that she was responsible, old Zeke would let her have driving lessons. She'd go check out the little town of Canooga Springs. Maybe she could buy a cell phone there.

Three beautiful elven girls stepped onto padded stools, high above the human women below. Then another girl stepped onto a cushioned ottoman, tossing golden curls over her shoulder. Elia, who considered herself perfect.

Keelie froze. The Perfect Elf Girl sneered and whispered to her companions. The thought of having to even speak to Elia sickened Keelie. She was the one who had cursed Ariel. The hawk's courage inspired Keelie; she wouldn't be afraid.

They hadn't spotted her yet. She just had to snag the Plumpkin costume and get the hell out of there. But then the elven girls all turned to look at her with matching disdain. They stood unembarrassed in their underwear, like swimsuit models ready to pose for a photographer, sure of their perfection. Keelie turned away. She was embarrassed, even if they weren't. The woman with the tape measure returned, arms full of silks and brocades.

"All right girls, let's try these on. No pins this time. The seams are all basted. Let me know if you need help."

"Am I to fasten this costume myself?" Elia's snooty voice made Keelie grit her teeth.

The costumer's shoulders slumped. She'd only gotten five feet away, but she returned to lace Elia in, puff out her sleeves, and tug her skirts into place.

The costumes were beautiful. Elia's was a plum-colored silk skirt with alternating panels of purple and gold brocade, and glistening amethyst-colored beads that decorated the joining of each panel and the edge of the hem. Her bodice was a work of art with three different strips of purple brocade pieced together. It looked like a modified Francesca.

Wistfully, Keelie thought about the job at the Francesca shop. Life was so unfair!

Then she noticed that Lady Annie sat on the floor, tracing an outline of one of the girl's feet. Miss Evil Elfpants and crew were getting custom boots. She tried to keep her jealousy from showing.

Lady Annie looked up and smiled. "Keelie, nice to see you again. I cut your boots this morning. Told you I'd get busy. Are you here to pick up a costume?"

"Yes, I've got a job." Keelie hoped she sounded normal.

"Oh, so the little Round Ear has come to work like the peasant she naturally is." Elia's voice carried over those of the elven girls, who shushed her, giggling.

Keelie imagined the seamstress choking Elia with a roll of lace and smiled. "Who are you supposed to be? And working, too, I might add." She would have added "Pointy Ear," but she'd promised Dad that she wouldn't give away the elven secret, no matter what the elf girls did. Besides, Elia would take it as a compliment.

"I'm the Princess of this Faire." Elia flounced her silk skirts. "And it's scarcely work. More like pleasure."

Her little clones twittered like birdbrains.

"I play Princess Eleanor of Angouleme, Prince John's betrothed." She picked at her full skirts and preened.

Keelie was unimpressed. "What a boring job. You get to watch everyone else have fun. You don't even get to ride a horse. I heard that Tarl the Muck and Mire man is playing Prince John. Isn't that great?" She smiled inwardly, knowing exactly what vain and self-important Elia thought of Tarl.

Elia stamped her foot and swung around, accidentally clipping her elbow across the seamstress' jaw. The seamstress shouted "Ow!" and dropped her scissors, which landed sharp-end-down in the toe of an elven girl's slippered foot.

"You oaf, you've cut me!" the girl shrieked. She slipped out of her shoe, hitting one of the other elf girls in the chest with her flailing gestures. That really had to hurt, Keelie thought. The elf girl's feet were narrow and white, and in dire need of a pedicure.

Another of the snooty crew nearly swooned when she saw the scissors. "You're going to lose your foot."

"Shut up, I am not!" the elf girl shouted back fearfully.

"Quiet down, girls. You sound like fishwives." Finch glared at them. She had a sad-looking fuzzy purple suit with glittery scales draped over her left arm, and a bottle of Febreze in her hamlike fist.

With her free hand, she pulled the scissors out of the girl's slipper and handed them to the red-cheeked seamstress. With every move, glitter from the costume's scales rained on the floor.

Elia's shoes got a liberal dose of it, and she wiped her shoe on the ottoman as if the glitter were dog poop.

"You need to fire her." Elia parked her pale fists on her hips. "If she's going around maiming people with scissors, then she shouldn't be working in here. She's a klutz, and I don't want her near me. And while you're at it, fire Keliel Heartwood. Wherever she goes she brings curses. See what just happened? It was her fault."

The other girls started murmuring to each other, looking like an angry mini-mob of elven fashion divas.

Finch's eyes flashed, and her lips pursed. "Princess, plug the cakehole!" Her last word echoed around the room.

The elf girls were stunned into silence.

Finch shoved the stinky dragon suit toward Keelie. "Here. Wear this, and wear lots of deodorant, because it's going to be hot tomorrow. I've used an entire bottle of Febreze; that's the best we can do."

The red-headed elven girl wrinkled her nose. "Eww, that's the suit that nasty Vernerd wore last year."

One of the other elf girls backed away. "Verminous Vernerd was the squire who spread head lice around the jousters. He got demoted to dragon after that."

Keelie stared at the deflated dragon suit. *Demoted*? *Lice*?

Elia plunked her hands on her hips again. "Then that suit could still be infected with lice." She motioned with her hand. "Keep away from me, peasant girl."

Finch growled. "Lice don't live more than forty eight hours without a host, and I said plug the cakehole because if you don't, you're going to be Princess Whine-a-Lot in the pony-and-kid parade with Plumpkin, here."

Two thoughts hit Keelie at once: Elia could be Princess Whine-a-Lot, which suited her; and Keelie was going to be in the pony-and-kid parade. Panic and laughter hit her at the same time. It sounded a little hysterical.

"Put on the dragon suit," Finch commanded.

"Now?"

"Yes. We can't wait for Halloween to get here."

Keelie started to unbutton her La Jolie Rouge shirt, flashing back to the first day of gym in seventh grade. Laurie had been there for support when she and Keelie had stripped down to their underwear and bras. Keelie hadn't had much in the way of cleavage then, and Laurie had yelled out at the girls who smirked, "What've you got in your bra? Toilet paper? Let's see."

Keelie had grown up and filled out since then. While she still didn't have as much as Laurie in the boob department, she had more than Elia. And thank goodness she'd had a shower in Sir Davey's RV this morning.

As the cold air hit her chest, one spot stayed warm. Keelie looked down at the wooden heart-shaped pendant that lay against her skin, soothing her with its magic.

Elia gasped.

Keelie looked up. The girls were gazing at her with wide eyes. One openly pointed at her and whispered to another.

"What?" Keelie asked, staring them down.

Elia's eyes were narrowed. "You don't deserve that."

"You're nuts."

Elia stamped her foot. She almost hissed. "*I* should be wearing that pendant, and you know why, *Round Ear*."

"I earned it. It was a gift. Get over it." Keelie reached up to her throat, feeling suffocated. It was the talisman. She had to take it off, or it would choke her. She was about to unclasp it when she glanced over at Elia, who now wore an expectant grin.

Sir Davey had taught her to breathe deeply whenever she experienced any type of magical attack. Earth magic helped, too. Keelie knew what she needed—the rose quartz. She walked over to her jeans and grabbed the smooth rock from her pocket. Immediately, the choking feeling was gone.

Thwarted, Elia stamped her foot again.

Keelie glared at her. The little witch had tried to manipulate her with magic. Holding the rose quartz up, she wondered what it would do if she aimed it at Goldilocks. Maybe the elf girl would implode.

Finch walked in front of Keelie and blocked her view

of Elia. But the formidable woman held the elf girl's gaze. "Hey, you two, whatever damn issues you have between you, don't bring them here, don't bring it to the Faire, and don't parade it in front of the mundanes, 'cause if you do, I'm going to kick your butts out of here and into Canada. Understand me?"

"Yes ma'am." Keelie knew better than to say what she really thought.

Elia muttered something.

Finch held her hand to her ear. "Can't hear you, Whine-a-Lot!"

Elia sighed. "Yes."

Finch glared directly at Elia. "Yes what?"

"Yes, ma'am."

"Good. Now, let Mona finish up with your dress. Elianard will be here searching for you pretty soon. I'd rather not see him, and he'd rather not see me."

Wondering if Finch might have been a pirate in a former life, Keelie put her feet into the Plumpkin suit and nearly hurled as she smelled what had to be eau de dried-up vomit. "Gross. What happened in here?"

"Nothing. The suit has been cleaned." Finch leaned over and sniffed, then frowned and spritzed Keelie and the costume from her spray bottle. "Vernerd liked to party, and sometimes he didn't get out of the suit in time. He was fond of beer and mead, but it didn't like him. I'd hoped dry cleaning would get rid of the smell." She sniffed again. "Seems the Febreze doesn't work, either."

"Can I wear the unicorn suit?" Keelie pointed. It was really cute and fluffy, sort of looked like the unicorn puppets Lulu had in her shop, something little girls would love to come up to and hug, whereas Plumpkin's button eyes spun round and round in counterclockwise directions, making the dragon look like he'd been smoking crack.

"I wish." Finch sighed. "We lost the bottom half to a disgruntled wench last year. She took off to be a showgirl, so it's probably in Vegas with her. The purple dragon suit is what we've got, and the kiddies are expecting to see Plumpkin. You're it. So, hold your nose and zip up." If dragons could assume human form, Finch was one of them.

Elia and her elf gal pals had gathered together and were whispering to one another. The looks they were giving Keelie would've made even a dragon nervous.

After making sure the head fit, and handing her a script, Finch retreated to her office. Keelie dressed in her own clothes again. The Vernerd smell lingered.

Smelly costume in hand, Keelie left the building and walked past a small trail covered in pine mulch. This was the road that bordered the forest and led back to the campground. She could take the Plumpkin suit back to Sir Davey's RV, or walk through the Faire and show Dad the stupid suit. Maybe he would have sympathy for his poor little girl, who had to wear a costume in which some former lice-infested idiot had puked his hung-over guts out. If Keelie ever met the disgruntled wench who'd stolen the bottom half of the unicorn costume, she would kick *her* butt into Canada. Great, now she was quoting Finch.

A shadow crossed the path and blocked out the sun. Keelie stopped, chills of anticipation dancing up her back. *Oh please, be the unicorn*!

The figure stepped out of the forest, still in the shadows. Keelie recoiled. It was Elianard, Elia's elf-lord father.

six

Elianard stepped into the dappled sun of the path, dressed in luxurious robes embroidered with trees. His perma-sneer was plastered on his face.

The afternoon was eerily silent. The road between Admin and the food courts was usually busy, but she and Elianard were alone. Ol' Sneer-a-nard didn't intimidate Keelie, but if a yard gnome with sharp teeth and a red cap appeared with him, she'd bolt.

"I thought that after your last experience, you'd learned your lesson about following paths that lead you into the deep, dark woods, Keliel." Elianard's voice was deep, deeper than usual.

Keelie wondered if he'd taken villain voice lessons to make himself sound more menacing. It wasn't working. He should ask for a refund.

"What do you want? Looking for a book you might have buried?" She suspected that Elianard had used a forbidden book of elven lore and magic to summon the evil Red Cap to Colorado. Both the book and the Red Cap had been annihilated, but with the book destroyed, there had been no proof of Elianard's involvement.

The Plumpkin suit was getting heavy. Keelie tossed it to her other arm, its eyes rattling.

"Never speak to me in that tone—" Elianard sniffed and wrinkled his nose. "What is that smell?"

"You?" Keelie replied. She wasn't about to admit that her costume stank.

"Impudent child." Elianard scowled. "Let me give you some advice. Stay out of the woods. It's not a place for half-breeds." His brows furrowed as he leaned toward her and sniffed again.

"Yeah right. The trees talk to me. I'm a tree shepherd, remember?" Of course, her father had forbidden her to enter the forest, too, but he didn't need to know that.

Elianard wrinkled his brow as he studied the purple dragon suit she held in her arms. Glitter sprinkled the ground around her. "You're a freak of nature. In the old days, we would've left something like you on a mountainside and let you die of exposure."

"That explains why the elven race thrives in such large numbers," Keelie answered. "You killed off your best ones."

He ignored her jibe. "At least our bloodline is pure, or rather, it is if we ignore your existence."

Keelie didn't have to stay here talking to this creep. She tried to move her foot to walk away, but she couldn't. It was as if her legs were encased in invisible concrete and wrapped in chains. She glanced at Elianard, who smiled back at her.

"I haven't finished speaking to you," he said. "Do not go into the woods. If you do, people near and dear to you may be harmed."

"Are you threatening us?"

"No. I'm suggesting that if you do enter the woods and interfere, then the consequences will be felt by anyone associated with you."

"What do you mean, interfere? With what?" As she spoke, instinct guided Keelie. She had to use the rose quartz to break the magic Elianard was using to bind her in place.

She tossed the costume over her shoulder, reached into her jeans pocket for her protective rock, and pulled it out. She held out her clenched fist to break the spell. Nothing happened. Not the reaction she'd expected.

Elianard's eyes narrowed. "Earth magic will not stop me. Do you think that your little quartz will chase me away, like garlic to a vampire?" He laughed. "Of course, that won't work either. Ask your father."

"Ask me what? I have warned you, Elianard, to stay away from my daughter."

"Dad!" Keelie's knees were watery with relief, or maybe it was the breaking of the spell, because suddenly it was as if her legs had been freed from the invisible concrete and chains. She stepped back to regain her balance.

Elianard walked away.

Dad frowned. "The idiot! He's getting more and more careless. Stay away from him."

"I did. I was minding my own business and he stopped me."

"I want you to stay in the Faire. Stay out of the woods."

"He said the same thing. Does this have to do with the unicorn?" Concern for the unicorn, along with a sense of protection, washed over Keelie. If Elianard harmed one hair on it, she'd...

She didn't know what she would do, but she'd do something. She'd protect the unicorn. She didn't want another creature hurt because of Elianard or Elia, the way Ariel had been. For once, Keelie was glad the hawk was in Pennsylvania and not here in the Wildewood.

"Maybe. Elianard's magic seems stronger." Zeke frowned, and his thoughts suddenly seemed far away. "Unicorns are very powerful in their own right."

Keelie shuddered, remembering the glowing horn she'd glimpsed that night and Elianard's comments about pure bloodlines. What kind of magic would it take to hurt a unicorn? Dad was right. Elianard *was* an idiot.

"Where's Knot? He's supposed to be with you at all times." Her father peered into the bushes, as if Knot had disguised himself as a shrub.

"I dunno. Maybe he went to check out the pubs."

Dad glowered toward the woods. "I'll find him, and when I do he has a lot of explaining to do."

Keelie rubbed her temple.

Dad wrinkled his nose. "What's that smell?"

"Probably Elianard."

Dad arched an eyebrow and the corners of his mouth lifted into a smile. "Isn't that the Plumpkin suit that Vernerd wore last year?"

She gave him a wide-eyed look. This was the moment she needed if she was going to milk sympathy from Dad. "Yes, it is. Can you believe they're making me wear this? From what I heard he had lice, too." Dad didn't have to know that Elia was the source of this bit of information.

Dad stroked his chin, a pensive look on his face. "I think I remember hearing about that." He started walking toward the campground.

Keelie easily kept up with his long stride. Like father like daughter, she thought. "So?"

"So what?"

Subtlety wasn't working. "How could you let your only child wear a stupid dragon suit that's infested with lice and smells like puke? Where's the concern? Where's the love?"

"I know Finch had the suit dry cleaned; so it's no longer infested with anything. As for the smell, there's nothing I can do about that other than possibly asking Janice to recommend some herb or essential oil to vanquish it. Let's hang your costume up at Sir Davey's camper. Maybe it just needs a little airing."

"A hurricane wouldn't help this mess." But maybe Janice could help. She could work miracles with her herbs. "Can't we bury it, and tell Finch it finally died? Besides, if we air it outside, then everyone in the campground is going to know I'm Plumpkin. I can't wait to get the tent up. Being inside the Swiss Miss Chalet is not going to work."

"Bad news about the tent. I pulled it out to air it, and it was covered in mildew. It even had mushrooms growing on one side. Luckily, Davey says we can bunk with him."

Keelie almost forgot about the stinking purple disaster

she was holding. Hot showers! And no sleeping in a moldy tent or, worse, in the fairy-tale outhouse on wheels.

Zeke smiled. "Wearing this purple dragon suit will teach you a great lesson, more than anything I can say or do."

"Yeah?" What was it with parents and life lessons?

"Not to go around making impulse buys and not thinking your decisions through to the end. By the way, I made the three-hundred-dollar deposit for your custom boots. Now you have to work it off, and pay off the balance, too. That means you have to wear a smelly purple dragon suit. Welcome to responsibility. And I need you at the shop, too. I just heard from Scott. He isn't going to make it."

"What? I can't do both jobs." She had a mental image of herself at the Heartwood shop, selling furniture while wearing the hideous purple dragon costume. Then what he said sank in. Scott, her father's apprentice, was a little stiff, but he was one of the good guys. "Is Scott okay?"

"Finch gave me a couple of messages. Scott's accepted a position at a Faire in California, and won't be fulfilling his apprenticeship with me."

"That turd! He's gone and left us high and dry. Are you going to hire someone else?"

"Not unless the right person comes along. I have to feel the trees' approval." Dad made furniture only from downed trees. He soothed their passing into a new form, giving his furniture a spiritual glow that was apparent even to the mundanes.

"You know, Zeke, that sounds very woo-woo even for you." Despite everything that went down with the Red Cap in the forest outside the High Mountain Faire, Keelie still wasn't totally comfortable with her newly discovered elven heritage and magic.

"I noticed I'm back to being Zeke."

"As long as I have to wear this suit, *Zeke*. As for the trees' approval, hire someone until the right person shows up."

"What can I say, Ke-li-el?" He emphasized all of the syllables in her elven name. He shrugged. "I am the Tree Shepherd. And the trees love you, Keelie. You are the natural choice to aid me. Besides, I don't have to pay you."

"Gee, I'm so lucky. Can't I just work for you, and skip the Faire job?"

"No. You've committed yourself to the job, and you're going to see it through. By the way, the other message was for you. Your friend Laurie called. She's coming in on the eleven o'clock train next Friday."

Keelie looked at the smelly costume draped over her shoulder. She had two jobs and lived in an RV with a dwarf, an elf, and Knot—or whatever he was when he wasn't being a cat. Laurie was the only person who remembered her old life in Los Angeles, a life filled with tennis lessons, private school, and mall shopping. She was going to have a good laugh when she saw Keelie's new life. Keelie hoped they could laugh about it together. Laughing with a friend was so much better than getting laughed at.

■ ■ ■

The suit smelled awful. There was no getting used to Plumpkin's stink. Keelie stood just outside the Faire gates, surrounded by milling wenches, knights, and bleary-eyed Merry Men. The Faire workers were supposed to interact with the gathering crowd, getting them excited about the coming fun. Some of the Merry Men were clearly not up to it.

Lulu, dressed in a white gown and white gauzy fairy wings, was handing out candy to little kids, some costumed and some dressed in everyday clothes. They danced around her like little butterflies drawn to a cluster of sweet-smelling flowers. Keelie enjoyed watching the kids, but that was as much interaction as she wanted to have with them.

Lulu had a unicorn puppet on her shoulder, one of the ones that was weighted to seem as if it were perched on her. She used a long, hidden wire to move its head. The little unicorn glittered in the sunlight. As if Lulu knew that Keelie was staring, the ivory-horned head twisted to look her way. It closed an eye in a slow-motion wink, then turned back to the children.

Keelie blinked, wondering if she had really seen that or if it were a trick of the light. The puppet lady was really talented—and the kids seemed to love her. She moved on, still surrounded by her little followers, except for one girl who, fairy wings askew, was staring off into space.

Keelie stepped aside to allow a family to walk by, and Lulu's little unicorn turned its head again, its black button eyes staring sightlessly right at her. Okay, this was getting creepy. She wondered how Lulu did it. Maybe she could work at the puppet shop and find out. Anything would be better than being Plumpkin the dragon.

Sweat dripped down Keelie's back; she'd worn a leotard and yoga pants to keep her body from touching Plumpkin's fuzzy insides. Irritating globs of glitter from the scales had drifted down inside her bra, and she itched. She couldn't scratch. A huge crowd had gathered outside the gates, and it was still thirty minutes before the opening trumpets. Keelie rolled her eyes. They should go get a life, a latte, something.

Several little girls in pink tutus, pink leotards, and tie-dyed fairy wings rushed toward Lulu, almost knocking Keelie over.

She was desperate to scratch. Even though Zeke (she was still mad at him), Finch, and several other Faire employees had reassured her over and over that there were no lice inside the suit, Keelie wasn't convinced.

This could be her last day on earth. She might die from itching combined with claustrophobia. She could see only through the mesh in the dragon's mouth. She certainly wouldn't die from hunger, because the vomit smell had permanently eradicated her appetite. She'd never eat again. She'd have anorexia, and it would be Zeke's fault. If he'd let her withdraw her inheritance money to pay for the custom-made boots, then she could be helping him at the shop. She hoped he was swamped with customers today.

She turned her back to a skinny maple tree and rubbed up and down, using the zipper's hard edge to quell the itch at her shoulder blade. It felt so good she almost moaned; then she stopped, horrified. She was acting like Knot. Something was squashed up inside the suit, under her right foot. She wiggled her toes against it. A cloth something.

A group of mothers talked in the shade of a tree, surrounded by a herd of small children and babies in strollers.

A little boy dressed in black plastic armor stared at her and shouted, "I'm going to kill you, mean dragon."

Keelie had been instructed by Finch to make exaggerated gestures, like a cartoon character, when engaging with obnoxious kids. They loved it, as did the parents. Keelie stepped back and held her hands up as if she were afraid.

Plumpkin was a wuss!

With the mood she was in, if Keelie had been a real dragon, she'd roast the kid. A man dressed in beggar's rags stumbled toward her. He smiled.

Ew! Those cavities in his front teeth didn't seem fake.

"Hello, Dragon."

Keelie sidled away. He followed her.

"Dragon, wait up."

Keelie stopped and turned around, and put her claws on her waist and tapped her foot, the one with the cloth wadded up in it.

The beggar came closer. "I'm Vernerd the beggar. Just wanted to ask if you might have found any personal items inside the suit?"

Keelie shook her head. Plumpkin's googly eyes rattled in their plastic sockets.

Vernerd cocked his head. "Ah, good. Let me recommend something. Don't let the Merry Men push you around on the Bedlam Barrel ride after the Faire-is-over party."

She didn't speak, hoping he didn't know who was inside the suit.

The minstrels gathered at the side of the clearing and began playing a sprightly Celtic tune. Vernerd smiled, again exposing his rotten teeth. Keelie made a note to use extra floss tonight.

"That's my cue." Vernerd hobbled away.

A knight walked past Keelie. He stopped and spun on his boots, then walked in a circle around her. He was nice to look at, with long dark brown hair pulled back in a tie. He wore a long green tunic over green tights, and black leather gloves covered his hands. "Ye dragon, begone from Sherwood

Forest, for the good folk of Nottingham must deal with evil more vile than thee."

Keelie held up her hands in mock surrender. The knight removed his sword from his scabbard and pressed the sword tip near Plumpkin's neck. "Should I kill the dragon?"

There were shouts of "No!" from the crowd. One little voice rang out louder than the others: "Kill the dragon." She knew who it belonged to. The little brat in black armor.

"Dragon, what say you?"

Again, Keelie held up her hands, or rather, her purple claws, in mock surrender. She could hear the black plastic eyes spinning round and round inside the round clear covers as she shook her head, pleading for her life. Maybe if the knight killed her now, then she wouldn't have to do the parade. She'd better still get paid.

The handsome knight motioned toward the crowd. "Good people, your kindness allows me to let this dragon live, but evil Prince John will not be so fortunate."

A fanfare erupted from atop the wooden gate. Long, pointed banners hung from the yard-long golden trumpets that the trumpeters blew in one direction, then another.

The handsome knight ran and hopped atop a stone. "Good people of Sherwood, be forewarned, rumor says that evil Prince John brings his new bride-to-be, the Princess Eleanor of Angouleme, to our fair town. You are safe, however. The Merry Men and I will save the good people of Nottingham from the treachery of Sir Guy of Gisbourne and the Sheriff until Good King Richard returns. So say I, Robin Hood!"

Loud clapping erupted from behind Keelie. She scooted to the side and ran into one of the Merry Men, who shoved her out of the way. She would've landed on her butt if she hadn't grabbed the trunk of a maple tree. The branches reached down to steady her just as a breeze kicked up. Keelie looked up, and the branches in all the nearby trees began to sway. Good cover.

Thank you, Keelie thought.

A comforting green filled her mind. She didn't sense any anger, or other emotional issues, from the maple like she had from the oaks.

A man in red, probably playing Will Scarlet, shouted, "Dragon, are you with the Merry Men or Prince John?"

How the heck did she know? She hadn't read the script, and she hadn't taken any improv classes, either.

From atop the wooden platform, Tarl, the former Muck and Mire man, waved to the crowd below. He was now dressed in royal velvet finery. He cleaned up well, but Keelie shuddered, remembering his naked, potato-shaped silhouette on a tent wall when he'd been "entertaining" a Faire goer at the High Mountain Faire. She'd be scarred for life—the image was burned into her mind.

Cheers erupted again.

Tarl raised his arms. "Greetings citizens and visitors, to the Wildewood Faire. Today is a most joyous occasion; for it is the day my betrothed arrives. Let us give her a Wildewood welcome."

Another round of fanfare. *Yeah, yeah, get on with it.* Keelie hoped she'd have a moment to slip into a privy and remove her bra. That might help the itching. Through her mesh mouth-netting, she saw an ATM and suddenly remembered her ATM card. If she could find her old card, she might be able to withdraw enough money to pay Zeke back as well as the remaining amount on her boots.

Whack! Something hard hit her on the knee. She almost toppled over from the pain. She looked down, and saw that the sniveling little brat in plastic armor had hit her with a wooden sword. Now the little cretin was running back to his mommy.

Keelie leaned against the tree, trying to ease the throbbing in her knee. Another fanfare blared overhead. Keelie watched as Princess Eleanor and her ladies-in-waiting joined Prince John on the platform. Elia looked beautiful. Keelie took in every detail enviously, from her sweeping skirts to her sleek, braided hair.

Elia did her dumb blonde routine and held out her dainty hand for Prince John's kiss. The kiss made her twitch. Keelie smiled inwardly. Elia had human cooties. She thought of Elia tongue-kissing Tarl. Eww! Maybe being a dragon wasn't so bad.

Prince John released her hand and gestured to someone behind him. "And let me introduce my lovely ward, Maid Marian." A young woman in a green cloak walked past Elia, sneering identically. Darn, an elf girl was playing Maid Marian. She waved to the crowd. There was something weird about her, but maybe it was just part of seeing the world through Plumpkin's eye-screens. Maid Marian's face seemed blurry.

Robin Hood shouted up to Prince John. "You're not the true ruler of England. Good King Richard will return and claim his crown."

"Robin, my love," Marian shouted down to him.

Oh brother. Who wrote this stuff?

Robin held his hand out toward Marian. "Dear heart, take courage."

"Oh, how sappy!" Ugly looks turned to her. Oops. She'd spoken out loud. Nevertheless, Keelie had to admit she would melt under Robin's loving gaze, which she should feel guilty for thinking because of her relationship with Sean. Even though he hadn't called her since they left Colorado.

Prince John stepped forward. "Enough. Marian is under my protection."

Damn! Tarl was really good as Prince John. Keelie was impressed with his acting skills. Marian dropped her cloak, revealing a scarlet gown. Nearby, the similarly dressed Will Scarlet nodded approvingly. Maybe Marian and Will shopped at the same booth, Hose to Toes. Speaking of toes, she couldn't wait to get rid of whatever it was wadded up at the end of her foot. It was making her own toes itch. One of those really nail-digging scratches would relieve the irritation. She just had to get over the itching, and the throbbing pain in her knee, and move through this day.

Maybe paying attention to the show would help. Maid Marian had broken free of Prince John's knights, and threw herself into Robin Hood's arms. Keelie watched enviously, imagining herself in the beautiful elf girl's place.

Prince John leaned down and shouted to Robin Hood. "At this day's end, I shall give my bride your head as a wedding gift."

Robin Hood, arms protectively around Marian, shouted, "Nay, rather, you shall surrender the crown to Richard."

"Then at the hour of ten and thirty, we shall decide the fate of England on the jousting field. What say you?"

"I agree." Robin Hood held his sword high in the air and the crowd cheered, "Huzzah."

Finally, Prince John told the crowd to enjoy the Faire

and their day in Sherwood Forest. The gates swung open majestically.

Yeah, yeah. Big fun coming up. Keelie resisted scratching herself as the crowd surged toward the gates. You'd think there was a prize for being the first one into the Faire. She motioned with a purple claw and waved people toward the gates. Most of the kids stuck their tongues out at her as they passed, or they shouted "You stink!" She had an overwhelming desire to kick some of them.

All the Faire workers were lining up. Ah, the stupid parade!

Keelie had no idea where she was supposed to go. Finch had said only "show up at the gates."

In the line, she walked behind the Ladies of Laundry, a comedy group that presented dirty humor at the Mudville Stage. They turned around and pinched their noses with their fingers and one said in a faux English accent, "Look, Molly, it be a dragon that needs washin'."

The other girl shook her head. "Not enough money in the kingdom for me to wash this wretched beastie."

A blocky guy built like a troll stepped in front of her. He had strawberry blonde hair and peach fuzz on his cheeks. He carried a large quarterstaff, and burped. "'Scuse me. We did a bit of merrymaking last night, and me stomach needs a bit of mead to cure what's ailing it." He patted his overhanging belly, its bulge fortunately covered up by his brown tunic.

Keelie stepped back because she didn't want to be downwind of the burp, but recognized this guy's deep baritone voice from the singing she'd endured while camping in the Swiss Miss Chalet. From the looks of the baby-faced giant, this had to be Robin Hood's sidekick, Little John.

He glanced at her, then did a double take. His eyes narrowed.

The fanfare began, and the parade started to move. She followed Little John. Inside the gates, all of the Merry Men had assembled in the courtyard along with their leader, Robin Hood. Prince John and his knights were on the other side of the clearing, giving them the evil eyeball as a crowd congregated to watch the show.

Maid Marian had gathered an admiring crowd, including seven little girls in princess dresses. She whispered to them, and they giggled. Maid Marian pointed in the direction of Keelie, who waved to them.

None of the princesses waved back. Instead, they picked up sticks. Before Keelie could react and run, Maid Marian and the little princesses rushed toward Plumpkin.

The princess ninjas attacked Keelie. They pounded her over and over, hitting her on the back, the legs, the arms. She swung her foot at one, intentionally missing. The kid squealed with mock fear and hit her in the knee. The point of her little light-up wand dug through the Plumpkin suit. Keelie was ready to take out a princess for real when she saw Robin Hood and Little John heading toward her and the mob of little hellions. Reinforcements. She was saved.

Little John arrived first, and, yelling like some sick animal, walloped Keelie on the butt with his quarterstaff. "Take that, you verminous scalawag."

"Ow! That really hurt."

The reinforcements had arrived, all right. For the wrong side.

seven

Keelie tried to rub her sore backside with her purple mittened hands while also trying to fend off her attackers.

In scarlet tights and satin cape, prissy Will Scarlet yelled, "Little John, stay away from the dragon. I will kill it for you."

One of the little princesses piped up. "That dragon stinks."

Robin Hood shouted, "Stop!"

Little John grabbed Keelie's dragon head and pulled. She kicked him in the kneecap. She was aiming for his privates, but her leg wasn't long enough. Will Scarlet stomped on her foot. She'd had it.

She screamed at him, and as she stepped back, Little

John gave a really hard tug. The head came off. Keelie inhaled fresh air for the first time that morning.

Little John raised Plumpkin's head in the air and gave a victory shout as if he was on the Renaissance Wrestling Channel or something.

Loud shrieks and screams pierced the Faire gates area as the little girls ran toward their parents. Little John turned around and looked at Keelie in shock, as if she'd roasted the little princesses. Then he dropped Plumpkin's head onto the ground. Obviously, the line between what was pretend at the Faire, and what wasn't, had blurred for Little John. Keelie wasn't going to wait around for him to figure it out. She ran.

■ ■ ■

Ms. Finch was on the telephone, having a not-very-pleasant conversation with someone, while Keelie stewed and looked at the photos on the wall. They were pictures of the employees of the Wildewood Faire, as well as some of the acts. Her father and Janice were in one. Dad was holding a turkey leg. She tried not to eavesdrop on Finch's conversation, but it was hard not to.

"Well, you're welcome to come here, we have nothing to hide. But just don't bring testing equipment that'll scare the visitors. Can you come on a weekday?"

Finch arched an eyebrow and grabbed a notepad and a pencil. "Okay, I'll be on the lookout for Dawn Valentine of the City Council. Sure, bring the EPA. I understand. Yes, this Wednesday." She nodded again, and her eyes seemed to bug out at whatever the person said on the other end of the phone. "Thank you. I'll be looking forward to your visit."

She slammed the phone down. The pencils in her pencil case jumped.

Keelie stepped back.

"What kind of name is Dawn Valentine?" Finch asked, her neck as bright red as her face.

"Ah. Not sure."

"I'll tell you. It sounds like a damn stripper, not a councilwoman. Like I don't have enough to do. Now I need to accommodate this Ms. Valentine and her staff, or our non-cooperation will be noted, thank you very much, and in the future the effing permits needed to run the Faire might not be granted. Does that not sound like a veiled threat to you?"

"Yes, it sort of does."

"Why am I telling you this? And where's your Plumpkin head?"

"I lost it." Keelie tried to sound unafraid. "Little John ripped it off."

"What?"

"Lost it to Little John."

Finch gritted her teeth and smacked her hand loudly on the desk. "Why did you let him take it?"

"He hit me with a quarterstaff and took it. I think he's got issues with reality." Keelie wanted to scratch.

"I know, but he brings such a sense of realism to his performance." She picked up her walkie-talkie. "Okay, let me get security."

There was some static, then a man's voice. "Jackson, here."

"Hey, Plumpkin is missing her head. I need it."

Please let it be gone. Please let it be gone. Please let it be gone.

"We got it here. It's at First Aid," Jackson replied.

"Good. Bring it here to the office."

Finch placed the walkie-talkie back onto her desk. "You're going to need to be at Lulu's puppet shop at eleven thirty. You're supposed to help her attract little kids into the shop."

Keelie groaned. "Is it really necessary for the kids to hit me with sticks?"

Finch furrowed her forehead. "Kids are hitting you with sticks? Funny. Usually the kids love Plumpkin. No one has ever hit Plumpkin. Must be something new. The smell?"

"What should I do when kids start attacking me?"

"Do?" Finch's voice rose even louder. "Do? Do whatever you have to do to bring a smile to their faces. Don't scare them, entertain them."

There was a knock at the door. "Come in."

In walked a stocky, bearded guy with a yellow shirt with "Wildewood Security" written across the chest. He shoved the dusty Plumpkin head at Keelie. It spun its eyes at her. She wanted to hit it. Maybe the kids were on to something.

Her "thank you" sounded insincere.

The security guy smirked. "Anything else, boss?"

"No, just keep an eye on Little John. Seems he's really back in Merry Olde England."

Keelie stood there holding her Plumpkin head and staring at the googly eyes. Whoever designed this costume had mental issues, or a sadistic streak.

Finch had turned her attention to her paperwork. She looked up at Keelie. "You still here? Get your ass out there and entertain the kids at Lulu's. It's already ten forty-five." People skills were not Finch's strong suit.

Keelie ran, but still was late getting to Lulu's. The Enchanted Lane was bustling. Every time and everywhere an actor engaged an audience, it became clogged with mundanes. The Heartwood shop was full. Keelie stopped, wondering if she should show Zeke the costume. She imagined him tearfully removing her Plumpkin head and telling her he was so wrong, and that she could have the money for the boots. Hardly. He would likely say, "You've got to learn responsibility, now get to the puppet shop."

A young woman with a stroller called to her. "Plumpkin, I want to get a picture of you and my baby." Sitting in the stroller was a ten-month-old with a nose that dripped green goo. The baby slurped a sippy cup, then threw it down and reached out for Keelie. Okay, she liked the kid. It wasn't screaming its head off, and in a weird way that made her feel better, after a morning filled with rejection.

Knot chose that moment to come sauntering out of the Heartwood shop. He stepped in front of Keelie and sat at the foot of the stroller, then turned his green eyes toward the kid and blinked. The baby began bouncing up and down in its seat, opening and closing its grubby little hands and saying, "Kitty, kitty, kitty."

Knot turned his huge orange head to Keelie. She could've sworn he was grinning. Then, the small white cat from the other day scampered out from the oak trees. It sat down on the edge of the lane and watched. It had bright blue eyes, but its fur was patchy and it seemed extra skinny.

A family with two little ones stopped and admired Knot as if they'd never seen a cat. The little boy reached out to Knot, who was strolling toward Keelie with his tail high in the air. This usually meant "kiss my butt." Knot sat down on Plumpkin's paw, his warm weight spreading to Keelie's toes. She couldn't see her feet with the Plumpkin head on.

The baby's mom reached down, pulled her squirming kid out of the stroller, and walked over to Keelie.

Zeke stepped out of the booth, looking down angrily at Knot. "That's better. You stay with her, and don't let her out of your sight." So much for sympathy from Dad.

Knot's tail twitched, then he purred even louder. Not a good sign. It meant he was going to do something knotty.

Zeke bowed graciously to the surprised mundanes. He swept his hand in the direction of Plumpkin. "This enchanted cat has been ordered to guard the dragon and keep it safe."

Everyone clapped. Knot yawned. Keelie placed her puffy claws up to her mouth and shook her head.

The mom handed her camera to Zeke and asked, "Will you take our picture?"

Zeke smiled and the woman blushed. She leaned against Keelie and the baby tugged on Plumpkin's googly eyes.

"Say turkey legs," Zeke encouraged. Keelie noticed dark circles under his eyes. He hadn't had dark circles under his eyes this morning.

"Turkey legs." The mom had a goofy grin on her face. The baby sneezed his icky baby grossness onto Plumpkin. Zeke clicked the camera. An outcry pulled her attention to Lulu's.

"You little jerk! Leave my shop alone." Lulu was one angry woman. Red-faced and waving a fist in the air, she threatened a pudgy little man in a gherkin-shaped hat and skintight green hose who was running away, one hand holding the floppy hat to his head while the other clutched a wooden contraption to his chest. A girl in green golf pants huffed and puffed after him, pushing a two-wheeled cart.

Lulu's steps were littered with pickles. Poor Lulu. First acorns, now dills.

Lulu vanished into her shop and reappeared in her white fairy wings, dancing a Dragon marionette in front of her gorgeous white gown. Chiming music filled the air and the kids in Dad's shop ran out toward her, followed by their confused parents. Keelie hadn't thought puppets were that popular. She watched as the baby turned his head toward Lulu. His bright eyes glazed over, and he pointed toward the puppet lady dressed in her fairy godmother splendor.

Knot sauntered over to the puppet shop. Lulu seemed confused when he entered, followed by Keelie, who was followed by the white cat. Her smile seemed a little forced. "There you are, Plumpkin."

Keelie pointed in the direction of the Admin building. She hoped Lulu understood that Finch had sent her to the puppet shop.

More and more little kids assembled in front of Lulu's shop. It seemed they were drawn to it like the children of Hamelin were drawn by the Pied Piper's enthralling music.

Lulu looked uncomfortable, and her skin was breaking out in those weird, red, irritating and itchy-looking bumps. Keelie could so relate. Between the aggravating cloth in the foot of the costume and the glitter, she was still super itchy.

The trees began to sway.

Green magic tingled through Keelie. Great, now something was up with the oaks. They were wide awake. She hoped they didn't pummel the mundanes with acorns. It was time for Zeke to do some tree shepherd therapy.

Knot carried a stuffed unicorn in his mouth, price tag dangling. He dropped it.

"Hey, stop that cat." Lulu pointed at Knot.

Blinking at her with his big green eyes, Knot placed his paw on the stuffed unicorn. Lulu stepped out into the Enchanted Lane. Before Keelie could shout out a warning, a shower of acorns cascaded down on the puppet-maker. The families who had gathered to see the puppet show ran, but they hadn't been the target of the oak trees' ire.

Keelie searched for her father. He needed to put the oaks back to sleep. She didn't know how.

As she shuffled quickly toward the shop, wishing she could run in her ridiculous costume, the little brat in plastic armor appeared. He ran up to Keelie and began beating her with his wooden sword.

"Die, stinky dragon. Die, stinky dragon."

Where was his mother? Keelie tried dancing from foot to foot. The kid hit the back of her knee, and she fell on her face. He hit her head, over and over. The costume's foam rubber deflected the sword, but she couldn't get up.

In pain and frustration, Keelie shouted a single word—one that began with "F." She realized her mistake the minute it left her lips. The boy vanished from her Plumpkin-eye-socket window, replaced by a woman whose mouth was shaped in a soundless "O" of shock.

Knot ran into Heartwood, the unicorn still in his mouth. All around, horrified parents covered their children's ears.

Lulu dropped her dragon marionette and began hopping up and down. "Out. Out. Out. These kids don't need to hear your filthy talk! Don't think I won't report you to Finch!!"

Keelie found herself on her way back to Admin, steeling herself to face the real dragon.

eight

"Take it off!" Finch's strident voice rang in Keelie's ears.

"What?" Startled, Keelie tried to look behind her, but all she could see was the back of the dragon head's cave-like interior.

"You heard me. Take the damn costume off. Now!"

Keelie ripped the Velcro fastenings at her neck and removed the Plumpkin head. Cool air rushed against her face. The air conditioning was heavenly on her skin and smelled fresh and sweet, especially compared to the stink of the costume.

Finch didn't seem to be feeling the AC's effect. Sweat dripped down her face and unruly sprigs of red hair stuck out all over her head. The woman looked as if she were going to burst into flames. She grabbed a yellow walkie-talkie off her desk and pressed a red button on its face.

"Mona," she yelled. "Bring me one of the costumes for the Steak-on-a-Stake booth." She must have heard an answer in the garbled sounds that came through the static, because she threw the walkie-talkie onto her desk and glared at Keelie.

"Are you intentionally trying to screw up? You know better than to use that word in front of the mundanes."

Keelie was embarrassed that she'd lost control, but she hated to be scolded even though she'd expected it. She raised her chin. "It's a period word. Its roots are Anglo-Saxon."

Finch lowered her head like a bull getting ready to charge. "Disemboweling miscreants is period, too. You'd better be damn glad that we use common sense around here, and that I'm famous for my even temper, or your head would be decorating the effing front gate." Her face was getting redder and redder. She seemed to be stoking an inner fire, about to blast anyone near her.

"Having our one animated character, our children's favorite, drop the F-bomb is wrong!" Finch yelled. "Get out of the damn Plumpkin suit. You don't deserve to wear it. From now on you're working the Steak-on-a-Stake booth." The windows rattled from her yells. Keelie could almost see the woman's sweat turn to steam.

She quickly slipped out of the Plumpkin costume, afraid that otherwise, Finch would turn her upside down and shake the suit until she fell out of it. She wondered if she'd subconsciously screwed up because she hated being Plumpkin. Whatever. Keelie was ecstatic. How bad could the Steak-on-a-Stake booth be? No more stinky old costume. But what had been inside the bottom of the foot? She reached down and pulled out a soft, yellow-streaked wad of black cloth, then shook it to see what it was. She screamed and dropped it.

"Now what?" Finch shouted.

Keelie pointed to the dingy, tiger-striped men's briefs on the floor. A couple of the tiger stripes went in another direction, suspiciously like skid marks.

Finch sighed. "Vernerd was looking for those." She handed Keelie a bottle of hand sanitizer. "You might want to use this stuff twice."

Keelie accepted it, shuddering. This was worse than lice. Her foot had been on top of men's underwear. Worse, Vernerd's obviously used underwear.

Finch sat back in her chair. "I might retire Plumpkin. I was thinking about maybe having fairies. Know anything about fairies?"

Keelie grimaced. "More than you want to know."

Finch's complexion was returning to a more human pink. "Good. Draw some pictures and give them to Mona. She'll start on the costumes next week. Not like we don't have other things to handle around here. If I have one more complaint from Princess Whine-A-Lot, I'll personally sew her lips together."

Keelie was beginning to like Finch, despite her temper. At least one person didn't think that Elia was perfect and beautiful. "I can't draw."

"Can you draw a stick figure?"

"I guess." How much did Finch know about the *bhata?*

The little fairies looked like sticks and leaves and bits of moss, but most humans couldn't see them.

Finch shrugged. "Come back later, and I'll give you some crayons and computer paper and you can have at it."

There was a knock at the door. "Come in," Finch bellowed.

Mona entered the room with a bundle under her arm. She seemed to have shed yesterday's stress. Although her face was still creased and worried-looking, her shoulders weren't hunched up. "Here's the costume you asked for."

She held up a full red skirt and a black bodice printed with white cow spots, and, to top off the horror, a short black vampire cape with a tall, stiff collar.

Keelie thought that this Count Von Bovine getup was almost worse than the old yellow Muck and Mire skirt, with the red handprints on the butt, that she'd had to wear when she'd first arrived at the High Mountain Faire. She cringed. "You've got to be kidding me."

"No. Get dressed and haul your ass to Steak-on-a-Stake. It's just past noon." Finch snapped her fingers several times in a row. "Lunchtime crowd. People are hungry. Move it."

"What about shoes?" Keelie wiggled her bare feet. The thought of steak was enticing. She hadn't eaten all day.

"Mona, get her some hose and boots."

"Follow me." Mona pulled a pair of green tights from a shelf stacked high with them. "We've got lots in stock because of the Faire's Robin Hood story line." She gave Keelie an apologetic smile. "And these are the only shoes left in your size."

Keelie put on the hose, even though they seriously clashed with her costume. She looked like a used-up Christmas ornament.

The shoes were something else. They didn't just totally clash, they looked like something from a genie-reject pile: glittery gold booties with stuffed fabric curlicues that swirled over the toes.

Once dressed, Keelie gathered up the sweaty leotard and yoga pants she'd worn under the Plumpkin costume. Mona called out, "Wait a minute. Don't forget your mail." She pointed to the stack on a chair.

"Thanks."

Keelie scooped up the untidy heap of envelopes and paper, then walked down the steps, treading carefully in the weird shoes. And she'd thought it was tough to negotiate the acorns in her regular shoes—she was going to break a leg. She made it past the path that skirted the woods and led to the campground, wondering if Elianard was hiding out in the forest, watching her.

Thinking of the forest made her long for the green coolness of the deep woods. A sudden need surged through her—she had to find the unicorn. Right now. She glanced down at the envelopes and papers in her hands, tempted to ditch them and run into the woods. The top sheet was torn from a notebook and covered in handwritten phone messages.

The pull of the unicorn faded as she saw Laurie's name. She slowed down and read. Laurie said she couldn't wait to see her on Friday! Keelie's skip of joy ended abruptly as the flipped-up curlicues on her gold booties tangled together. She struggled to regain her footing, then looked around quickly. Luckily, no one seemed to notice.

She hurried along, growing accustomed to walking in the funny footwear, her head spinning with plans. It suddenly occurred to her that with Laurie here, she couldn't spend her free time helping Dad.

Her happiness deflated as she thought of her overworked father. Just a while ago he'd looked pale and tired. She couldn't say no to him, but she wanted to show Laurie a good time, and to prove to herself that her new life wasn't the lame-fest she often accused it of being. She had a sinking feeling that her life would get insane in the coming days.

A family passing by laughed as their toddler pointed at Keelie's outfit and said something in baby talk. She gritted her teeth and shuffled on. This bites, she thought. Scott was at the California Faire, and she was stuck with a one-way ticket to Steak-on-a-Stake. But she couldn't screw up this job. There was more to the Faire than food service and ridiculous costumes, and Steak-on-a-Stake was just a step toward good money and a fun gig—maybe even the Francesca job.

To keep from looking at the Faire goers' reactions to her garb, Keelie rummaged through the rest of the mail. Business envelopes addressed to Zeke Heartwood, although a couple of them looked as if they'd been made from homemade paper, the kind you buy at museum shops, and were addressed in faded-looking calligraphy.

One of these was addressed to Zekeliel Heartwood, and the return address was the Dread Forest. She recognized the handwriting from a package she'd received earlier in the summer. Sadness seemed to seep into her fingers from the envelope. She knew that Grandmother Keliatiel, her dad's mother, hadn't written to her. Her elven grandmother didn't feel for her the way Grandma Josephine had. Her maternal grandmother had liked to spend time with her, and had taken her shopping and sent her funny cards for no reason.

She'd died before Mom did, and now it seemed like everything that remained of Keelie's old life was dead—except for Laurie.

She didn't expect the same warm feelings from Grandmother Keliatiel. After all, Grandmother Keliatiel was an elf, and elves were very different from humans. She wondered if elven anatomy was different. She'd probably find out in the fall. As vain as most of them were, maybe they had mirrors where their hearts should be. She wasn't like them. Like her rounded right ear, her heart was totally human. Too human, judging from the pain that had haunted her in the months since her mother's death.

Keelie tucked her grandmother's letter into the back of the stack and headed toward Heartwood. At the shop, she was surprised to see no Dad and no customers. Weird. In Colorado, the furniture shop had always been crowded with people. The lane outside was filled with tourists, and Lulu's shop next door rang with laughter, but in Heartwood, the only movement came from Knot, who lounged sideways on the counter, grooming the stuffed unicorn he'd stolen from Lulu's shop.

"I hope Dad makes you get a job to pay for that." Keelie dropped the mail next to him. "So, did Dad leave you in charge?"

To a mundane walking by, Knot probably seemed like any ordinary shop cat. Knot meowed, a sweet cry that ended on an up note as if he were asking a question.

"No mail for you, Knotsie."

She reached out to pet him. He swatted at her, claws extended, and she pulled her hand back just in time. "Don't worry, I'm not going to take the 'ittle kitty's toy away from him."

Knot growled.

"Love you, too. Not." She laughed at her lame pun. Knot didn't seem to think it was funny, although who could tell with cats? And that's when she saw the white cat curled up in the doorway that led to the back room.

Her father walked into the shop, trailing oak leaves. He leaned heavily against one of the posts of the open display floor and lifted a shoe to peel off a leaf that was stuck to the sole. "Keelie, glad you're here. I need your help ... "

He stopped talking as he got a good look at her. His gaze trailed down from the top of her head to the tip of her gold curlicued toes. The edges of his mouth twitched. "I see you've got a new job, but where? I don't recognize the, er, outfit."

"At the Steak." She pointed to her jersey-cow-printed vest. Then she moved her index finger to her vampire cape. "On a Stake."

He snorted, but swallowed before the guffaw that was building escaped and, instead, coughed into his fist. "I'm very proud of you for working so hard to repay me for your boots, but I'm also going to need your help here. Until I hire a helper, you'll have to fill in."

"After work? No way." Keelie protested out of principle. She'd suspected he'd need her, but she'd thought she'd have at least a few days to herself before she had to dive into the world of wood. She gritted her teeth. On the other hand, if she didn't fight this, then maybe she'd have more time to herself when Laurie arrived.

"Okay, fine. You can tell me the details later." Keelie

shoved her leotard and yoga pants under the counter. "Do you mind if I leave these here? I'm late."

"Sure." Dad sounded tired. "Thanks for not making a fuss. And good luck with the job."

"It'll be a piece of—steak." The job would be easy, if not for the humiliating costume. She waved goodbye and stepped onto the lane, immediately sinking ankle deep in oak leaves. Branches rustled above her and a few more leaves drifted down, as if the trees were laughing at her.

She tossed a stern look upwards, then headed to work, shuffling her feet to keep the acorns to the sides of her flimsy-bottomed shoes. It would be treacherous to walk normally around here. The hidden acorns were like marbles.

Knot sat at the shop door watching her dance through the acorns. Keelie frowned at him. "Laugh it up, fuzzy. And don't even think of coming with me."

He blinked up at her in kitty eye Morse code. She knew the cat. He meant, "Can, will, and you can't stop me."

She ignored him and hurried toward the food court area, walking as fast as she could while trying not to slip. He kept pace with her, and she noticed that people pointed at them. "That's right," she muttered. "No one's ever seen a vampire cowgirl and her strange kitty bodyguard before. Stand in awe, tourists."

The Steak-on-a-Stake booth was in the King's Food Court, along with about twenty other colorful food vendors all squashed together. It was very much like the booths in the Enchanted Lane, except for the delicious smell of all kinds of different food.

Keelie's stomach grumbled as she caught the tantalizing scent of roasting meat. Long lines of people overflowed into the clearing from the front of each booth. There would be no rest for the weary food servers, nor food for the hungry that didn't have cash. She couldn't pretend she'd missed the Steak-on-a-Stake booth: the sign that hung over the counter featured a fanged, dancing cow wearing a black cape.

Knot had vanished, thank goodness.

Between the Steak-on-a-Stake booth and the Death by Chocolate booth was a wooden fence with a narrow door marked "Peasants Only." She pushed on the rickety wooden slats and found herself momentarily disoriented by the sight of modern-day delivery trucks parked at the rear of the shops. The illusion of the Middle Ages didn't extend to back here, where big refrigerated metal lockers hummed.

A burly, unshaven man wearing an apron over soiled blue jeans yelled to her. "Hey you, Steak Girl, get up to the booth. You're late. Peggy's been waiting for you."

Keelie knocked on the plain, metal-clad Steak-on-a-Stake door. It opened a crack and a woman with a pinned-up braid of gray hair poked her head out. "About time you decided to show up for work." A strong, calloused hand grabbed Keelie by the wrist and pulled her into the kitchen.

"I'm sorry. I had trouble with my uniform." Yeah, it made her nauseated.

Skinny girls in Steak-on-a-Stake T-shirts were grilling strips of meat. As fast as they could get the steak off the grill, a young man with carroty hair poking out of his hair-net grabbed the strips, sprinkled some herb-looking stuff on them from a transparent spice canister, and threw them into a two-foot-square metal serving pan that was then quickly shoved out through the serving window.

"They gave you the wrong costume, girlie. Take that cape off and grab a hairnet."

"Hairnet?" But she gladly pulled off the cape and tossed it aside. It instantly flared up in flames.

Screams erupted as Keelie tried to stomp the flames out, then stopped, afraid her gold lamé booties would melt to her feet.

Peggy threw a pitcher of water on the flames and put them out, drenching Keelie in the process. Now she was a scorched, wet vampire cowgirl. Great.

Curious eyes peered at her from the pass-through window. The counter help were the ones who wore the vampire cape outfits with the cow-spot bodices. There must have been a bra size requirement, too, because all of the girls were bodaciously endowed.

"Get back to work," Peggy barked, and the assembly line began once more.

A buxom blonde grabbed the tray of cooked and skewered meat that perched on the pass-through and turned to serve the customers. In the kitchen, all of the steak workers were hot and sweaty and moving as fast as they could.

Peggy ignored Keelie's dripping outfit. "I need you to take Jimmy's place and sprinkle the 'rub,' as we call it, onto the meat. Don't touch the food, just hold it by the stick."

Peggy shoved the canister of "rub" into Keelie's hand and shouted to Jimmy, "I need you on the grill." She turned to the others. "Come on people. Move it. Move it. Customers want their meat before the joust."

Keelie sprinkled the spicy rub on the meat as fast as she could. She'd seen an identical clear plastic jar of spice at a warehouse club. In seconds she had become part of the meat-moving line, which reminded her of a cartoon factory. She had just gotten into the rhythm of it, or she thought she had, when Peggy yelled, "Come on rub girl, move it. Move it. Move it."

Toss in a couple of swear words and she'd be convinced that Peggy and Finch were related.

Keelie shook the spice jar faster over the meat. A cloud of rub floated around her. A tickle started up in her nose. Don't sneeze, she thought. *Don't sneeze.* It was useless.

She turned her head to avoid the tray in front of her. Her sneeze blasted through the noise and sprayed the tray of finished meat about to go out the window.

Silence.

As if that wasn't enough to stop the Steak-on-a-Stake production line again, a tiny meow filled the quiet. Keelie looked down. So did everyone else. Knot sat at her feet, green eyes wide and kitten-like. He placed his paw on her leg, gazed up at her, and purred.

Something was up. She could tell from the tone, because it wasn't his usual sadistic purr, but a sweet soft purr, the kind that made you want to pet him if you didn't know him.

Someone said "awww," but was quickly shushed.

Peggy strode over to them, armed with a broom. "No cats. No filthy, mangy cats!" Knot's tail twitched back and forth, narrowed eyes focused on the angry woman. His purr changed, becoming louder and more intense. Peggy lifted her arm, ready to whack.

Knot was a pain in the butt, but she couldn't let this woman pound him with her broom. "I'm so sorry. I'll get him out."

Peggy lowered her broom and glowered at her. "This is your cat?"

Keelie nodded. No use denying it.

"I see." Peggy's face relaxed and she leaned on the broom.

For a moment, Keelie was hopeful, but a second later the woman waved her hand dismissively. "Take your cat and yourself and get out of my booth."

"Okay. I'll be right back." It wouldn't take long to drop-kick Knot into the forest and scamper back.

"Don't bother coming back."

Her heart stopped. "But, but I just learned how to sprinkle the rub faster." No fair.

"Out." Peggy pointed at the back door. The other girls stared at her, looking about as smart as the costumed cow on the sign out front. "We have a three-strike rule. Setting a fire, sneezing on food, bringing your pet—you're out of here, missy."

Knot's muscles gathered. He leaped into the serving window just as Jimmy passed the next heavy serving tray of grilled meat to the buxom blonde. The girl with the overflowing bodice shrieked as Knot appeared on the serving tray, cutting off her cry of, "We need more steak!"

Knot had landed squarely in the middle of the steak strips, tilting the tray sideways just as the blonde placed it on the serving counter. A customer wearing khaki shorts and a spotless white polo shirt jumped back, but steak grease still splattered his tube socks and white Nikes. It was raining grilled steak-on-a-stake.

Peggy's eyes bulged. "I told you to get out of here!" she yelled.

Keelie ran, with Peggy right after her, broom in hand.

nine

Keelie was sure she'd feel Peggy's broom on her head or her backside, but the woman had turned to run out the peasants' exit. Keelie heard her apologizing profusely, probably to the spattered man.

She looked around wildly for Knot, then spotted him hightailing it toward the woods with a spear of steak chunks in his mouth. She ran after him, lifting her feet high to keep from slipping, then stared at the rub canister still in her hand. Now was not the time to return it.

Behind her, the crowd laughed and cheered as if the mayhem were part of the show. Keelie ran on, trying to keep Knot in sight. She slipped past the end of the shops, where delivery trucks lined a small gravel road leading to the employee parking lot.

On the other side of the parking lot, several picnic tables were grouped under a small stand of sycamores. A distant fanfare blasted the air and she heard cheering. The joust was starting. She plunked down on the wooden seat of one of the tables and dropped the rub on the grease-stained tabletop. No guests would see her here, and everyone else was too busy working. She'd be alone for a while.

Maybe Elia had cursed her. She'd been fired from two jobs in one day. But Elia wasn't that smart. And with the dumb decisions Keelie had been making, she didn't need a curse to make her life go bad.

She should head back to the Admin building to return the uniform, endure another fiery butt-blasting from Finch, and beg for a new job. She'd either get another post, or else Finch would outright fire her, and Keelie would have to go work at the shop with Dad for no money. She had to do that anyway.

Keelie needed a break. She'd been yelled at by just about every adult she knew, and she had to keep taking it in order to repay her father. It was all about the dollars.

Knot leaped lightly onto the picnic table and scraped his head up against the rub container, purring loudly. His mouth was shiny with rub-daubed grease. His little tongue licked out to taste it.

"Thanks to you, we're going to be on the Most Wanted List at this Faire. Or worse—the Least Wanted."

Knot hopped off the table and looked back at Keelie. It was as if he wanted her to follow him. "That's great. Now you're doing dog tricks like some kind of feline Lassie."

He meowed and looked at the Faire buildings, then back at her.

"Okay. I'll bite." She had nothing else to do.

Knot led her toward the front of the Faire, stopping to let her catch up when the crowd got in the way. She thought she saw Elianard, but it was a man in a wizard costume, staring intently at a group of children. He was either a magician looking for an audience, or he was about to get his butt reported for extreme creepiness. He didn't notice her as she passed by, but she saw that the trees above him swarmed with the *feithid daoine*. The bug fairies seemed to be having a little party up there.

Knot negotiated the crowd as if they weren't even there. His bushy tail, its tip crooked over, was the flag that she watched for as she dodged strollers and slowpokes, her feet sore from the curlicue shoes that weren't exactly made for sand and gravel.

They were headed in the direction of the Admin office. Keelie slowed down. She so didn't want to go there yet. Knot stopped, swished his tail, and ran ahead on the path. The trees swayed, and Keelie thought she saw the *bhata* moving among the leaves of a low-lying branch of a nearby tall maple. She heard their excited buzzing. They were probably laughing at her outfit.

Finch had said she wanted fairies. Well, now she had them. She'd regret her words, if these were anything like the ones in Colorado.

The breeze shifted, and suddenly Keelie's mind filled with a picture of the glowing white unicorn, tossing its head, mane flying, silvery horn gleaming in the moonlight. Again, she had a sudden compulsion to find him. The image had come out of nowhere, and with it an urgent desire to run through the woods. Suspicious, she looked around. No sign of magic—not that she knew what to look for, but at least nothing seemed out of place. Other than the stick people in the trees.

Knot seemed to be encouraging her, as if he knew where the unicorn was. Bet Dad—Zeke!—was going to love that, especially after warning her not to go near the "mythical" beast. Nevertheless, something was summoning her, and she knew it had to be him.

Knot meowed and started walking, looking over his shoulder at her.

Finally, curiosity and the insistent cat convinced Keelie she needed to find the unicorn. She stepped onto the path, hoping that Elianard wasn't lurking around. She only had her Queen Aspen pendant with her, which wasn't of any use against obnoxious elf lords.

In the woods, sound dimmed and the air was different, thick with the spicy earthiness of green living things. Knot walked ahead, his steps almost soundless despite the usual debris of the forest floor. She opened her senses to the trees, anticipating the flow of greenness that would wrap around her, enveloping her in its welcoming shelter.

What she sensed was very different. Her throat constricted and her stomach seemed to rise, ready to toss its contents. She fell to the ground, shaking her head, trying to lessen the pressure inside. She was nauseous with the overpowering sense, the painful ache, that built until she thought she couldn't breathe. The trees were sick, all of them. Something was weakening them.

A dark energy willed her not to go any further. The

Dread. She forced herself past it. The trees were sick, and they needed help. The part of Keelie that was elven reached out to them, not able to bear their pain.

"What can I do to help?" She spoke the words aloud. She looked up as Knot thrashed through the leaves and jumped onto a huge granite boulder covered in lichen. He meowed again to Keelie.

She climbed up. The wind lifted her hair. It was warm, like spring, on top of the rock, and the scent of flowers wafted through the air. The unicorn was like spring. She imagined he'd been here for the first spring on Earth, when the world was new and bright.

And then she saw him. He stood in a shaft of afternoon sunlight, his horn sparkling, glorious in its beauty and radiance. Each spiral gleamed as if it had been dipped in iridescent moonlight. He looked at her, then danced skittishly, hooves digging into the loam.

She squatted and dropped from the boulder.

He wheeled and ran, darting impossibly between the trees.

"No, don't go."

A bird shot out of a nearby bush, joined by others. The air was briefly darkened by rushing wings.

The unicorn stopped and turned, tossed his silver mane, then galloped away. Knot leaped after him, and Keelie followed. She wasn't about to be left behind.

Around her the trees entreated her to stay. "Don't go. Be our shepherd. Help us."

Keelie drove the tree thoughts from her mind and focused on the unicorn. A small part of her noticed that it wasn't a conscious effort—the tree thoughts had faded into the background. The unicorn had taken over her mind, had become a singular compulsion. She ran on, thinking that she must not lose him. She belonged with him. On and on through trees, through thickets of bushes, she ran as if in a trance, pulled like a puppet by a magical string.

Her skirt snagged on a branch, ripping. She pulled the skirt up and knotted it at her waist, then slipped out of the ridiculous shoes and ran barefoot, the green hose in tatters around her ankles, hardly feeling the rocks and twigs she stepped on. She forced herself to move faster, always keeping Knot and the unicorn in sight. Her side burned and she pressed a hand against her ribs to rub the stitch away.

The unicorn leaped across a stream, tail rippling, and landed lightly on the other side. Keelie grabbed a sapling to keep from falling in.

"Help me, shepherd. I grow weak..." It was a young oak, sick, like all the others.

She took her hands away from the treeling, and its entreaties for help faded. The unicorn pawed the ground lightly, but didn't move. Keelie crept forward slowly, deliberately, like a cat stalking its prey. A small part of her mind wondered why she hadn't stopped to help the little tree.

Knot sat upright at the water's edge, staring unblinking at the silvery white beast before them. Without looking away from the unicorn, Keelie lowered her foot, feeling for the stream bottom. When her toe touched sediment she dropped the rest of the way. The water was numbingly cold, and the pebbles that formed the streambed bruised her feet. The unicorn tossed its head, but made no move to leave. The water soaked the hem of her skirt, making it heavy, but the cold finally woke her up enough to realize she'd been somehow enchanted. She took a step forward and ran into an invisible wall.

A frisson of fright rushed through her body. A magical force held her in place. Fear did not override her desire to follow the unicorn, but a sane part of her mind awakened, freed from enchantment.

Knot meowed, and his low cry turned into an angry growl. He stared across the water, unmoving, but Keelie couldn't tell if he was under the spell, too, or if it was just a kitty's natural aversion to water.

The unicorn's eye glowed with intelligence.

"What do you want?" she whispered. It tilted its head and moved its ears forward. Keelie stepped back, and the spell released her. It was as if she'd walked out of a spider web, and thin tendrils of the spell tickled her with the compulsion to be still.

Move, don't move. A breeze blew softly through the forest, blowing thin strands of the broken spell around her.

She climbed back onto the bank, grateful that her feet were numb, because when the cold wore off they'd probably hurt like crazy.

Behind her, the unicorn whickered, the cry so horse-like that she turned to look. Was he calling her back? The glow around him faded, and suddenly she could see that his hide was bare in spots, and his horn was dull and yellowed. His neck was thin. As if he knew that she could see the truth, he hung his head, then backed away until he faded into the bushes behind him. This did not look like the guardian of the forest.

Keelie's tears dripped into the stream. The little glade where the unicorn had been seemed dimmer now. The afternoon sun had dipped lower, and the light would fade faster in the forest. Her heart ached with sadness, and she wanted lie down on the decaying forest floor and cry.

She wondered what could hurt a unicorn, and whether the forest had sickened it or if it was the guardian's illness that was affecting the forest. According to Dad, unicorns were very powerful. What evil could do this? Dad was the Tree Shepherd. She had to tell him, although he had warned her to stay out of the woods.

The forest seemed gloomy and sinister.

"Come on, Knot. Let's head back."

Limping, she retraced her steps. The little oak at the bank's edge seemed small and sad. She gently grasped one of its branches, and with her other hand touched the Queen Aspen's heart. Her fingertips tingled, the signal of rising magic. She couldn't help the unicorn, but she could save this tree. The magic bubbled up, like heated sap, and spilled over. She guided it to the tree's feeble roots and felt them thicken and throw out rootlets, reaching deeper into the nourishing earth. Leaves burst from the branches and its bark grew smoother.

As the magic deepened, she heard the singing of the sprite that lived in the stream, and the voices of the tall trees around her, begging for a sip of her magic.

There wasn't enough for all of them. *I will return*, she promised. A tug pulled her toward the magical stream, and she cried out as her hand brushed against bark and stuck fast, her magic usurped by the wide oak that branched over the water. He drank deeply of the Queen Aspen's magic. But the magic was not just the pendant's—it was Keelie's life force as well.

She fell to her knees, pulse racing. Her heart beat like a mechanical thing gone wild. Other trees protested above her, clamoring for a taste. Keelie fell over, numb, and as her vision grew fuzzy she watched an ant walk the edge of a leaf. Her world had been reduced to this, the march of the tiniest creature.

With an effort she turned her head. Silvery forms sprang to being around her, a ghostly forest that cried out to return to the earth. She heard the echo of saws and the shouts of men, and the cracking and thunder of falling brothers.

Suddenly, she couldn't breathe anymore. This is it, she thought. I'm dying, because I didn't listen to Dad. A roar filled her ears, like a wind machine beating against her eardrums. The saws had come for her. She closed her eyes, ready for whatever came next.

Someone was sandpapering her eyelids, and the horrible feeling of being siphoned dry lifted. She opened her eyes. Knot's face loomed large, revealing the reason why she couldn't breathe. He was sitting on her chest, purring, and he'd put his paw on her forehead to anchor himself as he groomed her.

She pushed him off and sat up. He purred and rubbed against her arm. "I thought I was dying, Snot, and it was just you." She laughed shakily, aware that she might have been really dying, and that just maybe the cat had done something to stop the trees from draining her.

The ghostly forest had faded, but it was still visible. She shivered. It had been real. This was the forest Dad had told her about, the trees that sought rest, the sisters and brothers of the oaks, themselves so sick that they might join them in death.

She glanced at the young oak, now in full leaf and healthy. One spot of vibrant health in the haunted and dying forest. Her good deed had almost killed her.

Nauseous, she got to her knees and then stood up, careful not to touch any trees. She needed to tell Dad about this. Maybe the haunted forest was the reason he looked so ill. It could be that he'd let the trees take his energy, but she doubted that he'd deplete himself so much. He probably knew a better way. No, he hadn't allowed himself to be drained. This was bad magic.

She was already in a lot of trouble. She'd been fired from her second job, she owed Dad and Lady Annie hundreds of dollars, and Laurie was coming. Her life was so messed up that she didn't know what he could do to make it worse.

Then it hit her. He could call Elizabeth and tell her not to let Laurie come to New York, he could say that Keelie couldn't drive. He could tell Lady Annie to sell the boots. She needed to stay in Dad's good graces, and that meant that her forest misadventure would remain a secret.

She looked down at Knot, who was blinking up at her. "Don't you tell him. This has to be our secret."

In answer, he stalked past her with his tail held high. Keelie followed his furry booty, and he led her to her shoes. She never would have believed she'd be glad to find the hideous gold lamé gnome booties, but almost cried with relief when she put them on. Her sore feet still kept her progress slow. Behind her, in the deep woods, the unicorn neighed, and the trees above whispered songs of sorrow and regret.

ten

Keelie thrashed her way clear of the last bush. The sunlight had faded into dusky twilight. Twilight and dawn—the times when the fairies came out, or so it was said in the fairy tales she'd read. But Keelie knew better. Fairies caused mischief no matter what time of day it was.

A cloud of them had surrounded Knot and he'd vanished, leaving her to fight her way through the unknown woods. She could forgive him that. The evening air chilled her exposed shoulders, and she wished she still had the vampire cape. At least she had the Robin Hood hose to keep her legs warm. They'd helped protect her skin from scratches, and she'd been careful not to touch any trees.

She remembered that weird spell in the water. And something was terribly wrong with the trees that had pulled her energy. A normal human, or even another elf, would not have been in danger from the trees. She pushed away the thought that she wouldn't have been in danger, either, if she'd listened to her father and if she hadn't helped the sapling.

She couldn't understand why anyone would put a spell like that in the water. It hadn't been in the trees, so it wasn't to keep people from falling in. It was to keep them from crossing the stream.

She saw the Admin building ahead and glanced down at the torn Jersey-cow bodice, the wet and muddy skirt, and the trashed glitter-gnome shoes. She couldn't face Finch tonight. Keelie's head was still buzzing from the spell, and she was fatigued, weak from the weight of the trees' illness.

Maybe Dad was so sick that he didn't know how bad off the trees were. The greenness of the hurt trees pressed against her, and she could smell moss and loam as if she had her nose to the ground, instead of aimed at the gravel walkway that gleamed in the dim light. The trees had called to her and she'd run, frightened that they could take what she had not offered.

Her shoulders ached from hunching them, not that it had helped to keep her from hearing their pleas. Dad would have to be in a coma not to notice that the trees were in distress. Maybe he couldn't help them, either. It would take an army of tree shepherds to solve their ills, or maybe a unicorn in full power, not the sad specimen that haunted these woods. She needed to find Dad, and quickly. He had to know what was going on, and she couldn't keep her forest adventure secret if she was to discover how to help him.

She hurried down the path, wincing as the gravel bit

through the thin-soled booties and into her sore feet. Sir Davey needed to be told about the forest, too, and especially about the unicorn. She shivered as she recalled his patchy coat and his dull horn, after she'd seen through his glamour. The oaks across the lane from Heartwood were so sad, and they had reason to be. Between the logging and the unicorn's decline, they'd had a rough century. She wanted to help them, but she didn't know where she could summon that much power—not to mention time, since she had to work, help at Heartwood, and show Laurie around.

Keelie crouched down, hidden below the level of the bushes as she passed the Admin building. She didn't want to get caught by Finch. Tomorrow, she would swallow her pride and take the next job. She still had to pay for those Lady Annie boots.

A few of the last-minute guests, probably from the pub, were dragging down the path out of the Faire, still singing. She got some odd looks, and no wonder. She was too exhausted to care.

All around, artisans were packing up and food vendors were cleaning their areas. A crowd of tall men was ahead of her on the narrow path, and Keelie slowed down, stuck behind them. She was about to tap one on the shoulder and ask him nicely to move aside when she realized that it was Little John, carrying his thick staff. He seemed to sense her and turned to look. She slowed, afraid he'd hit her, but he winked at her and walked on, his long legs striding easily next to Robin Hood and Will Scarlet. Maid Marian walked more slowly, dragging behind.

From here, Keelie could see the blur that seemed to

hover over Maid Marian's face. She squinted. Some sort of magic, but she couldn't tell what.

Then she overheard Will Scarlet say, "Hey Jared, I'll meet you down at Rivendell."

The guy playing Robin Hood waved his hand in a see-you-there motion.

Tired as she was, Keelie still summoned up a big dose of healthy appreciation for the guy playing Robin Hood. If she had been playing Maid Marian, she would've had her arms and lips locked around that hunky piece of work in green. Keelie thought of the party at the Shire, at the High Mountain Faire, and Captain Dandy Randy's wandering hand. She blushed at the memory.

The other Merry Men sang a bawdy song, with hand gestures, about Robin and Marian being fruitful and multiplying in Sherwood Forest. Maid Marian's long black braids, wrapped in green velvet and criss-crossed with leather cords, swung behind her like twin pendulums. Her skirts swayed with her steps. She was gorgeous. Keelie wondered how old she was. Eighteen? Ninety-two? You couldn't tell with elves. Dad might know.

Keelie made a face behind her back. Maid Marian was responsible for starting the attack of the stick-wielding princesses earlier in the day. Then the elf girl turned her head and Keelie almost gasped. The blurry effect was hiding her true face, and Keelie had seen right through the blur when she turned. The girl's beauty was a mask, a trick. Underneath the spell she looked sick, all hollow-eyed and pale.

As they neared the main performance stage, they passed Elia and her elven entourage—the girls who had accompanied her yesterday at the costume shop. A slender knight stood beside them, his armor stacked next to him. He had his head turned to one side, and Keelie admired his profile. His nose was straight as a knife, and strands of his long, butter-colored hair moved gently in the breeze. Keelie caught a glimpse of a pointed ear. An elf, of course.

Keelie hadn't yet checked out the jousters here, the stud muffins of every Faire. Some of them were sick. Her own favorite jouster, of course, was at the Florida Faire. He was part of the reason that Elia hated her so much. Sean o' the Wood had dated Elia, or whatever the elven equivalent of dating was, until Keelie had caught his eye.

She kept wondering why Sean hadn't returned her calls, or emailed her through the Admin office, since he'd left for his new jousting gig. It'd been almost two weeks! He was probably busy, but it still hurt that he hadn't contacted her. He was the most handsome guy she'd ever seen, and he'd smiled at her as if she was the most beautiful girl in the world. It made her warm inside to remember his kiss the last night of the Faire. It had been so romantic. Well, romantic until Knot used Sean's leg as a scratching post.

Still, since he hadn't called, she wasn't feeling guilty about her Robin Hood lust. Ahead, Maid Marian hurried toward the elven girls, joining them without a word of goodbye to her fellow actors. Elia greeted her, then stepped out in front of Keelie. "Well. Well. What are you supposed to be?" She smoothed out her skirts and preened at the Merry Men, who grinned appreciatively as they passed by.

Keelie didn't blame them. Elia was glowing. She looked as if she'd spent a week at a spa. Her friends, on the other hand, looked pale. If there was a bug going around, then it had totally missed Elia and hit them head on.

The Merry Men didn't slow down, so Keelie walked faster to catch up. She liked being a part of their tipsy parade, and she was too tired to banter with Elia.

But Elia caught up with Keelie, and smiled as if they were the best of friends. "I heard you stank like a human sewer earlier today."

Keelie ignored the elf girl and kept walking. Maybe she could give Elia to the trees in the forest, to use like a battery. She wouldn't last long. Then again, the trees might toss her back.

Elia pinched the back of her arm. "Hey, I'm talking to you, Round Ear."

The parade stragglers turned to glance at her. Keelie pulled her arm close and kept her gaze straight ahead, and soon the others did, too. Tuning Elia out was easy today. There was nothing the elf girl could say that would make things worse than they already were. At the intersection to the Enchanted Lane she turned, and the Merry Men walked on, still singing. As their voices faded, the Lane lost its enchantment. It looked sad without the bustling tourists, and this evening there wasn't even the usual hum of voices as merchants discussed their day.

Lady Annie's was already closed. Keelie walked past her shop, carefully stepping over the acorns that littered the sandy dirt path. She was afraid to look at her feet. They ached horribly from her barefoot forest run, and were probably bruised and cut.

Heartwood seemed deserted, too. Glancing next door, Keelie noted that Lulu's place was shuttered for the night. What a relief. She didn't want to face Lulu. She couldn't exactly blame the puppet lady for losing her temper. Yelling the ultimate swear word in front of little kids, no matter how obnoxious they were, had been pretty bad.

Keelie closed her eyes, and to her relief discovered that the oaks were asleep. A heavy green slumber blanketed their consciousness. But a pang of sympathy stabbed her, because even in sleep, grief cloaked them.

A loud voice boomed from the front of Heartwood. "Your shop was closed and whenever someone approached it, they were attacked by acorns." The voice was so earsplitting Keelie was surprised that the oaks hadn't awakened and started running for the nearest mountaintop.

Her father answered, sounding weary. "I'm sorry. I . . . "

Keelie wanted to dart into the shop and defend her dad from the bawling Faire director, who would've scared a shipload of Vikings, but she hung back when Finch resumed her loud harangue. This time she bellowed.

"You were closed today. Where were you? We've never had so many problems with the Enchanted Lane. I received over a hundred complaints about the number of acorns on the paths, and it's not even fall! And after I had them swept, they've come back."

Dad seemed lost. "The oaks . . . I'm trying to find the source."

"The oaks! Let's talk about those demented trees and the real world. You don't have liability insurance to cover injuries due to falls, but I have to have it. And when the insurance adjustor sees all of the acorns, then the rates go up. Head Office will want an explanation, and then I've got to haul my ass into Head Office and explain why I haven't cut down all the trees. I sure can't tell them that the Tree Shepherd couldn't control the oaks. And when I come to discuss it with you what do I find? Your shop is closed!"

Dad bit his lip. Keelie couldn't believe he was letting her talk to him like this.

"You said you'd take care of the oaks. Now do it! Now let's talk about your cat. Lulu went ballistic on me today because your hairball stole a puppet or something."

"I've paid for the toy unicorn. Lulu and I spoke about it." His voice was almost inaudible.

"Glad to hear it. Make sure I don't hear any more complaints about Knot because I swear, if I do, I'll personally tie a knot in his tail that he'll never be able to straighten out. Put that cat in your camper, get a television, and tune it to Animal Planet."

"I'll find a way of restraining him," Dad replied in a tired voice.

"Yeah, you'd better, because he wreaked havoc at the Steak-on-a-Stake booth earlier, and your daughter was a part of it."

Dad made no sound. Keelie wondered what he was thinking. She'd wanted to break it to him herself. In a way, though, she was relieved. The thought of Knot locked up in the Swiss Miss Chalet was a lovely one. Heh! Not that it would humble the hairball. More likely he'd just have the opportunity to trash Keelie's belongings, as he had in Colorado when he'd peed in her suitcase and ruined all her underwear.

But Knot had to stay free, because he was Keelie's link to the unicorn. Without him, she might not find it again.

"Do something, Zeke; otherwise, I'll have to."

Retreating, stomping footfalls meant that Finch had to be leaving. But Keelie waited a few minutes to be absolutely sure.

She finally tiptoed to the back of the shop. Suddenly,

something furry rubbed up against her legs. She jumped and swallowed the squeal that wanted to escape from her lips, just in case Finch was still around. Placing her hands against her thumping chest, Keelie she realized that the furry-something was the white kitty. She lifted the sad cat in her arms, but he struggled to be free. She released him, and he jumped from her arms and ran back outside. Did the cat belong to one of the Faire workers? They shouldn't let it run free.

Keelie stepped out from behind the furniture that was lined up against the wall and put on her chirpiest voice. "Hey Dad, what's going on?"

He startled. He was leaning against the counter, and in the fading light he looked a lot paler than he had earlier in the day. Poor Dad. Scott had a lot to answer for. If the turd had honored his agreement, her father wouldn't be worked to death and getting reamed out for not keeping the shop open.

Keelie looked at her father and her heart clenched as the light shifted outside, illuminating him. He looked really sick. Finch's demands were probably making him feel worse. Just being around Finch stressed Keelie out. The woman had the aura of a volcano ready to erupt at the slightest provocation.

"Where have you been? I've been looking for you all afternoon. I had a very disturbing message from Finch."

"I followed Knot into the woods. He wanted me to follow him."

Her father's expression changed to surprise.

"Don't yell about me going into the woods. The forest is sick, and the trees need our help." Keelie motioned toward the large oaks across from the shop. "It's not just the oaks. Can't you feel it?"

In reply, Dad drew in a sharp breath and leaned back against the counter, his shoulders slumped as if a huge sack of life's burdens had been placed on them. "I went searching for it, today. The unicorn. The trees blocked his energy from me."

And you're not looking so hot yourself, Keelie thought. "What are we going to do?"

"I know about the forest, Keelie, although the unicorn ... " He looked up at her with a strange look, as if he was trying to be angry but couldn't summon the energy. "Dark magic is poisoning the forest. Sir Davey and I are working on it, but Keelie ... You need to stay out of the forest. What if you'd been hurt?"

She walked closer. "Dad, I've already been in the forest. Knot led me there. He really wanted me to help the unicorn."

Her father's face went still. "What happened?" His voice was a whisper.

"There's a spell on the water, on the stream, and I got caught in it, like in a spider web. It was like the Dread, but it wasn't just a fear spell. It wouldn't let me cross. The unicorn jumped right through it, but then it wasn't beautiful anymore. It looks like a mangy old horse. His horn is all yellow and worn and cracked, and he's so skinny. I think he's dying, Dad."

Zeke rubbed a hand over his face, and Keelie saw tears in his eyes. "Is that all?"

"No." Her voice was very low. She didn't want to tell about this part. "There was a little oak, and it needed my help. And I thought I could help just this one little tree."

"No—" Her father's cry was strangled. "Keelie, you can't help just one tree in a dying forest."

Keelie continued, afraid that if she stopped, she'd never

say it. "I used the Queen Aspen's heart, I drew her power, but the other trees wanted it, too, and then I kind of passed out, and Knot brought me back."

Dad's arms went around her and he pulled her close. "Oh, Keelie."

She hugged him back, sinking into his embrace. The only family I have left, she thought. His rib bones were like ledges under her hands, and her cheek hurt against his sharp collarbone. He's fading away, she thought, fading like the unicorn. She shivered.

"You really truly saw it." Dad stared at a chair in front of him, as if its crystal-bedecked swirled branches could tell him what to say. Footsteps sounded on the wooden floor. Keelie turned quickly, peeved.

"Hello? Anyone here?" The voice was soft.

"It's Janice," Zeke said.

"Back here," Keelie called. Dad placed his finger against his lips. "We'll talk about this later. It's better others don't know about the forest being sick."

Janice might know what was ailing Dad.

The herb lady bustled in, bracelets jangling, surrounded by the delicious scents of the plants she worked with. She smiled at them. "Hey, you two. I want to invite you to dinner at my place. Nice stout stew in the crock-pot, crusty bread, and lots of hot tea. With Raven gone, it's very lonesome in the teeny-tiny closet that serves as my apartment here."

"Thank you, Janice. You're very kind." Zeke nodded as if his head was the only part of him flexible enough to bow.

Knot hopped onto the counter and rubbed his head against Dad's elbow.

"Keelie, what happened to you?" Janice frowned. "And what are you wearing?"

"You must not have gone to the food court yet. I worked at Steak-on-a-Stake. Briefly." She glared at Knot, who blinked once, as if in answer. "Knot got me fired."

"Did he chase you through a rose bush, too?" Janice shook her head. "Come on. I have some salve that will take the sting out of those scratches. And you don't look so good, Zeke. Goodness. The two of you need looking after. Follow me." Janice bustled off, looking happy to have someone to care for.

Keelie followed her in relief. "Food sounds great." Just being around Janice comforted her. "How's Raven doing?"

Janice waved her hand. "She's having fun. I'll catch you up with what's going on when we have dinner." She put her arm through Zeke's and he leaned into her a little. Knot trotted next to them, his ill-gotten stuffed unicorn hanging from his mouth.

"Hey, about Laurie," Keelie blurted out. "She said she'll be here Friday. Can we pick her up?"

"We'll arrange something," Dad promised. Keelie's heart sank at the thought of driving up to the train station in the Swiss Miss Chalet.

Janice's booth was smaller than the one she'd had in Colorado, but it had the same wonderful herbal smell.

"The privies are close." Keelie was trying to be diplomatic.

"That's both good and bad, Keelie," Janice replied. "The traffic is always great here, because people swarm by at all hours. But when it's hot, the smell is not the sweetest."

"Good thing you have all these herbs, then."

Janet laughed and ushered Zeke in. Keelie was about to

follow when she heard a sound that drew her to the back of the little half-timbered building. The forest grew close here, and she heard the sound clearly. A single note, sustained for so long that she couldn't tell what instrument made it, or what throat.

She stood with her arms crossed over her chest, and then moved closer to a straight, slender oak. She stopped well away from it, but something was scratching her head, tugging at her hair. She reached up and her fingers touched the stick hand of a *bhata*. "Stop it, or I'll freeze you."

Faint laughter, like sticks rubbing together, came from above, and was joined by more laughter from the bushes that bordered the forest. The little people were partying tonight. Fine. She had no desire to get caught up in their wicked games.

The breeze carried the scent of cinnamon. Keelie sniffed appreciatively, until she realized that it wasn't coming from Janice's herb shop. It was coming from the forest. Anxiety gripped her. As if the thought of the woods had conjured up a spell, Keelie suddenly couldn't breathe. She grabbed at her throat, trying to peel off the invisible hands that choked her. Her heart thudded against her ribs.

She turned and ran, gasping, for Janice's door. She pounded on it, unable to turn the knob, unable to scream for help.

The door opened, and Sir Davey stood before her awash in golden lamplight.

"Hey, ho. You'll be late for dinner!"

Keelie fell at his feet, choking. She heard Janice and Dad running toward her, and the last thing she heard before all went black was Sir Davey's grim voice.

"The Dread."

eleven

Trapped. Enslaved. Confined. Detained. Keelie thought of all the words that applied, but it meant the same thing no matter how she said it. She was stuck helping Dad. She hadn't thought he'd actually take her up on her offer to help him, but here she was, cutting off bits of tree branches (Yellow pine from Georgia) to make blocks, and nursing sore muscles from the hand saw. This was not her vision of "helping." She imagined herself at the door to the shop, greeting customers and looking really cute in a Francesca outfit.

Her hand stilled, making full contact with the log, and she was drawn into a vision of the tree's home, a warm, fragrant, piney woods. She heard the mockingbird's song and the cry of a swooping blue jay. She wished she were there, in that muggy, overgrown forest, instead of chopping up this tree, but this was the way trees should feel—their ring memories caught in the wood, happy visions of their native forests.

A pull of energy tugged at her from within. She dropped the saw and backed away. This was different from what she'd experienced a few days ago in the forest with the Wildewood trees. She remembered the cedar that she'd helped her father cut at his workshop in Colorado, how it had shown her its past, a memory that would be a part of everything created from its wood. She picked up the saw once more. This was normal. For a tree shepherd, that is.

Her encounter with the Dread on Saturday night had left her a little woozy. Keelie had passed out halfway into Janice's shop. She'd come to a few hours later in the tiny upstairs bedroom, with Janice's worried face looking pale and shadowed, haunted in the candlelight.

When she'd tried to sit up, a rock fell off of her forehead, and other crystals and pebbles rolled from her chest. Sir Davey's doing, no doubt. "What happened?"

"The Dread," Janice whispered. "Someone put a spell on the forest behind the shops, and it reached out and squeezed you. I was so afraid." Tears glistened in her warm brown eyes and her hand tightened on Keelie's.

Keelie patted her with her free hand. "I feel okay now. Earth magic, right?" Although Janice knew about the elves and all the rest, Keelie would still feel better in the rock-shielded RV.

Janice nodded. "Yes, Sir Davey's. And your father's in the forest now, trying to find the source of the spell."

The memory of the hungry trees, the haunted forest, and the gaunt, patch-coated unicorn came back to her. Dad had said that the unicorn was the guardian of the forest. Whatever had done that to the unicorn could probably kill a tree shepherd, and she'd fallen victim twice in one day. She swallowed to rid herself of the catch in her throat. "I don't think it's safe for him to go out there."

Janice uttered a short laugh and pulled her hand free. "Your father is the Tree Shepherd. No one is safer in the woods!" She stood up, bending over a little to keep from smacking her head on the low roof. "How about some veggie stew?"

Keelie wasn't really hungry, but she forced herself to smile. "Sounds great."

Her father and Sir Davey returned a while later and joined them for dinner, but she noticed when she turned in early, exhausted, that they did, too. By Sunday morning he'd put her to work, then returned to the forest. Keelie knew he was searching for the unicorn. She hoped that the trees would lead him, or that the unicorn would reveal himself. The only thing she could do was work hard in the shop.

The table next to her was stacked with the little bitty rounds that would soon be labeled as Heartwood's All-Natural Blocks. Dad said that Heartwood building blocks were popular. A woman had asked about the blocks, claiming that her daughter had a set growing up, and now she wanted to order another set for her granddaughter. Dad didn't have any in stock, and he thought it would be an easy project for Keelie to work on. Yeah, right. He needed her to help with the unicorn, but he was too stubborn to admit it.

Worse, he was making himself sicker every day by opening himself magically to the trees, especially the oaks.

Part of Keelie wanted to run back into the forest to be with the unicorn, now more out of compassion than a magical compulsion. But another part of her wanted to remain within the sanctuary of the Faire. It felt safer to be around people like Janice—humans.

Keelie touched a round of wood, thinking how strange it was that she'd never noticed a green tint in the wood grain of the other pieces. Another energy zing zapped through her body. She looked out at the oak trees across the lane, and closed her eyes. She sensed they were asleep.

Glancing down at the round, Keelie noticed that most of the green tint had flowed to the center. Okay, maybe this was a freaky little piece that had missed some elven de-magicking ritual Dad did with the trees. She dropped it onto the worktable, and it fell on its edge and spun around and around like a coin.

Dad needed to hire another assistant, ASAP. She was fine with going into the woods to talk to the trees, hear about their problems, be a kind of woodland mediator, but actually making stuff out of trees wasn't on her agenda.

Keelie held up her hand. Sticky blobs of pinesap clung to her skin. She peeled a gummy piece off and shook her finger to flip it away, but it held fast. This stuff was stickier than superglue. She finally got the blob off, and threw it down onto the worktable. It landed on the green wood round. Keelie heard a slurp.

Like water on a dry sponge, the sap was absorbed by the wood round. Within seconds, a small pinecone sprouted from the center of the round. She backed away, remembering that in Colorado, a branch had sprouted from a cedar fence when she'd leaned against it.

Right before her eyes, and just as Dad entered the work area, the pinecone morphed into a small pine seedling.

He stared at it. "Not again. Your tree magic is out of balance—dead wood is using it to regenerate. Come on." He hustled her out of the shop and down to Janice's for a tincture concocted from her herbs, as well as for a mysterious compound from Sir Davey that tasted like it was made from privy dirt. Beyond gross.

When she went to bed, Keelie was still scratching at sawdust that clung to her despite a thorough soaping. The following morning she showered again. Taking a shower in Sir Davey's camper was great, but she had to bend down really low to shampoo her hair or else she'd conk her forehead on the showerhead.

By the end of the day, her sore muscles protested. She'd been sawing, grinding, and sanding wood for four days. This was all Scott's fault. He should be here. Instead, he was in her old state, while she was stuck here in Nowhere, New York.

The only reason she hadn't screamed bloody rebellious murder about everything going on was because Dad looked as pale as the gourmet sheep cheese that Mom used to nibble when she drank wine with friends. Dad was wiped.

On the other hand, business was so good that he couldn't keep up with the work all by himself. This was a mixed blessing, since Keelie wasn't as useful as Scott was. Still, she had managed to sell six chairs and a dresser, and had taken orders for several custom pieces.

They weren't just making stuff for the Ren Faire, either.

With Christmas just over four months away, there had been a run on orders for dollhouses like the one Dad had made for her when she'd been little. This irked her, since she'd always thought hers was special, and now she was helping him to cut out its clones.

That night Keelie dreamed about a dollhouse. But it was life-sized, in the Wildewood, and it was nighttime—sunrise would be coming soon, and glimmers of pink shimmered on the horizon …

The unicorn galloped up to the front door and knocked with his horn. Knot answered the door, standing on his hind legs and wearing his Puss-in-Boots outfit. He stepped outside and walked with the unicorn to a mountaintop. In the background, Keelie heard something that sounded like turbine engines—the hydroelectric dam.

Bears, deer, wolves and every animal imaginable emerged from the surrounding forest and formed a circle around the unicorn and Knot. With a flourish of his paw, Knot removed his hat and bowed before the unicorn. In the first rays of the morning sun, the unicorn rose upon his hind legs. The horn shone with a blinding radiance. Keelie covered her face, and smelled coffee …

She awoke and blinked in the dim light that filtered through the RV's curtains. That was a weird dream, even for her.

Luckily, the smell of coffee was real. Thank goodness. Sir Davey was up. She walked to the kitchen and poured herself a cup, the dark brown liquid reminding her of the tincture Dad had made her take.

Dad came into the kitchen, long hair flowing. Keelie almost dropped her cup of coffee. She'd never seen it loose.

He always kept it pulled back, even when they'd been in the forests. Keelie studied him from the rim of her cup as she took her first sip.

He sat down heavily on the bench opposite her and closed his eyes. His hair moved slightly, revealing a pointed ear tip that reminded her of Elia's friends. They hadn't looked well either, the other day.

On the table was a copy of *Ye Wildewood Gazette*, the Faire paper. Keelie picked it up and read the headline aloud: "'Two More Jousters Sick, Lodge Quarantined.'" She looked up. "Dad, what's going on at the lodge? Is it some kind of elf flu?"

Dad lifted his head. "There is no flu, but I'm not surprised that some of the elves are sick." He covered his mouth and coughed.

Sir Davey checked the oatmeal and gave it a stir, his eyes on her dad. "Any luck, Zeke?"

"No. I'm exhausted." Dad leaned into the bench corner, and Keelie remembered how he'd leaned against the counter in the shop for support. He hadn't done that at the High Mountain Faire. He noticed her watching him, and sat up straight. His eyes cleared and he smiled. "I don't have the flu."

She smelled cinnamon. Her oatmeal didn't have any added spices, so his sudden healthy appearance had to be magic. He was trying to whammy her. Her worry briefly deepened into panic. He must be worse off than she thought. She would not lose Dad, too. She'd work harder in the woodshop to give him a break, and she wouldn't complain. Meanwhile, she would check in with Janice to see what sort of natural remedy she could suggest for Dad.

Beads of sweat dotted his skin.

Strange. She'd never seen Dad sweat. Keelie didn't know if it was an elven trait, either. Only the jousters worked hard enough to break a sweat, and they were hidden in their armor.

Dad patted her knee. "It may be that I'm working too hard. We've got a lot of orders to fill."

"Why did you take all these extra dollhouse orders?" She didn't do a good job of not sounding grumpy.

"I've got a daughter to support, and bills need to be paid."

Guilt swamped Keelie as she thought about her extravagant boot purchase. "Did you take all the dollhouse orders to pay for the boots?"

"Partly, although you promised to pay for them."

He needed her. It's why she worked so hard. She had a purpose. It was sweet of Dad to take on extra work to make sure he had the money to support her. It showed that he really cared. Even though he said he was thrilled to have her in his life, she still wondered sometimes. He'd gone from the most eligible bachelor to Daddy in two months, and maybe he regretted losing his freedom.

"So how do you get that smooth corner on the dollhouse roof?"

He reached over and ruffled her hair. "You're faking an interest, but I appreciate the effort. Let's walk to Heartwood."

"You look like you couldn't walk from here to the bathroom."

"I'm fine, but we have something important to do on our way to the shop. Take me to where you saw the unicorn."

Her heart raced as if she were about to see a guy she had a crush on. "Sure. It's not far."

"I'll stay and finish my research." Sir Davey's eyes met Keelie's. He was worried about Zeke, too.

Dad stood, swayed a bit, then walked steadily toward the door. Keelie followed. If he fell, she'd have a hard time getting him out of the woods. "Dad, are you up to this? You look like you should be headed to bed, not the forest."

"I'll feel better when I'm in the trees, when I'm in the evergreen part of the forest; they've been supplying me with the extra energy to keep the oaks asleep. The leader of the evergreens and conifers is a Douglas fir named Tavak. He'll be making contact with you soon."

Keelie hoped this Tavak was intelligent like Hrok, the aspen she'd befriended in the meadow near the High Mountain Faire. Dad put an arm over her shoulder, and she wondered if it was affection or to steady himself. "If we're near the unicorn, I'll feel its power, but I won't be able to see it."

"No loss, let me tell you. I was disappointed when I got a good look at it."

"Were you expecting something out of a cartoon?" He smiled down at her.

"I wasn't expecting to see it at all. But the first time I saw it, it glowed like a big firefly. It was gorgeous, just like an illustration."

"With our help, he'll look like that again."

Keelie straightened. *Our* help.

On the road to the forest, Knot leaped out from behind a bush and raced across the path and up a tree on the other side. He clung to its bark and meowed piteously. Despite the burst of energy, he did not sound like his usual arrogant-kitty self.

Dad nodded. "I see. I guess it's time to use the legendary Heartwood charm. Keelie, we need to go to the shop first."

Okay, there it was, right there in front of her. Evidence of what she'd long suspected. "You were talking to that cat," Keelie said accusingly.

Dad arched an eyebrow, and though he looked tired he had a mischievous twinkle in his eyes. "You talk to Knot, too. Every morning you call him a 'snotball wad of fur,' and tell him that he doesn't need to pollute the Earth with his drool."

"Yeah, but I don't expect him to answer me. What did he say?"

"Keelie, he's meowing because he's a cat."

"No, this is more. He's an *elven* cat. You're an elf. So, tell him to talk so the human can understand him."

Knot jumped off the tree and sauntered away.

Dad had the nerve to laugh. "I think that's your answer."

"Yeah, if that's the way you're going to be, furball, I won't dump your litter box for a week."

His loud purr wafted back. She wouldn't really do that to him and he knew it. The vindictive kitty would probably use her clean laundry for a litter box if she didn't keep his box clean. She'd think up something else to annoy him. It had become one of her favorite pastimes.

Near Heartwood, voices floated toward them from a bend in the road. Through the trees, she caught glimpses of a small knot of people. Dad placed his finger against his lips, which was code for *we don't need to talk elven stuff.*

"Whatever happens, I don't want you to interrupt. Do you understand?"

Keelie nodded, remembering Knot's warning. She caught a whiff of cinnamon, and wondered if it was magic or just the smell of nearby baking scones. Her stomach growled. Magic didn't seem as scary in the daylight.

When the group came into view, Keelie wanted to run. Finch was at their head, heavy boots pulverizing acorns as she stomped toward them. The woman looked unhappy—no change from her usual expression—and she was followed by three men who were either spies or FBI agents. They wore jeans and polo shirts, which was very normal, but their extreme work boots, mirrored sunglasses, and robot attitude did not say "fun Ren Faire weekend." Neither did their toolboxes.

A fifth person strutted into view, and she was definitely out of place. The woman wore a pink skirt-and-jacket outfit out of a 1980s sitcom. Her maroon high heels didn't match her outfit. A color-blind fashion victim. She wouldn't survive a minute in LA.

She carried a camera, and she was looking around and snapping photos.

Finch's red hair was piled in a tumbleweed of a bun, and her face and neck were flushed to almost the same color. The dragon was stoking the flames. Finch must be going to barbecue Keelie for getting fired again, or maybe for not returning her Steak-on-a-Stake costume. She hoped she wasn't going to have to pay for that loser outfit. The cape had gotten burned, and the rest, including the ridiculous gold gnome booties, was ruined.

Dad bowed elegantly as they approached. "A beautiful day, is it not?"

Finch's color went from hot sauce to peaches and cream, and the lady in pink smiled brilliantly.

The odor of cinnamon was heavy now. Either the tea shop had gone into overtime, or this was elven magic.

twelve

Dad took Pink Suit's hand and bowed over it. "I have heard that there are magical beings in this forest, and truly I believe it now, for such beauty cannot be mortal. My first glimpse of you will be forever etched in my memory, and I will define my waking days from the second I saw you. You must tell me your name."

Okay... hand out the barf bags. But Dad had said not to interrupt.

The woman smiled, exposing more of her flashy white teeth. No wonder those dudes wore sunglasses. The glare from Pink Suit's teeth would've blinded them. "My name is Dawn Valentine."

Finch had taken a step toward him, as if she thought his words were for her. Dawn Valentine, the town councilwoman with the stripper's name, seemed hypnotized. Keelie was going to have to save her father. He had to be truly sick to be making lovey-dovey eyes at this woman.

Pink Suit flicked her hand toward the three men in sunglasses. "Go check out the privy at the end of this lane." She pulled a Ren Faire map from her clipboard and gave it to the first guy.

He nodded and motioned with his head at the other two guys. They automatically followed him, focused on the sensors they'd pulled from their toolboxes. Even their steps were in unison.

Dad's smile widened. "Dawn Valentine. Lovely. A name for a goddess."

Goddess! Keelie felt a little nauseous.

Pink Suit pulled the hairpins from her bun and released her mousy brown hair, which fell limply to her shoulders. Highlights, volumizer, and a decent trim, stat! She looked Dad up and down. "And you are ... ?" Her tone had gone all girly and coy. Barf.

"How remiss of me. I'm Zeke Heartwood." He extended his hand once more in an elegant gesture. The woman placed her hand limply into his.

Very nice, except Dad didn't let go of her hand, and the woman didn't look like she was in any hurry, either. Definitely elf flu. Either that or he'd gone insane.

Dad turned to Finch. "What are you ladies doing on such a lovely day?"

Finch gestured toward the woman. "Ms. Valentine's with

the Canooga Town Council. She's here accompanying the gentlemen with the EPA." She shot Pink Suit a dirty look.

"Have you found anything?" Dad looked into her eyes.

"They want to check out some unusual air readings near the mountaintop. There's a power plant on the other side." Ms. Valentine gestured toward the departing men. "And they're setting up groundwater testing."

Finch pointed in the direction of the forested hill behind the Enchanted Lane. "We were on our way up."

That was where she had last seen the unicorn, Keelie realized. She doubted Dawn Valentine would be able to see a unicorn, but she was afraid that the EPA dudes had something that could sense the unicorn's magic. She needed to get up to the mountain. With Dad busy, this would be a good chance to check it out.

"Can I join you? In addition to being a master carpenter, I am very knowledgeable about the forest."

"No thanks. We have two scientists working with us," Dawn Valentine replied.

"I have degrees in biology, geology, forestry management, and medieval poetry."

Three hundred years gives you a lot of time to get an education.

"Wow!" Dawn Valentine seemed to have melted. She was looking at Zeke as if she was ready to give him everything he asked for.

Instead of looking disgusted at her reaction, his smile warmed. "May I escort both of you lovely ladies up the hillside?"

Dawn simpered like a homely high school girl who was being loved on by the quarterback. "I would love it, but I know Ms. Finch has a lot of work to do, and I've taken up enough of her time."

Finch, who seemed immune to Dad's charms, nodded and looked relieved. "I do have a mountain of paperwork. I'll let the two of you investigate the hillside."

"It will be my pleasure." Dad offered the hypnotized Dawn Valentine his elbow, and she linked her arms through his. They strolled down Enchanted Lane together. Keelie looked up expectantly at the oaks, hoping they would dump acorns on them, but none came.

Finch sneered as she watched them go. She glanced at Keelie. "Your dad can sure pile on the Heartwood charm."

"Yep."

"Doesn't work on me!" She laughed. "Your dad is doing me a favor by getting Valentine out of my hair, so I'll overlook the fact that you didn't return to Admin after you got fired from Steak-on-a-Stake. I heard all about it. Turn your costume in bright and early on Saturday morning, and be ready to grovel, and just maybe I'll give you another job."

Keelie felt sick.

The costume was trashed. Her life would be over on Saturday morning. But Janice probably had a needle and thread; she could fix it. If not, then Keelie would have to write out her will this week.

Finch glanced at her illegal, anachronistic watch and frowned. "Gotta haul my butt over to the campground to make sure Little John has taken his medication. I swear all I do is babysit actors, artists, and whiners." She started marching down the path. The dragon was back.

Dad was nowhere in sight, and Keelie returned to the shop to eat lunch. She needed to come up with a plan. She needed to be smart about this, and not go charging into the woods and possibly lead the EPA to the unicorn.

To her delight, the white cat sat atop the counter waiting for her. Knot was on the other end of the counter, purring his head off. The two cats were like furry bookends, except that the white cat didn't purr. Keelie scratched its head. The more she thought about it, maybe now would be a good time to go and search for the unicorn.

"Have you seen my mystical friend in the woods?"

The cat closed its eyes and tucked its tail under its body.

She could walk in the woods to clear her head, and maybe if she ran across the unicorn, she could warn him about the EPA people and tell him to be careful. There had to be something she could do to make him better.

As she stepped out of the shop, Dad returned. "Where do you think you're going?" He reached for Keelie's elbow and guided her back inside.

"I was going to look for the unicorn, to warn him."

"I don't want you going into the forest alone." His green eyes sparkled and his skin glowed. He leaned against one of the shop's posts. The cinnamon scent faded, and with it, his glow, until he looked as worn and sick as he had at breakfast. Worse, even.

"Dad you look awful. Let me find the unicorn. I know I can do it."

He sighed and rubbed his forehead as if his head ached. "You know, the elven have a saying: 'As the forest goes, so go the elves.' We're not doing very well."

"Then how come I'm not sick?"

He reached out to touch her rounded right ear. "Thank your mother."

"That doesn't explain Elia and Elianard. They look like you do when you put on the elven bling."

A pathetic twitch of his lips was probably supposed to be a smile. "Elven bling?" He frowned. "So, those two are unaffected? Curious. I'm trying to discover what's going on, and I'm convinced they're part of it."

"Does that include acting like a gigolo with that woman in the hideous pink suit?"

"A gigolo? That's insulting."

"You actually know what a gigolo is? Astonishing."

"Don't look surprised. I read. And I was merely charming Miss Valentine, and redirecting her attention away from the unicorn."

"You didn't do it with her, did you?" Keelie didn't really want to know the details of how he'd redirected her attention, but she blurted out the question as soon as it popped into her mind. "That would be so gross."

Dad's face grew as red as Finch's. "Absolutely not! You don't ask your father a question like that. To reassure you and your overactive imagination, Miss Valentine isn't my type, and I wouldn't glamour a woman for romantic purposes. I don't need to. Come on. We have to get back to work."

"Work? In your condition? You dragged me to the herb shop for the tincture, and now I think it's your turn to go there." Maybe Dad was affected by the woods cursed with the Dread. But the Dread wasn't here, and she was still getting that creepy, anxious feeling that made it hard to breathe—which preceded the paralyzing fear.

"What's wrong, Keelie?"

"Yes, Keelie, whatever is the matter?" asked an oily voice.

Elianard entered the shop and Keelie grimaced. Cinnamon was still the smell of the Dread. And of Elianard.

Elianard was a Ren Faire god in his flowing, embroidered robes. He lowered his gaze to the blocks on the worktable and smiled. "Your daughter is making your toys? How gratified you must be, Zekeliel. She is just like you. Well, the elven part." He looked up, green eyes full of malice. "The forest dies around us, and you make toys, Tree Shepherd."

Ouch. He was saying exactly what she'd been thinking. How disturbing to share opinions with evil Elianard. Keelie stood with her hands on her hips, determined not to let him get to her anymore. The magic rose in her. She stepped away from the walls and furniture, seeking distance between herself and wood. The hair on her arms stood on end, and Elianard's long silvery locks starting to float around his head. He looked like a dandelion puff she could magically blow.

Dad stepped between her and Elianard, blocking the haughty elf's gaze. "What do you want?"

"I'm here to deliver a message from the Council." He smiled. "They'll be arriving from Florida and Oregon. You've been summoned to answer for the oaks and for the status of the Wildewood. In the meantime, three of us wish to speak to the evergreens. We want to hear from them personally what ails this woodland realm because the Dread will soon be following the same pattern. You will be our guide, Tree Shepherd."

"If I refuse?"

Elianard smiled. "You have no choice. Keliatiel commands it, as she should, given your family's history."

Dad flinched as if Elianard had punched him in the face.

"We're meeting tonight at moonrise, in the old oak glade in the shadow of the three mountains. You've been summoned … " Elianard raised an arm and pointed toward the hills that towered over the river's edge. His long sleeve swept back, the end trailing the ground, the embroidery shimmering in the soft light. All of him seemed to glow with some type of luminescence. " … To take us to the evergreens."

No wonder Dad looked shocked. His own mother had sided against him. Normally, Keelie couldn't stand Elianard, but there was something about him today that intrigued her, a charisma that hadn't been there before. Was Dad's charm magic still lingering in the air? She couldn't tell. The Dread smelled of cinnamon, too.

"And you volunteered to meet with the evergreens?" Dad arched an eyebrow. "Why? What do you really want?" Keelie knew he suspected Elianard of bringing the Red Cap down on them in Colorado, and wondered why he didn't just accuse him.

Elianard put a hand against his chest, frowning as if injured. "Don't you trust me? Surely you do not think that the unfortunate series of circumstances at the High Mountain Faire had anything to do with me?"

Dad nodded solemnly. "I cannot accuse where there is no proof. Yet you are the only one who knows the lore books well enough to call upon the dark fae."

"One could likewise accuse your daughter. Perhaps it was her tainted human half that lured the Red Cap to us."

Yeah, right. Keelie had been there. She'd almost died trying to save the trees of the High Mountain, and Sir Davey had been injured.

Dad lowered his head, his eyes still on Elianard like a

bull about to charge. He seemed stronger. "Whenever you're around, magic is blighted. I can't prove to the Council that you are the cause, but I can prevent you from harming my daughter. I warn you, stay away from her."

Elianard's face hardened. "Is that a threat, Zekeliel?"

"If that is how you choose to interpret my words, so be it."

"I should report your irrational behavior to Lord Niriel," Elianard said stiffly.

"And risk exposing yourself? An empty threat, Elianard." Dad stepped forward. "If the Council wishes to inform me of a meeting, they'd best send another messenger. It is difficult for me to accept your words as truth. And as far as being your guide to the evergreens, speak to them yourself."

Whoa.

Elianard's voice dripped with restrained contempt. "You'll guide us to the evergreens whether you want to or not. We must know what is going on in the forest. Have you been feeling a little under the weather, lately, Zekeliel? If so, you're not the only one of the Faire Folk to feel sick."

Dad shrugged. "There's a bug going around, as my daughter would say."

"The elven are not the only ones falling prey to the illness. The Council has issued a mandatory quarantine at the lodge and a curious journalist is investigating why some of the humans are getting sick. She's noticed some odd differences between some of the Faire workers, and is calling attention to the EPA's presence at the Faire."

Dad's expression went from nonchalant to pensive. "This goes along with information I received this afternoon from a human scientist. I'll send a message to the Council.

The EPA was indeed here, and they're going to investigate even more closely."

Elianard's complexion whitened a shade or two. He reached for the worktable and steadied himself, then looked at Dad, who had crossed his arms over his chest. An understanding glance passed between the two men, as if they'd declared a truce. They'd probably realized that they were going to have to work together against the EPA.

The turbulent energy in the shop settled down. It was still tense, but calmer. Keelie turned away, but stopped—"Lulu?"

The puppet woman stood at the shop entrance wearing full fairy godmother gear, including sparkling wings. Dad and Elianard turned at the same time and stared, open-mouthed, at Lulu.

She came inside, but stopped when she saw Elianard. Keelie noticed that Lulu's costume exposed quite a bit of cleavage; she looked more wenchy than fairy godmothery.

With her gaze glued on Elianard, Lulu leaned against a post and spoke in a smoky, seductive voice. "Hello. What is your name?"

Dad's eyebrows shot up in surprise. "Lulu? Is everything okay?"

"I'm fine. Never better, but you must introduce me to your handsome friend here." Her voice became even darker and sexier.

Keelie turned to look at Elianard. Again, there was something about him today that just drew you into his energy. It was like being mesmerized by a candle flame and wanting to reach out to touch the fire.

Lulu did a va-va-voom saunter over to Elianard, who

seemed very uncomfortable to have a human woman openly flirting with him. This was good. Keelie was still miffed with the puppet lady after the Plumpkin incident, but all would be forgiven after this little spectacle.

Dipping her shoulder seductively, so that Elianard could get a good view of her chest, Lulu lifted her skirt to expose some calf from beneath her white sparkly dress. "Oh, baby, I've been looking for a man like you. You've got power unlike anything I've ever sensed before, and I'm looking for a man with energy like yours. You can handle me."

Mother Goose was on the loose, and she'd found her an elfman to keep her warm. Keelie clapped her hand over her mouth.

Elianard looked like a deer caught in the headlights of an oncoming tractor-trailer.

Lulu placed her hand on his shoulder and whispered in his ear.

Dad walked over to Keelie and smiled at her with a mischievous twinkle in his eye.

"There's something about you that I find deeply attractive. Want to come over and play with my puppets?" Lulu gave him a seductive pout and made kissy motions.

Elianard grimaced and removed Lulu's hand from his shoulder, a scornful look on his face. "I must pass on your, er, eloquent invitation."

"Oh, baby, don't say no, come down to my camper and I'll bake you my special chocolate cupcakes with cream cheese frosting. You won't be able to resist my cupcakes. They're so yummy." She waggled her shoulders, giving a different meaning to the idea of baked goods.

Elianard turned and left the shop, walking quickly. The amorous puppet lady trotted at his heels, making kissy noises.

Dad's whisper interrupted Keelie's enjoyment of the sickly fascinating scene. "I need to save Elianard."

"Don't you mean save Lulu?"

"Not really. Interesting comment Lulu made about Elianard being a powerful man, but for the moment let it suffice to say that Lulu is a witch, and Elianard is Elianard. Even though they deserve one another, we need to discover the source of the elven flu."

"Lulu's a witch?"

Dad nodded. "Have you noticed the way children flock to her booth? It's not just because of the toys she sells. I was going to inquire about her with the WWA."

"WWA?" Keelie frowned. "Sounds like some television wrestling league."

"It's the Wizards and Witches Association. I think Lulu is enchanting children and stealing their energy."

"That is so vile." Keelie remembered the kids with blank faces who trailed around after the puppet lady.

"The Faire isn't just a good cover for elves. A great many beings find it convenient ... "

Lulu, across the lane, was plastered against Elianard, body to body. The veins in his forehead popped out like thin purple rivers. He bit down on his lips as if he were trying hard not to scratch a really bad itchy rash in public.

The ground seemed to surge and billow around Keelie, and the oaks seemed to be walking toward her. Clammy, cold, and disoriented, she tried to breathe, but cinnamon clogged her nose. The Dread was hitting her like a tidal wave.

thirteen

Keelie gasped for air, and then Dad's hand was on her shoulder. The world righted itself.

"Watch this," he whispered into her elven ear. "Your old man is about to show off." He motioned with his hand, fingers spread wide. The leaves in the oak trees swayed, and suddenly a volley of acorns launched at Elianard and Lulu.

The trees had awakened. The majority of their missiles landed on Lulu's head. She screamed and ran back to her shop. "Oh, those accursed trees!" she wailed. "I'm going to hire a woodcutter to chop them down."

Keelie heard howls of indignation from the oaks. She

covered her ears with her hands. Everyone else heard the agitated rustling of leaves.

Elianard inclined his head toward Dad, apparently in gratitude for ridding him of Lulu. But he didn't count on the oaks. With Lulu safely inside the sanctuary of her booth, Elianard was now the prime target, and they had really good aim.

Too bad there wasn't a tree version of baseball for them to play. Elianard lifted his robes, revealing pale, skinny legs clad in custom-made Lady Annie boots. Life was so unfair!

That night, Keelie washed the dinner dishes in Sir Davey's camper. Dad had left after dinner to take Elianard and two other unnamed elves to meet with some evergreens. Keelie didn't trust Elianard, but Dad had reassured her that he'd be fine.

Sir Davey was at the tiny dining room table, comparing the inventory he'd done that day to a computer printout.

Keelie's upper back ached from leaning over to reach the Davey-sized sink. She had forgotten to remind Dad about Laurie coming in the morning. She hoped he remembered.

Sir Davey looked up from his papers. "Talked to Janice. Raven's coming to the Faire to help her mom. She sends her love."

"Right, but not for weeks yet. I can't wait to see her." Her glamorous older friend would probably be wearing designer clothes and have a great haircut, along with exciting stories about her internship at Doom Kitty. Whereas Keelie so far had failed at a number of dead-end jobs, and was reduced to sawing branches into blocks.

"Apparently, something went wrong with her job at that Squirrel of Doom place." Sir Davey sounded pleased that Raven's city life hadn't worked out. "She'll be here in a couple of days."

Keelie felt a dread more frightening than elf-magic Dread wash over her. Raven was not going to want to hang out with her. She was a college student and had worked at a cool company—she'd think Keelie was a loser. Along those lines, how was Laurie going to react to the "new Keelie"? Maybe she'd changed too much to have anything in common with her old California friend.

Glumly, Keelie imagined Laurie and Raven meeting. They would be wowed by one another and talk about their exciting lives. In her worst nightmare, her best friends would hit it off and ditch her, while Finch screamed at her to work some strange dork job and Elia and her elven friends sneered and pointed. Maybe Sean would show up and fall in love with Laurie.

She must be under too much stress. Keelie dried the last plate and placed it on the rack. She plopped into the booth seat across from Sir Davey, and sighed. He lowered his papers and studied her.

"Need some good news?" He waggled his eyebrows at her. "Janice said Zeke could use her Jeep Wagoneer to pick up your friend tomorrow morning at the train station."

"Great." She sighed again.

"Worried?"

"About what?"

"About how your friend is going to react to the Faire?

And what if she discovers you have tree magic? How are you going to hide that from her?"

"I don't know." Keelie put her chin in her hands. Davey had totally hit on her dilemma, and she had no solution.

■ ■ ■

Keelie looked at the spot on the couch where Dad crashed since they'd started sleeping in Sir Davey's camper. He was not there, and it was already 9:00 AM. The pillows were still in the same position as last night. Fabulous. Dad hadn't been to bed yet, or if he had, it wasn't here. They were going to have to leave in one hour to go get Laurie at the Canooga Springs train station, and Dad was nowhere around.

Sir Davey was missing, too. Indignant, Keelie realized that they might have left without her. She was beginning to understand why Finch was so dragonish. You depended on people to follow through, and what happened?

Keelie sighed. She grabbed the rose quartz from where she'd placed it by the sink last night when washing dishes.

She needed an alternative plan. Janice had said they could use her Wagoneer, but she'd thought that Zeke was available to drive. For all Keelie knew, Dad was still with Elianard and the evergreens. Maybe Janice would take her. She sure wasn't going to ask Finch—she was too young to die. Keelie thought about the Council meeting again. She was starting to worry.

This waiting was so frustrating. She walked over to the pillow, picked it up, and punched it. She threw it back down on the sofa. This was exactly why they needed cell phones. Real ones, not ones connected to trees. She opened the door to the camper and stepped outside, blinking up at the sunny sky. At least the weather was good. She needed to find out how Dad was doing, and let him know she was going to talk to Janice about taking her into town.

Keelie walked over to the hemlocks and closed her eyes. She tightened her hand around the quartz. It shielded her with a pink light, and then a bright green glow surrounded the pink light. Keelie opened herself to the tree energy, but this time she was able to gauge it. It didn't overwhelm her. One tree in particular answered her summons. Its name was Tavak, the Douglas fir Dad had mentioned.

Tree Shepherdess, you call?

Where is my father? Is he with you?

No, he left our meeting at the rise of the sun. He is with the other elves.

Elianard?

No, but others who seek his wisdom on matters concerning the Wildewood.

Now she was mad. Dad knew they needed to be at the Canooga train station. Where was he? Still hanging out with the elves, talking shop.

She knew some of the elves were sick, but this was so much like Mom putting a client's needs ahead of Keelie's. She couldn't leave Laurie stuck in town waiting for her. It wouldn't take long to drive into Canooga Springs, collect Laurie, and skedaddle back to the Faire, and then Dad could get back to his meeting.

Tell him we need to go to town to pick up Laurie.

Keelie to town to pick up a Laurie.

It was cryptic, but okay. Dad would get the gist of it.

Keelie suddenly wondered whether, since the trees could

send a message to Dad, they could send one to the unicorn. He was the guardian of the forest, so they should be able to communicate with him. She hadn't seen the unicorn for almost a week, and was worried about him—especially now with the EPA guys in the woods. She should have thought about telepathically corresponding with him before, but talking to unicorns was all new to her.

Keelie liked this Tavak. Dad was right; she sensed a keen intelligence from the tree.

Thank you, Tavak. I need you to send one more message—to the unicorn.

Lord Einhorn is fading.

So, that was his name. And she knew he was fading after getting a glimpse of him.

Tell him the humans are searching the woods. He needs to find somewhere to hide.

Silence.

Then Tavak spoke again. *Lord Einhorn wants you to meet him in the circle of oaks on the path past the building you call Admin.*

What time? Keelie would have to sneak out. With Laurie around, that might be difficult.

Be there and he'll find you, Tavak said.

I'll do my best.

Einhorn says you must. Or it might be too late.

No pressure. *I will meet him.*

Tree Shepherd's Daughter, your father's consciousness is not open to us. Though we sense him, we cannot communicate your message to him.

Great. Dad had put the trees on hold. Keelie was getting a headache from all the telepathic communication.

We will continue to try to reach him. What more may the forest do to aid you, Tree Shepherdess Keliel?

Nothing, but as soon as you to talk to him, let me know.

As you wish, Tree Shepherdess.

The green glow disappeared, and Keelie opened her eyes. Her trembling hands were warm, and the rose quartz glowed like a teeny-tiny pink night-light.

Was Dad hurt? Maybe Elianard and the other elves had him imprisoned somewhere. Surely the trees would have sensed this, unless . . . ? She turned wildly, looking in the direction of the Swiss Miss Chalet. The battered truck with its ornate camper was gone. Her fear eased. No wonder the trees couldn't find him. She made some mental notes: A) if they'd had cell phones, they could have communicated; B) if she had a driver's license, she could drive Janice's Wagoneer to Canooga Springs herself, and Dad could stay wherever he was, location unknown because (see A) she had no cell phone.

How many times had she told him that she had to pick up Laurie today? Wherever he was didn't matter now. Maybe Janice could take her.

Keelie heard the wheezing before she noticed Knot trotting up to her. He sneezed, eyes squeezed shut, then looked up at her as if she'd caused it. Great, now the cat was sick.

"I'll bet you're contagious. Stay away from me." Except for rabies, she didn't know of any diseases that cats and humans could share. But he wasn't really a cat, and she wasn't totally human.

Knot didn't come closer. Good thing, since Keelie was wearing a cute top and pants, and she wanted to stay presentable for Laurie.

The white cat crept over from behind the RV's wheel,

sat near Knot, and gazed up at Keelie. She opened the door of Sir Davey's Winnebago. "Breakfast is inside. It's some of that cat kibble Dad bought in Jackson Hole, all-natural yummy cat food." Knot lifted a hind leg and began washing his butt.

"Fine, don't eat, but let your little pal have some breakfast." Neither cat went in. She couldn't stand here holding the door forever. She brought the two bowls outside, and a third full of fresh water, and arranged them in the shade behind the tire. "All right, when you two are hungry, you know where the food is."

Knot sneezed, and the white cat looked at him briefly, then returned its grayish gaze to Keelie. She didn't have time for finicky felines, not when she had to find a way to get to the station to pick up Laurie.

She hurried toward the Faire, cutting through the spaces between the Faire workers' tents. Many were deserted, while the inhabitants got their booths ready for the weekend, but others bustled with activity. Keelie ignored them all. She hadn't planned on a trip to the Enchanted Lane.

Knot followed her, his silent steps occasionally punctuated with sneezes and snorts. This was worse than the endless licking. Keelie spun around, and was about to yell at him to get back to the Winnebago when she saw that the white cat had silently tagged along. The poor thing was desperate if he was hanging out with Knot the Snot.

She rushed up the path that intersected with the Enchanted Lane, thinking that she had bigger things to worry about than her cat's social life. What if Laurie thought that she'd changed so much they couldn't return to the way they'd been in California, sharing clothes and make-up and talking about boys? Keelie couldn't tell Laurie everything about Sean. She could describe his hot bod, and the kiss, and how Elia had claimed Keelie had stolen him from her. But she couldn't tell her best friend that he was an eighty-five-year-old elf. Or that she herself was part elf, or that all those times they'd played lacrosse in the fields at Baywood, the short trees next to the field had sung to her, and she'd stumbled as she tried to block them out.

Sean's age still made *her* feel strange, and sometimes she pictured him as he would be if he were an eighty-five-year-old human, all wrinkled and stooped. Worse yet was the realization that he'd experienced things she couldn't imagine. He must think that she was an infant, although he hadn't kissed her the way you kiss a baby. The thought of his kiss made her shiver. He totally made her forget that she was only fifteen. Maybe that was what books called an ageless feeling.

She couldn't wait to see him again. That was the one bright part of spending the coming winter in the Dread Forest, the home of elves in North America. She was to pass the time in elven studies, surrounded by her father's people—feeling like an outsider.

Anxiety sped her steps, and her breath came in short gasps. The press of the trees' unspoken pleas pressed against her. This was no panic attack. Keelie glanced up at the tree canopy. Talking to trees had its downside.

She reached for the rose quartz in her pocket and a wave of calm sluiced through her, hiding her behind its Earth-magic shield.

"Keelie. Hey, Keelie, wait up." Sir Davey's shout brought her back to the present. The little man was hurrying toward her, his satin musketeer's cloak swirling around him and the white plume on his hat bobbing with each step. He refused to go along with the Robin Hood theme, but no one seemed bothered by the sight of the miniature musketeer in the midst of the Merry Men.

"Have you seen Dad? He didn't come home from that Council meeting last night, and the truck is gone."

Sir Davey stopped, breathless, and bent over, bracing himself with his hands on his knees. He held up his index finger. "He's." Breath. "At." Another deep breath. "The lodge."

"I thought they were meeting in the woods."

Davey straightened. At full height, he reached Keelie's nose. His hat evened the score a bit. "They decided to continue the meeting today at the lodge. He's just under the weather, thought he'd stay in his camper. You know how elves are. They sleep, then wake up and feel better. Their immune systems are stronger than rocks."

"My dad is alone and sick, sleeping in a parking lot, and no one told me? Take me to him."

"Can't. He doesn't want you to catch what's ailing him, and many more of the Faire folk from what I've seen. The lodge is starting to look like a hospital ward. You're to stay in my RV with your friend from California. I'll bunk with some of the Merry Men in their tent."

At least she could be grateful that they'd be staying in modern surroundings. Exotic, but twenty-first century.

Knot opened his mouth, then sneezed in mid-meow.

Sir Davey met the cat's green gaze with his own steel-gray one. His forehead furrowed. "Get some rest, old man, and I'll look after Keelie. Take the day off."

The cat blinked, then seemed to nod. He walked away,

his tail dragging on the ground, pine needles clinging to his fluffy underside.

Keelie had never seen him sick. Not that she'd admit it aloud, but she was worried about him. She called out, "Hey, you'd better sleep in your cat bed and stay off my pillows." He ignored her and padded on. She turned back to Sir Davey. "Knot talked to you, and you understood him." She kept her tone casual, but this cat/person dialogue that she was excluded from was really bugging her.

"He meowed," Sir Davey replied. "You talk to him, all the time. You were just yelling at him as if he understood."

"Yeah. It's one thing to talk *at* the cat, but it's another to talk *to* the cat."

"It's the same thing."

"No, it's not. Dad does it, too."

A glimpse of white drew her attention to the ground. The snowy little cat sat at her feet, its delicate head lifted toward her as if to say, "save me." She reached down and patted it on the head. Tufts of white fur floated away. In the distance, Knot meowed.

The white cat's ears twitched and it followed Knot's path, as if he'd called. The pitiful thing was looking worse instead of better—she noticed two small bald patches on its haunches. "Poor abandoned kitty. We need to take him to the vet."

"We don't have time to take care of a feral cat right now." Sir Davey was all business. "Let's get to town. Later we can ask Janice about the poor beastie, and Knot as well. Right now if we don't move it, your friend from California is going to be standing at the train station wondering if she's been forgotten."

They were entering the parking lot. It was comfortable walking with Sir Davey. She didn't have to hurry to keep up, the way she did with Dad. "Can I drive to the train station?"

"No." He answered matter-of-factly, as if she'd asked, "can we have bologna sandwiches for lunch?"

"How am I going to learn how to drive if no one will teach me?"

"I don't know, and it's not a priority." Sir Davey brightened. "Ah, look, there's Janice, right now. It's your lucky day. Maybe after she heals your adopted cat, she can give you driving lessons."

Adults thought they were so funny. Janice was at the Wagoneer with her car keys. She wore a purple sweatshirt that had "Earth Mama" embroidered across the chest in flowery blue.

"Are you excited about your friend coming?" Janice's kindly face radiated good-mom vibes. Raven was so lucky.

"Yeah. I can't wait to see her. I just wish Dad wasn't sick."

"Let him sleep for about twenty-four hours, and he'll be fine." Janice sounded reassuring. "There's some weird bug going around, but those things come and go."

"I hope so. Would you take a look at the little stray cat that's been hanging around with Knot? Knot's just sneezing, but the white cat's losing the fur on the back of his legs. They're headed toward Sir Davey's camper."

Janice glanced up the path. "I'll check on him. Poor baby, left alone out here to fend for himself in the forest." She spoke with so much emotion in her voice that Keelie didn't know if Janice was talking about Dad or the stray cat.

"His hair loss could be from malnutrition. I'll look in on him this afternoon."

Keelie felt better knowing Janice was going to examine the cat. "And don't forget Knot's sneezing. He's either got a cold or he's allergic to something around here."

She smiled. "I'll check on him, too. Any other under-the-weather animals I need to know about?"

"No." Keelie looked up toward the hills and thought about the unicorn. Not unless Janice had an herbal remedy to make him better.

"She wants driving lessons." Sir Davey rolled his eyes.

"What?" Janice frowned.

"I *need* driving lessons."

The frown vanished, leaving Janice's face as blank as a mannequin's. "Oh. Well—" She glanced at her wrist. "Look at the time! You two had better get moving, or your friend is going to be waiting all alone in that train station, wondering where you are."

Sir Davey grinned. "Come on, Keelie."

As they hurried toward the parking lot, Keelie remembered that Janice never wore a watch. She could have just said no. Adults were hard to understand sometimes.

fourteen

Despite being too short to reach the pedals, Sir Davey drove the Wagoneer. The gas pedal just went down automatically when he needed to speed up, and the Jeep slowed down as he drove around a sharp curve. The brakes engaged whenever they came to a stop sign.

Keelie watched, amazed, before asking, "How are you doing that?"

"I'm using Earth magic, of course." He pulled a stone from his pocket. "Remember, an object helps you focus the energy, and acts as a conduit for the magic."

Keelie reached for the stone and Sir Davey yanked it

away. "Don't touch it," he said, panic in his voice. "I'm driving." He placed the stone back into his coat pocket.

"Geez. Okay, I guess it's your special rock."

"No. It's tuned to my magic. This rock's energy pattern matches my own. If you touch it, you'll damage it."

"Wow. How can I get a special rock?" The possibilities of having a rock tuned to her were tempting. She could bypass driver's ed, and maybe she could help the trees and the unicorn. "Does Dad know about this?" She fingered the rose quartz in her jeans pocket.

"You don't *get* a rock. The rock chooses you. You'll know when you feel a vibration from it. It's like a hum. A disturbing vibration at first, and then it settles into a soothing hum. It also filters out dark magic."

A few months ago, she would have laughed at his words. Now she nodded. She could use a rock that powerful.

Sir Davey furrowed his eyebrows. "I want you to have your special rock, too, because lass, with what's going on at the Faire, you need it."

Cold swept through her body. "What's going on? This seems worse than the Red Cap."

"Different." Davey pressed his lips together and motioned ahead. Conversation over.

They wound through a twisting, narrow road that cut through dense forest. Keelie whispered comfort to the trees as they passed, until the forest thinned and the cries of the wood folk drew faint. A few houses were set way back from the road, and then they passed a gas station straight out of an old movie, with uncovered pumps weathered to pink and gray and a man by the front door, chair tilted back against the wall. The town of Canooga Falls was smaller than your average L.A. neighborhood.

"Here we are," Sir Davey said, pulling over and putting the truck in "park."

Keelie looked around in astonishment. "Here? There's nothing here. You're kidding, right?" They were parked two buildings away from the moldering gas station, in front of a beauty shop that promised anything but. "Sally's Clip and Curl. Holy cow."

"The train station is around the corner. I'm heading to the rock shop. As soon as the train pulls in, you girls come find me, and I'll treat you to lunch." His eyes glinted excitedly, as if the prospect of bins of dusty rocks was the best treat ever. "You might find your special rock there. If not, there's more shopping in this charming town."

"Really? Like an awesome thrift shop? Or a used appliance store?" There was no point trying to make this dead place into some sort of shopping haven. Besides, she didn't have any money, and any money she would earn from her jobs was going for those boots. And a Steak-on-a-Stake costume.

Sir Davey rolled his eyes.

Keelie wished that they could at least window shop. It was something that she and Laurie had enjoyed together, and shopping with her old friend would have been a good transition to the Faire world—because Laurie was going to have an Alice-in-Wonderland experience when they returned to Wildewood.

The train station was a one-story platform with an ornate but rusty ticket booth facing the street. The train chugged and smoked on the tracks while a few people milled on the wide flagged platform. Keelie couldn't see her friend, but she knew she must be here. The stack of Louis Vuitton luggage gave her away.

Keelie's stomach became a mushy lump as she realized she'd have to keep Knot away from Laurie's luggage. If he didn't like her, he'd use them as the world's most expensive litter boxes.

Then she heard Laurie's familiar voice. "This town is so *quaint.*"

And there she was. Long, sun-streaked blonde hair, big blue eyes, and wearing an adorable gauzy top, low-slung jeans, and striped wedge sandals. A warm wave of sisterhood, of friendship, flowed through Keelie. Laurie was from her old world, the world she shared with Mom, and now that Laurie was here, memories hit Keelie like an asteroid.

Laurie turned and saw her. Her eyes widened and she shrieked. Keelie screamed, too, and ran toward her, arms opened wide. People stared as the two hugged and jumped up and down.

"Keelie, you look fabulous."

She wasn't quite expecting to hear that from Laurie. Her hair had gone curly and grown out, and her new clothes had suffered from the Faire's substandard laundry facilities.

Laurie stared at her face. "My God. Have you like been going to a spa? Whatever treatment you're doing, you've got to share the secret with me. You've got, like, this glow that is so *au naturel.* I would pay to glow like you."

"I . . . " Keelie started to tell her that she hadn't done anything different, but Laurie cut her off.

"This is the coolest town, ever. I mean, L.A. is so full of concrete and unnatural. I mean, you can juice all you want and take colonics, but I swear just stepping off this train,

I'm, like, breathing pure air. They should bottle the air, like they bottle water, and sell it in L.A."

Had she always been such a chatterbox? "Laurie . . . "

"Oh, and do you want to know what else? I'm dying to hit the little stores in this town. I bet it's full of darling shops. Is there a Starbucks here?"

"I don't know. This is my first time here." Keelie wasn't ready to admit that the place was a dud. On the other hand, Laurie'd see it for herself soon enough. "Dad and I went straight to the Faire when we drove through here." Coffee would be good, though. Keelie's blood sang at the thought of caffeine pumping through it. She was going to need it if she was going to keep up with her friend. "Let's look for one." And hope there aren't, like, geriatric hikers and scout troops hanging out in it.

"Hello? What about my luggage?" Laurie rolled her eyes toward the huge stack of designer bags. "Where's your car?"

"It's a few blocks away." Keelie's heart sank as she thought of how Laurie's expensive things would look in the back of the old Jeep.

"What are you driving? Daddy bought me a Prius, not the snazziest, but it's so eco-friendly, you know? And all the kids are driving them. Mine was silver, but I had it redone in light blue, because it goes with my eyes. Where are you going?"

Keelie flagged down a railway employee. "Excuse me, can we stash this luggage here until later?"

The man tugged at his chin as he looked at the pile. "There are lockers inside the ticket office, but none of them are big enough to put all of this in."

"I'll stay with the gear. Just get the car and come back here, Keelie. Geez. You're going all New York all of a sudden."

The man gave Laurie a sour look and walked away.

"Great idea, Laurie, but I don't have a driver's license."

Her friend's eyes widened. "What? Did you flunk the test? It's, like, the easiest test in the world."

"I haven't even learned how to drive yet. My dad hasn't had time to teach me," Keelie said through clenched teeth. *And just shut up about it.*

"Oh." Laurie looked embarrassed. "I'm sorry." She gazed helplessly at her suitcases. "I brought a lot of stuff, huh?"

"A lot," Keelie agreed.

"Well, how did you get here? You're acting like you took a bus!" Laurie said "bus" the way most people said "sewage."

"No, a friend of my dad's drove me here. Sir Davey. He's at one of the stores."

Laurie perked up. "Sir? He's British? That is so cool! I've never met a real knight."

"And you won't meet one now." Keelie laughed. "I think he's just called Sir Davey because of the Renaissance Faire. It's like a character he plays. His real name is Jadwyn Morgan, but nobody calls him that."

Well, her grandmother did. That was nobody, right?

Laurie's delighted expression didn't change. Obviously, to her, a Ren Faire knight was as good as the real thing. She tossed her blonde hair over her shoulder and flounced after the railway employee, who was at the other end of the platform.

For a second, she'd looked just like Elia. A human, friendly version of Elia. Keelie grinned. Wait until the two of them met. Laurie could be just as mean, but for a good cause. Life was about to be much more interesting.

Laurie tipped the ticket seller to store her baggage in his

office, and the two girls browsed their way to the end of the street, giggling at the hopeless, dusty-windowed shops until they came to one that looked like a piece of a castle that suddenly landed in upstate New York.

The shop's front was covered in stone, and above the wide doorway swung a wooden sign that read "The Canooga Crystal Shoppe." A little stone gargoyle leered down at them from the top of the sign. Keelie rolled her eyes. She thought the pseudo-medieval décor was limited to the Renaissance Faire, but apparently it had spread to the town, just like a virus.

Laurie stared at the building's façade. "Totally cheesy."

"Yeah. Let's go inside." Keelie reached for the painted metal door. A strong buzz traveled from her fingertips up her arm. She pulled back and stared at the door.

Laurie pushed through the doorway, unaffected. Keelie followed, after hesitantly touching one of the rocks that protruded from the wall. It was real. The buzzing hum tickled her fingers through the stone, but it didn't talk to her the way wood did. She shrugged. Maybe it was just bad wiring, because if rocks started talking to her, there wouldn't be any place safe for her on this planet.

■ ■ ■

The Canooga Crystal Shoppe's interior had purple walls decorated with hand-painted murals of mermaids, unicorns, dragons, and other fantastical creatures, which gave the place an ethereal, fairy-tale feel. The humming grew louder and more focused.

Wooden shelves lined the store, some holding baskets

full of small rocks, others holding stones as big as her head. Geodes filled one shelf, split open and gleaming. The quiet was soothing, and Keelie realized that it was because, in here, the trees were a faraway whisper.

Even Laurie seemed to sense the heavy pull of Earth magic. She'd stopped talking and was walking silently through the shop, taking everything in.

The buzzing shot through Keelie again. It wasn't like insects. It was as if her blood had suddenly become sandpapery, and she was filled with the raspy throb as it moved through her veins. She followed the sound.

"Do you feel that?" she asked Laurie. "That buzzing?"

"What buzzer?" Laurie was examining a display of crystal sculptures.

"I don't think it's a buzzer, but it sure is annoying." Keelie walked over to Laurie. The humming lessened. She looked at the ceiling, but didn't see anything that would generate the sound.

"I don't hear anything." Laurie walked toward the rock displays, and Keelie trailed after her. The sound became louder. This was like playing a game of Marco Polo.

Laurie picked up a spray of amethyst crystals. "This place is cool. It's a lot like this store where I hang out, the Dolphin Cottage? It's a beach cottage that was turned into a feng shui shop. Mom loves to buy love stuff there." Laurie threw an arm over Keelie's shoulder, laughing. "Last thing she bought there was a book of love spells. I think she might have the hots for the cabana boy at the club, not that she thinks it's true love. Permanent relationships should be based on cold green cash, not warm feelings, at least according to her."

"So, what does she need love spells for?" Keelie wondered

if Laurie's mom had always been like this. She hadn't really seen it. Had her own mom seen it? But after hearing about the Wizards and Witches Association and witnessing Dad work his "charm" on the EPA agent, a love-spell book seemed like a harmless toy.

"She thinks she's losing her looks, and love spells are cheaper than plastic surgery." Laurie's voice was matter-of-fact.

The humming had turned into a ringing that echoed in Keelie's head. She covered her ears, shrugged out of Laurie's arm, and looked around wildly for the cause. Laurie was sorting through a basket of rocks as if nothing was wrong.

Keelie stopped in front of a counter filled with glass-like rocks. She reached a hand toward it and the ringing escalated into a shrill whine, like the fire alarm at school. One of these rocks was the cause of the noise, and she was ready to heave it through a window. She backed away, then turned around and walked quickly to the back of the store, anxious to put distance between her and the noise. With every step the sound lessened, and the tension between her shoulder blades eased.

Back here, the décor was totally different. Cool, almost heavy, air filled the dark room. Keelie turned around to make sure she hadn't stumbled into another store. The wide airy room behind her glowed with blues and greens like the inside of an aquarium.

The buzzing called to her from the counter where Laurie still stood, staring at her. Keelie walked back slowly. Laurie didn't sense it, so it must be something magical.

It seemed to be coming from a glossy black stone, the size of a walnut and shaped a little like a jagged snail. This rock must be special; it was on top of a square of thick red felt in the center of the glass counter. Now that she was closer, Keelie's hands grew cold. The buzzing sounded like a warning. Maybe it was dangerous.

"Oh, you are so totally cute!" Laurie's declaration was followed by her laugh, and then Keelie heard Sir Davey and the man behind the counter laughing, too. She shook her head. Laurie and Sir Davey sounded like old friends.

She looked down at the sharp-edged rock, her fingertips inches away, and slowly withdrew her hand. Maybe she was learning something after all. She was not going to touch the thing until Sir Davey told her it was okay.

Sir Davey strolled over to her, stroking his beard. "Seems like you've found your rock, Keelie."

"Can you hear it, too? What is it?"

"Tektite. How interesting that it called you." He stared at the rock.

"What's a tektite?" Laurie touched the rock with a fingertip. The store didn't blow up.

Sir Davey arched an eyebrow. "Don't schools teach geology any more?"

"They might have." Laurie looked embarrassed.

Sir Davey turned to Keelie.

She shook her head. "Some kind of mineral?"

"Tektite is a natural glass object, usually found in meteorite impact areas."

"No fair. If it's from outer space, then it's not technically Earth science. It's a star rock, and a really ugly one." Laurie looked down at the tektite with distaste. Ugly was never a plus in Laurie's world.

"What does it do? Except make me crazy?" Keelie figured it had to do something, or else Davey wouldn't be so excited.

"Girl, if you think this rock is making you crazy, then don't blame the rock." Laurie laughed.

"It is used metaphysically..." Sir Davey winked at Keelie. "...to stop certain types of transmitted ailments and to strengthen the energy of whoever carries it."

Keelie frowned at the chunk of tektite. "I thought my rock would be something more earthy. As in, from the Earth."

"We're all made of stardust, aren't we?" He pointed to the mythical creatures on the wall, stopping at a unicorn. "Some of us have more stardust in us than others."

Stardust. Maybe that was what made the unicorn glow, unless it was just a metaphor. Maybe Sir Davey was following up his Earth science lesson with a little bit of poetry.

"How much is it?" Keelie asked, but she knew whatever the price was, she couldn't buy it. Besides, why would she want it? It would drive her nuts.

"I'd buy it. I totally need some cosmic stardust at my house." Laurie glanced over at another counter. "Check out those killer earrings." She abandoned the tektite to look at a display of silver jewelry.

"Keelie." Sir Davey's voice was low. "Your father told me to let you buy what you needed, and you need the tektite. Can't you hear it calling you?"

"Is that what it's doing? I don't need anything that makes my eyeballs vibrate and my fingernails itch."

Davey laughed. "Then you haven't touched it."

Keelie stared at the glassy rock. "Are you sure it won't hurt me?"

"Positive."

Her fingers hovered over the rock. The buzzing made her shiver. She lowered a fingertip and let it rest on one of the jagged edges. The vibrating noise stopped, as if she'd suddenly gone a block away. Peace filled her, as if she were floating in the ocean. "Whoa." She picked up the rock. No buzzing.

Davey smiled at her expression. "See? You need it."

"Is it expensive? It's out here like it's really special."

"It's special to you. But I think Ben just put it out because it's different."

"So this will help me with the Dread?" Keelie put the tektite into Sir Davey's hand.

He winked at her. "It will. It'll help you in many ways."

"Thanks."

"You are most welcome." He bowed. "And if you'll allow me to keep it, I'll etch runes on it to strengthen and focus its power."

"Sure." She didn't doubt anything Sir Davey said.

He handed her a basket holding a folded green velvet bag. "Now let's do something to help your father." He pointed to the wall holding baskets of tumbled stones. A painted dragon hovered on the wall next to them, looking a little like Finch.

"I want you to create a medicine pouch using the stones in those baskets. Whatever stone calls to you goes into the bag to help protect your father from illness."

"Keelie, come over here." Laurie was jumping excitedly by the jewelry counter. "You've got to come over here and look at these earrings. You're going to want to buy several pairs."

"Be there in a bit." Keelie went to stand in front of the baskets filled with healing stones. It was like a candy store, every basket holding a different color and identified by a little calligraphic card. Keelie went from basket to basket, choosing stones for the properties identified on their cards. When she had room for one more, she hesitated.

The seventh basket on the third shelf was full of smooth brown and white rocks, with rings banding them like tree rings. Keelie looked at the rectangular card. Petrified wood. Should've known. She picked one up and sensed the faraway echo of an alien forest. She quickly put it into the bag.

The card said that it was a grounding stone that provided strength during ill health. Perfect for dear old Dad.

She drew the drawstring closed on the full bag and joined Laurie at the jewelry counter. Sir Davey was sitting on a tall stool at the end of the counter talking to Ben, the proprietor. She handed the bag to him. He hefted it and smiled. "Feels rock solid."

"Ha, ha. Rock solid, very funny. I hope they work."

"They should." Sir Davey nodded to Ben, who rang up their purchases.

Laurie looked at the lumpy sack. "Maybe I should get some of those."

"Next time, girls. We have to return to the Faire."

"And pick up my luggage, too."

Keelie grinned at Sir Davey. She couldn't wait to see his face when he caught sight of the stack of suitcases.

"You're not getting any earrings?" Laurie dangled her silver butterflies, crescent moons, and hearts.

"No. I don't need any." Keelie yearned for a pair, but every time she thought about earrings, she saw the pair of boots she'd ordered. But she was pleased with her tektite and her bag of healing rocks for Dad, even if he'd paid for them himself.

"Well, duh. I don't *need* any either." She put the silver moons into her ears and admired her reflection in the countertop mirror. "I just *had* to have these."

Keelie shook her head. "Dad is into this less-is-more philosophy. I've got lots of earrings. I just haven't unpacked all of my jewelry yet."

Laurie's eyes met Keelie's. "I don't know if I could live with the less-is-more thing, but then, sometimes I wonder if shopping is just a way of trying to find the right thing to make me happy. You know. Once the thrill of the purchase is gone, I'm onto the next thing that might make me happy."

"I'm learning that."

At the checkout counter, Keelie's eyes immediately zeroed in on a tiny oak-leaf navel ring in a display of silver body jewelry. It was perfect for her, even though she didn't have a pierced navel. Maybe this was a sign that she should finally get hers pierced.

Keelie hoped that Laurie wouldn't buy the oak leaf for her own piercing. Instead, Laurie reached for a navel ring with a unicorn charm attached to it.

"Less is more, maybe, but this is too cute!" She dangled it in the air and pointed to the painting of the unicorn on the wall. "Looks just like it, doesn't it?"

Keelie stared at the painting. The unicorn glowed like silvery moonlight, and the artist had painted little starbursts all around it and at the tip of its horn. Keelie wondered what Laurie would do if she knew what a real unicorn looked like—and that Keelie had seen one.

fifteen

On the way back to the Faire, Sir Davey drove while Keelie and Laurie sat in the backseat. Keelie made sure Laurie sat behind the driver's seat so that she didn't notice that Sir Davey's feet didn't reach the pedals. At least he was going through the motions of pretending to drive. Keelie hoped that this wasn't how Laurie's whole stay would be, with Keelie trying to keep her from seeing her new, hidden world.

"So, will I get to meet your man, Sean?" Laurie's eyes crinkled with curiosity. "Last I heard, he was working at a Florida Renaissance Faire."

"Yeah, and I haven't heard from him. Nothing's changed." The thought of Sean, far away, made her glum. Their kiss seemed long ago, not just a few weeks past. And not hearing from him made the time seem so much longer.

"I can't believe you haven't touched a phone since St. Louis. How do you exist? So does Sean email? Is he on MySpace?"

"I don't go online much anymore," Keelie admitted. More like, at all. Laurie would find out soon enough that they were practically living in the Middle Ages. "How are things at Baywood?"

Laurie made a face. "I failed most of my classes, even though Mom redid my room in 'get good grades' colors. She moved my furniture all around, too, because she said the bad feng shui was holding me back. I think it was spending time at the mall with Trent. I passed history, though, which is good because Mom said that if I studied she'd buy me the peridot-and-amethyst necklace and earrings that I really wanted." Laurie's stream of words dried up and her expression turned serious. "It's not the same without you. School's not the same. Shopping's not the same. I miss you."

Keelie's chest tightened. "I miss you, too." She was about to get teary, but Laurie let out a laugh and punched her shoulder.

"Yeah, right, last time we talked, you were on the road with your Pops and totally excited about something. You said you were going to tell me what it was all about, but so far, nada. Was it about Sean?"

"I wish." She couldn't tell a mundane about the elves and the other world. For one, Laurie would think she was nuts. "Maybe it was about the pirates." The High Mountain Faire had been infested with pirates, handsome ones who were mostly very naughty. As in, a-girl-could-really-get-into-trouble-hanging-with-them kind of naughty.

"Oh! Details."

Sir Davey had an ear cocked their way. Not that he would overhear on purpose, maybe, but he was her dad's best friend. But she didn't want him to know just how friendly she had been with the pirates, especially Captain Dandy Randy. Keelie whispered, "We'll talk later."

Laurie raised her eyebrows. "Gotcha."

As if on cue, Sir Davey inserted a CD and a rollicking drumbeat started, joined by flutes and fiddles.

Laurie's eyes widened. "I love Irish music!"

"This is Rigadoon. They play at the Faire." Keelie had heard the band at the Fletcher's Row stage when she'd been in the Plumpkin costume. She whispered, "They're also famous for doing the music at the drinking parties at Rivendell, the Faire's party spot. Dad says they're as bad as pirates." She laughed. "He called them rogues."

Laurie grinned, eyes twinkling, and wriggled in her seat belt as if she were already dancing at the party.

Keelie thought that with Laurie along, she might gather up the courage to join in the merriment. It would be great to get away from all the tree troubles, and with the elves sick and at the lodge, maybe Rivendell would be more fun—not that the elves ever mixed with the humans.

"Rogues." Laurie shivered, smiling. "They sound exciting and scary. What do these Rigadoon rogues look like?"

"They're all different. Tall, short, fat, skinny, bearded, and bald. All of them are incredibly talented and incredibly weird, and *so* not boyfriend material."

"So, where *is* the so-called boyfriend material around here? I'm ready for a summer fling."

Sir Davey made a noise that might have been a snort of laughter. Laurie glared at the back of his head.

"Some of the actors are really cute. You should see the guy who plays Robin Hood. Yummy." Keelie hugged herself to show how totally delicious she found Robin Hood.

Sir Davey's eyes met hers in the rearview mirror. He was sending her severe parental vibes.

Keelie smiled innocently at him, then turned to look out the window. She was catching snippets of each tree as they passed by, one big blurry sense of leafy green flashing in her mind. Unlike the forest around the Wildewood Faire, everything seemed to be fine in the forest around Canooga Springs—except for a few distressing seconds, when she'd picked up a sense of desperation in the trees, wanting her, calling out to her for help. And then, like a dropped call on her cell phone (when she'd had one), it was gone.

Maybe she was stressed. She wondered how she was going to hide the tree magic from Laurie. Did she even want her to know? Laurie was her last tie to her old life. If she knew about the other world, then it would blur the line between her old life and her new one, a line already shaky since she'd remembered seeing the fairies and feeling the trees as a child. Keelie thought of the times she wanted to remember, and the moments slid through her mind like the passing landscape: she and Laurie at the beach with the cute surfers in the background, at the mall trying on goofy hats, and talking and teasing about Trent. Laurie was still living this life, which was now closed to her.

Sir Davey pulled into the Faire's main parking lot instead of the campground. "I have a meeting with some of the performers in a few minutes. Show Laurie around, Keelie. I'll drive the car around to the RV when I'm done, and you girls can help me unload."

Keelie steeled herself. Time to introduce Laurie to her new life. Things would never be the same between them. She hugged her friend, and Laurie hugged her back, surprised.

"You dope. It hasn't been that long." Laurie jumped out of the Wagoneer. "Thank you for coming to pick me up, Sir Davey." She curtseyed, a movement that should have looked dumb in street clothes, but instead looked natural. Watch out Elia. Laurie's California-blonde good looks would rival the elf girl's any day of the week.

"Everything is quiet until the weekends," Keelie told her friend. "But most of the folk live here and camp by the river. It'll get livelier tomorrow."

They strolled through the gates, and Laurie looked up, interested in the towers and the medieval-looking architecture. Keelie saw it through her friend's eyes and was struck by how pretty it was, with flowers bursting from window boxes and brightly colored banners and shop signs everywhere.

Their trip toward the campground took them near the Admin building. Keelie shivered and looked up the path, dark from the forest canopy above it. She looked around for Elianard. She hated the way he popped out of thin air, his derisive tone of voice being the only warning he was there. Keelie shuddered. Of course, it could be because of the Admin building, lair to the living, breathing, human dragon. She'd have to face Finch tomorrow, and with Elianard lurking around in the woods, Keelie would stay away. Right now, she'd just enjoy the moment with Laurie.

Heartwood's simple wooden structure was deserted, but Dad had left them a little note tacked to an outer post: "Come to Janice's for lunch. Dad."

Dad was back! Suddenly lighter, Keelie thought he must

be better. She grabbed Laurie's hand. "Come on. You'll love Janice."

They passed Lulu's shop, and Laurie's feet slowed. Her mouth hung open as she stared at the gingerbread house. "I want a puppet."

Alarmed, Keelie pulled her past the enchanted building. "Believe me, you don't."

Laurie shook her head as if to shake a bad feeling off. "No, I don't. I never liked puppets. They're creepy." She looked back at Lulu's shop. "For minute there I really wanted one. Weird."

Keelie glanced at her friend. Most humans would fall under the spell and then out again without ever noticing, but Laurie had sensed its passing. Interesting.

Ahead was the thatched roof of Janice's two-story cottage. "Janice runs the herb shop, and she's so into herbal cures and remedies. You'll love her."

"You told me about her. She's Raven's mom, right? Is Raven here?"

"Not yet. She had a summer job in New York, at Doom Kitty, but she's leaving there early to come help her mom." Keelie didn't want to say any more until she found out the whole story.

"Wow. Doom Kitty? That must be incredible. I'm glad she's coming." Laurie looked around at the little wooden buildings. "This place is amazing. I've never been to a Renaissance Faire. Do people live in these little fairy houses?"

"Fairy houses are mostly moss and sticks, like little nests. These are cottages, and yes, some of the merchants live in the back or above their shops. Just like in the real Renaissance. Although, strictly speaking, this is a Medieval Faire, since the theme is Robin Hood."

"Don't go all geeky on me, girl," Laurie cautioned.

Keelie's face got hot. She totally was geeking out. She knocked lightly on Janice's door, then pushed it open. Redwood from California gave off the sunshine of home, and the spicy smell of the forest floor.

They walked into the tiny vestibule. To the right, the shop was dark, with the counters covered in cloth to protect them from dust. The smell of herbs, soaps, and potions was intoxicating. She glanced at Laurie to see if it had the same effect on her.

Laurie's eyes gleamed in the dim light. "Can we go in here?"

"Maybe later. Let's go upstairs." The bare wooden stairs led up to the tiny loft apartment.

To Keelie's relief, Dad was up and dressed. He sat on the futon, buttoning a white poet's shirt, its billowing sleeves and ruffled cuffs very different from his usual straight, woodsy tunic. His dark blue jeans were tucked inside his Ren Faire boots, and he'd pulled his hair back loosely, his ears still covered.

"Hey Dad, feeling better?"

Knot sat on the futon beside him, purring. A day of sleep had done the two of them a lot of good. There was no sign of the stray white cat.

"I'm much better." Dad rose, smiling. "Are you going to introduce me to your friend?"

Keelie gave him a look that she hoped he would read as, *don't use elven charm on Laurie.* She'd talked to him in her head once before, when they'd battled the Red Cap in the High Mountain meadow.

To introduce Laurie, Keelie swept her hand in a "ta-da" gesture. Her friend's mouth was hanging open. Apparently,

Dad didn't need to use elven charm to impress her. His looks were enough. Keelie sighed loudly. "Dad, this is Laurie. Laurie, this is my dad."

He held out his hand. Laurie stopped gaping and looked back at Keelie, mouthing "Oh my God" at her, then turned to accept Zeke's hand. "Nice to meet you, Keelie's Dad. Mr. Heartwood. Sir."

He smiled as he gently removed his hand. Laurie looked at Keelie, then back again at Dad. "Thank you for letting me visit," she said. "I've really missed Keelie. We used to get into all kinds of trouble together. It's tough when you lose, like, your partner in crime."

Dad arched an eyebrow and cleared his throat. "I'm glad your mother allowed you to come. When I spoke to her, she was interested in the educational opportunities the Faire had to offer, along with the experience of traveling out east."

Laurie motioned with her hand. "Mom was thrilled when you called and invited me to come out."

Dad had called to invite her? Like melting chocolate chip cookies fresh from the oven, Keelie's insides went all warm and gooey. He'd remembered how much Laurie meant to her.

Janice appeared, wearing her beautiful purple and white gown and holding a bowl full of fragrant loose herbs. "You're back."

"Laurie, this is Janice, herbalist extraordinaire." If Keelie's voice was a teeny bit frosty, it was because she was still a little miffed about the 'no watch, oh, look at the time' incident. "Why are you in costume?"

"Photo op for the newspapers." She straightened Zeke's collar.

Laurie's elbow dug into her ribs. Yeah, so the Zekester

and Janice were an item, even if he didn't know it. So what? She cleared her throat. "What did you give Dad and Knot to make them better?"

"Dragonberry tea."

"Dragonberry tea?" Laurie laughed. "That sounds so My Little Pony. Remember playing My Little Pony?"

"Oh yeah. I had the stable, but you had the ranch, and when you got mad you wouldn't let my ponies come over and play." Keelie hadn't thought it was funny at the time.

"Yeah well, you never let me play with your old wooden dollhouse. You always shrieked if I touched it."

"Oh, yeah." Keelie's cheeks burned with embarrassment. She never wanted any of her friends, even her best friend, to touch the dollhouse Dad had made for her. How she'd longed to have him in her life back then. She turned to him and smiled. Now she had him, rather than a substitute dollhouse.

He was smiling at her, pleased to hear how she'd valued the toy he'd made for her.

"Dad, I almost forgot. I bought these for you." She reached into the plastic Canooga Springs Crystal Shoppe bag and pulled out the green velvet pouch of healing stones. "Sir Davey helped me pick them out for you."

Dad tugged at the drawstring and let the stones fall into his other hand. "Thank you, Keelie. I may have more need of these than you know."

"Sir Davey brought the car around to the parking area," Janice said to Laurie. "I'm going to have some of the Merry Men unload your luggage and put it in Sir Davey's camper. Keelie, why don't you take your friend on a tour of the Faire before it's crowded with mundanes?"

"We were actually in the middle of a tour when we found Dad's note." Keelie wasn't anxious to go outside again.

"Lunch is just sandwiches, but I thought you girls would be hungry." Janice produced a platter piled high with them.

"I'm totally in love with the Faire." Laurie took a sandwich. "It's so picturesque. I even like the terminology. Mundanes—how medieval. Like serfs or something."

"You said it." Keelie helped herself to a sandwich. "So this photo op, is it for the Faire?" She thought of the reporter the elves were worried about.

Dad smiled reassuringly. "It's a promo shot for an ad, Keelie." He stood up. "And we need to get going."

Janice patted the girls' shoulders as she headed to the stairs. "Laurie, if you need garb, just say the word."

"I'll say the word, all right." Laurie looked at Keelie. "Garb?"

"Costumes."

"Oh. Cool."

They finished lunch, then cleaned up, working cautiously in the tiny space to avoid a concussion.

"Ready to continue the tour?" Keelie glanced around the little space, spotless once more.

"Totally." Laurie jumped up.

Knot bolted from the futon, ran to the door, and stopped, waiting for them to open it.

"You can't go with us." Keelie glared at Knot.

He blinked up at her. His tail swished back and forth on the floor like a fuzzy samba dancer.

"Cute kitty. Is he yours?"

"This," Keelie swept a hand dramatically toward him, "is Knot."

"The Evil Kitty? No. It can't be. He's so cute and fluffy. I can't believe you called him a demon cat straight from the pits of the feline netherworld." Laurie smiled down at him. "Cutie."

Knot lifted his head to stare up at Keelie, eyes narrowed to slits. His tail swished faster, kicking up dust motes.

Keelie knew he was mad, and that she would pay for that comment. She nudged Knot to one side with her tennis shoe. "Stay here, Snot."

He purred and shifted to sit on her foot.

"Get your fuzzy butt off my toe, Knot the Snot."

"I think he's sweet." Laurie snapped her fingers at him. "Come on, Knotsie."

"Knotsie? Oh, gag." Keelie opened the door and pushed her foot forward, launching Knot down the stairs. He flew down, legs outspread, purring loudly, then flipped in the air and landed on the bottom step. He blinked up at them, unfazed.

"Keelie, I can't believe you did that." Laurie seemed ready to run to Knot's rescue. "You used to be an animal lover."

"He's fine." Laurie didn't know what Knot was capable of—that he wasn't a cat at all, but some fairy, um, thing.

Knot's buzz-saw purr rose up to meet them.

"You don't have to live with Pickles, the demon cat." Laurie's cat was famous for snagging bare toes by the pool. Not even close to Knot's level of evil.

Knot batted at Keelie's pant leg as she walked past, then the orange hairball ran in front of her just as she reached for the door.

Laurie had turned into the bigger room and spun around in a circle, taking in Janice's apothecary shop. Her face was etched with wonder as she tried to drink in the sight. Dried bunches of herbs hung from the exposed ceiling beams. Cobalt blue glass containers filled with healing elixirs sparkled in the sunbeams that shone on the back wall.

Knot reached up on his hind legs and touched the doorknob with his paw. And the door opened.

Laurie turned around in time to see Knot's latest trick. "Whoa, that's a smart cat. This place is so cool. My mom would go nuts in here. By the way, you didn't tell me that your dad is way good looking. He's like the Johnny Depp of the Renaissance Faire."

"Eew, Laurie, you're talking about my dad."

"Hey listen, if my mom and her friends ever lay eyes on him, then it's going to be like *Desperate Housewives*."

Keelie smiled. Through the window, she saw a *bhata* climb up to a higher branch in an oak tree, and then like a woodland acrobat disappear into the leaves of the oaks. Thank goodness the oaks were still asleep. No acorns.

She glanced over at Laurie—and for a moment panic set in, because Laurie's eyes were wide with wonder. But Keelie relaxed as she realized that this was still Laurie's reaction to Janice's shop.

They stepped outside and closed the door after them. The woodland setting gave the place a fairy-tale feeling. Admin had cleared off the acorns and leaves that had littered the dirt lane.

Infused with enthusiasm, Keelie danced ahead. "Come on, I'll show you the inside of our shop. This is called Enchanted Lane. You've seen Lulu's puppet shop. Over there is the blacksmith's building, and over there is Lady Annie's boot shop, and here is ours. It's not like our really cool shop in Colorado, but it works."

The carved Heartwood sign swung from a spear-shaped pole. They stepped off the dirt path onto the wooden floor, and Laurie looked around at Dad's creations. She was wide-eyed. "I've never seen anything like this."

Keelie ran her hand over one of the crystal-embellished chairs by the front entrance. Elm, from fallen branches. Not that Laurie would be able to sense it, since she was one hundred percent normal. Human.

"You know, Keelie, not only does your family have a shop on Enchanted Lane, but you're living an enchanted life."

"Let's see if you say that after you've been here for a while and you're stuck feeding bits of rat to a hawk."

"That's so not happening." Laurie laughed and walked farther into the shop. She stopped and turned a quizzical eye to Keelie. "Is it?"

"Welcome to my world."

sixteen

The unicorn shone bright against the dark pines. He stared at Keelie, as if trying to communicate. Keelie stepped toward him, hand outstretched to touch the luminous horn. It was slightly curved, like a strung bow.

As her fingers brushed the cool ivory, he reared, hooves flashing past her startled face, and galloped through the trees.

Keelie awoke, gasping, sitting up in bed. Her breathing slowed as she realized that she was safe in Sir Davey's camper. Laurie turned over, pulling the covers with her. Keelie grabbed the edge of the blanket as it left her legs and tugged it back, smiling. Still a total bed hog.

No unicorn. It was a dream. She was about to lie down again when a green whisper tickled her mind.

It was Tavak. *Tree Shepherdess. It is time.*

Keelie bolted upright. She touched her Queen Aspen heart, and the tree's telepathic connection became stronger.

Tree Shepherdess, Keliel, Lord Einhorn needs to see you—now—it is most urgent.

Einhorn. One horn. Keelie gazed at the alarm clock: 3:00 AM. Whatever happened to "he'd be there when I was ready"? He must be getting sicker.

Knot sat at the end of the bed, watching her with eyes that glowed like two round green lanterns. He meowed.

Keelie glared at him. "I'm not talking to you." She glanced down at Laurie. Still asleep, thank goodness. She sent her thoughts to the forest.

Where do I meet Lord Einhorn?

In the forest, near the human merrymaking place.

Merrymaking place?

Images of a huge white merchant tent, much bigger than anything in the staff parking lot, filled Keelie's mind, as did mental pictures of the Merry Men and the handsome actor who played Robin Hood, and she heard the familiar music of Rigadoon. She understood. The unicorn wanted to meet near Rivendell.

Tavak, I've never been to Rivendell from the campground. Will you show me the way?

The path glowed in her head, as if seen from a great height. Duh, of course. Tree height.

Keelie eased out of bed and dropped her rose quartz into the front pocket of her pajama top. She wished she had the tektite, too, but she didn't know where Sir Davey had stashed it. After the sapling incident, she wasn't going anywhere near a tree without her rose quartz. Plus, she had a feeling it might be needed to heal Einhorn. Keelie slipped her feet into her tennis shoes and tiptoed to the RV's door. Laurie would freak if she knew she was sneaking out to meet a unicorn.

Keelie slipped outside, latching the door carefully behind her. The air was crisp and cool and, above, the almost-full-moon's light blocked the stars and illuminated the ground before her like a giant lantern. Farther away, stars shone like little diamond points in the sky. Keelie thought of the starbursts on the unicorn painting at the crystal shop. She touched the rose quartz, easing the flutters in her stomach, missing the tektite she'd left behind. She stopped to get her bearings. The path the tree had shown her started behind the RV. The campground was quiet, and few lights glowed in the tents.

Tree Shepherdess, follow the cat.

Knot ran before her, then stopped and looked back as if she were being too pokey. The walk to Rivendell was easy, and they didn't encounter anyone but a few *bhata* who followed along in the bushes by the path. Keelie ignored them, knowing from experience that if she looked at them they might attack, pinching and tugging her hair. It was nothing deadly, but neither were wasps, for most folks.

Party central at Rivendell was a canvas tent, which sat at one end of the fenced pasture where the jousting horses were corralled at night. Large bodies shifted, and ears on massive heads twitched as she and Knot went by. It looked just as Keelie had imagined it.

Outside the tent, someone strummed a guitar, and the

notes seem to linger in the air as if Keelie could reach out and touch them with her fingers. Magic was all about her. Her body tingled with it. She skirted around the edge of the tent, staying out of sight, and entered the forest. Knot hurried, and she sped up to reach him. Twenty feet into the woods she could no longer see the lights of Rivendell when she turned.

Then, a dim glow ahead resolved itself into the unicorn. He was standing in a ring of pines, and seemed brighter as her eyes grew accustomed to the dark. The scent of forest loam tickled Keelie's nose, and the thick bed of old needles was like a cushion under her feet. It broke her heart to see the unicorn. His coat seemed even more tattered and lackluster; he looked like a sick, ill-used horse, with a fake horn stuck to his head. She had to help him.

"I'm here," she said aloud. "What can I do to help you?"

He nodded his head and pawed the ground, but said nothing.

She opened her mind and the trees crowded in hungrily. She quickly pulled away.

She had no idea how to talk to a unicorn. She may as well chat with Knot. She pulled the rose quartz from her pocket and held it up. Closing her eyes, Keelie opened herself to the trees. *Help me to speak with him.*

A chorus of green filled her mind. *We are here for you, Tree Shepherdess.*

Why can't I speak with the unicorn? What does he want of me?

Tavak's voice crowded out the others. *He does not speak directly for fear the others will hear him and know he is here.*

What others?

Those who seek to capture him for his power.

Someone was out to catch the unicorn, but there weren't many who could even see him. She had an image of a group of evil virgins chasing him. Maybe she could just cure him and go back to bed before Dad found out she was gone.

The rose quartz glowed as she held it out. Earth magic and tree magic might be the combination to cure Einhorn. These were the only kinds of magic that she knew. She grasped the amulet on its silver chain. From the charred aspen wood, warmth flowed through Keelie's hand. Magic, green magic, streamed through her body, tingling sharply.

Tavak warned, *Someone comes.*

The tingling increased, becoming a stabbing, shocklike pain. Keelie released the amulet; the warmth faded away, and with it the magic did too.

The unicorn pawed the ground. He tilted his head, staggered a bit, and then gathered himself and ran past her, heading deeper into the forest. The horses at Rivendell whinnied to him as he galloped away.

The light of the rose quartz grew fainter until it was completely extinguished, like a dying candle flame.

A stick snapped nearby. She jumped and whirled, expecting to see Elianard. But it was Laurie, standing in her red plaid pajama bottoms and her Baywood Academy T-shirt.

"What are you doing here?" Keelie asked.

"I knew it. You're a Wiccan, and you're doing some ritual. You going to show me?"

"I'm taking a walk."

"At three in the morning? You're doing something, I know it. Margaret Seastrunk is a Wiccan, and she says she performs rituals under a full moon, but I don't think it's real, because she learned it from a book. Plus, she sings in the choir at Greater L.A. Unitarian."

Keelie interrupted her babbling. "What did you see?"

Laurie frowned. "Chill, Keelie. I heard you leave, and followed your pink flashlight. You don't have to get all huffy."

Pink flashlight. The rose quartz must have been giving off light the whole way. She'd been visible to anyone who cared to look. "You didn't see anything else?" The unicorn must have sped right past her, within touching distance.

"Just that crazy white horse. Did you let it out of the pasture?"

Keelie stared at her friend. Just a horse? Who was keeping secrets now? Her mind swirled with a thousand questions she wanted to ask. Laurie would've told her if she'd had sex. Something like that was monumental, the kind of event that best friends shared. They'd told each other everything growing up. Suddenly, she was sad.

"Hello?" Laurie waved her hands in front of Keelie's face. "So are you going to tell me what you were doing out here?" The jousters' horses whinnied in the background.

"My cat. I was following Knot." It sounded lame.

"Uh-huh, right! What's the big secret? I'll bet it's a guy."

"I was following Knot. That's all. " Keelie was beginning to sound like Dad when he denied he could speak to the cat. She lifted her gaze up to the treetops, and she saw the silhouettes of several *bhata* moving in, around, and among the tree limbs. To the unknowing eye, it appeared as if a breeze were blowing.

The horses turned and ran to the center of the pasture, spooked. A dark figure came out of the Rivendell tent, and as it moved away from the tent's shadow, she saw that it was one of the jousters. He circled the perimeter of the fence, sword in hand, and watched the horses run.

Laurie inched closer to Keelie and grabbed her hand. "Is that him? Your secret boyfriend?"

Keelie rolled her eyes. "He's just a jouster. Probably in charge of the horses. I don't have a secret boyfriend."

Laurie moved forward, releasing her hand. "A real jouster? Like he does it for a living?"

"Yes. They travel from Faire to Faire. Kind of like a medieval PGA Tour."

Blessed by the moon's silver glow, the meadow with its ivory-colored tent looked like a medieval tapestry. It was oddly quiet, though, even for this time of the night. Back in Colorado, the Shire's night owls had kept the music and conversations going until dawn, especially on weeknights, when no one had to perform the next day. Were that many people sick? Of course, she didn't know how many actually stayed on site, and how many were at the lodge in town.

The figure returned to the tent, as the tent door opened, the light from inside briefly illuminated the man.

The lone guitar's music began anew and added to the mystical ambience, but it brought Keelie back to the reality of her situation. She and Laurie needed to sneak past before the man with the sword noticed them and got word back to Dad. They'd said they were going to work together to help the unicorn, and if he found out that she'd come out here alone, especially after the last tree incident, he'd be furious. She didn't want to worry him, even if he was feeling better.

Laurie climbed up onto the pasture's wooden fence. "Listen, Keelie. Hear that music? Someone's playing the guitar out here in the middle of nowhere. This feels like a dream." In the moonlight, Laurie's face changed from dreamy musing to comprehension, as if she'd just figured out a piece of a missing puzzle. "You are so lying, Keelie Heartwood. Your secret boyfriend is down there in that tent."

"I am not! I was trying to find the stray white cat that's been hanging around and I thought Knot would lead me to him, since they're buddies now. I've been worried about it."

"Prove it." Laurie crossed her arms over her chest.

"Prove what?" Keelie answered. "I don't have to prove anything."

"That you don't have a secret boyfriend at this Faire. I mean, Sean's in Florida, and he wouldn't know if you were seeing someone on the sly."

"Sean and I weren't really dating." Keelie's face burned, because she had been having some naughty thoughts about the Robin Hood actor. Not that it was a crime to think about someone else, but it seemed to be sort of cheating to think about someone—you know—naked, when you'd been out with a guy you really liked and were desperate to hear from again.

"Okay. Don't be so touchy. I mean, you never know when someone will cheat."

Keelie definitely picked up an undercurrent of bitterness. Sounded like Laurie might be talking about Trent. They'd been tight when Keelie had to leave after Mom's death. Funny how Laurie hadn't mentioned his name since her arrival. Of course, Keelie hadn't asked, but maybe he'd been the one. Laurie hadn't seen the unicorn.

Her friend was looking longingly at the golden lights of

the tent. "Let's just go down there and check it out. Who knows, there may be a party."

"I don't hear one. Besides, I can't. Dad will kill me."

"He doesn't have to know. We'll stay an hour, and then rush back to the camper. Who's going to tell him?"

"Knot."

"Yeah right, the cat." Laurie trucked off toward the tent. "I'm going."

"Laurie," Keelie whispered as loudly as she could from the safety of the trees' shadows. "Get back here."

No answer. Once Laurie got started partying there would be no stopping her.

Knot glared accusingly at Keelie, as if she could control her friend or had put the idea of going down to the tent into Laurie's head. She glowered back down at him. "This is your fault. I need your help to get her back to the RV."

He blinked at her, then sauntered off after Laurie, his fuzzy orange tail held high. Laurie pushed aside the heavy canvas door of the tent with her hand, and a soft golden glow from inside illuminated her. She held the tent flap back as Knot entered, like a VIP guest at a Hollywood party, then followed him. The flap dropped behind them and the light was gone, leaving Keelie in darkness.

She pulled herself over the fence after them and crossed the meadow, glancing back toward the dark woods. Einhorn was gone, and she was going to be in so much trouble. She already imagined the conversation she would have with Dad: "I had to follow her. Laurie's not used to Ren Faire party types." As if Keelie was. The unicorn would be no excuse, either. Dad would be furious and frightened that she'd tried to help Einhorn by herself. But the trees had called to her, not to Dad.

She entered the tent. Inside, lanterns hung from hooks atop long, twisted iron poles that were stuck in the ground. The floor was a jumble of bamboo mats, revealing meadow grass at the tent walls. An area had been partitioned to one side with wooden screens, and at the far end of the tent, long panels of colorful gauze hung down, forming another room. The warm light of the lanterns cast a flickering spotlight on the Faire actor who played Robin Hood. He strummed a melody Keelie recognized: "Scarborough Fair."

Tonight, Robin Hood wore jeans and a light blue polo shirt with a black, long-sleeved T-shirt underneath. Whether in tights or mundane clothes, the guy was hot. He sang, looking into Laurie's eyes as she stood watching him adoringly, like an idiot fan. Any minute now she'd start drooling.

Suddenly self-conscious, Keelie wondered what this guy, who had hundreds of girls swooning at his feet every weekend, thought of two teenage girls wandering around in the middle of the night in pajama pants and T-shirts.

The song ended. Robin Hood smiled up at Laurie. "You're new."

Laurie's lips curved up. "Please keep playing. I'm Laurie. What's your name?"

Robin Hood grinned as if he'd been offered a box of candy. "Hey there, Laurie. I'm Jared. What are you and your friend doing out in the middle of the night?"

"Stargazing." She batted her eyes.

The flirt! Keelie quickly sidled up to her.

Robin Hood arched an eyebrow. "I know you. Weren't you Plumpkin?"

“What’s a Plumpkin?” Laurie frowned, unhappy that his attention had strayed.

“I’ll explain it later.” Keelie blushed all the way down to her toes. “Yep, lost the head and almost lost my job. You wouldn’t happen to have seen a white cat? He belongs to my cat, Knot.”

“Your cat has a cat.” Laurie rolled her eyes.

Keelie wanted to stomp on her friend’s foot for pointing out how ridiculous it sounded. Laurie didn’t know the half of what Knot could do.

Jared laughed. “I haven’t seen a white cat, but I did see you and that white horse. He came right to you. He’s a wild one. A lot of the jousters have been trying to catch him, yet he seemed charmed by you.”

Keelie suppressed a gasp. It occurred to her that she might be giving off that cinnamon smell, too, when she worked magic or communicated with the trees. She realized Laurie and Jared were looking at her, expecting a reply, and shrugged. “I just have a way with animals.”

He smiled, and dimples popped out in his cheeks to match the small indentation in his chin. Too cute. “Your cat likes to come down here and listen to the music.” He gestured toward Knot, who was washing his tail. “He likes to hang out, although he hisses at the jousters sometimes.” Knot rubbed up against the guitar and purred.

“Really?” Life wasn’t fair, Keelie thought. First, Knot had hung out with the pirates at the High Mountain Faire, and now here he was with Robin Hood at the Wildewood. Of course, he’d traveled with Dad for decades. He’d probably seen lots of fun acts at Ren Faires throughout the years.

"Well, if you haven't seen the white cat, Laurie and I need to get back to the campground."

"No we don't. It's a lovely night—live for the moment. Knot knows how to have a good time." Laurie lowered her voice. "You've really gotten uptight since you left California. This is like something out of a movie: two teen girls wandering in the woods meet up with a really awesomely cute dude playing a guitar."

"Yeah, just before the guy with the chain saw shows up," Keelie muttered.

"Wrong movie. The only thing missing to really make it more fantastical is for a unicorn to show up, like the one on the wall at the Canooga Crystal Shoppe. Or maybe some fairies dancing around in a circle, leaving mushrooms behind to show the world they were here."

Keelie's laugh was shaky. She rubbed her hands over her arms to warm up.

"What?" Laurie picked up on Keelie's unease.

"I'm just cold."

Laurie rubbed her hands up and down her arms, too, squeezing them tight to her torso to deepen her cleavage. "You're right; it is getting cold, and we still have to hike back." She smiled at Jared. "It was nice meeting you. I'll look for you at the Faire."

"Would you two like some coffee before you go back? I just made a fresh pot. I have to stay awake to babysit the horses since all the other jousters have the crud."

"Are you kidding? I'd love some coffee," Laurie replied before Keelie could utter "no."

Hearing about the sick jousters, Keelie wanted to rush back and check on Dad. And she didn't want him hearing from the Faire workers she'd been hanging out in Rivendell.

Jared placed his guitar to the side and rose. Maybe one cup of coffee wouldn't hurt. But since there was no fire pit with a coffeepot on it, and no roaring generator outside disturbing the night, the coffee probably wasn't brewed. But maybe Laurie would lose her glazed groupie look if he served her the instant dreck.

"Come over to the Kasbah. That's what we call the inner room of our tent."

They followed Jared through the colorful strips of gauzy fabric and into a room straight out of the Arabian Knights. Fat silk pillows littered the carpet-covered floor, illuminated by flickering candles in tall iron holders. The room had a sexy Silk Road caravan feel.

This had to be party central. The plump pillows had probably seen a lot of action, but Keelie didn't feel in danger. It was two against one.

She sat back against the pillows. It was really very comfortable. Laurie sprawled next to her, bright-eyed and looking like an invitation to a jail sentence. Maybe this hadn't been a good idea.

seventeen

Jared didn't throw himself down between them, to Keelie's relief. Instead, he went to the tent's corner, where a Mr. Coffee sat on a wooden table. The "on" light glowed bright orange.

Keelie frowned. "How are you powering your coffeepot?" If she kept the focus away from Laurie, maybe they'd get out of here quickly.

Jared paused and pushed the tent wall back. A power strip was rigged to a huge plastic square. "Battery. We don't use it much, to conserve power. But I've got to stay up to watch the horses." He grinned at Keelie with his dimples set on high. "Can't leave civilization behind, can we, little dove?"

Little dove? Keelie smiled weakly at Laurie, who shot her a mock venomous look. Jared poured some coffee into a small green porcelain cup. Keelie smirked at her friend's reaction. She'd been called little dove, and Laurie hadn't. The scent from the cup wafted out to greet her, like a siren's call to her taste buds.

She accepted a green china cup with a chipped handle. Jared gave Laurie a white cup painted with delicate roses. Laurie's grateful smile was way over the top.

"Sorry about the random mugs. With all the traveling, we end up with a jumble of dishes."

"You travel from Faire to Faire?" Laurie blew on her coffee. "That's so gypsy-like."

Keelie could have kicked her, but Jared might notice.

Jared smiled. "Yeah, I'm on the circuit."

"Are you Robin Hood at every Faire?"

"No, different Faires have different themes. I audition just like everyone else. It depends on the role. Sometimes I just joust, and play the Queen's Champion or the Black Knight."

"I hear auditions are tough. At our school in L.A., our friend Ashlee was always auditioning for TV roles."

"Are you both from L.A.?" Jared sat down on a tall stack of pillows with his own steaming cup of brew.

"Yes, and I live still live there." Laurie probably thought he'd be impressed.

"And I'm living with my dad," Keelie replied with a grin. She was glad he wasn't falling for Laurie's flirtation.

Laurie leaned forward, still trying to act cute. "Are you doing another Faire after this one?"

"Nope. This is the last one of the season for me." Jared

sipped his coffee and looked at Keelie. "How about you and your father?"

"This is our last Faire for the season, too. Dad spends the winter making furniture, so we're going to his home in the Dread Forest when this Faire closes."

"The Dread Forest?"

Was she supposed to keep the place a secret? Keelie couldn't remember. "I know it sounds like it's located in Transylvania, but it's in Oregon."

Knot sat next to Jared, who reached down absentmindedly to scratch the cat's ears. Knot closed his eyes contentedly, but his tail swished back and forth like a furry snake.

Laurie gave Keelie a "back off, he's mine" look. "So, are you alone here? We thought you were having a party."

"This is the party tent, but only the person on watch with the horses sleeps here. Something's been spooking them, so I'm on watch all night."

Keelie grinned at Laurie. "It was probably a bear."

Jared laughed. "I'm pretty sure there aren't any bears around here. It was probably that wild white horse. They get really upset whenever they see him."

"*I* saw him!" Laurie exclaimed. "Can't you catch him?"

"Not yet. I was amazed that he let Keelie get so close."

He seemed ready to talk more about the mysterious white horse, so Keelie changed the conversation. "I can't wait for Laurie to see the Faire in action. You're very convincing as Robin Hood."

He preened. "Thanks. Have you seen the entire Robin Hood and his Merry Men story line played out?"

"No, I've been busy working as a Jill-of-the-Faire for Ms. Finch, and in my dad's shop."

"Ah, Finch, aka the Faire Dragon." Jared rolled his eyes and made a face. "Yeah, she's got all the acts scheduled to appear at the Maypole tomorrow. It's going to be a traffic jam, and if Sir Brine the Pickle Man shows up, then I'll shoot him with a bow and arrow myself."

"Faire Dragon?" Laurie looked confused. "Sir Brine?"

"I'll explain it all later." Keelie wasn't sure she understood it all herself. "Suffice to say, Finch is my boss, and you'll get the dubious pleasure of meeting her tomorrow."

"You're working?" Laurie's eyes were wide. "Like, a job?"

"Don't act all shocked." Another round of heat flushed Keelie's skin. "I have to."

"Well, I'm here to have fun. It's summer vacation." Laurie scooted closer to Jared and linked her arm through his elbow. "You're an actor *and* a jouster. That's so cool. Sounds like I'm going to have lots of free time tomorrow. Maybe you could show me around."

Jared cleared his throat. "I do have to be Robin Hood, so unfortunately I won't be able to tend thee, my fair lady."

"Well, I'll be sure to say 'hi' to you. Tell me, what's the most exciting thing that's ever happened to you at a Faire?"

Jared smiled and began telling Laurie tales of Rennie life. Keelie wanted to hit her with a pillow. It wasn't fair. Laurie could come to the Faire and play, and then return to her life in California. She'd waltzed into Keelie's new life, enchanted Sir Davey, and was now flirting with Robin Hood, while Keelie had been working her ass off. The only thing she had to show for it was more work ahead, thanks to Dad and his ideas about learning values and building character.

Then a realization hit her like a cold slap. Dad would be waking up soon. Very soon.

"What time is it?"

Jared glanced at his watch. "Four thirty."

"Laurie, we need to get back or we're going to be grounded."

"Grounded by your dad? He's too sweet." Laurie gave Jared a syrupy smile. "So far I'm very impressed by the handsome men at this Faire."

Jared's gaze bounced from Keelie to Laurie. "Keelie's right. Her dad is tough. He sent a memo out to all the jousters saying they were to stay away from his daughter."

Keelie sat straight up, outraged. "He did what?"

"He wasn't fooling."

For the umpteenth time, Keelie blushed. "Laurie, it's time to go." Laurie cuddled closer to Jared.

"We're already in trouble just for leaving the RV. So what more can he do to us?"

The aspen heart talisman grew warm against Keelie's skin. She put a hand up to touch the T-shirt covering it. Was Einhorn back? It hadn't reacted to the unicorn before.

"Are we having a party?" The deep baritone voice came from just outside the colorful cloth wall. A man stepped through, and Keelie stared. He was a stranger, but he seemed familiar.

"Lord Niriel. I didn't know anyone else was up." Jared looked uncomfortable.

Laurie giggled. "It's so cool the way everyone calls each other Lord this and that."

Lord Niriel didn't seem amused. "You're supposed to be watching the horses, not entertaining ladies."

Keelie poked Laurie in the back, trying to get her to shut up. The man looked young, but there was something about him that said he was much older. He was in shape, with broad shoulders and a small waist, and he had a majestic face with an aquiline nose. Although the only sign of age was a couple of wrinkles that creased at the corners of his eyes, wisdom clung to him like a cloak. He looked as if he should be wearing long robes, but he was dressed in jeans and a long-sleeved polo shirt with a shiny leaf embroidered on the left pocket.

Jared stood with athletic grace and bowed from the waist. "Lord Niriel, you were right, the white horse returned." He motioned to Keelie. "I saw it go to Keelie."

Lord Niriel arched an eyebrow. "Ah, Keelie Heartwood. So your charm extends to stray horses. I would think collecting jousters' hearts would be work enough for you."

Jared looked at her with renewed interest.

Keelie's heart raced. "I don't know what you're talking about." He meant Sean, of course. Her palms were sweaty at the thought of him. She wiped her hands on her pajama pants and hoped she didn't smell like cinnamon.

"Hi, I'm Laurie. I'm staying with Keelie." Laurie's hand stuck out, daring Lord Niriel not to shake.

He took it and bowed slightly over it, then released it and turned back to Keelie. "I'm speaking, of course, of Sean o' the Wood."

"You know Sean? Have you spoken to him? Is he still in Florida?" Sean must have mentioned her to this man. He'd been thinking of her.

Jared motioned to the cushions. "Please, milord, have a seat."

Niriel did so, sitting close to Keelie. "He is in Florida, and was well when I left him. I drove all night to get here, when I heard that most of the jousters in my company were sick."

"You must be the head of the Silver Bough Jousters." That accounted for the leaf crest on his shirt.

He bowed again.

"My dad mentioned you. He said you were on the Council." That explained the elven-sounding name. "If you just got here, then you missed the meeting."

Lord Niriel looked quickly at Jared and Laurie, then raised an eyebrow at Keelie, as if cautioning her to stay quiet.

"Sean's the guy you met at the High Mountain Faire, right?" Laurie pouted. "Too bad he's in Florida. I was dying to meet him." She smiled at Jared, as if reinforcing the idea that Keelie was taken, but she was not.

"Is he enjoying the Faire in Florida?" Keelie was starting to run out of conversation, and she was desperate to get back to the RV before Dad woke up.

"Somewhat, although he is confused." Lord Niriel looked directly into her eyes. "Sean is my son, and he tells me you haven't returned any of his letters."

Keelie stared at him, dumbstruck. She swallowed. "What letters?"

Before he could answer, the colorful strips that formed the wall were pushed violently aside and her father appeared. Gone was the mild-mannered artisan. He looked like an avenging warrior.

Keelie wished she could disappear like the *bhata*. But her father didn't even glance at her. His steely gaze was fixed on Lord Niriel, who returned the stare. No love lost there.

"Keelie, Laurie. Come with me."

The girls scrambled to their feet. Keelie's legs wobbled from nerves. Lord Niriel was watching her, his eyes secretive. Was her panic obvious?

"I need to speak to your father," he said. "And now is as good a time as any. Excuse me, ladies. Zeke, follow me." He pushed past Dad, crossed the outer room, then ducked through the tent door out into the night.

Keelie was amazed when her father followed him without a word. She saw a corner of Dad's blue tunic outside before the heavy canvas dropped into place once more. She ran to the outer room and leaned forward to hear their conversation.

"Zekeliel," Lord Niriel said, his tone frosty.

"I came for my daughter." Dad's smooth voice cracked.

What was wrong with him? Keelie had never been so afraid. Her father sounded angry, but he sounded sick, too.

Laurie stood up. "Are you okay?

"We should've left hours ago."

Dad's voice rose. "She's my daughter, and I will decide what happens to her."

"Uh-oh." Keelie looked at Laurie.

"He's just blowing off steam because he's worried." Laurie waved a hand dismissively. "Here's what you do when you're caught—you find a way to twist everything around and make it his fault. When Mom caught me drinking this spring, she was going to ground me and cut off my credit card. I told her if she did, I'd run away. I told her it was her fault I was drinking because she loved her new boyfriend more than me."

Keelie realized that her mouth was hanging open, and closed it. She couldn't believe what she was hearing, but she detected deep pain beneath her friend's nonchalant attitude. She wondered if this was how she sounded to others.

"Keliel Heartwood, out here now!"

Before she could move, the tent flap opened again. Dad appeared with a lantern held high, casting its bright glow onto Keelie and Laurie. This was all so surreal, as if she were one of those characters in a movie, just escaped from imprisonment, but now caught red-handed with all the searchlights focused on her.

Dad's forehead was deeply furrowed. The arm that held the lantern aloft trembled a little, causing the shadows around them to flicker. Jared started to back away from the older men, then turned and pushed past Keelie and Laurie with a muttered, "I need to check on the horses."

Dad looked them over, then turned. "Follow me."

Keelie and Laurie did. Outside, Lord Niriel stood to the far left talking to Elianard and Elia. Keelie hesitated, wondering what they were doing here. Was everyone up at this time of the night?

The elf girl scowled at Keelie. This was probably the moment she had been waiting for. A sick feeling hit Keelie in the pit of her stomach as she envisioned Sean's handsome face when Elia told him she'd been in the Rivendell tent with Jared—of course, leaving out the fact that Laurie had been there, too.

Dad motioned to them. "We're going home." He looked exhausted. His shoulders drooped, and he wiped his hand across his forehead. Guilt slammed Keelie. She noticed how Niriel, Elianard, and Elia, even in the glow of the Rivendell lantern light, shone with radiant health. They weren't sick like the other elves, or even tired like Dad. Very curious.

Unable to take her father's silence and the weight of his disappointment, Keelie started to speak, but only managed "I . . . " before Dad cut in.

His voice held a mix of controlled anger and restraint. "We'll discuss this later."

Keelie was silent.

"Keelie snuck out to find that stray white cat." Laurie's voice was pitched high; she wasn't immune to the strained atmosphere. "I mean, she worries about him, and then she freaks when this white horse gallops past from the woods."

Elia gasped.

Keelie wanted to kick Laurie in the knee for opening her big mouth. Elianard and Elia didn't need to know about her involvement with the unicorn. From their reaction, they'd put two and two together. But this probably wouldn't put Einhorn in danger… all the elves knew about the forest guardian.

Dad's stare was fixed on the elven trio.

Lord Niriel lifted his head. "How interesting." He walked closer to Dad. "Zeke, since I arrived too late for the Council meeting, let's get together at the lodge to discuss the illness that has befallen us." He glanced at Elianard. "Can you join us?"

Elianard nodded.

"Good. Then let's say in about three hours. I have to meet the Faire director first and go over available jousters for today's show, but it will be a short meeting."

Dad's eyes narrowed, and he gave a resigned sigh. "I'll be there."

"See that you are." Lord Niriel's authoritative voice told Keelie that he was accustomed to being obeyed. Even though he was Sean's father, she didn't like the way he ordered her father around.

Elianard strode forward with Elia following in the wake of his robes. He stopped with a smarmy smile on his face. "Until our meeting at the lodge, Zekeliel."

Dad gave a slight nod.

Something was up with the elves, and fear for Dad made Keelie forget her own situation and the fact that she'd probably be grounded for life. She wondered again if there was a connection between Einhorn's failing health and the elves. As Dad always said, "as the forest goes, so go the elves."

Elianard walked past her, and Elia, like a dutiful daughter, trailed after her father. She lifted her head slightly and glared at Keelie, then sneered at Laurie, the lowly human.

"Your face will freeze that way," Laurie said casually.

Elia looked dumbstruck, as if a chair had insulted her.

Dad started down the path, his lantern steady in the darkness. "Let's get back to the RV."

On the hike back to Sir Davey's, Keelie couldn't take her father's silence and his disappointment. "Dad, I…"

"Why were you in the tent?"

"It was cold and dark outside."

Dad stopped and held the lantern high above her head, making it look like he had a halo. "Keelie, you're old enough to be responsible for the consequences of your actions. There are consequences, dire ones, if you take the wrong path. It can lead to darkness, to loneliness and despair. I trust you, Keelie, not to break the hearts of those who love you, those who will have to live with the aftermath of your actions for the rest of their lives."

Shocked, for a second Keelie couldn't find any words to

make a reply. It sounded so extreme. She glanced at Laurie. She couldn't explain about Einhorn in front of her friend. "Tavak called me. I had to go." Dad's expression didn't change. It seemed to be a mix of love and pity and fear.

There was more going on with the elves than the unicorn and the illness afflicting them. Lots more. Maybe that was what Dad had been hinting at. Dire consequences. Right. It wasn't as if she were about to turn into Darth Vader or anything.

At the RV, Sir Davey greeted them with a weary smile. "Coffee's brewing."

Laurie yawned. "What time is it?"

"Six," Dad answered.

"Can you get me up at, say, twelve?"

"You'd better stay awake." Sir Davey bustled over to the coffeemaker. "Going to bed now is pointless, since the Faire opens in two hours. Lots to do."

"What? My mother would never . . . "

"If you can stay up all night, then you can stay up all day." Dad didn't appear ready to stay up another second.

Laurie seemed at a loss for words. Keelie was sure that if they'd been in full daylight, her friend's face would be pasty white from shock.

"I suggest if you want a hot shower, you go and take one now. Last one in will probably get a cold one." Dad turned to Sir Davey. "Let's start the oatmeal."

Keelie's stomach turned over. Elf politics, unicorns, trees, fairies, and Sean's dad. And the missing letters from Sean. She needed quiet time to process everything that had happened tonight. She needed sleep. And in a few hours, she'd have to face Finch.

eighteen

Laurie took Zeke's hint and headed for the shower. Keelie stayed by the RV door and watched as her father dropped onto one of the sofas and shook out a wrinkled copy of *Ye Wildewood Gazette*.

Sir Davey winked at Keelie and walked into the kitchen area. "Oatmeal coming up. What's today's plan, Zeke?"

"I've got a Council meeting to attend at eight o'clock, and I've got to check on the oaks, go to the woodlands near the stream, and open the booth." Dad popped the paper in angry emphasis.

Knot hopped up beside him, placing an orange paw on

Dad's knee in a comforting gesture. Stupid cat. Acting all lovey-dovey to get on Dad's good side.

Sir Davey whistled as he looked at the counter. "I'll print out the information you requested about the forest before the dam was built. You're going to need it."

Peering up from his paper, Dad glowered at Keelie. She sensed tension flow toward her like an invisible electrical current connecting them. She reached for the rose quartz in her pocket and closed her hand over its familiar contours, but it didn't help.

She served herself a cup of coffee and watched Sir Davey. He was busy at the computer keyboard on his office desk, which was converted from the rollout pantry at the far end of the kitchen counter. His attention was focused on a crystal orb attached to his computer. A topographic map flashed across his screen, some areas heavily outlined in green, others beige like a desert. The bottom of the screen read, "Wildewood." The image grew as Sir Davey zeroed in on a pale rectangle of a rushing river and woodlands as far as the eye could see.

"This is an image of the Wildewood as an Old Growth forest, before it was logged."

Keelie's heart ached at the vision of beauty before her. She thought of the oaks in the Faire, the only remaining survivors of this ancient forest—no wonder they were so emotionally scarred. She glanced over at her father. *Say something,* she thought. *Anything.*

The sound of the shower running, followed by a sharp yell, broke the tense silence. Laurie had probably hit her head on the low-hung, Davey-sized showerhead. Good! If they hadn't gone into the tent, Keelie wouldn't be in this mess. Dad wouldn't have to attend this stupid Council meeting, and she might have had time to help Einhorn. It was just like back in school, when Keelie got in trouble because of Laurie's not-so-bright ideas. Funny what you forget when you're away from someone for a few months.

Dad folded the paper. "Keelie, time to talk. Outside."

She let her shoulders slump and kept her head down; if her body posture conveyed that she was being very humble, maybe he would go easier on her. She closed the RV door behind them, then held her coffee cup in front of her like a shield.

Dad looked at the trees at the edge of the clearing and blew out a sigh. "I know that Lord Einhorn summoned you. Tavak told me."

Keelie frowned. "I don't understand why Tavak sent me to help the unicorn. You totally outrank me. What could I do that you couldn't?"

"He trusts you," Dad said softly. "Lord Einhorn has reason to distrust elves. He chose you."

Keelie's hands tightened on the cup. "Okay, explain this to me, Dad. I'm about to turn sixteen. Elia, who's like, sixty, called me a mutt, and she's not wrong. I'm not elf, I'm not human, and I just found out about all this 'other world' stuff. So why me? Why can't you help? Why can't the other elves? Or Sir Davey's Earth magic? Or Janice with her herb lore? I mean, if Lulu can do magic, why the heck am I the chosen one?" She realized she was waving her arm, and sat down on the RV's steps. "You never explain anything. I need answers."

Dad sighed. "I can't protect you. I thought I could, until you knew more, but your magic seems to draw trouble. As for why you, only Lord Einhorn knows, but I suspect it's because you are a child of two worlds and are apart from our struggle."

Keelie frowned. "So the answer is that there is none? You don't know, and that's it."

Dad untied the green velvet bag of rocks from his hip belt. It pleased her that he had them.

He closed his hands into a fist, then absentmindedly rubbed the rocks together, making them click against one another. A verdant glimmer glowed from between his fingers. Her aspen heart talisman felt warm. Keelie didn't think she was doing any magic. Normally, tingles ran through her body. It must be Dad.

She pointed at his rocks. Instead, he placed his left index finger against his lips. He didn't want her to say anything. He opened his hands and the rocks, cocooned in green energy, levitated one by one like little space satellites floating above the Earth. Keelie inhaled sharply.

Dad looked at her. "Why was Laurie out in the meadow with you?"

"Laurie followed me. I told her I was looking for Knot and the white cat."

"Did she believe you?" The rocks, glowing green, still suspended in air, hovered above his outstretched hand.

"No, she asked if I was going to do some type of ritual. She heard Robin Hood—I mean, Jared—playing the guitar, and saw the party tent. Off she went. Laurie is a real social butterfly."

"I spoke with Laurie's mom." The rocks dropped one by one in his hand. He clasped his fist around them. "That woman is a piece of work. I tracked her down using tree magic. She's in Lake Tahoe with her boyfriend. She didn't want me to send Laurie back, told me if I wanted to ground her to go ahead; that it may make the girl think about consequences. I can't believe you wanted to go live with that woman." Dad's expression turned glum as he tightened his fist around the tumbled stones, and the green glow faded away.

Time to do some damage control. "That was back then. I was desperate to get back to what I thought would be the closest thing to having Mom."

Dad reached over and ruffled her curls. "And now?"

"I'm home." Keelie leaned into him and he wrapped his arm around her shoulder. "What happens next?"

Sighing, Dad looked up at the trees as if the *bhata* might be holding up a cue card as to what he should do with a teen daughter and her wayward friend. "Don't discuss the unicorn with anyone, and Keelie, don't go into the forest without me. I told you that Einhorn has reason to distrust the elves, and you do, too."

"That sounds like a warning."

"It is. I can't lose you again."

"Then clue me in, Dad." She stepped away from him, angry. "You're treating me like a kid. If there's real danger, then tell me what's going on. This 'only Einhorn knows' is bullshit."

His eyebrows rose in surprise. "I'm trying to protect you. You've been through a lot in the last few months. Magic is new to you and I'm still trying to deal with how powerful your magic is. The best thing for you is to stay out of the forest, and stay away from the unicorn."

"The unicorn, the jousters—sure, I'll stay away from everybody and everything. Just lock me up in the Swiss Miss

Chalet and call me Rapunzel. I heard about the memo you sent the jousters. Jared told me."

"Stay away from him, too."

"What? Okay, who can I talk to?" Her voice rose with each frustrated word. "You, Janice, Sir Davey, Knot, and I guess the trees."

"Not the trees."

"Great." The word came out in a shriek. "Let me know how to keep them out of my head, Tree Shepherd."

He ran a hand over his face and leaned against a chestnut sapling, as if taking comfort from it. "I don't know what to tell you. I want you to be safe."

"Ever since we got to this Faire, you've changed, Dad. We talked all the way here, and then suddenly you clam up. You were teaching me about the trees, about the elves, and ever since I saw the unicorn you've said nothing except to tell me stay out of the woods. Hello? Teaching opportunity. I can't learn everything from osmosis."

"There's something very wrong with the forest here, something that could be dangerous to you. You don't know enough about your magic, and I can't help you now. I've got the forest and the unicorn to deal with." The tips of his pointed ears were red, and his face was pale, making the dark circles under his eyes starker.

"I stopped the Red Cap, didn't I?" The murderous little creature had almost killed Sir Davey.

"We were lucky, and there's no guarantee that you'll win the next time it happens. So please, Keelie, stay out of the woods."

Keelie had been ready to yell at him again, but she stopped.

Fine. She'd stay out of the woods. For now. But the next time the unicorn called her, she would go.

Dad's leaf-green eyes looked glazed. She hugged him. "We'll talk about it later." She'd do what she had to do. "I know you were sick yesterday, and you're not looking so good."

He hugged her back. "I'll be fine. Just tired. I'm not looking forward to this meeting. I think I may drink some of Davey's coffee."

Shocked, Keelie couldn't believe that Dad would even consider drinking coffee. He must be on the verge of exhaustion.

"Well, hello, Laurie." Dad was looking over her shoulder.

Keelie turned around and saw Laurie standing at the RV's door, wearing jeans, and—Keelie couldn't believe it—Keelie's Vampire Girl shirt, the one she'd bought with her own money at La Jolie Rouge. "What are you doing with my shirt?"

"I found it. Looks good on me, doesn't it?" Laurie stepped down and turned to model it.

She was going to kill Laurie. That shirt had been neatly folded in a suitcase, tucked away where Knot couldn't find it, which meant Laurie had been digging through Keelie's stuff. "You have mountains of new clothes, so why are you poaching on mine?"

"Your clothes are new to me. Come on, girlfriend, you and I always share clothes. What's the diff?"

The "diff" was that thanks to Knot, her fashionable clothes could fit in a Ziploc bag, and now Laurie was wearing part of Keelie's pathetic little fashion stash. But Keelie let it drop. Laurie was staring at her dad as if he were about to cut her head off.

"Are you going to make me go home?" Laurie looked like she was used to adults discussing her as if she were a traveling piece of luggage, to be shipped to whoever would take her. Earlier, Keelie would have been on her side, but that shirt made her think it would do Laurie some good to sweat it out.

"You may remain with us, but you will have to obey my rules, the same rules that Keelie has to follow." Dad looked grim.

Laurie exhaled, obviously relieved. "I will. I'll follow your rules to the letter. Thanks for letting me stay."

Keelie was glad Laurie was staying, but they had to talk about her rules, too. Keelie would never violate her friend's privacy. They'd shared clothes and secrets in the past, but those had been freely given, not taken. She had to establish parameters with Laurie, especially if she was going to help the unicorn. Balancing magic with real life was tough.

"Today's my first day of the Faire, so what are we doing?" Laurie rubbed her hands together.

Annoyed, Keelie noted how quickly her friend had shifted from acting like the repentant teen to being a resort guest expecting to be entertained. "This is not Club Medieval."

"Keelie has to go to the Administration building to meet with Finch, the Faire director. Keelie has a job, whereas you, Laurie, will have a chaperone to escort you around Wildewood."

"Chaperone?" Laurie rocked back in her Converse sneakers as if she were going to faint.

"Who's going to chaperone her?" Keelie asked, equally horrified. "Knot?"

"Your *cat*?" Laurie had a *can this get any worse?* look on her face.

"Me," answered a voice Keelie hadn't heard in weeks.

"I got in late last night, and got recruited by Sir Davey to babysit some kid first thing this morning."

Keelie spun around and, to her delight, found herself face to face with her friend Raven. Shrieking with glee, she ran to hug her.

Raven was dressed in full gothic Renaissance couture, like a Goth fairy queen. She wore a shiny vinyl bodice, which emphasized her trim figure and looked sleek against the soft white of her off-the-shoulder blouse. Her ruffled black skirt cascaded down into red-trimmed scalloped edges, which were pulled up on one side and tucked into the skirt's waistband to show off her black-edged, white-ruffled petticoat and velvety black-suede boots.

Raven laughed, hugging Keelie tightly to keep her from jumping up and down. "Stop. Stop. Stop. I'm glad to see you, too. But I have to tell you, I'm not one bit happy about being here. My God. Who gets up this early in the morning?" Raven pressed her hand to her head as if she suffered from a hangover. She took her hand away and batted her eyelashes, making it obvious that she was just fooling around. She grinned at Laurie. "And you must be the famous Laurie. I've heard a lot about you."

"Nice to meet you, I think." Laurie looked to Keelie for help.

"I heard you girls snuck out to Rivendell. I'm impressed. But you know the party doesn't start without me." Raven snapped her fingers and struck a pose.

Dad cleared his throat. "Let's not encourage them."

Raven nodded as if in agreement. "Of course, Zeke." She winked at Keelie. "But you owe me."

Keelie was suddenly in heaven. The two girls she cared

for most in the world, and they were right here with her. She would love to go to the Faire, and just be carefree and have a great time. But she couldn't. She had a job, and she had a unicorn to save, not to mention the trees.

Dad furrowed his eyebrows. "Right. Girls, I have eyes and ears all around the Faire—and in the meadow." He said this while staring directly at Laurie, who seemed oblivious to Dad's *this means you* gaze because she was too busy gawking at Raven. He gave Keelie a stern look, then gave up and headed toward the parking lot.

"Be careful, Dad." He'd told her to trust no one, and she wanted to give him the same warning. The meeting with Lord Niriel sounded unfriendly.

He waved. "I will."

Laurie didn't notice that he'd left. Her eyes were still glued on Raven. "I love your outfit, Raven. Where did you get it?"

"I bought this at the Francesca booth by the front gates," Raven replied. "It's from their Dark Ages collection. You have to be a real badass to pull off the look. Sorry, babe, you're too blonde to do that."

Laurie gasped. "I can wear black."

"Tell you what, we'll hit Francesca's and see what works for you."

"What? You're going shopping without me?" Keelie would be slaving away while her two best friends went shopping together. They were going to need her to be a referee, especially at the Francesca booth. Totally unfair.

"It sucks that you have to go to work." Raven looked sympathetic. "But welcome to the real world."

"I'll miss you." It didn't look like Laurie really meant it, but even the fake sympathy made Keelie feel a little better.

"Yeah, I'll be busy with whatever kind of torture the Faire dragon has for me today."

Raven grinned at her. "Don't pout. You have to work because you went shopping first, right? I heard about your designer boots. What possessed you? You have your mom's boots and the ones my mom gave you at the High Mountain Rennie. It wasn't like you needed another pair."

"I don't know." Keelie shook her head. "They were so gorgeous that I couldn't resist."

Laurie's excitement grew. "You bought designer boots here? Do they have any left? Where?"

"In the Faire." Keelie wondered if she could keep Laurie from finding out about Lady Annie's. Laurie'd just whip out her credit card, and then she'd have a pair, too.

"Sometimes impulse buys come back to bite you in the ass, don't they?" Raven said, grinning. Then, as if they'd exhausted the subject of Keelie's boots and job problem, she turned to Laurie. "Hey, do you belly dance?"

"No, but I've always wanted to learn."

"Good, I can introduce you to Rhiannon Rose. I really don't want to spend the day just shopping. Maybe Rhiannon can give you some belly dancing lessons or something."

Keelie glowered. Laurie had never said anything about wanting to learn how to belly dance when they were at Baywood together. Besides, belly dancing was what she and Raven did together. Not Laurie and Raven. Just thinking of their names together made her feel miserable.

"Rhiannon is performing later at the Fletcher's Row stage, and she's totally awesome. You'll love her." Raven noticed the glare Keelie was aiming at her and grinned even more widely. "Don't be a baby, Keelie. We'll stop by to see you wherever you're working. Once you've paid for your boots, you can have fun, too. I have to work and pay for my own stuff. Mom says it builds character."

Laurie shrugged. "My mom isn't into building character; she just gives me her credit cards."

"Oh, come on, California, around here characters are just assumed personas. Maybe you can buy one." Raven swept her hand toward the Faire, its colorful flags and pointed tower tops visible through the trees. "And if you give me any grief, I'll arrange for you to be a volunteer at the Grime and Slime Show."

Laurie looked aghast. "I don't know what that is, but it sounds awful."

The RV's door opened and Sir Davey stepped down, holding onto the door for balance. "Still here? Oh, it's Raven come for breakfast."

"Hi, Sir Davey. Got any coffee? If I don't have some soon, I'll be crankier than Finch."

"Speaking of Finch, I came out to tell Keelie that it's time to get to Admin." Davey vanished into the RV again.

Keelie knew she needed to concentrate on working off the cost of her boots. She couldn't lose another job, no matter how jealous she was of Raven and Laurie's friendship. Time to face the dragon.

nineteen

The Admin building was bursting with activity. Keelie pushed past the people coming and going in the narrow, carpeted hall leading to the costume fitting room. Finch's office was empty, but Keelie heard her voice echoing above the din. A man was yelling back. The smell of pickle brine permeated the hall.

Keelie entered the fitting room, then stopped, astonished. It was the man who had made Lulu so furious last week. He was a walking fashion disaster. Someone should be arrested for letting him wear his revealing hose so tight, not to mention the hideous green poet's shirt. He was suicidal, too. He was right in Finch's face, gesticulating dramatically.

"I need help," he yelled. He looked like a tall leprechaun with his ruddy complexion, strawberry blond hair, and big bushy mustache. "My second Dilly in two weeks, and she's sick. I can't have a barfing Dilly. I need help, I tell you!"

He needed help with his costume. Or better yet, he needed to buy the *Buns of Steel* DVD, because his tights exposed his disgusting cottage-cheese butt dimples. Keelie turned away before she got totally grossed out. The Renaissance fashion police should outlaw hose and codpieces.

She forgot about him when she saw Lord Niriel at the far end of the room. He must be here to talk with Finch about the jousters. But he was leaning comfortably against the wall, ignoring the drama, his attention on the clipboard in his hands. Even in the daylight Lord Niriel looked young, almost as young as Sean. All of the elves had that ageless quality, but he blended into the human world even more easily than Dad.

He wore a polo shirt tucked into jeans. His long, sandy brown hair was tied back with a brown ribbon, but loose enough to cover his elven ears. He had a businesslike, efficient air about him, nothing like his son's blond, relaxed-surfer look.

Keelie blushed when his gaze caught hers, and she turned away when his glance turned to questioning scrutiny. She needed to talk to him about Sean's missing letters, but she wouldn't be able to once Finch saw her. Lord Niriel was about to find out that she was the Jill-of-the-Faire, and he'd probably overhear whatever Finch had in store for her. What if Elia had already told him about her job fiascoes? This would be a great time to be anywhere else.

Finch caught sight of her and motioned with her hand.

"Heartwood, over here." She was still almost nose-to-nose with the oversized leprechaun—who was having a conversation with himself because Finch wasn't listening to him.

Warning shivered through Keelie's body as she looked from Finch to the green nightmare. No. Life couldn't be that cruel. Her luck couldn't be that bad.

"Keelie, this is Sir Brine of Cucumberton. You may be just the person that he needs to play his assistant, Dilly of the Dale."

Brine. The green suddenly made sense, and she remembered the path strewn with mutilated pickles and the poor girl pushing the cart after him. The Pickle Man. Oh God, she was going to work for the Pickle Man. Her feet seemed frozen to the hardwood floor.

She dreaded the reaction if Raven and Laurie saw her working with Sir Brine. At least neither of them had witnessed the Plumpkin fiasco or the Steak-on-a-Stake disaster. Laurie would go back to school and tell all of their friends at Baywood Academy that Keelie had a job as a pickle vendor. How humiliating. Finch pursed her lips and rubbed her hand against her temple as Sir Brine of Cucumberton talked. Maybe Plumpkin would come out of retirement.

Then Finch pointed to Keelie, and the Pickle Man turned toward her. He looked her up and down, then sneered and shook his head. "I need a strong worker. This skinny kid can't push the cart."

Keelie sighed with relief. Okay, give the guy some credit. He knew by looking at her that they wouldn't work well together.

Finch lifted her hands as if to say "that's it, take her or leave her."

Lord Niriel's eyes went from Finch to the Pickle Man to Keelie. She smiled weakly at him.

Sir Brine placed his hands on his hips and tapped his foot, eyes squinting as he checked her out. Then he nodded.

No, don't nod, Keelie thought. Frown and look for someone else.

Finch grinned widely, certain that she'd won the argument. She always did.

Oh God. Maybe they'd give her a mask to wear.

Lord Niriel walked over to her. "If your proclivity toward bad luck with Ren Faire jobs runs its course with the Pickle Man today, then come see me. Since you can charm a special kind of horse, then you can no doubt charm the regular horses. You'd make a great squire."

Keelie didn't know whether to be shocked, relieved, or honored. Absolutely everyone at the Faire must have heard about her disastrous job record, but now an elven lord, her boyfriend's father, had offered her a job in the jousting company. But before she could answer him he walked away, humming and studying his clipboard as if he'd forgotten she was there.

Finch snapped fingers in front of her face. "Pay attention, Heartwood. Sir Brine of Cucumberton says you'll do. Thank God, if I had to listen to him drone on and on for another second, then I was going to shove a cucumber in his mouth just to shut him up."

Keelie had a sour feeling in her stomach. Something bad was going to happen. "Are you sure? I mean after the Steak-on-a-Stake incident, do you really want me working with food?"

Finch harrumphed. "Are you kidding me? With everyone

getting sick, I'm just glad to have some warm bodies to fill some of the posts. Be glad you're not jousting. You'll love this job. You're going to be pushing the pickle cart as Sir Brine does his song and dance. Then he'll collect the money and you just serve the pickles to the paying customers. It should be all kosher." Finch chuckled at her stupid joke. "By the way, your dad said he talked to your cat. He understands about the Faire restrictions now, and we shouldn't have any more kitty trouble."

See, even Finch knew about Dad talking to Knot, not *at* Knot.

Sir Brine of Cucumberton arched an eyebrow, "Your father talks to your cat?"

"Long story." Keelie shrugged.

He made a sweeping motion with his hand. "Hurry up and get your costume. The gates open in thirty minutes. I hope you're good at improv, Heartwood. Or should I say, Dilly?" He laughed, a weird little chortle.

Thirty minutes later, Mona the costumer had stuffed Keelie into a stained peasant shirt and green, calf-length, broadcloth pants. Keelie stared wistfully at the Plumpkin head, which now lay abandoned and forlorn next to the unicorn head. She realized that she was nostalgic only because she wasn't close enough to smell it.

The pickle cart was parked outside. It was a heavy, tipped-over pickle barrel, with two big green wheels on each side and long wooden handles that seemed to be made so that a donkey or pony could pull it. Sir Brine trotted ahead, and Keelie grabbed the handles and pushed the heavy cart down the graveled path after him. Sir Brine of Cucumberton sang, "Do you know the Pickle Man, the Pickle Man, the Pickle Man? Do you know the Pickle Man, who walks down Nottingham Lane?"

Even though Sir Brine had a good baritone voice, his stupid pickle song was already getting on her nerves. Worse, now that she was outside, Keelie sensed that something was different; something was wrong. It wasn't the Dread, but something akin to it that tainted the morning. She couldn't put her finger on it, but her skin tingled and her head ached like it did in the aftermath of too much tree magic. Her vision was distorted, and the air was hazy as if a thick fog of discord blanketed the Faire.

Keelie thought she must be the only person who could feel the weirdness, because they sold dozens of pickles. People seemed to love Sir Brine. She wondered if they actually ate the pickles or only bought them because they thought the vendor was funny.

They'd made their way in a big circle, from the front gates to the jousting ring and back down Enchanted Lane. They were almost at the Heartwood shop when she saw it was closed. Dad must still be at the lodge. It was then that Keelie realized that something was very different about the landscape.

"Dilly, hurry it up. I want to break for lunch after we do this bit." He broke into his song for what seemed like the one-thousandth time.

Keelie rolled her eyes and bent over to push the cart over the acorn-strewn path.

"Watch out, lass, you're going to run into that tree." The pickle man tsked and grabbed the front of the cart to pull it to one side.

Keelie stopped pushing and the cart rolled back toward

her, hitting her hip. She barely felt the jolt, her attention fixed on the tall, slender oak in the path. A tree where one had not been this morning. One of the oaks from across the lane had moved, and was now standing between Dad's booth and Lulu's puppet shop.

She looked around at the shops. No one seemed to notice the tree. She put a hand out toward the bark, then pulled it back and instead opened herself to the forest. *Anger.* She was surprised to feel strong animosity flow to her, along with a really icky feeling. Sickness. Even these trees were sick. Queasiness made her knees weak. As she felt wildly for the pink quartz that would neutralize the effect of the tree magic, she realized that her costume didn't have pockets. Her quartz was back at Admin in her jeans pocket. She felt wide-open, exposed to the magic around her. She was going to have to find a way to get away from Sir Brine and return to Admin.

Sir Brine looked around. "We may as well set up here for a while."

"Stay here?" If Laurie and Raven went to Janice's herb shop they'd have to walk right past her.

"Surely. We move up and down the lanes, then stop for a while. We can stay here about twenty minutes and see how business is." He pushed the cart to the side of the path and started to sing again.

They were in front of Lulu's building. Lulu had company, a stern-looking man in wizard's robes she'd seen watching Lulu by the front gates on opening day. He sat in a chair behind the counter as Lulu glumly waved at the children passing by her shop. Her costume was crumpled and her wings frumpled, hanging limply down her back as if they'd been left in the rain. She picked up a bottle wrapped in a brown paper bag and swigged from it.

Lulu then noticed the cart, and came to her shop door. She hadn't seen Keelie yet. She sneered at Sir Brine. "Get out of here, and sell your pickles somewhere else, you green jerk."

Sir Brine glared at her. He placed his hands on his hips and sang out, "Old Mother Puppet went to the cupboard, expecting to find Elianard, but when she got there, she found it was bare, and now she's all alone."

"Aw, shut up." Lulu chugged whatever was in her brown bottle.

Keelie couldn't believe that Elianard's rejection of Lulu's home-baked goods had broken her heart. She didn't think that a witch who preyed on children's imaginations could have a heart.

A crowd of Faire goers gathered round and watched, laughing as if the vendors' battle was part of the show. Sir Brine smiled and began his Pickle Man song. He moved his hands as if he were directing an orchestra, then turned to Keelie. "Okay, Dilly join in on the chorus. 'Yes, I know the Pickle Man, the Pickle Man, the Pickle Man, who walks down Enchanted Lane.'"

Keelie stared at him with her arms crossed over her chest. She was not going to sing.

He smiled at her and again animatedly moved his arms in big gestures. "Sing it, Dilly." No way she would sing. Not her. Not happening. She pointed to her ear and shook her head, miming that she was deaf.

He arched an eyebrow, placed his hands on his hips, and tapped his foot. Keelie grinned at him, then reached into the pickle barrel with her large silver tongs and removed a huge, warty green pickle. The tangy smell of vinegar and spices filled the air. Maybe if they displayed the product she could divert attention from Sir Brine and his song and dance.

A little curly-headed girl, dressed in a pink fairy outfit, pointed at her with a chubby finger. "Ickle."

Aw, how cute!

The girl's mom searched her purse for money. "She loves pickles. How much?"

Keelie pointed to the wooden market pickle sign that had "$1.00" carved into it. She wanted to ask how old the little girl was, but she had to stay in character.

The mother gave Keelie a dollar, and Keelie handed a napkin-wrapped pickle to the little girl. From the corner of her eye, she saw three of the oak trees across from Heartwood lift their branches in perfect synchronization, as if they were taking stage directions from someone nearby.

The little girl's face scrunched up as she stared at the trees, and Keelie followed her gaze. The bark on the tree trunks had formed faces. Dark green eyes blinked from the bark. Uh oh. This was not normal tree behavior, even for a unicorn's forest. She had to contact Dad before more people noticed.

The little white cat ran across the lane and onto the steps of the Heartwood booth. Keelie wondered if Knot was close by, too. He could get a message to Dad. Better yet, she could do it herself. She closed her eyes and opened her mind to the trees, searching for that green sensation, like sap running through her veins. For a second it was there, then it quickly cut off and she was queasy. She staggered and grabbed for the cart to steady herself. Shocked, she realized that the oaks had blocked her telepathic attempt to communicate with them. The aspen heart was cold against her skin.

The oaks swayed to and fro as if a strong wind waltzed through their canopies, the hiss of their leaves as loud as if a storm was approaching. People were looking up, searching the sky for clouds. Keelie looked up, too, but she surveyed the uppermost treetops for any sign of the trouble-making *bhata*. She closed her eyes, opening herself to the trees once more. Still, the aspen heart was cold, and this time the nausea that followed brought her to her knees. She sensed hostility. The trees didn't want her around.

A single lovely note rang through the air, and Elia stepped into a beam of sunlight in the middle of Enchanted Lane. She strummed her harp and sang,

"Here's the song of the Pickle Girl, the biggest loser in the world. By day she smells of pickle juice, beware when she is on the loose—"

It was just Elia. Keelie could handle her, although the elf girl was badly in need of a poetry intervention. She had some nerve, calling Keelie a loser when her rhymes were so awful.

As Elia neared, the little girl in the fairy outfit dropped her pickle and hid her face in her mom's blue-jean-covered leg.

Sir Brine walked over and picked up the discarded pickle, now dusty. "Dilly, give this fairy princess another one."

Elia sauntered closer to the pickle cart and played another chord on her harp strings. The hairs on Keelie's neck stood up.

The little girl kept her arms tightly wrapped around her

mother's leg. Keelie noticed that Elia's gaze was focused on the child. Behind them the trees swayed together in the same direction, like choreographed woodland dancers.

Instinctively, Keelie ran to stand in front of the little girl and her mother as all of the oaks acted like living slingshots, sending a barrage of acorns flying toward them. She extended her hand, palm outward, and visualized a shield of green magic to protect them. Tingles of magic flowed through her as her talisman, the heart of the aspen queen, grew warm.

Sir Brine's voice rose over the crowd. "Everyone stay calm; it's just the wind blowing."

Keelie telepathically summoned Tavak. *I need your help.* She allowed the tree to see through her eyes, as if she were a video camera.

Tavak answered immediately. *Tree Shepherdess, their fear has made them wild.*

Fear of what?

Tavak's answer was muffled; then he went silent. Keelie wondered what was going on around here.

A scream erupted behind her. She turned, fearing the mom and little girl had been hurt, but it was Lulu who had screamed. Hundreds of acorns covered the entrance of her shop. Acorns were rolling down the shop roof and red welts covered her face where she'd been pummeled by the nutty projectiles. The wizard dude, who'd been keeping watch over her, glowered at Lulu as if the acorn blizzard were her fault.

The oak that stood between Heartwood and Lulu's shop seemed to become more alive, more animated. A face formed from the knots in its trunk. Keelie stared, fascinated. She'd seen a tree's face before, in the meadows of the High

Mountain Faire, but she'd considered Hrok her friend. This tree was a stranger.

The little girl gasped and pointed at the closed eyes, nose and lips that had formed on the bark. The mom looked, but apparently didn't see anything. Keelie watched the girl, wondering what she could do to lessen her fear.

Keelie waved to get the mother's attention. "Ma'am? There's a petting zoo over there with sheep, chickens, and ponies." She pointed at the sign that marked the way to the zoo.

"You can talk," the child said accusingly.

Keelie placed her index finger against her lip and winked.

The little girl giggled.

We're with you, Tree Shepherdess. Tavak spoke again in her head. *Touch the oak. Lord Einhorn will use his magic to help you contact him.*

She shivered and wondered where he was, wishing that he didn't trust her. That's what Dad was here for. She looked around, but saw only the busy Faire and the avid faces of the crowd around them. The unicorn was so sick that his guard might be down. If he came out of the forest, maybe the child would see it, as well as all the other innocents here. If only Dad were here. He'd want to know that Einhorn wanted to talk to her.

The little white stray meowed at her feet. Keelie bent down, picked it up and placed it on the railing that bordered one side of the Heartwood booth. "Silly kitty. You could get hurt. Go back to the camper and stay with Knot."

She reached out to the oak tree and it opened to her, allowing their thoughts to touch. She didn't need the unicorn to talk to a tree, especially this poor oak. It was hurting. She stretched out a hand and brushed its rough bark. Pain filled her mind. Reeling, she pitched forward, bringing both hands into full contact with the tree as she tried to catch herself. She cried out as the oak's pain coursed through her. Falling to her knees, she tried to shake her thoughts free from the tree's. But she was trapped.

twenty

In the green darkness, Keelie's mind was trapped in the tree's mind, her movements tree-slow. She throbbed with pain and thirst and despair. She felt Lord Einhorn, and saw that he was frail and almost transparent. He'd given up everything for the forest. He stood between it and the dark evil that threatened them all.

Keelie was the tree. Voices surround her, like the rustling of leaves before a storm. She had to find the Tree Shepherd, even if he did not heed their calls. The Tree Shepherd's child was too young, although she had deep roots. As if she were the tree, she felt its roots shift. Where her left leg would be was a twist of roots that reached, thick and deep, into the nourishing earth. Her mind was one with the tree. She tugged, and the root moved again. She pulled harder now, and it pulled out of the ground and snaked across the top of the earth. The pain was excruciating.

Keelie tried once more to separate herself from the tree as it pushed its roots further out, and the tips and rootlets sought the soil and sank deep again. Her canopy moved forward, then back again. As if she were the tree, she thrust out her branches for balance, and an abandoned robin's nest broke free of her shoulder and fell, turning over and over to splinter on the ground below. Around her roots the humans swarmed, running back and forth. She saw herself at the base of the tree.

Bruk, the tree's name was Bruk, and she was a sapling of the mighty Silak of the ancient place, the untouched forest that felt no pain except the sky fire that sometimes came before the rain.

"Dilly! Aw, lass, are you sick, too?" She heard the words and understood them, but had no voice to answer.

She was back. Keelie opened her eyes. She was lying in the middle of the dirt path. Sir Brine stood over her, a paper-wrapped pickle in his fist and a worried expression on his face.

"Are you back with us? I think you knocked your noggin on the tree." He grinned nervously. "Don't want you to get sick, girlie."

Over his shoulder she saw Bruk the tree. The oak had become more lifelike, more human in appearance. It was looking down at her, and sitting on a massive branch by its eyes was the white cat, chin pointed up and eyes slit shut as if he was smelling the air. The face in the oak blinked, then the eyes, nose, and mouth formed back into knots. The cat shook itself, then seemed to collapse, draping itself onto the branch. The scent of loamy earth and deep forests on a cool spring day surrounded her, as did a sense of calm. The oak tree was quiet; asleep and pain-free.

Keelie sighed with relief. The cat looked down at her and meowed piteously.

Sir Brine rubbed his head. "I could have sworn I saw a face in that tree. What is the Faire administration thinking? We pay more and more to run our businesses, and they're spending the money on fancy animatronics instead of putting in a decent bathhouse."

Keelie ignored his rant, but she couldn't ignore the fact that he'd seen the tree. Where was Dad? She couldn't handle all this by herself. On top of everything else, how was she going to get that idiot cat out of the oak? Not that she had to. The first thing was to get some aspirin, because her head was throbbing. Keelie got up and dusted off her pickle costume. She should never have touched the tree without the rose quartz. She knew that. Being inside a tree was an all-new experience, though.

"Back to work, Dilly."

Sir Brine was working it, and Keelie dutifully handed out pickles to buyers. Elia walked up, her harp in one hand, and placed her other hand on the barrel lid as if to keep Keelie from getting another pickle. Her long golden hair twisted in bright curls, cascading down to her little waist. She wore a long, fitted gown with wide, sweeping oversleeves in blue, and tight, gold-embroidered green sleeves underneath. The green sleeves were loosely laced over a fluffy, thin white cloth. A low leather belt was clasped around her waist, worked all around with oak leaves and acorns. It hurt Keelie that Elia was so beautiful on the outside and so hideous inside.

As if to prove her point, the elf girl leaned forward and hissed, "Tell me where the unicorn is, and I won't hurt the little human girl."

Keelie glanced around. The little girl and her mother had not gone to the zoo yet. They were coming down the steps of Lulu's shop. Lulu seemed pathetically happy to see them.

Keelie removed Elia's hand, then lifted the lid and reached in and grabbed a pickle. "I thought elves weren't supposed to use magic in front of humans."

"We're not, but I need to know where the unicorn is. If you don't tell me, then I'm going to follow that little girl to the petting zoo, and I will make sure that all the animals hurt her because you were nice to her. All kinds of odd things are happening at the Faire today, are they not?" Elia plinked a harp string for added emphasis and smiled insincerely.

Keelie matched her fake grin as she wrapped the pickle in wax paper. "I don't know where the unicorn is."

"He is here. I can sense him. And he summoned you last night."

Keelie remembered Dad's warning to not discuss the unicorn. No worries there. "Were you hoping that he would come to you, Elia, and he didn't? Maybe you scared him away."

"So amusing. But if you don't get the unicorn here right now, then I'm going to follow through on my threat. Don't forget I cursed your bird, and I can curse that ugly little human pig."

Keelie slammed the barrel lid down on Elia's fingers. The elf girl yelled and snatched her hand back, dropping her harp. She glared at Keelie. "That hurt!"

Keelie grabbed the harp and held it close to her chest.

"Get your filthy human hands off my harp," Elia screamed.

Sir Brine watched them, wide-eyed, from a crowd of Faire goers that had gathered thinking the girls were putting on a show.

Not missing a beat, Elia cradled her hand against her chest as if she were hurt. Her voice rose, plaintive, over the crowd. "I have to find Prince John, and I will see that this wicked pickle peddler is punished. Now give me back my harp, you villainous wretch."

Keelie shrugged, pointed to her ear, and shook her head.

Elia stomped her foot on the ground and shrieked. "Get over the lame act. You can talk. I want my harp back."

"Dilly, you must return the harp to Princess Eleanor." Sir Brine grabbed one end of the harp as Keelie clung to the other. His voice lowered to a hiss. "You idiot. What do you think you're doing?"

For a few seconds, a tug of war continued between Keelie and Sir Brine, while Elia held up her hurt hand and pretended to cry.

"What is this?" Little John's familiar voice boomed over the clearing. He wrapped his burly arm around Elia, who glowered at him. Then she smiled, as an evil idea had popped into her brain.

"Oh, Little John, save my harp," she squeaked like a maiden in distress. "I was attacked by this beastly pickle peasant, and she's stolen my harp."

Little John's face reddened, and his eyes narrowed as he shot Keelie and Sir Brine a very nasty look.

Keelie had seen that overzealous look before. Here was someone who was still Little John after the Faire was closed and the mundanes had gone home.

Sir Brine released his end of the harp and pointed at Keelie. "She stole it from Lady Eleanor."

What a wuss!

Little John released Elia and held his staff before him. The crowd had grown, and now they cheered. "Little John. Little John. Little John."

He punched a fist into the air, then turned on Keelie. "Peasant, are you going to give Lady Eleanor her harp back, or am I going to have to persuade you?" He twirled his staff as if he were a member of the Sherwood Marching Band. And he was looking straight at Keelie.

Yup. Somebody hadn't taken his medication this morning and had slipped back into his own little make-believe medieval world. It wasn't worth a broken arm.

Keelie shoved the harp toward a smirking Elia, who hissed "round-eared peasant." She took her harp and made a big show of examining it for damage, before tossing her curls and leaving in a swirl of skirts.

Victorious, the rogue and delusional Merry Man held his staff up and the crowd cheered.

Little John made a "V" with two fingers and pointed toward his eyes, and then at Keelie. He marched away, accompanied by his growing band of admirers. A dark figure peeled away from the crowd and walked toward them, applauding enthusiastically. It was Raven. She laughed as she turned to watch Little John's parade go around a corner, then whirled back to face Keelie and Sir Brine.

"And to think that just weeks ago we could hardly get you into a costume. You've gotten to be quite the drama queen."

Behind Raven was someone in a Francesca costume. If Keelie hadn't been green on the outside before, she surely was now. Laurie wore a scrumptious Francesca gown in green and gold brocade with long flowing sleeves. The front skirt panel was printed with rich, deep golden leaves against a green fabric background, and she had a garland of matching flowers in her hair with ribbons flowing down the back.

Keelie groaned inwardly and steeled herself for a litany of pickle comments. She waited for them to start rolling off Laurie's tongue.

Instead, Laurie did a twirl and ta-da stance. Keelie wanted to throw a pickle at her. Let's see how she liked a little vinegar with her brand new outfit. But she pasted a smile on, just like Mom used to do when she ran into a client she didn't want to talk to outside of the office, and choked the words out. "That's really gorgeous."

"Isn't it? It's so much fun shopping with Laurie. She doesn't even look at the price tags." Raven rolled her eyes. "We're on our way to the braiding booth. Woo hoo!"

Dad was really, really, really going to owe Raven big time.

Laurie grinned. "Where are you going to be? I want to show you my hair after I've had it done."

Keelie looked at Sir Brine, who beamed at Laurie. "We'll be by the Maypole, mistress, and I'll have a big pickle for you."

Gross. She wondered if Finch knew that Sir Brine was a perv.

Laurie clapped a hand over her mouth, either to keep from gagging or laughing. Before Keelie could find out which, Lady Annie stepped outside her booth and hung more of her gorgeous boots on display hooks.

Laurie's eyes widened. "Oh. My. God. Look at those cosmic-stellar boots. I've got to have a pair."

Keelie's heart dropped down to her toes. Laurie was already crossing the lane to Lady Annie's. Life just wasn't fair.

Sir Brine clapped a hand on her shoulder and shouted, "Move it, Dilly. We need to get to the Maypole."

Raven leaned closer to Keelie. "I saw the face in the oak. There's some bad vibes going on around here. A little while ago, the Bedlam Barrel ride went berserk. It took fifteen Faire workers to stop it, when normally it only takes two."

"It's more than bad vibes. We'll talk later."

"Dilly, move it," Sir Brine yelled, then turned his cry into a pickle yodel.

"Dilly?" Raven asked.

Trying to maintain some of her tattered dignity, Keelie lifted up the handles of the wheelbarrow. "I have pickles to sell." At least the boots had kept Laurie from commenting on her job, but that would come, she was certain. Laurie didn't miss a thing.

She turned the cart around, anxious to get to the Maypole before Elia had a chance to possibly follow through on her threat against the little girl. Elia had seemed obnoxious, but not evil.

"Looks like you're going to be pickle splatter, kid. He's going to use the catapult." Lulu was on her porch. She took a swig from her bottle, then kicked acorns from the top step. "You're that Heartwood brat that played Plumpkin. I've had the worst luck since I moved next door to your booth; it's like a never-ending psycho circus around here. I even saw your cat paw a number into a cell phone and meow into it the other day." She snorted and took another long pull.

Knot on a cell phone. Even Keelie had trouble believing that one. Maybe a certain puppet maker had been hitting the mead for a touch too long.

Keelie hoped Dad would get back from the meeting soon. She wondered how much he'd sensed of the tree's pain. Bruk had been struggling to get to him, and knew that the unicorn was sick. They had a lot to talk about, and if Finch found the shop unattended, her skull would split open and the inner fire-breathing dragon would explode from her head.

The white cat sat on the steps to the booth.

"Hey, bad thing. How did you get out of the tree?"

It stared at her intently, and for a moment Keelie saw an iridescent gleam in its fur. When she blinked, he looked like an ordinary white cat. This is what happened when you stayed out all night chasing unicorns—you started seeing things that weren't really there. Or maybe one of the Rennies had put glitter lotion on the poor cat's fur.

"Dilly, come along." Sir Brine was way ahead of her.

Keelie pushed the barrel, and he began singing. "Do you know the Pickle Man, the Pickle Man, the Pickle Man. Do you know the Pickle Man, skipping down Pottery Row?"

If Sir Brine thought she was going to sing after that incident with Elia, forget it. She had touched Elia's harp, had held it in her hand. Now that the elf girl had it back, there was no telling what she would do, which meant more work for Keelie.

She was beginning to see the tree shepherding tasks as her own work. Not only did it entail keeping the trees in line, and in balance, but also protecting them from harm—including from humans. Strange that she'd started thinking of people as "humans."

She thought of Bruk, the Oaken Prince. He'd been hurting so much, and still he'd struggled to reach Heartwood. Keelie touched the aspen heart, which pulsed warm on her chest—a tangible sign of her heritage. She quickly let go of it as the cart, off-balance, pivoted to one side.

"Dilly, hurry up." Sir Brine's shout echoed embarrassingly from the faux stucco of the nearby buildings. Sweat dripped down Keelie's back. People stopped and looked at her as she pushed the heavy cart uphill. She checked out the trees as she huffed up the path. The conifers that lined the wide, sloped track were calmer than the oaks by Heartwood had been. Her talisman was still warm against her skin, reassuring her that she was connected to the magic. Keelie hadn't liked having her mental link to the forest blocked by the oaks on Enchanted Lane. She had to get back to Heartwood as soon as possible, to check on the trees and to make sure Dad had returned from the lodge. She glanced back and saw Raven disappear into Lady Annie's, where Laurie probably was waving her credit card. Life sucked.

twenty-one

Keelie caught up to Sir Brine at the intersection of Lincoln Green and Sherwood and stopped, panting. She watched as he twirled the curlicued end of his huge mustache between his fingers and bowed to the Faire patrons as they passed by, particularly the women in low-cut summery tops. He glanced at Keelie. "Not speaking, huh? Good, you're staying in character. You won't give me any grief then."

What she wanted to do was let the stupid pickle cart roll back down the hill, and then watch Brine push it back up. He needed the workout.

They'd passed the jousting field, the food court, and the petting zoo, and were now at the back of the Faire in an area where there were lots of artisans' booths. Sir Brine led Keelie to a very small booth, nothing more than a converted wooden barrel. A wooden sign, which was swinging from a two-by-four nailed to the barrel's side, was carved with a dancing pickle that had big, round, googly-cartoon eyes.

"Home sweet pickle barrel." Sir Brine surveyed his minute domain. Keelie leaned closer to get a better look at what was painted around the dancing pickle's waist, then quickly backed away.

Gross. The dancing pickle wore a codpiece.

She wiped her hand across her forehead. It had to be close to noon because a lot of Faire goers were sitting in the shade eating turkey legs and drinking from paper cups that dripped with condensation. She was so thirsty. After pushing the heavy cart, standing at the pickle booth in full sun would give her heatstroke if she didn't get a break soon.

Sir Brine unlocked a door that had been cut into the barrel and pulled out a wooden contraption made of hinged and jointed wooden planks. He made a sweeping motion over it as if it were his most prized possession. "Behold the pickle chunker. I'm going to entertain the crowd, so be prepared to accept their money and give them their pickles. We always have big sales after pickle chunking." Sir Brine pulled a rubber mallet out and did some wildly exaggerated stretching exercises.

Curious folks were already gathering around. Some smiled expectantly. It couldn't be all bad if his past victims returned with a smile. Not knowing what to expect, Keelie examined the pickle chunker: a wooden box with a long lever attached to one end. A rope dangled from the end of the lever, with a small, pickle-sized platform attached to it.

"How does that work?" Keelie had never seen anything like it.

"So, now you're talking to me. It's a catapult, or sort of a catapult. I designed it myself. Might even apply for a patent for it. Couldn't you tell it's a catapult?"

"It doesn't look like any catapult I've seen in history books."

"History books! Don't they teach kids 'real' history these days?"

Keelie shrugged. In the distance she heard the jingling of bells and people singing. She thought she recognized Jared's voice.

Sir Brine lifted his head at the sound. He rubbed his hands together in manic glee. "Ah, this is going to be perfect, here comes Robin Hood and his Merry Men. Finch has screwed up the schedule and has everyone converging at the Maypole."

Jared, dressed as Robin Hood, appeared riding a white Arabian horse, with Maid Marian following on a black Andalusian with silver bells tinkling from its bridle. The girl on the horse this time was one of Elia's elf friends. The first Maid Marian must be back at the lodge, too sick to work. The Merry Men walked behind, waving at the growing crowd that jostled for the best view on both sides of the lane.

Sir Brine heaved his mallet up onto his shoulder. "I'm going to launch pickles at them. I'm hoping that Little John gets riled and comes after us. He doesn't like you, so he should get even angrier, and the crowds love it. I worked in front of Lulu's booth last weekend, launching pickles during her puppet show, and she went ballistic. I sold tons of pickles."

No way was Keelie going to get Little John "riled up." If

he showed up, she was outta here. The big man had it in for her, and he was nuts.

Sir Brine pulled a pickle, squashed at one end, from a vinegary-smelling five-gallon food service bucket and placed it on the platform. "Always check your angle—you don't want to launch the pickles over there." He pointed to his right.

Keelie peeked around the pickle barrel at The Heart of Glass. A stained glass shop. Glass fairies, glass dragons, and other fantastical glass creatures twinkled with fairytale splendor from hooks hanging from the shop's eaves. Her eyes were drawn to the shop's centerpiece, a beautiful stained glass window of a unicorn. Silver solder outlined the milky-white glass that formed the unicorn's body, and the iridescent glass of the mane and the horn glittered as if it had been dipped in starlight. A man with spiky, bleached-blond hair sat on a stool behind a wooden counter, watching for potential customers.

This was not good. Not good at all. Foreboding tingled over Keelie's skin, settling at the base of her neck.

"Hear ye, hear ye," Sir Brine shouted in a deep, booming voice. A small crowd of teenagers in jeans and T-shirts gathered. If Keelie still attended Baywood Academy, she would have classified them as geeks and wouldn't have talked to them. Now she thought they looked interesting.

Robin Hood dismounted and walked over to Maid Marian's mount. He held up his gloved hands, offering to help her dismount. She was riding sidesaddle, so with a little maneuvering of her right leg, she jumped into Robin Hood's arms, her skirts swirling around them romantically. She looked thrilled. Keelie would have been too, if she'd been offered the job. Why did she get stuck as the Pickle Girl?

If Sean played Robin Hood, Keelie could be his Maid Marian, and together they would ride through the Faire enjoying the adulation of the crowd. A picture of Knot riding on the back of Keelie's horse popped into her mind, intruding on her fantasy.

"Dilly, pay attention!" She startled at Sir Brine's shout. Maybe Little John would go after Brine.

Over at the Maypole, the girls who played Renaissance fairies in wispy, colorful costumes and sparkly makeup danced in and around each another, unraveling yards of colorful ribbons wrapped around the pole. That looked like a fun job.

Keelie clacked the pickle tongs in time to the music and gazed through her eyelashes at Brine. He was lining his pickle projectiles in a neat row next to the catapult. This was going to end badly.

Parents congregated around the perimeter of the Maypole. Little children were getting excited. Then the flute and drum of the Maypole band were overwhelmed by pounding drums and bagpipes. It was Rigadoon, the kilted band that played toe-tapping dance tunes, on their way to one of the pubs.

The Maypole band good-naturedly played along with Rigadoon, and the fairies matched their dance to the faster beat, unraveling yards of floating ribbon as the kids clapped their hands in tune to the music. The little girl who'd seen the tree was here, hopping excitedly next to her mom. Keelie waved to them and they waved back.

One of the Rigadoons began beating on a drum with a hard-pounding rhythm. A troupe of belly dancers threaded through the crowd and gathered in the dusty circle in front of the stained glass shop, gracefully moving their hips and arms in tune to the music. The tassels on their hip belts swung back and forth. Knot would go ballistic if he saw them.

A dancer dressed in shades of red took the center spot, coins jingling merrily from her scarlet hip belt. The others stepped back as the belly dancer moved in sinuous rhythm to the music. One of the other dancers yelled, "Go, Rhiannon!"

This had to be Raven's friend, Rhiannon Rose. Raven and Laurie had planned to catch her act, but Keelie was seeing her first. She couldn't really enjoy the performance, though, with one ear cocked for the plinking of Elia's harp, not to mention the imminent charge of an angry Little John.

"We will soon disrupt these Sherwood rogues. They'll find themselves in a pickle," Sir Brine chortled as he cranked back the lever and attached the taut rope to a hook at the base. The lever arched backward. He centered the pickle on the launching platform and readied his mallet to release the rope.

Nobody paid any attention to him.

At the Maypole, the ribbons were unwound and the Renaissance fairies motioned for the children to join them. The little kids ran to pick their favorite colors, and some of the belly dancers looked on as the others danced.

Keelie leaned against a slender pine and opened her mind, searching for any word of her father. The air around her was filled with nervous energy, and she felt the *bhata* above her and in the shrubbery that surrounded the clearing. The pipes and drumming excited them. The young pine was enjoying it too. She tried to ignore their buzzing and go farther, and finally found a thread of the unicorn's magic amid the woody greenness of the great oaks. Just as she was about to dive into that cool greenness, she heard a single musical note—the plucked string of a harp.

Keelie came crashing back to herself just as Sir Brine smacked his mallet against the hook, releasing the rope. It made a "kathunk" sound, and the pickle flew in a long arc toward Robin Hood. Keelie watched, horrified. Brine was definitely nuts. The pickle soared up, up, up, followed by dozens of eyes on the ground. It reached the pinnacle of its trajectory, then stopped and spun left toward the Maypole. The crowd gasped, eyes on the wayward pickle missile. Sir Brine's mouth hung open.

Keelie cried out a warning to her little fairy princess friend, hoping she'd hear and look up. But before she could reach the little girl, the white cat shot out in front of her. The pickle changed direction again, and landed on the chest of a very well-endowed woman wearing a leather corset with matching skirt. She carried a huge wooden sword over her shoulder. She glowered menacingly at Sir Brine, who now looked on in horror.

Removing the pickle from her chest, the woman squashed it under her huge boot, then unsheathed her wooden sword and swung it over her head. "Have a taste of my claymore, varlet."

It wasn't a real, bladed weapon, but getting smacked by the claymore would be like getting bashed with a baseball bat. Sir Brine went pale and backed up, hands in front of him as if he could ward off the angry woman.

Keelie's little friend jumped up and down, her glittering wings bouncing on her back. "I saw the magic kitty."

Keelie looked around quickly, but there was no sign of Knot.

Angry parents and faux fairies glared at the Pickle Man, who'd been backed up against a tree by the swordswoman.

Little John emerged from the throng. The swordswoman grinned and bowed slightly to the Merry Man.

"Hurling pickles at little ones, Evil One?" The crowd cheered as Little John positioned his quarterstaff in his hands in a battle-ready stance. "You'd better run for your life, Brine."

Sir Brine gulped and leaped to the other side of the tree. "Don't worry about me, Dilly." He sprinted back up the path. "Stay here and guard the pickles."

Little John roared, quarterstaff held high, as he pursued Sir Brine. The woman with the claymore chased after them. Keelie felt sorry for Sir Brine, but she was grateful that they weren't after her.

The crowd clapped, and some even raised their fists in the air and shouted, "Huzzah!"

Keelie was stuck on Pickle Patrol. Near the Maypole, a sweep of blue caught her eye. Elia. The elf girl scowled at Keelie and tried to make herself blend in with the Rigadoons.

Elia had to be the one trying to disrupt the Faire, to make Keelie tell her where the unicorn was. She hadn't succeeded, but she'd almost hurt people. Keelie was sure that Sir Brine wouldn't get away without some bruises.

She made a "V" with her fingers and pointed at her eyes and then at Elia, as Little John had done earlier, hoping that the elf girl understood what it meant: *I'm watching you.*

Elia wrinkled her nose, tossed her blonde curls over her shoulder, and joined the players.

The people walking by glared at Keelie, and no one bought pickles. One little boy booed her. Keelie hadn't been the one who'd launched the pickle at the Maypole, but she was getting the blame. "For shame," she heard a woman say, and another one shook her head as if she were really disappointed in her.

At least she was still employed. Her stomach rumbled. Even though she could've helped herself to a pickle, she never wanted to eat or smell one again.

Then she spotted Laurie, who looked beautiful. Laurie's hair was intricately braided, and despite the heat, she wore a green velvet cloak over her Francesca outfit, fastened at the neck by a gold clasp shaped like an oak leaf.

Keelie grinned, just happy to see a friendly face. "Did you catch the show?"

"Most of it, from the other side." Laurie waved toward the path on the other side of the Maypole.

Raven joined them, leaning against the pickle barrel in mock exhaustion. "That's it, no more shopping for me. I want food, then we're going to find a shady spot so I can take a nap."

"The braids look beautiful. What else did you get?"

Laurie smiled as if she had a big secret, then lifted her skirts. On her feet were exact replicas of the boots Keelie had ordered. Keelie's stomach sank all the way down to the ground and suddenly she wasn't hungry anymore. Betrayal could do that to a girl.

Raven pushed at the carved pickle sign. It squeaked as it swung back and forth. "That girl can spend some cash." Her voice was carefully neutral, but Keelie could tell she was jealous.

Laurie twirled. "I love this place. Lady Annie said these boots were just like yours. She'd cut them for someone who cancelled their order, and they just fit me. Isn't that lucky? She gave me a great deal, and voila, here I am."

Keelie gripped the pickle tongs very tightly. Laurie had every right to spend her money the way she chose. "Love the boots." Her voice sounded a little creaky from the effort.

"Thanks." Laurie smiled down at her new purchase.

Raven leaned forward. "It's okay," she whispered. "Remember, when someone copies you, it's a form of flattery."

Keelie snapped the tong ends in Raven's face. "No, it's not. Not when I'm having to slave away to earn my boots, and she waltzes in and just buys them. No. No. No. I'm not flattered, Raven. I'm mad."

Raven motioned for Keelie to calm down. Laurie's eyes widened. "Did I do something wrong?"

"No, Keelie's cranky because she needs lunch." Raven looked around. "Let's get her something that doesn't smell like pickles."

Laurie's face brightened. "I'm starved, too. Let's go to that really nice tea shop. We can sit down inside."

"I can't leave the pickle cart." Keelie hoped that Laurie would keep her long skirts down. She didn't want to see the boots again.

"Is Brine coming back?" Raven looked around suspiciously. "We can just get you a sandwich or something."

"The green twerp is hiding from Little John." Keelie smiled a little at the memory of Brine running away. "I was told to guard the pickles."

Raven shook her head. "Not good to be the object of Little John's ire."

Laurie watched a group of girls go by. Two of them had intricate designs painted on the backs of their hands. "Look, there must be a henna shop. Maybe they do belly button piercing, too. You can get yours pierced, Keelie."

"I can't. Dad will kill me."

"When did not having a parent's approval stop you?" Laughter tinged Laurie's voice.

For a moment, Keelie and Laurie glared at one another. Then the angry looks faded as both of them realized how much the other had changed. An awkward silence hung in the air.

Here Laurie stood, dressed in all the things that would make her fit in at Wildewood. It was like she was searching for something, trying to find a place she belonged. But once the Faire was over, Laurie had to go home to California, while Keelie had the real thing. She remembered how Dad had tousled her curls, the way he had smiled lovingly at her before he left this morning, even though he was really mad at her. Something melted on the inside, making her very aware of how much she was loved, and how much she loved Dad.

"Hey, stained glass. Maybe I can find something for Mom before we eat. See you guys in a bit." Laurie pushed her green cape over her shoulders and made her way to the shop, drawing admiring glances on her way.

Keelie watched her go, then stared at the wood rings on the barrel. She'd touched it before: oak from the Ozarks. She touched a small round indentation on the barrel and her fingertip glowed green. Whoa! Quickly, Keelie jerked her hand back. She didn't want any branches to sprout from the wood. She lifted her head to see if anyone had seen.

Raven was moving the pickle catapult up and down. "Have you launched a pickle? It might help with sales."

"Maybe it would." Keelie cocked her head. "You don't hear a harp, do you?"

"Elia up to her tricks again? I saw the pickle turn in

midair." Raven shook her head. "Why is she allowed to get away with stuff like that? Elianard must be really powerful. I don't think she's around now, though. Try one."

Keelie was tempted.

Laurie returned. "There are some seriously beautiful pieces in that shop. Mom would love that big unicorn window, but it costs a mint."

"I saw it earlier, and you're right, it's gorgeous." At least they were speaking to each other.

"Keelie's going to launch a pickle," Raven announced to some passersby, who stared curiously.

"I'm thinking about it." Keelie looked around. No sign of Elia.

"Aw, come on, Keelie, one pickle. I want to see you do it." Laurie checked out possible targets. "How about throwing one toward the Maypole? No one's there now."

Keelie wanted to impress Laurie. Earlier in the day, she'd been fearful that Laurie would think working at the Faire was a dorky thing to do, but now Laurie seemed genuinely interested. Keelie was still in touch with her human side. She could still have fun like Laurie.

She pulled the lever back, and held it down with both hands as Raven attached the end to the hook. Then she grabbed a pickle and placed it in the catapult.

Raven jumped onto the path and called out for attention. "Hear ye, hear ye. Come witness the amazing Pickle Launch. Catch the pickle and win another! Hear ye!"

Keelie rolled her eyes. Yeah, like people would line up to field pickles out of the sky. But when she looked up, a crowd had gathered and others were coming.

She lined up the catapult, making sure the pickle would

fly away from the shops, then picked up the mallet. She swung it toward the hook. "Pickles away!"

The mallet pushed the hook aside and the catapult arm swung up, rope flapping loosely, as the pickle flew skyward. The plink of a harp string vibrated all around her, as if she were inside a huge sound wave rather than at the Faire in the middle of the day. She watched in silent horror as the pickle arced to the side—and soared like a green missile straight for the Hearts of Glass booth and the stained glass unicorn window.

On pickle impact, the window shattered. It was as if time had been suspended. Hundreds of pieces of stained glass exploded and cascaded to the ground like a sparkling blizzard of deadly shards.

"Oh. My. God!" Raven's eyes were wide.

Laurie stood open-mouthed. "It wasn't even aimed that way."

Stunned, Keelie stared, wondering what to do. The poor shop owner lay stretched out on the floor of his booth. He'd fainted from the shock of seeing his masterpiece broken by a rogue pickle-missile.

"I am so dead," Keelie whispered.

Laurie smiled brightly. "Does this mean you get to go to lunch?"

twenty-two

"I shouldn't let you live."

Finch was red-faced from screaming, and she'd almost run out of steam. Keelie's ears rang from the eighty-decibel lecture she'd endured for the last twenty minutes.

"If this was the Middle Ages, your head would be on a pike at the gates as a warning to all other bumblers and fools. You've cost the Faire hundreds of dollars."

"I thought I was going to pay for it." Keelie regretted the words as soon as she spoke them.

Finch's hair, already standing on end, seemed to poke up higher, and her complexion went from tomato to firecracker.

She loomed over Keelie like a corseted dragon, ready to spit fire.

"Insolent child! Rude puppy!" Finch was probably choking off worse expletives. She threw her clipboard on the floor and stomped her booted foot on it, cracking the pressboard away from the metal clip.

Keelie swallowed. Mom would have said that it was good to transfer aggression to an inanimate object rather than to the real person. She wondered if she'd be paying for a new clipboard as well. She faced the Faire director, hoping Finch wouldn't kill her. Did the elves have Lorems for dead tree shepherdesses? Maybe Knot would even mourn for her. Dad would date again, if he didn't have a daughter around.

Finch sat down in her desk chair and lowered her head onto the palm of her hand. She said in a very low voice, "That window alone was nine hundred and fifty dollars."

The world narrowed and got dark. *I will not faint.*

On the other side of the room, the Faire medics were tending to the owner of the Hearts of Glass shop. He was looking better—the color was coming back to his face—but he had to keep breathing into a paper bag every few minutes, especially whenever he attempted to say "window." It kept coming out as "win, win," and then he had to breathe into the bag.

"Add that to the Steak-on-a-Stake costume," Finch continued. "The dry cleaning for the Plumpkin costume, an extra large bottle of Febreze." She punched some numbers—tickey tock, tickey tock—on her desk calculator. "That's forty-five dollars, added to the nine hundred and fifty, that's a total of nine hundred and ninety-five dollars.

Let's make it an even thousand. You have until the end of the day to pay it."

Finch's bun had come down, and strands of red hair were wild and loose. She looked like Medusa. It might have been easier to face Medusa at this moment than her. She reached into her desk drawer, pulled out a silver flask, and took a sip. "What are you waiting for? Get out of here, and don't come back until you have my money."

"Will I be assigned a new job?"

"No!" Finch roared, and the veins in her forehead popped out in excruciating detail. "You are fired."

Keelie ran. Outside, Raven and Laurie were waiting for her by the path that led to the campground.

"We heard every word," Laurie said, eyes wide. "She really let you have it."

Raven's expression was strange, as if she'd just discovered that a bug was crawling up her leg. Then she gave up trying to control her expression and guffawed. "You were Plumpkin?"

"It's not funny," Keelie grumbled. She shouldn't have to pay for cleaning that noxious costume. She'd burn it for them for free. "Humiliating, yes. Hilarious, no."

Laurie draped her arm over Keelie's shoulders. "I'll give you the money. You don't have to tell your dad about the thousand you owe."

A thousand dollars. Even if she'd worked full time all summer, she wouldn't have earned that much. Keelie leaned against a maple tree. It sent waves of comfort to her. She pressed her head against its bark. "I have to tell Dad. He'll find out."

"Yeah, he will." Laurie sighed, and then her voice became very cheerful. "One good thing is, if you ever move back to L.A. you can work as a theme park character. You know, I think I would like doing that. Meeting people at a theme park, you get to see real families that are happy and ready to have fun with their kids."

Keelie remembered thinking the same thing the first time she'd ever set foot in a Renaissance Faire. All the families had looked so happy. Her mother had just died and she was all alone. Laurie might be feeling the same way.

"And one more good thing is that you don't have to wear that hideous Steak-on-a-Stake costume ever again." Laurie shuddered. "I saw the girls in them, and you should sue the Faire for inflicting that tackiness on you. Heck, the customers had to look at them. You could make it a class action lawsuit. Better yet, thank your cat for screwing up that job."

Keelie smiled, and her eyes closed as she drew comfort from the tree. Laurie was working overtime to cheer her up. "I need to get back to the shop and tell Dad before he hears it from someone else." If he was there. She also needed to make sure the oaks were still quiet, although she would have heard if they had awakened.

Nearby was a kiosk specializing in silver jewelry. Laurie was looking toward it longingly. "Do you mind if I look at this jewelry?"

"No, go ahead." Keelie sat on the ground. She leaned back and soaked up the encompassing green of the maple's comfort. Green-magic hugs.

Tree Shepherdess, do you need us?

Tavak?

Yes.

Did you sense Elia use magic today?

She has gone to join her father at the lodge. The tree was evading her question.

Let me know if she returns.

Yes, Tree Shepherdess.

How are the oaks across our shop doing?

They sleep, but not for long. You need to return soon, Tree Shepherdess.

I'm on my way.

Funny. Dad should be there by now to keep an eye on the oaks. Maybe he was busy with customers. She should have asked Tavak. She recalled the dark circles under Dad's eyes this morning. Her bad news would not help him heal.

"Doing your tree thing?"

Keelie opened her eyes. Raven had a huge smile on her face. Keelie wanted to wipe it off.

"I'm glad my life is such comedic fodder for your personal enjoyment." She looked toward the kiosk, where Laurie was paying the silversmith for a purchase. At least her friend was good for the economic health of the Faire.

Raven shook her head. "I'm sorry I didn't think to tell you about the Plumpkin suit and Vernerd. They're legendary. But by next year, you'll think it's funny and tell everyone about it."

By then, Keelie would be part of the legend, too. She decided to change the topic. "Why are you here? Whatever happened to the Perilous Pirate marketing stuff you were going to do for Captain Dandy Randy?"

"The company that bought his game went with a large marketing firm out of L.A. He had no control over who did the advertising."

Keelie frowned. "Oh. But what happened, exactly, at Doom Kitty? Janice said you loved it there."

Raven sat down on a rock near the maple. She pulled a dandelion out of the ground and twirled it around in her hand. She looked up at Keelie. "I did. I came up with this really great promo thing for this group. The lead singer, Poison Ivy, loved it. She loved it. Then, the next day, she hated it, and it was like she had it in for me. I think she cast a spell on me or something, because everything I touched went wrong from that point on. If I filed papers, the filing cabinet drawer would slide out and crash to the floor. Sharpened pencils would fly through the air like arrows. If I made coffee, everyone would get diarrhea. There was a very bad vibe in the air. And there was this cinnamon smell everywhere. I never want a cinnamon roll, ever again. I associate it with bad things. They fired me. Told me I had bad mojo, and called in a shaman to exorcise the place." Raven looked at the dandelion, surprised. She'd shredded it. She dropped it and wiped her hands on her skirt.

The smell of cinnamon. Keelie knew it well, but she didn't think humans associated it with the presence of elven magic. She looked at her friend closely. Raven's ears were in full view, with rounded tops.

Keelie leaned close and whispered, "Do you have any elf enemies?"

Raven gave her a look. "Just the usual jealous elf girl. She's not exactly an enemy, though. She's that way to everyone."

"Besides her." Keelie stopped. "Unless you think Elia is powerful enough to put a whammy on you all the way in Manhattan."

"You know that Daddy's Little Girl gets whatever she wants." Raven's eyes narrowed. "Elia. It never occurred to me. But why would she? And what makes you suspect it was elven magic?"

"The cinnamon smell. It's a giveaway. Although—" Keelie hesitated. "I didn't think humans could smell it."

Raven's eyebrows rose. "Really?"

"Yeah, think about it. Did anyone else at Doom Kitty notice the smell?"

"No," Raven said slowly. "No one. It was pretty strong, too."

"Raven, what do you know about your dad?" Keelie held her breath, unsure how her friend would react to such a personal question.

"I never met him. Mom's kind of relaxed about stuff like that. It's always been the two of us. She always said it was a guy she'd partied with when she was young. I quit asking when I was ten or so. It didn't seem important any more. Do you think my father was an elf?"

"I don't think so. But maybe something else. I wish I could ask my dad. He's got a lot of stuff going on, though, plus being sick."

"Whatever's going around is rough. Some of the shops are closing."

Laurie came over to them, holding out her hand as if she had a three-karat diamond ring on her finger instead of a plain silver band carved with stars. "Don't you love it?" Raven and Keelie both nodded.

Keelie stood up, dusting off her pickle pants. "I need to get back to Heartwood. I need to talk to Dad. Raven, could you run in and get my jeans and T-shirt? They're under the clothes rack opposite the Plumpkin head. I'm afraid to go back in."

Raven laughed. "You're not afraid of much, but I'll do it for you." She marched off, black skirts swirling as she scooted through the door.

Keelie and Laurie watched and waited. No noise, no talking. Then suddenly, an outraged screech split the air. Raven appeared in the doorway like a bat in the air, seeming to fly, with Keelie's jeans flung over her arm. "Run!"

They turned and ran full tilt down the path, laughing and dodging Faire patrons until they got to the picnic tables. They fell on the bench, out of breath, still laughing, then ducked behind them as Finch whizzed by in her very nonperiod golf cart.

"What happened?" Keelie grabbed her jeans and pulled off the pickle pants, not caring who saw her underwear. The rose quartz was a comforting lump in her jeans pocket.

"Holy shit," Raven said. "Old Finch took one look at me and she fired up her furnace. You'd think Keelie's jeans were part of her personal hoard. Did I ever tell you about when I was Jill-of-the-Faire?"

"You?" Keelie hooted. "Oh, you have to tell all."

Raven waved both hands dismissively. "I can't top you, girl. You're going down in history as the worst Jill ever."

Laurie laughed, too, but she looked wistful. No stories to share. Keelie finished changing clothes and they walked back to Heartwood, leaving the pickle outfit draped over the picnic table.

As soon as they turned down Enchanted Lane, Keelie knew something was wrong. No birds were singing. She lifted her head to study the treetops, but there were no *bhata* around. Lulu's shop was shuttered, and there were just a few people walking down Enchanted Lane. Keelie opened her mind to the trees, to Tavak, but something blocked her.

"What's wrong?" Raven was studying her expression.

"I don't know." Keelie ran to Heartwood, followed by her friends. It was closed. Dad wasn't there, but Knot sat at the entrance, his fur bushed to maximum fluff. Tufts of white cat hair were everywhere. "Did you have a fight with the white stray?"

"Heartwood, come here."

Keelie froze. It was Finch. She'd caught up with them, or maybe she'd come for the money. Or was she here to tell Zeke everything herself? Raven slipped away, the white kitty at her heels.

Finch still looked like a human-dragon hybrid with a mean Viking aura, but she didn't seem to be about to barbecue anyone. Instead, she looked worried, and Keelie did a double take when she saw Sir Davey standing next to her, his face also lined with concern.

"Okay, Davey there she is. I've got to get back to the office." She sighed. "Now that I've got both the EPA and the CDC to worry about, the heat's on."

"The CDC? That's the disease people," Laurie whispered.

Keelie felt cold. "Sir Davey, where's Dad?"

Davey seemed to consider his words. "He's sicker than we all thought. He hid it from you and from me, lass."

Keelie's heart raced. "Where is he? He was fine this morning." Except for the dark circles. Except for the fatigue.

"He's with the others at the lodge."

With Elia and the elves. He wasn't safe there. "I've got

to go to him. He needs to be here with me. I'll take care of him."

"What's going on?" Raven reappeared as Finch left. "Is my mom okay?"

"Zeke has been quarantined with the others at the lodge. Janice is fine, Raven. The CDC is investigating the source of the illness, and they're trying to identify it."

Keelie knew her face was bleached white from fear.

"If the CDC runs tests on them, then—then it's good because they can find out what's going on," Laurie spoke confidently. "They can be cured."

Keelie met Davey's eyes. Not good, if they found out they weren't human.

Raven still looked worried. "What about the Faire workers, crafts people, and mundanes—are they in danger?"

"Some Faire workers have become sick, but it's mostly the folks at the lodge," Sir Davey answered. "Raven, the only ones still here and healthy from that, er, group, are Elianard, Elia, Lord Niriel, and Keelie."

All the elves were sick. Every one. Keelie was only half elven, so that might explain how she was not affected, but it didn't explain why Elia and Elianard looked better than ever. Lord Niriel, too. She wondered what the three had in common.

Raven raced out the door. "Keelie, I'm going to be right back. I need to make sure Mom is okay."

"Sure." Keelie heard a sneeze at ground level. Knot sneezed again and pawed at the door of the shop, then meowed.

Even though he didn't talk to her the way he talked to her dad, she understood. He wanted to go inside.

Sir Davey watched Raven go. "Zeke says work needs to go on as normally as possible. He says it will create a diversion for you. He wants you to remember that you're a Heartwood, and he needs for you to help with . . . ." He inclined his head across the lane.

Keelie understood. "But I want to go to him. How will I know he's all right?"

Knot meowed again.

Sir Davey seemed hesitant to leave. "I'll keep you informed. I'll be back to check on you in an hour."

"I'll help you, Keelie." Laurie put a hand on her arm. "I guess I get to be a working girl after all. This is going to shock my mom, and you know hardly anything shocks her."

Despite everything going on, Keelie couldn't help being totally surprised by Laurie's offer. "Are you sure?"

"Hey, I heard working builds character."

Keelie stepped into the shop and ran her hand across the wood of a nearby chair. Elm from Maine. She had to hold back the tears. "Dad."

Now was not the time to fall apart. Knot went behind the counter and scratched at a small cupboard, to the right of the shelves, that held receipt books, pens, and binders of furniture designs. Keelie opened it, and Knot pawed at something inside.

She bent down and reached for the object. It was a cell phone, or what looked like a cell phone—a flat wooden box decorated with a silver filigreed tree. When Keelie opened the silver-hinged lid, embedded, rune-like symbols glowed green. She could feel the chlorophyll from inside it.

She tilted her head and looked at Sir Davey. "Is this what I think it is?"

"Yep." Sir Davey removed a small crystal from a leather bag tied to his belt. "It figures that Knot knew where he hid it." He handed the crystal to Keelie. "This will boost your power signal. Zeke quit using it because it kept dropping calls."

Keelie looked down at Knot. "I should kick you across the Faire for hiding this from me."

Laurie leaned over the counter. "That doesn't look like any cell phone I've ever seen. What company do you use?"

"Earth Network," Sir Davey replied easily. "They're an underground company working with natural resources. Zeke uses Northwest Sylvan."

"Very eco-cool." Laurie looked impressed. "So green."

Knot placed a paw on Keelie's arm, his claws hooked into her cotton shirt. She looked down at him. His eyes were totally dilated. He released her and pressed his paw on a spiral-shaped symbol.

The world tilted. Keelie closed her eyes; she felt like she was traveling through a portal of green. She was connected from forest to forest down the Appalachian Mountains. The feeling was similar to getting on Google and viewing satellite pictures. Images of forests flashed across her mind. And then she heard Sean's voice.

"Hello?"

"Sean, is that you?"

"Keelie? Why didn't you answer my letters?"

"I never got them, but we can talk about that later. I need your help. Everyone here is sick and the CDC is going to run tests on them. Everyone's sick except me, Elianard, Elia, and your father."

Laurie was watching Keelie with wide eyes. "Sean? *The* Sean?"

Keelie knew she couldn't say anything about the unicorn in front of Laurie. She might already be saying too much.

"Keelie, you've got to stop the CDC. They cannot find out about us." His voice sounded urgent.

"How can I?"

"Go to my father," Sean insisted. "He's the—

There was a sound like the rustling of leaves, and the plink of a harp string, then silence.

"Dropped call?" Laurie was sympathetic. "And after all that time, too."

"You might say that." Keelie put the wooden cell phone on the counter. "Guess we'd better get to work."

twenty-three

Laurie turned out to be a terrific saleswoman, which was good, since Keelie had spent all afternoon and all that night keeping the oaks asleep. She'd channeled magic through the Queen Aspen's heart, and her head throbbed from the effort.

"No more Tylenol." Raven took the bottle away from her. "It'll destroy your liver."

Keelie sat at the sales counter of Heartwood, her cheek pressed against the cool wood of the countertop. "But my head still hurts," she moaned. Her fingers and toes were getting a green tinge, too, from spending so much time talking to the trees.

"Mom fixed you something." Raven pushed forward a dark blue glass bottle with a cork stopper.

Keelie opened one eye. "What is it?"

"Herb infusion with honey. Don't ask me what's in it, except for the honey. She said that was to make it taste good."

"I'm for that." Keelie sat up gingerly and pulled the bottle toward her. "How much do I take?"

"All of it."

She would have shrugged, but it would have made her head throb more. The cork was jammed in tight. Keelie tugged hard and it came loose with a loud pop. A sweet smell wafted up from the narrow bottleneck.

Keelie took a breath, then put the bottle to her lips and drank it down. There wasn't much in it, just about half a cup. It didn't taste very good, but the honey made it tolerable.

Raven took the empty bottle and recorked it. "Give it a while to work. Mom says it's foolproof."

"I'd say you're calling me a fool, but it would take too much effort." Keelie put her head back down and watched as Laurie walked by, leading three very well-dressed women in period costume. Playtrons. That's what the Ren Faire folk called customers in costume, patrons who enhanced the feel of the event for everyone by wearing costumes like the players.

Laurie smiled and gave them a finger wave. "These ladies didn't know about the handcrafted wooden furniture on this side of the Faire."

Keelie forced a smile. "Welcome."

The three elaborately gowned women smiled, looking like taller versions of the three fairy godmothers in Disney's *Sleeping Beauty*. One wore green, the other blue, and the third wore violet.

Knot staggered to the foot of Keelie's tall stool and collapsed in a furry heap. The green lady smiled and bent over to pet his head. "I love shop cats. They add such a welcoming feeling to a place."

Laurie motioned toward the back of the shop. "Ladies, if you follow me, this is where you'll find those custom-designed dollhouses I told you about."

The four swept away, literally. Their trailing skirts pushed leaves and acorns aside as they progressed down the aisle. Keelie watched them go, amused. Laurie actually enjoyed talking to shoppers. Who knew?

Her thoughts were interrupted by the trees. Something was moving quickly through the forest, and the trees followed its movements. Keelie couldn't tell what it was. Probably not a deer. The trees didn't care about the forest's usual inhabitants, which meant that this probably wasn't the unicorn, either.

Raven's eyes were on her face, tense and worried. "Is it a Red Cap?" She'd seen the damage that the evil fairy had caused at the High Mountain Faire.

Keelie lowered her voice. "No Red Cap, thank goodness. This time it's a unicorn. And Elia is looking for him."

Raven gasped, then grinned. "No way. You've seen a real unicorn? There were always stories about a unicorn in the Wildewood. I thought I saw him once when I was about eleven, but everyone laughed at me, so I figured I'd made him up. You've actually seen it? Or did you say him?"

Raven could be trusted with her secret. "Him, definitely. His name is Lord Einhorn, and he's really sick and needs my help." The white cat leaped onto the counter. It sat, tail curled neatly around its feet, and stared at Raven.

Raven stroked the little cat's head. "He's been around the Faire for years, or his ancestors have. I played with his grandfather, probably, because there's been one just like him since I was a kid." The cat closed its eyes and leaned into her caress. "Keelie, it's so cool about the unicorn. Not that he's sick, but that's he real." Raven looked like a little kid who'd just glimpsed Santa Claus on his throne at the mall. "What can I do to help?"

Laurie interrupted. "They asked if you took Master Card or Lady Visa."

Keelie stared at her blankly, her mind still divided between whatever was running through the forest and telling Raven about the unicorn. Laurie's question finally filtered in. "Dad has a credit card machine somewhere."

Raven walked to the other side of the counter. "Look under the shelves. Mom shoves hers under there when she's finished for the day."

She and Keelie poked through the shelves. Keelie's fingers paused to touch Zeke's green tea mug. Then she opened the cupboard door, seeing the vision of an Alabama pine forest, and pulled out a brick-sized machine covered in silver-filigreed tree branches. A plate at the bottom front read "The Bank of the Dread Forest" in calligraphic script.

"This must be it." She touched the top and the machine whirred to life, glowing with bright green light. Her fingers tingled from the chlorophyll. Great, as if she needed more. She knew it came from the trees, but it reminded her of radiation, and she knew that too much exposure would make her sick.

Raven stared. "Wow, you didn't have to turn it on. It just turned on when you touched it."

"Yeah, how about that. Must be wireless." Keelie poked at a couple of the buttons. The machine whirred like an insect.

The green-gowned woman came to the counter. "Can you have that large dollhouse in back delivered?"

"Sure," Keelie said, then stopped. She'd heard her father make shipping arrangements, but didn't know what to do next.

"Allow me." Raven pushed her gently aside. "Cash or charge?"

With Raven in control, Keelie went to the rear of the shop to see if Laurie needed help. She felt much better, thanks to Janice's herbal infusion. The woman in violet stopped her.

"This is darling. Did you make them?" She held one of the smaller dollhouses in her arms.

"No, my dad's the woodworker. Let me get you a box." Keelie went to the back to grab one from the small pile Dad always kept for customers. As she picked one out, a tree branch moved through the high, open window and touched her arm. Moving trees no longer freaked her out, a sure sign that she was no longer California Keelie.

"It'll be okay," she told the tree, patting its rough branches. She lied. She had no idea what to do, and Raven couldn't push her aside and help with this one. She needed Dad. The elves were sick, the unicorn was sick, and two government agencies were crawling all over the Faire site. She couldn't figure out how or if it was all connected.

She grabbed a box and started back to the front, where she packed the dollhouse while Raven took the woman's card. She ran it through the machine, and a receipt printed up. Thanks to the Bank of the Dread Forest, they were in business.

The woman signed the receipt with a wooden pen. "It's hard to find such enchanting, old-fashioned toys."

Raven laughed. "One thing the Heartwoods can certainly do is bring out the enchantment in wood."

The blonde lady in green exclaimed over a bag of cylindrical building blocks, and added them to her purchase.

Despite the chlorophyll wooziness, Keelie felt proud of her work. Her shoulders ached a little from all the sawing, but she'd made a contribution to the family budget. She couldn't wait to tell Dad. She blinked back tears and stepped behind a column so that the others wouldn't see.

"My best friend is going to have a baby," the woman said, pulling her wallet out again. "And she's going to love these blocks."

Laurie took her credit card. "You know, out in L.A. these would go for triple this amount. Your friend is going to totally love these."

Raven packed them in a brown paper bag with a raffia handle.

Knot left the adoring women, and padded over to Keelie. He placed his paw on her hand, then hopped off the counter and walked outside. He stopped at an oak tree, stretched up, and sharpened his claws on the bark. The oak tree lifted a root and kicked at him.

Darn that cat. After all the work to keep the oaks asleep. Keelie glanced quickly at the women, certain one of them must have seen the movement. They were still fussing over their purchases.

A small *bhata* climbed down the tree trunk, looking like

a woodland marionette made of branches and held together by moss. Knot's tail bushed out and he hissed at it. It tilted its face of leaves and examined him with its berry eyes.

One of the women glanced at Keelie, then followed her gaze and gasped. She pointed at the *bhata*, looking right at it. "What an amazing puppet."

The woman could see the *bhata*. This was totally wrong. Adults never saw fairies.

"Wow, I've never seen anything like that." Laurie's mouth dropped open.

Keelie groaned. Laurie, too. Then she noticed that Raven was staring at the creature in awe, probably the only one who had an idea of what this really was.

Keelie remembered what Dad said about diverting humans who saw magic. "That's a new puppet design my dad is working on. It's still in the planning stages, so it's not for sale."

"I don't see any strings, and it's so lifelike." The violet-gowned woman clasped her hands together in delight. "How do you make them?"

"It's a trade secret. Dad's applied for a patent." Keelie walked carefully toward the tree, a hand outstretched toward the *bhata*, which seemed to be waiting for her.

"It's like primitive art, but yet, so real." The lady in blue squinted, trying to see strings or rods.

"You're sure you don't have any for sale?" The green lady searched for an overlooked basket of *bhata* puppets.

Keelie shook her head. "Like I said, they're still in development." She lowered her hand and allowed the *bhata* to climb up her sleeve. It clung to her shoulder and patted her cheek with its stick hand.

"Wow." The blue-gowned woman grinned at her friends. She turned back to Keelie. "Do you have a mailing list?"

Knot meowed and vanished under the counter. They heard scrabbling sounds, then a thump. Raven glanced down at her feet, then leaned over and reappeared with a blank notebook.

"Here you go. Name, address, phone, and email, please."

Laurie seemed to be torn between looking at the *bhata* and watching for Knot, who was still under the counter with the supplies. "That cat should be in the movies."

As the ladies lined up at the book to scribble down their contact information, Raven gave Keelie a look over their heads. A "you have got to fill me in on the real truth" kind of look.

Keelie rolled her eyes. The *bhata* climbed onto her head and then leaped up and vanished into the shop's exposed rafters, blending in with the dark wood.

"This place is wonderful," the violet woman told the blue one.

The blue lady nodded emphatically. "We'll have to come back next year, and bring all of our friends."

After they'd left, laden with boxes and bags, Laurie and Raven high-fived and danced around the counter. Keelie looked at the totals. "In the last hour, we've managed to make close to two thousand dollars."

"Not bad for an hour's work." Laurie looked satisfied. "You can pay back the evil Finch person."

Raven reached up with a finger, and the *bhata* leaned down from the rafters. Red berries popped out of the moss-wrapped jumble that formed its face, giving it a lopsided berry smile. Raven smiled back. "Keelie, what is this?"

"Yeah." Laurie looked out the open front of the shop. "I think you need to explain some of this Faire stuff to me, because I think I see an oak tree walking across the lane. That's either serious animatronics, which—don't get me wrong—I don't think your dinky Faire can afford, or we've all been fed hallucinogenic tea."

Keelie's mouth dropped open. "Oh, no." An oak tree was indeed heaving itself across the lane. She gripped the pine counter. Several mundanes had gathered to watch the walking oak, probably thinking it was a performance.

Keelie rushed out of the shop and ran up to the trees, summoning up energy and magic. Her magical encounter with Elia yesterday had drained her, and the magic she'd used to keep the trees asleep was falling apart.

She closed her eyes and opened her mind. *Tavak, can you hear me?* Keelie allowed the tree to see into her mind and what was happening with the oak.

Create a shield. Channel your energy.

Keelie didn't think she had much energy left, but she pushed her hands toward the trees and felt for the slow-moving core of forest magic she had discovered deep inside of herself. Green energy flowed from her hands. The wind began to blow, and sand and debris swirled around the humans, encasing them in small cyclones. Green energy also surrounded the mundanes, but they had covered their eyes to protect themselves from the wind and didn't see the glow.

Tavak spoke again. *We are helping you, Tree Shepherd's Daughter. The humans won't see the trees.*

Are you kidding me? An oak the size of a two-story house was stomping down the side alley between the herb shop and the privies. Janice stood in her doorway, her mouth opened in a perfect circle of amazement. *I'm thinking they're visible to some.*

Help Oamlik, Tree Shepherdess. Tavak sounded stressed.

Oamlik must be the wayward oak. Keelie had an impression of great age, although Oamlik wasn't the tallest tree in the forest. Maybe not the brightest, either. She walked over to Oamlik and reached up. The struggling tree clutched her arm with what looked like twiggy fingers.

Janice watched them as Keelie walked Oamlik back to the grove across from Heartwood. It was like she was escorting an elderly person across a busy intersection. This is a first, she thought. And if she was lucky, a last, too.

As they made their way to the grove, dozens of *bhata* clambered down the trees and touched her, as if in tribute. One touched her eyelids, making her duck. She didn't want to get her eyes poked out by a stick fairy, but when she reopened them everything was bright green.

She'd heard of viewing the world through rose-colored glasses, but this was the forest version. It was like she was seeing two different realms stacked on top of each other.

The human world, the world in which she lived, was there; but with the magic sight, she saw the hidden world, too. Was this the way Dad saw the forest? Was this the difference between seeing with human and elven eyes?

There were *bhata* everywhere, all sorts of them. And the *feithid daoine*—the bug fairies that were smart and sometimes mean. Knot loved to chase them. And she could see the faces in the trees, the trees as they really were, and they were as different as you'd find among humans. There were some with wide faces, and some that were angular. Some had solemn expressions, with dour bark lips puckered together, while others seemed to have once been happy, with smile lines grooved into their bark. Their jolliness had faded, however, and many of the trees and some of the *bhata* and *feithid daoine* were smeared with a thick, luminous, dark blue liquid. Some of the trees had the stuff oozing down their trunks.

As Oamlik sank his roots deep into the soil, Keelie noticed that the old oak's roots were also covered in the sticky blue substance. She opened her mind to Tavak and to Oamlik. *What is this?*

We call it venumiel. Since Lord Einhorn has been sick, he cannot protect us from the poisons humans make.

Compassion filled her. The trees were tired, and they'd been sick for a long time. Keelie drew from Oamlik's memories, and saw the unicorn running through the forest. His magic protected the trees from the burning rains and the dark, dirty air, and from the painful throbbing vibrations of the humans' metal houses on the other side of the mountain. Keelie saw from the tree's memory how the unicorn touched his horn to the sick trees and extended his magic over all, protecting this woodland.

The unicorn stood in a clearing. This was happening now, Keelie saw. Far away, but happening this very minute. Buildings were behind him, and what appeared to be a smokestack. He staggered as he touched his horn to a leafless tree. Even now, sick as he was, he was trying to protect his realm. She would help him. She had to.

Keelie hugged the tree. He wrapped his branches around her, and then the green faded from her vision and she realized that she was surrounded by a small crowd, clapping.

She looked up, but Oamlik's face had formed back into knots.

Exhausted, Keelie bowed to the crowd, but not too low in case she pitched forward into the dust. She wondered what the people had seen, or thought they'd seen, and started back toward Heartwood.

The geeky boys who'd watched the pickle launch the day before followed her. "That's so amazing! Are you running some type of robotic program? That was cool how you and that tree never reacted to the jousters."

"Jousters?" She must have been totally out of it. Jousters always shook the earth as they galloped past on their huge, armored steeds.

"Yeah, when the two of you were walking across the street and the jousters came charging by on those great big horses, and you kept walking. Way cool! Where did the jousters go?" The boys looked around as if the phantom jousters would reappear.

Now Keelie understood what Tavak had meant; the trees had created an illusion of jousters so that everyone would think the walking tree was part of the show. "I'll bet they went to the joust."

A burly guy wearing a kilt snorted. "That wasn't a robot. There's some actor in that tree suit, ain't there, girly?"

Keelie shook her head. "No actor. Believe me."

"I say it's an actor, and I'll prove it." The man picked up a broom that was leaning against a nearby building and headed toward Oamlik. As he passed by one of the other oaks, a branch seemed to bob with a passing breeze. It snagged his kilt, revealing silky blue boxers with the New York Yankees' logo emblazoned in red on the rear.

Laughter burst from the crowd. The guy pulled his kilt back down, his face as red as the lettering across his backside. Keelie smiled. Trees with a sense of humor. Who would have guessed?

twenty-four

When Keelie returned to Heartwood, she found Laurie and Raven waiting on new customers. Knot lay on the counter in a beam of sunlight, which gave his usually demonic orange fur an angelic golden glow. He purred like a kitty Ferrari. People petted him as they passed and told him what a lovely cat he was. But Keelie could tell that he was still sick, and now she saw the blue that edged his kitty nostrils. She wondered if she'd see venumiel on Dad. He'd said the trees and elves were closely linked, and this would be a sure sign.

Even ill, Knot was enjoying the adoration of the customers he'd charmed. There would be no living with him now. Keelie wondered if it was a variation of the elf charm. Nah, that wasn't possible. Still, she sniffed as she passed, checking him out for the telltale cinnamon scent of elf magic.

Laurie was showing a cradle, made of twigs and encrusted with semi-precious stones, to a couple. The woman was enormously pregnant. The couple held hands and gazed adoringly at one another as Laurie told them what a special cradle they had decided to purchase. "Just like Sleeping Beauty's."

Keelie had changed into one of the long flowing gowns she'd bought at Galadriel's Closet at the High Mountain Faire. Wearing her own garb felt great after the assortment of weird costumes she'd endured. She was sure she could still catch a whiff of pickle from her skin every now and then.

Raven was working the credit card machine. Keelie sidled up to her, and Raven frowned. "Why don't you run back to the RV and take a nap? You haven't slept in two days."

"I can't. I have to keep the oaks from going on a rampage." Keelie slumped down on a stool and leaned her head against the wall. Her head was buzzing, and the thunderous headache was coming back.

"Hey, Laurie, why don't you get us all some coffee? I'll mind the shop for Keelie."

Laurie grabbed two fives from the cashbox and poked at Keelie's arm. "Is it Saint Patrick's Day?"

Keelie glanced down. Her arm was green. Not good.

"I agree with Raven. You need rest." Laurie frowned, but she didn't notice the *bhata* clambering up the shop columns. The magic was safe for a while longer, even if Keelie was turning into a human broccoli.

When Laurie returned with three coffees, Keelie accepted hers gratefully. Her old friend sat opposite her and watched her drink. "What's up with the trees, these stick puppets, and you turning green?"

Keelie swallowed the wrong way and started to cough. Laurie handed her a stack of napkins, as if she'd been ready for that very reaction.

She wondered how much she should tell Laurie. She'd already blabbed just about everything to Raven, but Raven was practically family and she'd grown up around the elves. "What do you know about magic?"

"Oh please. Don't go all *Lord of the Rings* on me." Laurie sat up straight, looking angry. "If you can't trust me with the truth, then just shut up."

Keelie sighed. "Do you think you really saw puppets?"

Raven met Laurie's eyes and slowly shook her head. After a moment, Laurie's eyes widened. "You can't be serious."

"What do you know about magic?" Keelie repeated.

Laurie shrugged. "Stuff I've read in the books I bought at the New Age store, and stuff Margaret Seastrunk tells me. I mean, she buys all these Wiccan books from the bookstore and brings them to school, and I confess, we've cast some spells trying to get the cute guys to fall in love with us. Doesn't work!"

Warmth for Laurie flowed through Keelie. Laurie had been her lifelong friend, and if they were going to stay friends, then she'd have to tell her the truth. Keeping the human world and elven world separate was going to be tough, and Keelie needed her friends if she was going to make it work.

"Look at my hands." Keelie held them up. Her cuticles were green, and the tips of her nails were green, too.

"What about them, aside from really needing a manicure?" Laurie asked. "That's not a nail fungus, is it?"

"It's chlorophyll."

"Chlorophyll? Like in Mr. Stein's science class?"

"Laurie, you really did see that tree walk across the street, and you really did see a stick person. They're called *bhata*." Keelie examined her friend's face, trying to gauge her reaction.

"Get out. Butter?" Laurie laughed.

"*Bhata*. And they're not the only weird things around here. Lots of the people with elf ears aren't wearing makeup."

Raven was leaning in close, listening.

"My father is an elf, and Elia, the girl with the harp, is an elf, too. Not a very good one, either."

"Get out!" Laurie squealed. "A real elf? That beats Margaret Seastrunk and her love spells any day. And it explains a lot—that ear, and how you always got way carried away playing fairies, and the way you snort when you laugh."

Keelie glared at her. "I do not snort when I laugh. But everything else is true."

Raven was nodding slowly. "And the unicorn?"

Laurie's mouth dropped open. "A unicorn?"

"Yes," Keelie said. "I went into the woods the other night because I was summoned by a unicorn."

"But it wasn't there?" Laurie stared at her. "I didn't see it, and I was right behind you."

Keelie regarded her friend. Laurie seemed more accepting of all this otherworldly stuff than Keelie had been when her father and Sir Davey had first told her about her true nature. "It was there, all right, waiting for me."

"You mean in the forest? That was just a white horse."

"Yeah, about that." Keelie paused. "You have to be a virgin to see it."

Laurie sat down hard, and then burst into tears.

Keelie rushed to hug her weeping friend, and Raven handed her Laurie's coffee and turned around to keep an eye out for customers.

"I'm not accusing you of anything, Laurie. You don't have to talk about it if you don't want to."

"I don't." Laurie sobbed and turned away.

Keelie returned to the counter, sad that Laurie didn't want to share her secrets. Not that she should complain—she had more than a few secrets of her own. She wished she could just go to bed and sleep off the rest of the day. Sipping her coffee, she waited for Laurie to pull herself together. Raven was suddenly busy straightening up the shop.

After a while the sobs turned into hiccups, and then Laurie rejoined them. Her face was splotchy from crying and her blue eyes were wide with shock, either from Keelie's revelation or her own. But before she could speak again, the wooden cell phone rang from the shelf underneath the pine countertop.

Startled, Keelie almost spilled the contents of her coffee cup. She reached for the phone with a trembling hand, hoping it wasn't Elia. Knot jumped up onto the counter, and placed a paw on her arm as she gripped the phone.

"Should I answer it?"

The orange cat blinked, his eyes fully dilated. Keelie didn't know if she was ready to face the elf girl again. Elia had used magic on Keelie's old cell phone, in Colorado, pretending she was Laurie. Back then Keelie had been plotting to return to California, desperate to regain the life she'd been torn from when her mother died. Life had certainly changed for her in the last couple of months.

Knot rubbed his head against her arm, which she took to mean that yes, she should answer the phone. It rang again. Maybe it was Dad.

"Are you going to answer that?" Laurie's voice had the shrill tone it took on when she was getting agitated.

"Yes." Keelie pressed the spiral button and the cell phone screen lit up. A zing tingled through her body and the room spun around. She steadied herself against the edge of the counter as her mind filled with the image of a wide, strangely illuminated forest filled with dripping trees and dim with mist.

Once her head cleared, Keelie noticed that the nails on the hand gripping the phone had become a darker green. "Hello, Heartwood."

"Who is this?" The voice was female, and demanding. "I need to speak to Zekeliel Heartwood immediately."

Knot hissed.

"He can't... come to the phone, but I can take a message."

"Is this Keliel?"

Only one other person would call her by her elven name. "Yes."

"This is your grandmother, Keliatiel. Tell your father I need to speak to him, now."

This bitchy, uptight woman did not sound grandmotherly. Irritation welled up inside of Keelie. She hadn't heard from her grandmother since she came to live with her dad, aside from a curt note.

"Hello? Hello?" Grandmother Keliatiel's voice echoed from the phone. "Keliel?"

"Yes, grandmother."

"Lord Elianard phoned me about the dire circumstances in Wildewood. How is my son?"

Her son! Feeling territorial, Keelie thought that while Dad may be Grandmother Keliatiel's son, he was her father. "Dad is sick. He's in quarantine with the other elves at the lodge in town. I don't know much more than that, other than what Sir Davey has told me."

Laurie had walked away and was straightening the dollhouses.

"Davey? You mean Jadwyn. That dwarf is always sticking his nose into elf business."

Keelie didn't like her grandmother's tone. At least Sir Davey was here with her, and not in some woodland in the Northwest.

Grandmother Keliatiel charged on. "I was disappointed to hear from Lord Elianard about your disrespectful attitude toward him and your abhorrent behavior toward Elia. That's no way for the Tree Shepherd's daughter to behave. I suspected that we'd have years of human education to overcome. We'll start as soon as you're home in the Dread Forest. In the meantime, I want you to mind Lord Elianard."

Keelie decided right then and there that she didn't like her grandmother. She was not looking forward to meeting her, and Keliatiel did not seem to have any love for her long-lost granddaughter. There would probably be lots of stern lectures and elven expectations of perfection, which Keelie would never be able to live up to. She couldn't believe that her kind, gentle father was raised by this human-hating shrew.

Knot reached up on his hind legs and batted at the phone with his paw. "What?" Keelie mouthed.

He snagged a claw on the silver filigree and tugged on the phone. She held it out to him, and he meowed into the mouthpiece. Then he lowered his front legs, closed his eyes, and purred as if he'd accomplished a mission.

Keelie lifted the phone back to her ear and heard Grandmother Keliatiel say tensely, "I understand that Knot is with you."

Apparently there was no love lost between Grandmother Keliatiel and Knot. Heh.

"Yes, he's here. He's my guardian, you know."

Laurie looked down at the cat in astonishment. Raven looked ill.

"I'll tell Dad you called when I see him." Keelie rolled her eyes at her friends.

"Please do, and have him phone me as soon as possible. Tell the others an emergency response team has left the Dread Forest. If you need anything, Elianard reassured me that he'll do whatever he can for you and for your father."

Bet he would. As long as I show him the unicorn, and then he'd push me off a cliff.

"I'll remember that. Goodbye, Grand—what do I call you?"

"Grandmother Keliatiel will do." Her voice became warmer, laden with concern. "If your father gets worse, let me know as soon as possible."

"I will."

"Until we meet in person, Daughter of the Forest, care for your father as best you can."

"I will." Daughter of the Forest? That was a new one.

She'd have to start a list of all her new names. "Goodbye, Grandmother Keliatiel."

Hanging up the phone, Keelie had this horrid premonition that life in the Dread Forest would truly be dreadful, sort of like an elven military academy, with Elia at the head of the class. Pain throbbed behind Keelie's right eye as she thought about how long she'd be in school. Elia was already sixty years old.

Laurie leaned over the counter. "Are you okay? You're looking kind of green. I mean, greener than before. You know, you used to turn that color when you were around a lot of trees. Is it your tree allergy?"

"There never was a tree allergy." Keelie held her hand up and gazed at it in the light. Yup, she was turning really green. If Sir Brine saw her now, he'd be overjoyed.

"Oh. My. God. You've really had this magic elf thing going since we were kids, haven't you?"

Keelie nodded. "I didn't know. Mom's the one who told me it was a tree allergy."

"What is it really?"

"It's a side effect of using tree magic." Of being whammied by tree magic, Keelie thought. She reached into the pocket of her gown for the rose quartz, but it wasn't there. Panic filled her, and she had to take a couple of deep breaths to calm her anxiety. She had to keep her head, but she desperately needed the rose quartz to neutralize her body's reaction to the tree magic.

The pain increased threefold behind her eye, and she leaned against the counter with her head in her hand. "I need to lie down, Laurie."

Quickly, Laurie walked around the counter and wrapped her arm around Keelie. "Where?"

"In the back."

Heavy footfalls thudded on the steps outside the booth. Keelie forced her head up, wincing as pain pounded through her as if she'd been clubbed by one of the oak's branches. She leaned against Laurie and steadied herself against the counter.

It was Finch who entered the shop—which was not surprising, given the thousand dollars owed to her. But Keelie was shocked by the Faire director's appearance. Finch's red bun drooped, and wilty curls framed her face. Her corset also drooped. A pasty complexion replaced the bright red angry one she normally sported.

"Close it up, girls. Just got word that the CDC and the EPA are shutting down the Faire, and from the looks of you, Heartwood, it's none too soon."

"What?" They couldn't shut down the Faire. Did Dad know?

"My orders from headquarters are to tell everyone to get the hell out of Wildewood. You have twenty-four hours to pack up your vehicle and all personal belongings, but since your father is sick and you're minors—" She sighed. "I think I need to alert the local child welfare services."

"That won't be necessary. The girls will be going with me." Sir Davey stepped into the shop with a huge amethyst geode in his arms. "Zeke said that since the girls are already staying with me, it'll be easy to drive somewhere close and wait out the quarantine until Zeke is released."

The scent of cinnamon permeated the air. The hairs on Keelie's neck rose in alarm.

Elianard had followed Sir Davey into the shop. "How do we know that those are Zekeliel's wishes, Jadwyn? I spoke to Keelie's grandmother, and she wishes me to be in charge of her granddaughter's welfare." Elianard's eyes darted about the shop as if he searched for something.

Knot hissed and his tail bushed out. Elianard backed up. "But you can take the cat."

What? No way was Keelie going with Smellianard. Knot, either.

Sir Davey's eyebrows rose. "You may have spoken to Keelie's grandmother, but it'll be the lass' father who makes the final decision as to where she goes."

Elianard didn't look pleased. His face became even more pinched than normal. The left corner of his upper lip lifted, and his eyes narrowed. He swallowed as if he were choking on his retort to Sir Davey.

"Her father is quite ill. He's in no condition to make such decisions. Keelie is part of my extended family, so to speak, therefore I am naturally the one to take care of her and her friend, and her father's business." Elianard ran his index finger along the edge of the counter. "Such as it is."

More cinnamon wafted toward Keelie. Maybe going with Elianard wouldn't be so bad...

She shook her head, wrapping herself in green tree magic to clear away the spell, but it didn't work. Cinnamon... Keelie realized that he was using the elven charm magic on her. Her fingers closed around the pouch at her waist. Of course. That was where she'd put the rose quartz. She held it tightly, and the smell faded. Her headache eased to a dull thudding.

"Obviously the child is not feeling well. She can rest,

and Elia can take care of her." He forced seldom-used muscles around his mouth into a smile. It looked really creepy on him. "We can make arrangements to send her friend back to California."

Laurie put her fists on her hips. "I'm staying with Keelie. She needs me."

"I want to go with Davey." Actually, Keelie didn't want to go anywhere until the unicorn was healed.

"Do you disobey your father's and grandmother's wishes?" Elianard's green eyes darkened. Something like smoke swam in his irises.

Keelie motioned with her hand toward the cell phone still on the counter. "Let's call him and find out."

Laurie reached back and grabbed it. "I'll dial the number for you."

"I know the number." Sir Davey held out his hand for the phone. "Let's ask Zeke." He held Elianard's gaze.

"Do you really want to wake your father up, Keelie? He needs his rest." Elianard's face was full of fake concern.

She didn't want to wake Dad up, but she didn't want to go with Elianard. She knew Dad wouldn't want her to go with him, but Finch needed to hear it herself.

"Call him, Sir Davey."

Finch arched an eyebrow. "Sir Davey, take the two girls. I know Zeke trusts you."

Elianard was about to speak, but Finch made a cutting motion with her hand across her neck. "Listen, I don't care what Grandma said, take it up with Zeke. Furthermore, I wouldn't subject a rat to your daughter's care."

Elianard's face reddened. He straightened and pointed a finger at Finch, who, in turn, thrust her corseted chest out and said very loudly, "I don't have time for this, Elianard. I have to go and tell everyone at this Faire that they have to leave, and it's going to take me hours to do it, and not only that, I'm going to have to listen to people whine and pitch fits like they're little kindergartners because they don't want to go, they're losing money, and because life isn't fair. So, I don't have time to put up with one of your tantrums, and if you keep pushing me, you're going to make me mad, and you really don't want to make me mad, do you?"

Elianard backed up.

Finch left.

Sir Davey looked around. "Do you girls need help closing up the shop?"

"You'll regret interfering, dwarf," Elianard said. "Keelie goes with me."

The inside of the amethyst geode began to glow with a bright purple light. Sir Davey placed it up on his shoulder like a bazooka. "If you don't get out of here, then your elven healers will be plucking purple crystals out of your backside."

Elianard kept a wary eye on Sir Davey as the dwarf advanced on him. Then he turned around and walked away—not in a hurried trying-to-get-away-from-a-dwarf gait, but Keelie noticed a quicker pace to his stride.

"A crystal bazooka. Mom would die." Laurie looked impressed. "You know, we have a fair amount of crime in LA."

Keelie pulled the rose quartz out of her pouch, tempted to kiss it. Elianard had almost succeeded. And who would have thought that Finch would turn out to be their hero?

twenty-five

That evening, at the RV's dining table, Keelie rubbed her tektite between her fingers and watched as Sir Davey used wire cutters to snip several strands of silver wire from a large roll. He wore glasses with magnifying lenses that really super-sized his eyebrows, making them look like mutant caterpillars.

Laurie searched through a basket of gemstones, picking out her personal stones at Sir Davey's urging.

"And don't pick one because it'll go with a certain outfit. You've got to get one that feels right, and you'll know it when you find it. Keelie did." He held his hand out for the tektite, and then lifted the leaf-shaped meteor fragment up to the light, examining it like a jeweler does a diamond.

A blue carafe, with a silver dragon etched on the top, sat upon the table between them. Keelie thought the dragon looked like Finch, especially the smoke coming out of its nostrils. She'd had to drink three cups of Sir Davey's super-strong coffee before her headache had dissipated. But her recovery time had drastically improved. The first time she'd used tree magic, it had taken her a couple of days to get over it, and this time it had been less than twelve hours.

"I think I found the one." Laurie held up a stone, then dropped it, disappointed. "No, I don't feel anything."

"Keep looking."

Keelie gazed out the small window and watched the trees blowing in the wind. There were dark clouds hanging in the horizon, reminding her of Elianard's eyes earlier. There was something menacing in the air. If there was a storm, she'd have to go out in it. She had to find Einhorn. She stared at the carafe and then poured herself another cup of coffee, thinking that she'd have to stay awake for the quest ahead.

Laurie shouted. "Whoa, I'm feeling the vibe from this one." She held up a white stone that reflected little rainbows in the light.

"Ah, a good choice, Laurie." Sir Davey smiled. "It's a moonstone. It'll protect you, but mostly it brings happiness to its wearer. And it helps the wearer accept changes in her life."

"Cool. After the stuff I've seen and heard today," Laurie's gaze held Keelie's, "I need some moonstone in my life."

"I'm going to wrap your tektite in silver wire so that you can wear it." Sir Davey unrolled thin strips of silver from the spool. "It's time to do some Earth magic."

He formed a silver wire net around the tektite and rolled

one edge over to form a loop, then handed it to Laurie, who threaded a leather cord through it and tied it around Keelie's neck.

The tektite pendant felt heavy next to the Queen Aspen heart, but Keelie didn't have to draw on it as she did the rose quartz. She felt enveloped in an invisible shield.

At eleven, Sir Davey put down his tools. "I'm exhausted. We'll clean up tomorrow. But remember, lasses, wear your protective stones wherever you go."

"We will." Keelie gave Sir Davey a kiss on his cheek, as did Laurie, who now wore the moonstone dangling from a pink silk cord.

By midnight everyone settled down to sleep, except for Keelie, who was determined to stay awake. Sir Davey had gone to bunk with the two remaining Merry Men next door.

Laurie lay in Davey's humongous bed, looking little and alone in the middle of it. She watched Keelie brush her hair. "You know, I should be freaking out about you being an elf and having magic. I should be running back to California. But you know, I've always felt that life wasn't always what we could see. I mean, I wanted fairies to be real. I wanted magic to be real, and it is."

Keelie turned from the mirror to face her friend. "Magic is real, but it's not all fairy-tale stuff like Cinderella. I mean, Elia threatened to harm a child at the Maypole, and at the High Mountain Faire, she blinded a hawk named Ariel."

Laurie yawned and shook her head. "That Elia is a wicked bitch. You can save the trees and your dad, Keelie. You have to find a way. I'll help you." She yawned again.

"Good night, Laurie."

No answer. Laurie was out already.

Keelie's eyelids were heavy, too. She was so tired. She thought about Einhorn, Oamlik the oak, and Dad. They all needed her. She sat at the foot of the bed and rubbed her eyes. She couldn't stay awake. As her eyes finally closed, Keelie heard the sounds of a harp echoing in her mind.

A picture of Elianard's face formed. He was twirling a cord with a thorn-wrapped acorn pendant at the end of it. The cord twirled round and round, and Elianard's patronizing voice asked over and over, "Where's the unicorn?"

A harp played, background music to his repetitive droning. Keelie couldn't wake up; she couldn't escape Elianard. She ran, but his disembodied head appeared in front of her. In one vista, she found herself on a mountaintop, and Elianard stood beside her and waved his hand.

"The unicorn uses his magic to conceal himself from me, and now the human scientists will find him before I can complete my work. I think you know where the wily beast is hiding."

An image formed of one of the EPA agents. They were in the campground on the other side of the power plant. Somewhere nearby was the unicorn. She had to get to him. She remembered the satellite images of the area from Sir Davey's computer. The forest area around the power plant had once been sentient, but now it was dead—because its guardian was dying.

"You're killing the unicorn." Keelie wanted to get away from Elianard, but she couldn't. His image loomed over her as if he were on an IMAX movie screen.

"I'm not killing him; I'm only borrowing his magic. The humans are to blame, with their poisons." Elianard's forehead furrowed. "I do not have to explain myself to an insignificant Round Ear. Tell me what I want to know."

"No." Keelie tried to cling to the vision of the unicorn, but it faded and vanished.

"Perhaps there is something else that can persuade you."

Suddenly they were in a candlelit chamber. The flickering flames cast tall shadows on the log walls. A small cot was in one corner of the otherwise empty room. Dad was on it, clammy and gray, and he looked very sick. Keelie ran to his side. "Dad, can you hear me? It's me, Keelie." She tried to touch him, but her hand passed through him. This was just a dream, she told herself.

She turned to look at Elianard. He stood before her, looking real enough to touch. Around them were the faces of tree phantoms. Their mouths moved silently, trying to speak to her, but she heard nothing.

"Tell me where Einhorn is, or your father's death is on your head." Elianard spoke as if her choice troubled him. The green of his eyes was rimmed with black, a darkness she'd seen before—the mark of dark magic. "If you help me, the sickness will go away, and you'll have saved the Dread Forest as well. What's one sad unicorn? It's a blessing to put him out of his pain."

She looked down at her father. This was more than a dream. Somewhere, Dad was lying sick, and she had no way of knowing where this cabin was in all the vast forest around them. She had to choose. Einhorn, or Dad. The forest might grow again, but she had only one father. Of course, maybe he wouldn't forgive her if she let the unicorn die.

The harp music increased in tempo, and the thorn-entwined acorn spun round and round in time to the music.

"Tell me, Keliel." Elianard walked forward and Keelie stepped back. It wasn't until her right foot hit air that she realized they were back on the mountaintop and she had stepped off onto nothingness. She fell, soaring through the air. This must be how Ariel felt when she flew. She hit the ground—

—and woke up. Something really heavy landed on her chest, and her breath whooshed out. Knot sat on her stomach and stared at her. His eyes glowed silver with reflected moonlight.

She gasped for air. "Crazy cat. I nearly jumped out of my skin."

Something was pounding the trailer with hard blows. It was rocking back and forth. An earthquake!

Outside, there were shouts from the Merry Men's tent. Keelie heard Sir Davey's voice in the mayhem.

She shook Laurie's shoulder. Her friend mumbled, "What?" Then Laurie sat straight up. "Earthquake!" Her California instincts kicked in and she rolled onto the floor and crawled to the doorway.

"It's not an earthquake. I think the trees are attacking the tents. Come on, we have to get out of here. We have to help the others."

She remembered Elianard's threat. Keelie knew that it had been no mere dream. Her father was in dire danger, but right now she was, too. She jumped out of the RV, Laurie right behind her, and leaned into the wind that blew in strong, hard gusts. It took her a second to make sense of what she was seeing. Screams and angry yells filled the night. Dark shapes moved all over the campground. To one side, a car fire burned, but no one seemed to take notice.

The air was filled with the smell of turned earth, mixed with the stink of burning rubber.

The looming shapes were trees. A giant crunch of metal made them turn. A branch lay in a crease on top of Sir Davey's RV. Keelie cried out as she realized it was still attached to the tree, which was lifting the massive branch to crunch it down once more.

Laurie looked up. "Watch out!" she screamed, leaping to one side. Keelie staggered back as a branch came down hard between them.

She grabbed the Queen Aspen's heart and opened her thoughts, but her mind boiled with the murderous rage of the forest around her. Keelie quickly released the talisman to break the bond. There was no reasoning with these trees. They'd gone crazy. "Run!" she shouted.

Laurie sprinted, but a tree sprang up in front of her and she quickly veered toward Keelie. Suddenly, a broad-shouldered figure blocked their path. "Get behind me, girls." It was Little John, wearing nothing but a kilt and boots, his quarterstaff in his hands.

He confronted the tree with his weapon, which was formidable for a human but looked pitiful against the huge oak that faced him. Behind the tree, no clouds marred the perfect black sky.

Finch's strident voice carried across the campground battlefield. "Davey!"

Davey. Where was he? Keelie glanced toward the campground's edge, where the Faire administrator stood looking more like a fiery dragon than ever, her red hair twisting in the wind and her arms out as if she would throttle the tree that dared come near her.

Finch put her hands to her mouth and yelled again. "Gather everyone and bring them to Admin."

Sir Davey appeared, dashing between lifting tree roots with a black bundle in his arms. Keelie called out to him, and he turned and ran toward them. Little John was engaged in battle, whooping a war cry as he clacked his quarterstaff against the branches that threatened him. Keelie was suddenly glad Little John never shed his Rennie persona.

Davey's face was covered in dirt.

"Jared and Niriel are taking the horses and people down to town on the main road," he said breathlessly. "We have to get to Admin. It has a stone foundation, so I can protect the building easily with Earth magic."

They started to run toward the road, where they could see the bobbing lights of people running with flashlights. A propane tank exploded, illuminating the site with ghastly yellow light. Keelie saw that Little John had joined them. He held a piece of his splintered quarterstaff, now more like a baseball bat.

A wooden cage suddenly appeared around her, and a bar hit her waist. She felt herself being lifted, as if she'd gotten onto a crazy carnival ride. Laurie screamed nearby. The tree had followed them. They were being lifted into the night.

twenty-six

Keelie saw Sir Davey and the others far below. They had run ahead, and were almost at the path that led to safety. The branches were tight around her but she didn't struggle, afraid that she would fall.

With a lurch, the tree turned. Now they were being carried in the opposite direction. Keelie remembered the feeling of flying in her dream, and of falling. She grabbed the branch around her with both hands.

Maybe she could connect with this one tree. They were headed back to the forest. The light of the burning cars showed that the Swiss Miss Chalet was undamaged.

"Laurie, shut up," she yelled, trying to be heard above

the screams, the shriek of smashing metal, and the crashing of wood.

Laurie's shocked face stared at her from her tree branch prison. "Shut up?" she bellowed. "I'm being kidnapped by a tree."

"I'm going to try something," Keelie yelled back. "Get ready to run."

She closed her eyes, trying to sense the tree's energy, but the only thing she could feel was its anger. Extreme anger and pain. A *bhata* crawled onto her shoulder and touched her eyes, and she could see through the magic. These trees were dying. The blue luminous liquid covered their trunks and oozed from open sores in their bark. They were trying to save themselves, but dark magic had twisted their pain into anger, and now they wanted revenge against humans.

Keelie summoned Tavak, but he didn't respond. She closed her eyes and opened her mind so that she could communicate through the trees' pain. All she saw was a sticky black mist enshrouding each and every tree. She listened, and this time the unmistakable lilt of a harp's music played in the distance. Elia.

Keelie closed her eyes and summoned the *bhata*, but none answered except for the one hanging onto her shoulder.

She called upon the evergreens in a valley several miles away. *I am the Tree Shepherdess Keliel, and I need your help.*

The lovely scent of Christmas trees surrounded her. Dark green energy filled her mind as a conifer named Evas answered her plea.

Tree Shepherdess, we will do what we can, but the only one who can stop the trees is Lord Einhorn.

Evas, I need the energy of the evergreens.

It is yours. We will do what we can to help our brothers.

She followed Evas' thoughts, and slid into the mind of the oak carrying them. His name was Ovrom. Keelie touched the pendants on her chest and felt, intertwined with the green magic, a dark, warm channel of Earth magic. The tektite. She pushed its earthy vibrancy into Ovrom, and felt his pain subside. The blue venumiel dried and flaked away. *I must help Lord Einhorn. You must stop attacking the humans, or I cannot help you, too.*

The tree stopped moving and the branches lowered until she and Laurie could touch the ground. They wriggled free of their spiky wooden cages.

You have healed me, Tree Shepherd's Daughter, Ovrom answered. *But I am compelled. Her music makes us hurt more.*

Keelie knew he meant Elia.

I will do what I can to stop her, but I have to find Lord Einhorn. Keelie was already exhausted, and she sensed the Dread building. If the humans became too afraid to move, and the trees began their attack once more, they would have no hope of survival. Keelie's lungs burned and head throbbed.

She touched the tektite around her neck, the rose quartz in her other hand. Calm, soothing energy flowed through her as if she'd been dipped in cool water, easing her pain.

The *bhata* clung to her hair.

"Keelie, we can't stay here. We'll die. We have to go."

"No, Laurie, that's just the Dread. I need you. We have to go on and find the unicorn, and I can't do it alone."

Laurie shrieked with fear and frustration. "I don't want to die!"

Around her, tall forms moved in the night. Keelie saw

green streamers rising from her friend's head. Chlorophyll poisoning. Keelie was okay, but Laurie wouldn't last much longer.

Someone shouted out above the wind's howling din, "Come on! Sir Davey said to get everyone to the Admin building."

Laurie let go of Keelie and started to run toward the voice.

"Come back," Keelie cried. "I need your help." She ran after her friend and tackled her. They rolled on the grass and watched as an oak smashed a pickup truck in two.

Laurie screamed and wriggled on the ground. Keelie knew the Dread had her in its grasp. The sound of creaking wood and smashing metal was deafening, and as she struggled to hold Laurie she saw others running toward the edge of the campground, where the path to the Admin building snaked beside the woods.

Laurie kicked out and connected with Keelie's leg. Keelie cried out and dropped the rose quartz. Immediately, she felt the paralyzing fear of the Dread.

She wanted to curl up and scream, but forced herself to scramble to her knees and run her hands over the ground, trying to find her rock. She couldn't breathe. She felt her fingers close around the rose quartz, but Laurie was on her feet and running.

Keelie cursed the trees and ran after her again. She'd never find Einhorn if she had to keep grabbing Laurie. A tree root swung over her head, and she ducked to the side, then channeled her inner track star and caught up with her friend, grabbing her long blonde hair and yanking her back.

Laurie rounded on her, eyes wide and panicked, and her

fist connected with Keelie's jaw. The rose quartz went flying again. Bright lights exploded as Keelie's head rocked back, but with one hand she kept her hold on Laurie's hair and wrestled her to the ground. She sat on Laurie's back, dodging her kicking feet.

She needed the rose quartz. She felt for it with her mind, remembering the calming effect it had on the Dread. A trickle of its energy remained in her hand, and she extended it toward the spot where she'd dropped it. Amazed, she felt it respond. She drew on that thread until the Dread backed away, and then she wrapped the cool pink energy around her friend.

Laurie's heavy breathing subsided and she turned onto her back, spitting out dirt and grass. "What the heck was that?"

"The Dread."

Laurie shuddered. "Now what? It's not over, is it?" The trees had followed the fleeing humans across the Faire ground, but the tektite had protected Keelie and Laurie. And with the rose quartz, they had overcome the Dread.

Keelie closed her eyes, pressing her hand over the tektite. She stood up and helped Laurie to her feet. The trail of the rose quartz seemed clear, and she found it in the grass a few yards away. It glowed pink when she picked it up.

"We have to get to the Admin building." Laurie was looking around nervously, as if the trees might be back. From the crashing on the other side of the campground, the Faire would never be the same again.

Keelie grabbed Laurie's arm. "We're not going to the Admin building. We're going to save the unicorn, and I need your help. Come on."

The *bhata* scampered back up onto her shoulder and Keelie suddenly had a clear mental picture of the unicorn in the circle of dead trees near the power plant. Then an image of the EPA agents formed, and she saw that their search had expanded up the mountainside to the power plant, where the unicorn was too weak to move.

The problem would be getting up there in time. She couldn't walk through the woods, which were dangerous now, full of pain-wracked trees and dark magic. Besides, it would take too long. But the path she'd hiked with Knot when she was fired from Steak-on-a-Stake was the old logging road.

"We can drive Dad's camper up the abandoned logging road. Dad's driven up and down roads that looked like water-park slides. We can do it, too. Or, you can. I don't know how to drive."

"Yeah, sure. We'll drive straight up the mountain in your dad's Jethro truck with possessed trees chasing us. And the evil witch will grant our wish and then we'll click our heels together—"

"It's not a joke, Laurie. It's the only way we can get there in time to save Dad and the unicorn."

As if on cue, Knot ran toward them, a jingling, shiny thing in his mouth. He dropped it at her feet. Dad's key ring.

"That cat is something else." Laurie looked down at him. "Where's your little white friend?"

"He's probably hiding out someplace safe." Keelie turned around and held the rose quartz up high, and in its pink glow she saw that her friend's eyes were still glazed with fear. The harp music sounded again from the forest, getting closer. Keelie grabbed the keys. "You go to Admin if you want. I'll drive."

"Do you think I'll see the unicorn if I go with you?" Laurie sounded hopeful.

Keelie knew she would not, but didn't answer.

Laurie sighed. "You can't drive. Give me those keys."

The Swiss Miss Chalet was, thankfully, unharmed. Keelie pulled dropped branches off the hood while Laurie cranked it up. Then Keelie jumped in, with Knot right after her.

"Drive to the end of the parking lot, then get on the little trail that goes toward Admin." Keelie could feel the *bhata* clinging to her hair like a weird woodland hair bow.

Knot's fur bushed out to maximum pouf. He hissed and looked toward the forest. Laurie turned the engine off. She hadn't even turned the headlights on.

"Why did you turn it off?" Was she crazy?

"Look." Laurie's voice trembled. She was pointing a shaking finger at Elianard, who had stepped out of the forest. He held a glowing silver rope, and at the end of it floated Dad, limp and unconscious.

"Let go of him, you bastard," Keelie screamed, opening the door.

Laurie grabbed the back of Keelie's shirt. "It's a trap."

Elianard glowered angrily, his hawkish nose harsh in the moonlight. "So very human to resort to name calling, but as you wish, I'll let go of him."

He twirled his amulet and Dad dropped, landing on the ground like a discarded marionette. "Oops, didn't mean to drop him so hard. I'm sure that wasn't very good for his internal organs, especially in his weakened condition. This is a nasty disease, especially for elves."

Keelie's heart skipped a beat. Laurie stuck her head out the window and yelled, "Yeah, well, how come you're unaffected?"

"This does not concern humans."

The *bhata* touched Keelie's eyelid, and she saw her father's image flicker. She remembered her dream. Dad was in a cabin up on the mountain.

More crackling leaves, and this time Lulu walked out of the woods. Elianard didn't look happy to see her.

"I can tell you why Elianard is able to resist the tree disease. He's using the unicorn's magic to protect himself and his daughter." Lulu smirked at Elianard, apparently unafraid of his powers.

"Shut up, witch."

Lulu almost hissed at him. "You think you're too good for me. Well, I'm taking the unicorn's horn for myself."

"Vain witch. How do you propose to capture him? With your *charms*?" Elianard sneered at her, but moved farther away.

Keelie noticed her father cast no shadow in the moonlight. It really wasn't him.

"You've caught him for me. Your daughter plays her harp and the poor beast can't move. You think I didn't follow you, to see for myself?"

"I should have known you would try to take his magic for yourself." Elianard glared at Lulu. "The unicorn belongs to me."

Keelie closed her eyes. She sought out her father, but his consciousness was blocked. She reached out to the trees who'd answered her before; she called out to Tavak. Nothing.

Evas. No answer.

Elianard pointed to Keelie. "Blame her. She has fought against us and strengthened the trees. Einhorn called to her to help him break the enchantment."

Lulu's face hardened, her mouth contorted into an angry scowl. "I should've known. Ever since you showed up, kid, I've had the worst luck."

"Laurie," Keelie whispered. "Can you start the camper up again? No lights, just aim for the road that Sir Davey took."

"But your dad—"

"I don't think that's really Dad. I think you're right—it's a trap."

Keelie heard shouts of men in the distance. "Hey Charlie, that strange light's coming from down here."

"It's the EPA." She felt panicked. "They're going to find us."

Laurie cranked the camper, and with a howl of triumph shoved it into gear and stomped on the accelerator. The old Swiss Miss Chalet surged forward, bumping over branches and bits of abandoned camping gear as Laurie aimed it at the road.

Elianard held his amulet up. The glowing silver rope faded, and so did the image of Dad. It *had* been an illusion. A silvery lightning bolt streaked toward them, and Keelie screamed, "Faster!"

The bolt hit the back of the camper, and bits of gingerbread trim went flying past the cab windows.

Knot's green eyes glowed with a hellacious hatred as they passed Elianard, who was just a blur in the darkness. The white figure of Lulu leaped back, and then they crashed over the curb and were careening down the path toward Admin.

Keelie watched the forest, feeling for the logging road. The ghost trees filled the woods with their spectral presence.

"Here," she yelled, and Laurie wrenched the wheel to the right, knocking Knot off the back of the seat. With a yowl of surprise he thudded to the floor, then crawled back up, hissing briefly at Laurie before squeezing onto the dashboard—an evil kitty dashboard ornament.

Then something totally unexpected happened. A figure rose from the bracken and stretched out a white hand toward them. Laurie shrieked, and would have turned off the logging road, but Keelie grabbed the wheel.

"Stop the car!"

Laurie stomped on the brake and they flopped forward against their seat belts. Lucky for Knot, he couldn't move anywhere.

The figure struggled through the undergrowth, and then stepped into the beam of the headlights. Bloody, gown torn, and hair hanging around her shoulders, she limped toward the truck. Despite her bruised face, she smiled when she saw who had stopped for her.

It was Raven.

twenty-seven

Keelie leaped out of the camper and ran around the front to help Raven climb in. "Are you okay? Where's Janice?"

Laurie was poking her head out the window, looking up at the ghost trees that were now crowding the haunted forest.

"Our shop took a pounding and I ran into the forest. The trees didn't seem to be coming from here." Raven looked awful, but sounded okay. "I'm really worried about Mom, though. She took Lady Annie to Admin after Annie's shop took a direct hit, and I don't know where she is now."

"Probably safe." Keelie was relieved at the news, although the destruction of Lady Annie's shop disturbed her.

She was right next door to Heartwood. "Sir Davey rounded everyone up and took them there, too. He'll protect them."

Raven leaned back in the seat and closed her eyes. A tear trailed down her cheek. "Thank God."

They needed to keep moving. "We cross there, Laurie." Keelie pointed toward the stream. She could see a spectral road, a silver shadow overlying the darkness. The unicorn was somewhere above them, on the mountain.

"Not that way." Raven opened her eyes. "There's a huge drop to the stream bed. But if you go about fifty yards left, it's like a beach. We go skinny-dipping there when it's really hot."

"Really?" Laurie seemed to want to hear more.

"Will we be able to drive across the stream there?" Keelie interrupted. "We have to get to the top."

"No one drives through the woods, Keelie. There's no road. You're insane." Raven held onto the dash with both hands.

"That's what I think, too, but we have to save the unicorn." Laurie steered around a huge tree stump. "I can make it. I've driven on the Los Angeles Freeway in rush hour, so driving through the woods is a piece of cake."

Keelie remembered the first night she saw the unicorn, and the sense of awe she'd felt. Now, desperation clawed its way inside her to get to him and save him. "Go for it."

They got to the stream and Laurie gunned the truck across the bed, not giving the tires a chance to sink into the soft, sandy bottom. Keelie touched the Queen Aspen's heart and tried to strengthen her magic sight. She felt queasy for a moment as the two worlds were visible at once, overlaid one on the other. "I can see the road. It's an old logging trail."

"Whoa. Your eyes are like glow-in-the-dark green." Raven looked at Knot. "So are his."

With Keelie guiding them with the magic sight, they drove up the hill, switching back and forth as Keelie focused on the road that was hidden underneath the growth. Branches thumped against the camper. Shadows of trees, the spirits of the old trees who had been logged from the forest, grew alongside the road with the living trees, whispery shades in the moonlight.

Keelie recalled the Tree Lorem ceremony that Dad had performed for Reina, the Aspen Queen in Colorado whose charred heart she wore. He'd released Reina's spirit so that the other trees in the forest could heal, and grow deep roots and tall limbs reaching for the sun. No such ceremony had taken place here in a long time.

Leaves from the trees slapped against the windshield. Keelie could see faces in the tree trunks, like she did with the oak trees at the Faire. It was amazing how individual they all were.

Laurie almost hit a tree; fortunately it jumped back in time, and she missed it.

"Whoa, pay attention to the road, Laurie," Raven shouted over the roar of the truck and the crashing underbrush. She clung to her seat belt and braced her feet against the glove box. The *bhata* had lodged itself in one of the visors and hung upside down, its berry eyes wide and fixed on the forest ahead.

"What road? There's no road."

Keelie had to focus on Dad. Save Dad. Save the unicorn. That would be her mantra.

"Why didn't you ever tell me you were an elf?" Laurie suddenly asked.

"Half elf. And I didn't know, until I came to live with Dad." A pang went through Keelie's chest. He had to be all right.

"Were you going to tell me?"

"I don't know."

"Oh, that's just great; keep secrets from your friend."

"Me keep secrets?"

Laurie gripped the wheel and glanced at her accusingly. "Yeah, you."

"You're one to talk. Hey, keep your eyes on the invisible road. Why don't you tell me about why you can't see the unicorn?"

Silence.

Again, Keelie looked over at her friend.

Laurie was hunched in concentration. "I didn't think I'd be outed by a mythical beast." She glared at Keelie. The truck shimmied and slid sideways.

Keelie pointed straight ahead. "Well, are you going to tell me? You know my secrets."

Raven groaned. "Guys, just fess up before we fall off the mountain."

Laurie gritted her teeth and stepped hard on the accelerator. The truck shot forward. "Trent and I were dating, and I was at his house, watching movies, and we kissed, and one thing led to another, and we sort of did it."

Keelie gasped as a tree motioned for them to turn to the right, like a policeman directing forest traffic with branches. She pointed and Laurie turned. The truck's engine whined at the steep climb.

"So you and Trent really love each other, right?"

"He broke up with me and started dating Ashlee."

"What a jerk," Keelie and Raven said at the same time.

"And Ashlee put the story on her MySpace page. She blogged about it."

"No. That bitch." Keelie slammed the dashboard.

Raven shook her head. "Unbelievable. Some people."

Knot meowed. Laurie patted him on the head, then put both hands back on the wheel when the truck swerved.

"This is very surreal," Raven said quietly. "We're talking about high school drama, driving up a road that doesn't exist yet somehow does exist, on our way to rescue a unicorn."

"And my dad," Keelie reminded her. "I've lost one parent, and I'm not going to lose Dad because of Elianard and Elia."

A white deer ran out in front of them, and Laurie pressed on the brake. They fishtailed to a stop, and the wheels toward the inside of the trail lifted a bit before coming back down.

Knot fell onto the floor, and Raven lunged sideways as she braced her arms against the dash. "Are you crazy?" she shouted.

"I've never seen a white deer before. Creepy." Laurie started forward again.

Keelie slapped her forehead. She pointed into the darkness. "White deer, white cat, white unicorn. He's a shape shifter!" She pounded the dashboard as she put the supernatural equation together. "The glowing white fur, the eyes, the white cat was the unicorn!"

"I saw the white cat and that white deer—maybe I'll see the unicorn, too." Laurie sounded excited.

Knot climbed back onto the dashboard and wedged himself against the windshield. He hooked his claws into the AC vents. Keelie wished she had one of Sir Davey's crystals to give the truck more power. Laurie pushed on the gas, and finally the lumbering ski chalet was on top of the hill.

On the horizon, the night sky glittered with thousands of stars. Keelie had never seen this many stars when she lived in Los Angeles.

From the corner of her eye, she saw a shooting star. She made a wish—*please let me save the unicorn and Dad*. It was two wishes, but maybe given the circumstances she could hope for a two-fer deal.

Laurie rolled down her window, and Keelie heard a roaring sound. Raven heard it, too. "We're getting close to the power plant." They were driving along the ridge.

Suddenly, they slowed. The trail seemed clear to Keelie. "Can't we go any faster?"

She glanced at Laurie, whose expression was strained. Her eyes were strange with some unexplained emotion. Raven called out, and the truck rolled to a stop.

Keelie watched, horrified, as her friends wailed and ducked, cringing as if something were swooping down on them. She knew what it was. She felt the Dread beating around her, renewed, stronger than ever before.

"Keelie, I can't move." Laurie brought her feet up to the seat and wrapped her arms around her knees. Raven shivered and leaned against her.

Keelie opened the door and jumped out. "Come on, it's not much farther."

"I can't go, I'm going to die." Laurie was gasping. "I can't breathe. Something bad is going to happen."

"Don't go, Keelie." Raven's eyes looked huge in her pale face. Her black hair blended into the darkness around them. "I don't want you to die."

The scent of cinnamon floated in the air. "It's the Dread, guys. It's not real. Fight it." Elianard must be using up every drop of power on the mountain to feed it.

There was a pounding of frantic hooves, followed by

a strangled whinny, and then a shrill scream. Keelie froze. "Please, don't be Einhorn."

"Einhorn, the unicorn?" Raven sat up straight.

"It feels so real." Laurie's face looked strained. "Let's get out of here."

Knot's ears were flat against his skull. He growled. The *bhata* yanked at Keelie's hair and pinched her ear, pulling her forward. "Ow, I'm coming."

"Who are you talking to?" Raven looked as if she wanted to crawl under the seat, but she forced herself to straighten. "I'm coming with you, Keelie."

Knot's tail whipped back and forth. He yowled, then jumped over Raven's legs and streaked away. The whine and roar of the power plant's turbines was overwhelming. Keelie could hear the intertwined notes of Elia's harp.

"Stay here if you're afraid." She hurried after the cat, the *bhata* clinging to her hair.

"You're more elf than human if you're not feeling this!" Laurie yelled after her, putting her hands over her ears and closing her eyes. She probably thought the turbine's throbbing was part of the Dread. There was no time to explain.

Knot looked back, his tail lashing wildly. Keelie saw him meow. He wanted her to follow him, but she couldn't without any light. She reached into her pocket and brought out the rose quartz. At first it flickered, but once it powered up, it shone like a super-watt flashlight. "I'm coming."

Behind her, she heard the camper door slam. Raven was clutching the fender and looking as if she was about to throw up, but moving steadily forward.

A faint tree voice sounded in her head. Keelie tried to

concentrate on the message, and when she reached the edge of the woods it came through. It was Tavak.

Einhorn has fallen.

Below her, the headlights went out. Keelie looked back and Laurie waved, a brief flutter of white in the darkness. She waved back, then, heart heavy, followed Knot.

The clearing was not far, but undergrowth tugged at her clothes. The trees were all dead here, and weeds had taken over. Keelie was overwhelmed by sadness; so many trees were dead and gone, and their spirits clung to the earth, trapped. She felt them call to her, but their voices were dim.

A light flickered ahead, and Keelie pocketed the rose quartz. She hid behind a boulder scaly with lichen. Elianard knelt in the clearing, at the foot of a huge, ghostly tree. A white form was splayed out at his feet. Lord Einhorn.

The unicorn faded in and out of consciousness as Elianard held his amulet over its horn. Nearby, Elia played her harp, tears streaming down her face, her eyes locked onto the failing unicorn.

Keelie stayed hidden. The tektite around her neck had grown uncomfortably warm, and so had her aspen heart talisman. Again, she looked up into the night sky, and she saw another shooting star. *Help me to save Einhorn.*

She ripped the leather thong from around her neck and held it aloft. The tektite, no longer black, glowed like a small, leaf-shaped star, each tiny rune picked out in brighter light.

Opening her senses to the trees, Keelie summoned Tavak and Evas.

Tavak answered, *Tree Shepherdess, I'm here.*

Evas replied as well. *Milady, we hear you.*

From the Faire, far below, Keelie sensed Oamlik and

the other sick oaks. She sent a message, but they were still under the harp's spell.

Near her, Knot paced back and forth. What had she been thinking? She'd fought her way up here, put her friends in danger, and for what? Einhorn was dead, the trees were immobilized, and she had no way of finding her father.

A sickening, meaty crack was followed by the unicorn's scream. Elianard rose, the lovely spiral horn in his hand. The silver light outlining Einhorn's body slowly faded.

Elianard turned to look toward the rock, and Keelie felt his penetrating stare bore right through to her. "Round Ear, you come too late. You cannot stop me."

He marched toward her. Fear filled Keelie, but she wasn't going to run. She stepped out, her voice shaky. "I stopped you once before, I can stop you now." But she could tell he was not fooled.

"You are too late. You are not one of us." Elianard pointed toward the power plant. "This is what your species does, it destroys, but the humans won't destroy our elven lands. You think me harsh to take the unicorn's magic, but it will save many." He held the bloody horn in one hand, unaware of the irony of his words.

Keelie clenched her fists. "You've hurt the people at the Faire, too. What justifies their sacrifice?"

Elia stopped playing her harp and stood up. "Nothing. They should not have been harmed."

Elianard turned to his daughter with raised brows. "Why did you stop? Continue. Our work is not yet done."

"No, father, please don't do this." Elia's haughty look was gone, and she seemed haunted and afraid. "Think of what will happen to you. Think of me."

"Don't be foolish." Elianard gestured impatiently. "Einhorn's magic can't save the Wildewood, but it can save the Dread Forest. His death is one of honor, and his magic will give me the power to save the elves."

He closed quickly on Keelie and snatched off the tektite and the charred heart, yanking the cords over her head. They snagged on her pointed elf ear, and Keelie cried out. She tried to hold onto the cords, but he was too strong. He threw them to the other side of the clearing and then grabbed her right wrist, squeezing until her hand went numb and she dropped the rose quartz.

He pushed her down, and Keelie curled into a ball, overcome by the Dread without the stone's protection. She would die here, alone, as her mother had died in a plane crash, as her father might now be dying somewhere in the forest. The unicorn was dead, and Elianard had won. All was lost. She trembled, thinking of all the ways that Elianard could hurt her.

A tiny voice in the back of her mind reminded her that if she had her rose quartz, she wouldn't feel the Dread. She remembered the way she'd pulled on the rose quartz even when it was far from her.

Elianard was pushing Elia back to her harp. The beautiful elf girl sobbed, but began to play again. Elianard resumed his place by Einhorn, holding the horn triumphantly over the unicorn's body.

The unicorn faded even more. The feeling of sorrow from the trees was unbearable. This wasn't the Dread, this was the combined grief of thousands of trees, living and dead, mourning their guardian.

Keelie's face was wet with tears. She couldn't do anything.

She was just a kid. If her father couldn't help, what hope did she have?

"No!" She thought of Dad dying as Mom had, alone. And leaving her alone, too. She was afraid to open herself to feel for the rose quartz. What if she felt the trees' pain instead?

A touch on her cheek made her cry out. Elianard glanced at her, then froze, staring.

Keelie didn't know what he was looking at. Would she die now? She thought of her friends, still by the camper. She didn't want to die alone. The touch came again, and Keelie saw that it was the *bhata*. It sat on her arm in a watchful pose. *Yes, you can feel for the rose quartz*, the tiny voice told her. She would find it.

Keelie opened her mind. Her fists closed around moist clods of cool earth—and she felt power.

Huge power. Power that yawned just under the surface of the mountain in a vast, unending pool. She gasped. This was not her little pink crystal. It was warm and earthy and yellow, like a molten sun, like a vast nourishing river that she could draw on, again and again.

Blind with grief, she picked up a strand of it and wove it around herself. The Dread abated. Keelie sobbed and took the power, channeling it through her body until she felt as if she would explode, her skin tingling and her blood pulsing with it. She pushed a bright ribbon of it into the unicorn, and his eyelids fluttered. She stood and ran to him. He had faded, his glow gone. She saw his worn fur, with the bare spots, the stump of his horn bloody and broken where Elianard had ripped it from him.

"Get away from him, misbegotten brat. You can do nothing for him now." Elianard seized her shoulders, but before he could wrench her away she pulled on the power thread and pushed the molten energy into the dying unicorn.

The power crashed through Elianard, too, and he cried out and released her, reeling back across the clearing. Elia stood and, eyes on Keelie, lifted the harp over her head and smashed it to the ground.

Keelie felt the Dread vanish with the harp's destruction, and at the same time, the trees sang out their release. She sensed their movement. They were coming.

Elianard turned and ran, crashing down the mountain. Keelie didn't worry. He was headed toward the approaching trees.

The power thread had wrapped tightly around the unicorn, and with her magic sight, Keelie saw him absorbing the molten energy. But still he lay, eyes closed. Had it all been for nothing?

She wrapped her hand around the unicorn's mane, aware that Elia was watching, and put her forehead against his cheek. A hand reached down to hand her the rose quartz. Elia smiled uncertainly, then stepped away. The rose quartz in her other fist, Keelie felt for the magic that had helped her before, the strong Earth magic that rose from the mountain beneath her. Then, from the unicorn, she guided it out, far out. She felt it spread like a river overflowing its boundaries. The forests for miles around soaked it in, and green sprang anew.

When there was no place for the power to go, Keelie sent it home, back into the earth below. She was conscious only long enough to hear the explosions on the other side of the ridge, as the power plant blew flame far into the sky.

twenty-eight

A cool whisper blew across her cheek. Keelie opened her eyes and saw the unicorn standing over her. She sat up and stared. He glowed as before, but where his horn had been was a jagged, bloody stump.

She turned and saw Raven standing by the boulder, her fist covering her mouth, crying huge tears from her wide eyes.

"Raven? Are you hurt?"

Raven shook her head. "I'm okay. I'm okay." But her eyes went to the place where the unicorn stood.

"You can see him." Keelie stared at her friend, surprised.

Raven took a tentative step forward, and the thing she

had in her hand glowed like a star. It was the tektite. The unicorn watched her approach, eyes intent.

"Give it to me." Keelie reached her hand out.

"No." Raven's eyes were fixed on Einhorn. "Don't be afraid, my lord."

Einhorn moved toward her, and she touched the tektite to his wound, his head nestled against her like a grieving child.

Keelie went to stand behind Raven and Einhorn, watching them together. The tektite wasn't enough. She could feel it. She placed her palm flat against Raven's back, feeling her heart thud, then reached down to the well of power and pushed it through Raven and into the unicorn.

Einhorn tossed his head, and Raven fought to keep the tektite on his wrecked horn. Her hands glowed, then her arms, as Einhorn's aura engulfed her until they were a single glowing object. Keelie felt herself burn, part of that shining space, and then she fell back into her own body and collapsed on the leaf-strewn ground.

Einhorn reared, glorious once more, his horn restored and gleaming. Keelie staggered to her feet, and Raven turned and hugged her. The two girls clung to each other, laughing and crying at the same time as Einhorn bowed his horn low to the ground, then galloped into the forest.

She'd never gotten to speak to him. A tickle in her mind formed itself into feathery thoughts.

Tree Shepherdess, in saving me, you have healed the forest, and in turn you have healed your father and his people from the humans' poisons. May they realize that they have in you a phoenix, bringing forth a new era and a new way for the elves.

"Keelie, are you okay?" Laurie stood behind her. "I heard the explosion and came running. The Dread is gone."

"I'm okay. Did you see him?"

"Your dad? No. Is he around here?" Laurie kicked at the shards of the smashed harp. "What happened here?"

Dad. How was she going to find him with Elianard gone?

Keelie felt a little shaky, but better than she had in days, as if she'd had a full night's sleep. The green tinge was gone from her skin. She looked around the clearing. Elia had vanished, and so had Einhorn's broken horn.

We have found your father, Tavak said. *Follow the bhata.*

The leaves above them shook, and *bhata* poured down the trunks of the trees and raced across the clearing. Hundreds more of the stick fairies flew and crawled around them.

Laurie screamed and climbed onto the boulder. Knot leaped off and streaked into the forest after them, with Keelie in pursuit and Raven right behind.

"Hey guys, wait up!" Laurie's voice was far away.

With a noise like a thousand castanets, the *bhata* led the way, and Keelie jumped over logs and dodged branches, racing with Knot beside her. The ghostly trees of the forest weren't scary now, and as they ran, the living trees grew larger until there were only the tall ancients around her.

Knot slowed, stopping on a giant root, and Keelie saw that the tree was prickly with *bhata*, their berry eyes focused on the roots below them. Knot leaped down, and Keelie clambered over and saw, nestled in the crook of the vast tree's base, her father's still figure.

"Dad." She jumped down and knelt beside him. He was breathing, and his skin was once more sun-browned.

You healed him, Tree Shepherdess, the old tree above her said. *He was safe here until you came.*

Thank you for guarding him, Ancient One. She wondered how she'd get him back home.

She nudged his shoulder. "Dad?"

He moved a little, and then he yawned, stretching wide. He opened his green eyes, a mirror of her own. "Keelie?"

"I'm here, Dad."

"Lord Einhorn . . . " He fell silent, his head cocked, listening to the forest. His eyes widened. "You've had quite a night."

"Don't listen to the trees, Dad. They're awful gossips."

He smiled and grabbed the tree root to pull himself up. It lifted, helping him. Keelie put her shoulder under his other arm and steadied him.

"Elianard?"

"I don't know. Last I saw, he was booking it down the mountain. Tavak came to the rescue."

You are the rescuer, Tree Shepherdess, the Old One said above them. Keelie could see that Dad heard it, too.

As a sign of our trust in you, we give you a great honor and a great responsibility. We offer you a treeling of our forest to root in your Dread Forest.

Dad seemed moved. He was actually showing a little eye leakage. Keelie wondered what the trees were talking about. A treeling. Sounded like some sort of Arbor Day project.

I accept, and thank you. If the trees wanted to give her a souvenir, why not?

The earth at her feet moved, and she stepped back,

alarmed. A huge acorn popped out of the ground and rolled, bumping to a stop at her tennis shoe. Its cap was banded in worked gold.

"Pretty," Keelie said. She bent over and picked it up. It was heavy.

Dad stood over her and touched the gold ring with a fingertip. *Welcome to our family, Princess Alora.*

Princess Alora. The nut had a name. She smiled as she realized that she'd heard Dad's greeting in her mind.

As they walked back to find the others, Keelie realized that she'd chased Knot through the forest in pitch blackness, using the magic sight to find her way. Raven and Laurie must have turned back. They found them back on the ridge, by the battered Swiss Miss Chalet. Dad insisted that they leave it there and walk down the mountain. By the time they reached the stream, the sun was rising.

Sir Davey was waiting for them on the other bank. He held his lantern aloft and shouted, "They're over here. Janice. Tell the others."

Keelie was the first to wade across. She felt fingers around her ankles as she forded the stream, and heard the silvery laugh of a water sprite. "If you knock me in the water, I'll bring beavers here to dam up your stream." The fingers withdrew quickly. "Just kidding."

Sir Davey met her, his expression grave. "Keelie, there's no easy way to put this. Your father is missing from the lodge."

"No, he's not. He's right over there." She pointed back across the stream, where Dad was helping Raven down the slippery side. As they watched, he staggered to one side, still weak.

Sir Davey's eyes brightened and he breathed a big sigh

of relief. "Lass, you've got a story to tell me, but the Emergency Response Team from Oregon is here, and they'll tend to your father now."

Janice arrived, worry lines wrinkling her forehead, her bracelets jangling on her wrist as she draped blankets over Raven, Laurie, and Keelie. "Girls, I'll get you something hot, and then all three of you need to get into bed and sleep."

Keelie didn't feel like sleeping. She watched Janice and her friends take the path that led back to the Faire, with Laurie quizzing Raven about skinny-dipping.

Several elves appeared, carrying a stretcher. "Where's the Tree Shepherd?" one asked.

Keelie pointed to the stream, where Dad was telling Sir Davey about the night's adventures, and Sir Davey was filling him in on what had happened at the Faire.

The elves passed her, mostly dressed in hiking boots and dark green cargo pants, with thermal T-shirts sporting the golden tree logo she'd seen on Dad's elven correspondence. One hung back, an elderly woman whose gray hair was pinned back in a severe bun. She was wearing a long embroidered gown, which reminded Keelie of something from the Middle Ages although she got the feeling this was not a costume. The woman stopped and looked at Keelie.

"Keliel Heartwood, come to me."

One of the elves leaned over to Keelie. "That's Etilafael. She's on the Council."

Keelie walked over to the elf woman.

The woman lifted Keelie's chin up, and turned her head to the right and to the left. "The blessings of the trees are upon you, child. I expect great things from you."

With that, she walked away.

Puzzled, Keelie turned to the enclosure the Emergency Response Team had set up. She couldn't wait to see the Response Team's faces when they saw that Dad was totally okay. They had set up barriers around a tent and the entrance was guarded.

Just as she was about to step through, an elven woman blocked Keelie's way. "You are not allowed."

"I am, too."

"Humans aren't allowed."

Keelie stood open-mouthed. "That's my dad in there."

"You are human. Entrance is denied." The woman closed the gate to the barriers, and turned away.

She'd saved the unicorn, the forest had given her a treeling, and she still wasn't considered an elf. If this was a preview of coming attractions, then life was still unfair. Keelie debated stomping back to the campground. No way. Dad owed her some answers.

She vaulted over the gate and marched into the tent where her father lay. The elf guard ran after her. "Stop. You must leave immediately."

Her father was pale, his eyes closed. He still had a blue tint to his skin and was weak from the venumiel.

Then he opened his eyes and saw Keelie. "I'm proud of you. I don't know how you tapped such Earth magic, but you've saved the unicorn, the Wildewood, and the elves. I was wrong when I said you couldn't handle it. But Keelie, I was so afraid, and you could have been killed."

"I think Elianard would have killed me. In case you haven't noticed, the elves don't exactly adore me. That woman wouldn't let me see you. I'm a Round Ear." She spat the word out.

Dad took her hand in his cool one. "Just as there are mean-spirited people, there are mean-spirited elves. Elianard and Elia for example. Don't judge us all by those two."

"I think they're totally evil. Just because Elianard wanted to save the Dread Forest, does that mean he was right to try to kill the unicorn?"

Dad flinched. "What?"

"Elianard said that he was trying to save the elven home forest. He thought that justified killing Einhorn, to take his power."

Dad's expression turned grim. He seemed shocked at her revelation.

"I don't think I can live in the Dread Forest. My human side seems to be the only part of me that they see."

"I need for you to be tough when you get to the elven forest," Dad answered quickly. "You have friends among the elves, but prejudice is in every culture and society, whether it be based on the color of your skin or the shape of your ears." He pointed to her heart. "As long as this guides your life, then you can face anything that is thrown at you, whether it be elf, human, magic, or injustice. You're strong like your mother." He closed his eyes, exhausted.

Keelie kissed his forehead. "Thanks, Dad. I love you." The answers to her questions would have to wait.

twenty-nine

Dinner the next day was an open-air feast. Because of the three-state blackout caused by the power plant's "inexplicable" failure, all of the Faire's freezers had been emptied, and a vast barbecue had been set up featuring lots of turkey legs and steak on a stake.

Raven had spread out quilts by Davey's RV, the only decent sleeping place around, and Keelie flopped down on one, exhausted. She had spent the day helping to clean up from what the papers were calling a "freak storm." But from the shell-shocked looks on some of the faces around her, everyone remembered the tree rampage and no storm story would convince them otherwise.

Janice's shop would need big repairs, but luckily most of the damage had been to the upstairs living quarters. Lady Annie had moved into Lulu's shop. Lulu had last been seen hanging by her feet from a spruce tree, her mouth sealed with resin.

Elianard's room at the lodge had been empty, and Elia's things were gone as well. Keelie wondered why the elf girl had helped her, and whether she knew what had happened to Einhorn's broken horn. No doubt she would run into her again in the Dread Forest. Keelie was not looking forward to it.

In the parking lot, Finch was in her element, barking orders and shouting at slowpokes. Sir Brine had turned out to be a hero, or at least that's what he told everyone as he recounted his valiant effort to hold back the trees with catapulted pickles. Dad was talking to him, because the little weirdo had his eyes set on the old Lady Annie booth right next door to Heartwood. No way would he set up his perma–pickle stand that close to them.

Keelie looked up at the blue sky, and listened to the sound of the river nearby and the murmur of the trees in the breeze. Gone was the oppressive feeling of the forest. Dad had scheduled a Tree Lorem for later.

Knot ran past, yowling, a *bhata* riding him like a stick cowboy.

She rolled over onto her stomach and laughed.

"What's so funny?"

Keelie turned over again, and looked up at the figure that was blocking the sun. She brought a hand up to shade her eyes, but he dropped down next to her. He brushed blond hair from his forehead, his blue-green eyes on her.

"Sean." He looked just as handsome as he had when

she'd last seem him in Colorado. She sat up, feeling shy and wishing she knew what had been in those letters. Had they been friendly, kind of "Hey how are you?" or had they been dreamy love letters? She was at a serious disadvantage.

"Your father told me you were coming. I didn't know if you wanted to see me again."

His eyes clouded. "I wasn't too sure myself. Why didn't you answer my letters?"

"I never saw them, Sean. Your dad said that you'd written. I thought you'd forgotten me, or that you'd met someone else." The last words faded in volume as he leaned forward, eyes fixed on her lips. This was totally okay. Life had suddenly improved more than one hundred percent. Her heart thudded, feeling as if it was fluttering in her throat. Did he feel the same? Their lips met, his mouth warm and firm on hers. His hand covered hers on the blanket and she felt his pulse, fast against her skin. Okay. That answered that.

Knot streaked by again, and this time ran right over the quilt, making Keelie and Sean pull apart. This was a good thing, since Dad appeared a second later.

"Sean, well met. Your father told me you were coming."

Sean stood and the two men bowed their heads to each other, elf fashion, and then shook hands. From the look on Dad's face, maybe he'd seen too much.

"You should go now. The feast at the lodge is starting soon." Dad looked meaningfully at Sean.

"You are coming, too, are you not?" Sean smiled at Dad, then down at Keelie. His smile warmed.

"I'll make an appearance," Dad said. "Keelie will not attend."

"First I've heard of it," Keelie announced, then shut up, as she realized she'd probably not been invited.

Sean looked from Keelie to her father, and back again. "Not attending? But it's in appreciation of what you did. You saved the forest."

"The dinner is for the Response Team," Dad said.

Keelie shrugged. "The dinner is for the full-blood elves, is what he means. No Round Ears need attend. I don't care. My friends are here."

Sean looked shocked. "If that is so, then I won't go either. I'll stay here with you."

Zeke's smile grew frosty. "Lord Niriel will not be pleased."

Keelie wondered if Dad was being snarky about Lord Niriel just because he was Sean's dad, or if there was another reason. Not that it would help to ask. He never told her anything.

Sean bowed again. "As Keelie said, my friends are here."

His words warmed her. With Sean beside her, the Dread Forest wouldn't be so lonely.

Laurie and Raven came flying up, laden with plates, and stopped, eyes wide at the elf face-off. Keelie patted the quilt beside her.

"Sit down, ladies. Raven, you know Sean o' the Wood. Sean, this is my old friend Laurie."

Dad raised his arms in surrender and headed for the lodge, leaving the girls to admire Sean.

After dinner, they all walked up the trail to an overlook that Raven remembered from previous stays at the Wildewood Faire. They could see down to Rivendell from here, and the lilting strains of Jared playing an instrumental version of *The Three Marys* floated up to them. They started back down when Rigadoon was tuning up. The dancing was about to begin.

Keelie's eyes caught a glimmer in the forest to their right. "Go on, guys. I want to look at something."

Sean stopped, too. "Need my help?"

"No, you go down. I'll catch up."

She watched Laurie and Raven converge on Sean and laughed. He loved the attention. She walked into the forest.

"Lord Einhorn?"

A beautiful man in a snowy white shirt and pristine white jeans stepped out from behind a great tree. His skin glowed, leaving no doubt that he was the unicorn.

"I didn't know you could be a person, too."

Einhorn smiled, and it was as if a star had kissed her.

He held out a hand. Dangling from his long fingers was the Queen Aspen's charred heart, and also a cord on which hung a silver acorn entwined with thorns. Elianard's amulet.

Keelie took the charred heart, but left the other. "Thank you."

He still held out Elianard's pendant. "This is for you as well." His voice was like chimes in a breeze. "You saved my life, you saved my forest, and you've brought me my mate."

Mate? She didn't remember that part, but she took the necklace and dropped it over her head, hiding it inside her shirt. It felt cold and sharp against her skin.

"Keelie? You here?" Raven's voice came from the path.

"It was my honor to be of service to you." Keelie bowed her head in the elven way. Dad would be so proud of her, even if she wasn't too sure about that mate business. Surely he didn't mean her? Or, worse, Elia?

Underbrush rustled behind her. "Keelie, is that you in

here? Who are you talking to?" Raven stepped forward. Keelie looked at her, wondering if she'd still be able to see the unicorn, or if last night had been part of a greater magic.

Einhorn extended a pale, long-fingered hand, and to Keelie's astonishment, Raven took it and went to stand at his side, her darkness striking against his light. He lifted her hand to his lips, and the two stared at each other for a long moment.

Then Einhorn shimmered, and the unicorn stood before them. He bowed low, so that his horn touched Keelie's forehead. It felt as if he were blessing her. Then he reared up, turned, and galloped away.

Raven brushed her fingertips over Keelie's brow and smiled gently. Then the old, no-nonsense Raven was back. "So, weren't we headed down to Rivendell?"

"You and Lord Einhorn?" She didn't have to speak the rest of the question. The answer seemed obvious.

"From the moment I saw him in the clearing. We have a date tomorrow night. He's kind of old-fashioned." Raven picked her way toward the path.

Keelie followed, her head still spinning from the idea of Raven being the unicorn's mate. "Married to a unicorn. That's just so weird."

"Not really. And hey, I won't have to worry about Rennie wenches going after him. They won't even see him."

Keelie laughed, then thought that maybe one day she wouldn't see him either. Sean waved to her from the bottom of the hill, and Laurie yelled to them to hurry.

Raven linked her arm through Keelie's. "What's really weird is that I'm grateful to Elia, if she was responsible for messing up my gig at Doom Kitty. Without her I'd still be there, instead of finding my true love."

Keelie laughed again. "Grateful to Elia. That *is* strange."

"Einhorn wanted to know where Elianard and Elia were. Did they just disappear?"

"Yeah, but I have a feeling they won't be gone for long. Dad thinks they're headed for the Dread Forest. He says Elianard has friends who share his views."

Raven looked troubled. "What does that mean for Einhorn? Will they be back?"

Keelie shook her head. "Who knows?"

"No one's going to hurt my mate, or the Wildewood," Raven said, suddenly fierce. For a second she looked proud and strong, a warrior queen protecting her realm.

Whatever sort of creature Raven's dad might be, he'd be proud of her. Keelie was relieved that she wouldn't have to worry about the Wildewood again, or Einhorn.

■ ■ ■

That night, the remaining elves held a Tree Lorem. It was a very different ceremony from the one they'd held for the Queen Aspen at the High Mountain Faire. There, the elves had praised Keelie, and she'd received the Queen's charred heart.

At this Lorem, she stood at one end of the tree that represented all the ones that had fallen. It was Bruk, the oak, and Keelie's cheeks were wet as she remembered the tree's pain when they'd been briefly mind-bonded. As her father laid his hands on the scarred bark, Bruk's face appeared, serene now, and then faded back into the wood. Keelie felt the forest lighten, as all the tree spirits faded into the Forest Beyond, leaving behind the green and the living.

Raven stood at the edge of the gathering, the white cat cradled in her arms. Keelie looked into its eyes and saw her pain reflected there.

Lord Niriel looked from Keelie to Raven, and down at the cat, and a curious expression crossed his handsome face. Even though he was Sean's father, she felt uneasy. Something about him reminded her of Lord Elianard. They were both tall and handsome older guys, but that should be the only resemblance. Lord Niriel was always polite. Even now, when other elves had sneered and whispered about Raven, who they thought was human, attending their ceremony, Lord Niriel had welcomed her graciously.

Keelie smiled at him, and he smiled back. Why had Dad said she should stay away from him? Lord Niriel was charming. Dad had told her to stay away from the unicorn, too, and good thing she hadn't listened to him.

Lady Etilafael stepped forward, and all eyes turned to her. "Keliel Heartwood, we thank you and your friends for your extraordinary efforts." She turned to Raven. "Lord Einhorn's lady, Raven of the Shining Ones—" A gasp went up from the elves and everyone craned their necks to look at Raven, who seemed puzzled by the name she'd been called. "You honor us with your presence at our ceremony. The Wildewood is in good hands."

Raven bowed her head, but her eyes shot over to Keelie as if to ask, "What the hell?"

Keelie shrugged. Yet another question for Dad.

Dad leaned close. "The Shining Ones are the high fairies," he whispered.

Keelie turned to stare at Raven. *Whoa.*

epilogue

Keelie propped her feet on the Swiss Miss Chalet's dashboard and prayed for deafness. Or a coma. The camper creaked and groaned with every rotation of its tires, battered from the trip up the mountain and Laurie's wild ride back down. Zeke had decided that he surely could not bring it back down himself, and Laurie, fearless with the Dread gone, had volunteered to show off her driving skills again. In a show of solidarity, Keelie had gone along for the ride, and had probably cut about ten years off her lifespan. Maybe she didn't need to learn how to drive quite so soon.

But Zeke was himself again, and Keelie was stuck in the cab of the creakmobile with Knot, and Laurie, and the *bhata* that would not go home, and the treeling—which had sprouted immediately after being planted in a homely terra-cotta pot and had been driving her nuts ever since.

Nuts was not a pun.

"When are we going to stop? I need coffee." Laurie sounded as peevish as Keelie felt.

"No coffee. We aren't stopping to go the bathroom, which we'd have to if you had coffee." Dad tapped his fingers impatiently on the steering wheel.

"Keelie, your father is an ogre."

"Nope. He's an elf."

I need to be watered. Do you have mineral water? Not that tap stuff that chaps my leaves. The aristocratic tree seedling was such a whiner. *And when am I getting a new pot? I'm a princess, you know. This one's ugly.*

Knot growled. The *bhata* clicked its stick arms at him, then climbed into Keelie's hair. She shifted uncomfortably. They were all crammed into the cab together because the back was stuffed full of her belongings taken out of storage, plus Laurie's mountain of luggage.

Keelie found herself looking forward to the Dread Forest. At least there, the elves would be rude and ignore her, and she could put some distance between herself and the Acorn Princess Alora.

"I could really use coffee. Come on, Zeke." Laurie wheedled like a pro.

"We haven't left the parking lot yet. Give me a break."

Keelie groaned and put her face against the window glass. It was going to be a long trip. And the second half would include a blind hawk, when they picked Ariel up on the way to Oregon. Maybe Ariel would eat Princess Alora.

She smiled at the thought as they bumped their way out of the closed-down Wildewood Faire. The road was already clogged with the vehicles of disgruntled shopkeepers and performers. Keelie was glad she hadn't seen Finch again, since the fire-breathing administrator had probably completed her transformation into a dragon.

Around them, the forest stretched, green and lush up the mountain. Keelie thought she saw a glint of white near the top.

Goodbye Einhorn. See you and Raven next year. If I survive the Dread Forest.

And in response, she heard his answer, echoed by a chorus of trees that extended far beyond the green Wildewood...

Farewell, Keliel Tree Talker, Daughter of the Forest.

About Gillian Summers

A forest dweller, Gillian was raised by gypsies at a Renaissance Faire. She likes knitting, hot soup, and costumes, and adores oatmeal—especially in the form of cookies. She loathes concrete, but tolerates it if it means attending a science fiction convention. She's an obsessive collector of beads, recipes, knitting needles, and tarot cards, and admits to reading *InStyle* Magazine. You can find her in her north Georgia cabin, where she lives with her large, friendly dogs and obnoxious cats, and at www.gilliansummers.com.

Look for Book III of the Faire Folk Trilogy in Summer 2009.